THE ★★★★ BREAKTHROUGH

A PRECINCT 11 NOVEL

JERRY B. JENKINS

Visit Tyndale online at www.tyndale.com.

Visit Jerry B. Jenkins's website at www.jerryjenkins.com.

TYNDALE and Tyndale's quill logo are registered trademarks of Tyndale House Publishers, Inc.

The Breakthrough

Designed by Erik M. Peterson

Library of Congress Cataloging-in-Publication Data

Jenkins, Jerry B.
The breakthrough : a Precinct 11 novel / Jerry B. Jenkins.
p. cm. — (Precinct 11)
ISBN 978-1-4143-0909-5 (hc) — ISBN 978-1-4143-3584-1 (sc)
1. Police—Illinois—Chicago—Fiction. 2. Chicago (Ill.)—Fiction. I. Title.
PS3560.E485B74 2012
813'.54—dc23 2012017820

Printed in the United States of America

18 17 16 15 14 13 12
7 6 5 4 3 2 1

To B. Doug Hallmark,
who sets the believers an example
in speech, in conduct,
in love, in faith, in purity.

1 TIMOTHY 4:12

Thanks to
Walt Larimore, M.D.,
for medical input;
and to
John White, John Li, and Steven Zhang
for an unforgettable visit to China

With Gratitude

I HAVE ENJOYED a long and fruitful relationship with Tyndale House Publishers, from the Left Behind series through the *Soon* trilogy, the Red Rock Mysteries and Wormling series (with Chris Fabry), *Riven*, Joe Gibbs's *Game Plan for Life*, *Midnight Clear* (with son Dallas), *The Last Operative*, and now the Precinct 11 trilogy, of which *The Breakthrough* is the third.

At the risk of leaving out many who should not be omitted, I would like to specifically thank President Mark Taylor, Ron Beers, Karen Watson, Jan Stob, Carol Traver, Cheryl Kerwin, and my editor, Jeremy Taylor.

It's been a great ride.

1

★★★★

DREAD

JUNE 21

The last time Boone Drake felt so sunny about life, storm clouds beyond the horizon unleashed a torrent that washed away everything he loved.

His wife.

His son.

His home.

His faith.

His passion for police work.

His reason for being.

That in just a few years he was back on top left him reeling. If Boone could only take credit for doing more than merely hanging on while his world slowly rebuilt itself . . .

Now he enjoyed a new wife, a new son, a new home,

a renewed faith, and an even deeper passion for his work. And all, it seemed, in spite of himself.

Grateful didn't begin to describe how Boone felt about everyone and everything that coalesced to salve his raw existence, to restore him. *Obligated* was more like it. At his most despairing, people who cared about him had seemed to conspire to force him to hang on until the arduous healing could begin.

Why was it, then, that being back to a pinnacle in his personal and professional and spiritual lives left Boone wary? Was it all too good to be true? Surely there was no guarantee that a guy could be metaphorically stomped to within an inch of death only once in his life.

What might be looming?

Was Boone's unease a character flaw, a chink in the armor of his faith? Didn't he deserve success and happiness?

Well, of course he didn't. He knew what he deserved. When he had gotten serious about his spiritual life, he had come to understand where he stood with God. He had deserved all the bad stuff. This abundance was grace, pure and simple.

It was not a wise man, Boone knew, who looked for trouble. One in his profession, however, had to be ever vigilant. With that alertness came intuition, street smarts. And Boone's were telling him he might be luxuriating in the tranquility before a tempest.

Even his pastor, a master of texting just the right Scripture reference at just the right time, had appeared to drop the ball today, the first day of summer. Boone's phone chirped a little after 8 p.m., just as he was preparing to leave his Major Case Squad office for home. He gathered his stuff with one hand

and thumbed the tiny screen with the other. The note from Francisco Sosa read: Job 5:7ff.

Normally Boone waited till he had a moment to look up the references, but this he had to see. Sosa had found some nugget of encouragement for him in Job, really?

On the elevator at the Area 4, District 11 stationhouse on West Harrison Street, with everything else tucked under his arm, Boone accessed his mobile Bible and brought up:

People are born for trouble
  as readily as sparks fly up from a fire.

On that cheery note, the youngest bureau chief in the history of the Chicago Police Department headed wearily to his car. The thermometer had hit triple digits that afternoon—which rarely, if ever, happened before late July in the Windy City—and Boone had had to endure a rare day in uniform.

He preferred a suit and tie, as did most detectives, but when Downtown decreed a uniform for some official to-do, even chiefs obeyed. Boone had wanted to decline, but he had to pick his battles. He had endured enough politics in his new role. The chiefs of four of the other five major bureaus within the department—Patrol, Detectives, Organizational Development, and Administration—didn't see the need for another. The fifth happened to be Jack Keller, chief of the Organized Crime Division (OCD), and critics said he backed Boone only because he had been his partner, then his boss and mentor.

Keller, steely gray and pushing a taut sixty, advised Boone to stay above the fray. "It's not your fight," he said as they worked out together one day. "It's what the super wants, and it's been approved by the city council's subcommittee, so it's gonna happen, end of story."

Boone put his uniform cap on the backseat, removed the leather Sam Browne belt that carried his handcuffs, ammunition, and service sidearm, and placed it on the floor. He hung his coat near the rear passenger door to keep it from blocking his vision when he drove. As he slid in and checked his mirrors, he was stunned afresh to see the single star on his collar. It likely hardly registered to anyone not on the job, but Chicago coppers knew what it meant. He was one of six chiefs, making him one of the nine top cops of more than thirteen thousand in the city.

The temperature was still in the nineties, though the sun had begun to sink, and Boone felt fortunate the AC kicked in fast in his brand-new BMW 760Li—a sedan he wouldn't have sprung for if not for his wife. Not to mention he was also driving to a house he would not have enjoyed but for her.

It wasn't that Boone had married into money. Well, he had, but he hadn't meant to. The former Haeley Lamonica's seven-figure settlement from the City of Chicago for false arrest had actually been won late in their courtship and paid early in their marriage.

Neither Boone nor Haeley had ever been people of means. She had been a single mother, struggling to get by. He had been well compensated for his age but certainly was not wealthy. His new role paid in the neighborhood of ten thousand dollars a month, but that was nothing compared to Haeley's windfall. It had resulted from a sordid case that had exposed corruption at the highest levels of the CPD. What to do with the money became a dilemma.

Boone had wanted nothing to do with it. "It's yours alone to do with what you want."

"I don't want it at all," Haeley had said. She took seriously the admonition that it was harder for a rich person to get into heaven than for a camel to squeeze through the eye of a needle. "I mean, who wouldn't want to be rich?" she said. "But it's not what we're about, and it terrifies me."

Yet Boone, along with Haeley's attorney—who was entitled to a third of the money—had persuaded her to take it. And they had all celebrated one warm spring evening the previous year on *The Settlement*, newly anchored at Belmont Harbor.

"You can give your two-thirds away for all I care," Friedrich Zappolo, Esquire, told her. "My third went for—"

"This boat, I know," she said.

Haeley told Boone she had finally concluded that she would accept the money because, for one thing, she was entitled to it. And she had caveats. "First, I want to give you a gift."

"No need," Boone said. "You and Max are all I want, and—"

"Don't deny me. When else in my life would I ever be able to give you anything really worth something?"

He had acquiesced, and she had bought him the car of his dreams—but one that wouldn't raise too many eyebrows at the department.

The second condition was that she wanted a nice, big home with a fireplace in a safe neighborhood. In Chicago that hardly meant ostentatious, but it did mean a place beyond the reach of even a bureau chief.

Zappolo, who had helped with tax ramifications, told her,

"You know, even after the house and the car, you still have well over a million left. You talked before about investing in a side fund to put your kid through college."

"Makes sense, Hael," Boone said. "Put a chunk away; let it grow for Max."

Zappolo had referred them to a lawyer experienced in family law, who had accomplished Boone's adoption of the beautiful blond boy.

"A college fund is nonnegotiable, Fritz," Haeley said, running both hands through her long, dark hair. "But it might not be just for Max."

Zappolo showed her on paper how she could ensure three kids would go to college and still have more than a million dollars left. "Plenty to treat yourself with."

"The rest goes to charity," she said.

"Sorry?"

"You heard me, Mr. Zappolo."

"I know I did. I just didn't want to. It's nice to be generous and all, but . . ."

"The balance," she said, "all of it, goes to our churches."

"Plural?" Zappolo said.

"Well, we're going to Community Life now, but I used to go to North Beach, and they're struggling."

"That so?" the lawyer said. "I advise you to be careful how much you give to a small nonprofit."

"I'm listening."

"How big is this church? What's their budget?"

She shrugged and looked at Boone. "Less than fifty people, a pastor who also works on the side. Maybe fifty thousand a year for everything?"

"Well, you know I'm not a church guy, but I've worked with a lot of nonprofits, and I'm just sayin', you give a place like this more'n, say, double their annual budget, and you're gonna have problems. I've seen little outfits go under because they just can't handle it. All of a sudden the director—in your case, the pastor—gets a new car or spruces up his office or quits his other job, and people start talking; you know how it goes."

"A hundred thousand would be wonderful for them," Haeley said.

"Okay, now you're down to about one and a quarter mil. Me, I'd be buying a place on the Continent. You?"

"Community Life. They have a multimillion-dollar budget and ministries all over the city. They'd know what to do with it, and they'd do it right."

"You're a bigger woman than I am," Fritz said. "I mean . . . you know what I mean."

So Haeley had been both generous and sacrificial. The only hard part for her in having married and relocated, she told Boone, had been giving up going to her own little church. He offered to go to hers instead, but she insisted. "Community is where you need to be—where *we* need to be. And I don't feel so bad about leaving North Beach now that I can give them a gift like this."

Haeley added one more condition. "The gifts are anonymous, Fritz. Nothing named after me or us, no announcements, no thank-yous. Can you make that happen?"

"You think these pastors live under rocks, girl? They watch the news. They know I defended you against the city. Everybody in town knows of the settlement. You're going to be hearing from friends you never knew you had."

"I can just say it's already all accounted for. I'm not a bank."

"That's the right line," Fritz said, "but I all of a sudden show up with big checks, and you don't think these pastors are going to put two and two together? There's no way around that they're going to know. Let's do this: I'll let the pastors know it came from you but tell them that if anyone else finds out, it's revocable."

Haeley held a hand over her rumbling abdomen as she closed the drapes for the evening. A small foreign car in the cul-de-sac didn't look like any of the neighbors', and they never parked in the street anyway.

It hadn't been that long ago that she had seen another strange car, twice the same day. She had taken Max back to their old church because Boone had had to work one Sunday. Max had been excited to see Aunt Flo, the black lady from North Beach Fellowship who had stayed with him often before Boone and Haeley married. They had spent the afternoon at Florence's apartment, where Haeley noticed the same car on the street outside the building that she had noticed in the strip mall parking lot after church—a dark-blue vintage four-door Buick with Illinois plates.

Haeley told herself she had become overly suspicious as the wife of a cop and decided not to mention it to Boone. But this one? Maybe she should.

Boone merged onto the Eisenhower Expressway as remnants of an orange sun played peekaboo between buildings. He was glad rush-hour traffic had largely dissipated, but that reminded him he would get home after Max was in bed. He hated that, as did Max and Haeley. Fortunately, it was rare with his new role. There were still occasional cases that saw him work into the night, but the hours were nothing like they had been in Organized Crime.

He looked forward to getting out of uniform, settling on the couch with Haeley, and enjoying the spacious house. Could life be better? Even his generous salary was not exorbitant these days, but without a mortgage, they were comfortable.

And that troubled Boone. He'd never done well with comfort. He should be on top of the world—and in many ways he was. But could it last? According to Job 5:7, maybe not.

Boone slipped his cell phone from his shirt pocket and inserted it into a docking station installed under the dash. At the last bureau chiefs' meeting, the head of Patrol had reported that the prohibition against texting and using other than hands-free phones while driving had reduced cell phone involvement in crashes. "But," the Patrol chief said, "to our embarrassment, our own employees remain chronic offenders."

It's hard to get the public to obey laws that you yourself flout.

Boone hit a speed-dial button and turned on his radio, set to an FM frequency that, in essence, broadcast his phone in the car.

"Hey, babe," Haeley said. "You close? Keeping your plate warm."

"A few minutes. Max down?"

"Yeah, and he wasn't too happy to miss you."

"Me either, but I can run him to school in the morning on the way in."

"How're you doing on your letter to him?"

"Still working on it. I'll get back to it. What's up, Hael?"

"Hmm?"

"You sound different. Anything wrong?"

"You're good, Chief. I've felt a little punky all day. Not hungry. And there's a car I don't recognize in the cul-de-sac."

"Anybody in it?"

"I think so. Hard to see."

"Can you see a plate number?"

He heard the rustle of a curtain. "Can't make it out, but it doesn't look like an Illinois tag. Dark background."

"What color?"

"Can't tell from here."

"What kind of car?"

"Foreign. Compact. Old, shabby."

"Hon, my binoculars are on the shelf in the front closet. See if you can give me a tag number."

He heard her set the phone down and rummage. She called out, "Found 'em!"

A few seconds later she was back on the phone. "Solid background, maybe a little lighter than navy, three white numbers and three white letters, can't make out the state."

"Indiana," Boone said. "Read 'em off to me."

"You won't be able to write them down."

"C'mon, Hael. Memorizing plate numbers is a hobby of old street cops."

She recited the numbers and letters.

"I'll run it, but don't open the door to anyone you don't recognize."

2

★★★★

UNWELCOME

THE MYSTERY CAR, a twelve-year-old Nissan Sentra, was registered to DeWayne Mannock, male, Caucasian, age twenty-nine, no current warrants, long history of suspended licenses for DWI, DUI, reckless driving, and even excessive lane changing. His license had been reinstated just four months before, restricted to work-related trips.

As Boone turned onto the street leading to his cul-de-sac, he phoned Haeley again.

"Any idea how DeWayne Mannock got our home address?"

"Oh, Boone! No!"

"Ever known him to be dangerous? Violent?"

"No, but be careful. He was a jock, you know."

"What're you, serious? I thought he was a skinny little loser."

"Uh, no. A loser for sure, but not always. He was once cut, strong."

Boone shook his head, recalling the mug shot of Haeley's old boyfriend, the father of her child. A mullet on a real man?

"I called for backup, but they'll wait around the corner until I need them. I want to talk to this guy."

"What could he possibly want after all this time?" Haeley said.

The sun was gone when Boone slowly pulled in and parked under a streetlamp about twenty feet behind the Sentra. The driver seemed to be studying his rearview mirror. Boone pulled a flashlight from the glove box, emerged slowly, and opened his back door. He laid the light on the seat and donned his uniform cap and coat. After buttoning it from the bottom, he cinched his gun belt tight, tucked the flashlight under his arm, and strode to the left rear of Mannock's car.

Boone stopped at the taillight and directed his light into the driver's outside mirror. The Nissan started.

"Don't even think about it!" Boone bellowed, free hand on the leather flap covering his Beretta. "Shut it off!"

The car died, and the driver left the key turned far enough to roll down his window. "Problem, officer?"

"Keep your hands on the wheel."

"You don't want my license or registration?"

"I want you to speak only when spoken to and keep your hands on the wheel."

Boone's shoulder radio squawked, "Backup in position."

"Ten-four. Stand by."

Boone approached the driver's side, staying back so Mannock had to crane his neck to see him. That would make it harder for DeWayne if he had a weapon.

"Where's your license?"

"Wallet. Back pocket."

"Slowly, under my light."

The wiry young man with greasy hair and a wannabe moustache handed his license to Boone.

"Registration in the glove box?"

"Yeah."

"Open it, but don't reach in till I can see in there with my light."

Seeing no weapon, Boone told him to grab the registration. As Mannock handed it out, Boone moved next to the man.

"You still live in Hammond, Mr. Mannock?"

"Uh-huh."

"Long way from home, aren't you, DeWayne?" Boone said, pronouncing it *Duane* on purpose.

"It's Dee Wayne, sir, and I know who you are."

"Don't be answering questions I didn't ask, DeWayne. Now what did I ask you?"

"Yeah, long way, I guess."

"Still dealing at the casino there?"

"Part-time. The economy, you know."

"Since you know who I am, you also know whose house you're sitting in front of."

Mannock nodded. "Wondering if I could talk to you guys."

"You don't have a phone? Why not call first?"

"Don't have a number."

"How'd you find the address?"

"That's easy with the Internet and everything."

"What do you want with us?"

"Well, it's more what I want with Haeley."

"That's not going to happen, DeWayne."

"You're not even gonna let me talk to her?"

"What do you want with a woman you haven't seen for more than five years?"

"My piece of the action."

"Step out of the car please, sir."

"Why?"

"So I don't have to put one in your ear and come up with a reason."

"Am I under arrest?"

"Not yet."

"For what?"

"You're asking me what you're *not* under arrest for?"

Mannock slid out of the car and looked warily at Boone. "What?"

"Follow me."

Boone led him to the back of the car. It appeared Mannock was trying to look nonchalant. He put one foot on the bumper and rested a tattooed forearm on his thigh. It read NEVER SAY DIE.

"Haeley has moved on. Stay out of her life."

"You can't keep me from talking to her."

Boone raised his eyebrows in the light from the lamppost and stared at Mannock. "Forget the uniform. Forget the badge. Forget the gun. I'm her husband, and you don't want to test what you just said."

"Why can't I talk to her?"

"Because she's my responsibility, and I don't see anything good coming from that."

"Well, she shouldn't keep all that to herself."

"All what?"

"Everybody knows how much she got."

"And you want a piece of it."

"Who wouldn't? Not much. Just some."

Boone could barely find words. He looked left. He looked right. He looked up. "Seriously, DeWayne?"

"She's got enough! She could give me twenty-five grand and not even feel it."

"You want twenty-five thousand dollars. For what?"

"I got business ideas."

"Good for you. And why would you be entitled to one cent of her money?"

"'Cause we were like common-law married."

"You lived together how long?"

"I don't remember."

"Not more than a few months. You find out she's pregnant and you're gone for good."

"Still, I'm the father."

"Yet you denied that under oath."

"A DNA test will prove it. The court'll say I'm entitled to half what she got, and here I am only askin' for seed money for my business."

"Now you *want* to claim paternity?"

"I'm the father."

Boone tucked the flashlight back under his elbow, crossed his arms, and shook his head. "Could you be dumber?"

"Why?"

"Have you ever before claimed to be the father? Ever asked to see the boy? Ever sent a dime of support? Anything?"

Mannock shrugged.

"You didn't even contest the adoption, and we know you were duly notified. And now somehow you and she are partners, entitling you to a share of assets she was awarded five years after you disappeared, and not that long after you told investigators she was a loose woman and you had about a one in ten chance of being the father."

"I didn't know what they were questioning me for! I thought maybe for child support. So I lied. I knew she was a virgin when we met. I'm the father; I know that."

"Any court anywhere would study your history and deny all rights."

"I don't want rights anyway. I just want a little of her settlement."

"I rest my case. You can't get any dumber."

"She might give it to me. She liked me once."

"Don't flatter yourself, DeWayne. She was rebelling and you were convenient. She's a different person now."

"You should still at least let me try to talk sense to her."

"Sense? You wouldn't know sense if it stole your car."

"What?"

"I've got a deal for you, DeWayne. You listening?"

"I guess."

"There's a squad around the corner, and the officers in that vehicle would love to collar a guy violating his probation."

"Who's what?"

"You don't have work-only restrictions on your license?"

"I was thinking of applying for a job at one of the Chicago casinos, so coming this way is just like driving to work."

"Is it? Should we deliver you back to Hammond and let a judge decide?"

DeWayne seemed to be trying to stare Boone down.

"You know as well as I do that that would be the end of your license and your part-time job. What would you do then?"

"That's why I need a little money."

"DeWayne, I'm hot, I'm tired, and I'm hungry. I'm going to give you ten seconds to get back in your car and get home, or I'll turn my guys loose on you."

"You're going to regret this, Drake."

"You want to waste time trying to find out if I'm bluffing, that's on you. Seven, eight, nine—"

DeWayne Mannock strolled past Boone and slowly slid into the car. Boone mashed the button on his shoulder transceiver. "Drake clear. Many thanks."

Mannock thrust his arm out the window and pointed at his tattoo. Boone snorted.

Haeley, pale and shaky, was waiting at the back door when Boone came in. She held him tight. "Can't wait to hear this," she said.

3

★★★★

MOUTHWATERING

JUNE 22

The next morning on their way to school, Max told Boone all about his recent visit with Aunt Flo. "I miss her."

"You miss that little church too?"

"Sort of. But I like yours better."

"It's ours now, bud."

"I liked the old one, but the Life church has so many more kids and things to do." He still found it difficult to pronounce *Community*.

"Aunt Flo lives a little far from us now, Max, but maybe we could see if she's available again a week from tomorrow."

"Where you goin'?"

"To a barbecue."

"I like barbecue."

"You want to come?"

"Will other kids be there?"

"Nope. Just six adults."

"Maybe Aunt Flo will cook me barbecue. She did before, you know."

"Did she?"

"Really good, too."

"Let's hope she's free then."

"I want to stay overnight again."

"We'll check with Mom on that."

When Boone dropped Max off, he reminded himself that he really must get back to his letter to the boy. He had written a letter to his first son the day he was born, telling him of his heritage and of his parents' love and dreams for him. The idea was that Josh would read the letter on his twelfth birthday.

Though Josh had died as a toddler, Boone still liked the letter idea. He had started his letter to Max the day he adopted him, but he had not finished and had not gotten back to it. *Soon,* he promised himself.

Haeley was okay with the idea of Max staying at Florence's, she told Boone that evening. "I could use the break."

"Not feeling any better?"

"Worse. And I'm late, Boone."

He shot her a double take. "Should I be excited?"

"Not yet."

"But there's only one reason for being late, isn't there?"

"I'm only going by how it was with Max. I wasn't even nauseated till several weeks in."

"So this is more than morning sickness?"

She shrugged. "Hope not. But something's not right. I made an appointment with Dr. Fabrie for a week from Monday. I tried to get in sooner, but she's away till then. You need to meet her."

"I don't want to get ahead of myself, love," Boone said, "but I'm already excited."

"I'm not even sure I'm pregnant. If I am, and if it's not right—"

"Can't you take a home test?"

She fell silent.

"Have you already taken one?"

Haeley shook her head.

"You're afraid?"

She nodded. "If I found out I was pregnant before I could talk to Kris, I'd be even more worried."

"You and your doctor are on a first-name basis?"

"You'll love her, Boone."

"If she delivers our baby, I sure will. What else could make you late?"

"No idea. I just want her to tell me I'm pregnant and that everything is normal."

"Me too."

"But wouldn't you think it would be the same as the first time?"

"I wouldn't know, Hael. You want to check with that Indian guy from church?"

"He not a baby doctor."

"But don't they all study this stuff? He could at least put your mind at ease."

"Maybe."

Boone found a home number for Dr. Murari Sarangan, the physician from St. Luke's who had been so kind to him when he lost his first wife and son in a fire.

He and the doctor traded pleasantries, and Boone apologized for bothering him after hours.

"Don't think a thing of it," Dr. Sarangan said in his lilting accent. "I have been so pleased to see you with your new family."

Boone put his phone on speaker and introduced Haeley.

"Yes, hello, Mrs. Drake! I have seen you at church with your handsome son."

Haeley briefly ran down her symptoms.

"As you know, this is not my field, but many factors besides pregnancy can cause this. You do not appear either overweight or underweight."

"I always want to lose a few pounds."

"But if I may say, that is just vanity. Your weight does not appear to be a medical problem, at least from my perspective. And you're sure you haven't miscalculated on the calendar?"

"I'm sure."

"Have you been under stress?"

"Not at all. If my life was any better, I'd feel guilty."

"That's wonderful," the doctor said, but Boone was sobered. Was this the other shoe he'd feared would drop? "Any change in meds?"

"I'm on nothing but a multivitamin."

"Good for you. That leaves just the symptoms. Illness itself can delay your cycle, but a pregnancy could also cause illness."

Haeley told him of her appointment.

"I know Dr. Fabrie," Dr. Sarangan said. "Excellent. She will be able to tell you for sure whether a pregnancy is causing your ailments or your ailments are causing your lateness."

Haeley asked him about a home test.

"My only hesitation is that a false negative could result if you do this too early. And I suspect that would only add to your anxiety."

"For sure."

"I would advise you to treat your symptoms over the counter until your doctor can give you a conclusive diagnosis."

JUNE 30

Saturday morning Jack Keller and his former live-in girlfriend, Margaret, arrived in separate cars about half an hour before they and the Drakes were to leave for the west side. They had finally accepted a longstanding invitation from Fletcher and Dorothy Galloway. The last time Boone and Jack had visited the Galloways had been in the middle of the night to involve the recently retired chief of the Organized Crime Division in one last case. Dorothy had lectured the pair and told them the next time they came to her house it had better be because their cholesterol was down a quart.

"And just so you know," she had added, "I will be speaking only to the women."

"Been looking forward to a ride in your new chariot, Boones," Jack said. "And have I got some questions for your wife."

"I can't wait," Haeley deadpanned. "Does decency ever give you pause?"

Jack and Margaret both laughed.

"Didn't think so," Haeley said. "But you need to know I don't feel obligated to answer."

"We'll see," Jack said.

"Well, we have to drop Max at the sitter's before we go," Haeley said, "so save it till he's out of the car."

She put a package of raw burgers and dogs on the console in the front seat, then secured Max in the middle of the back. Jack and Margaret sat on either side of him.

Both looked younger than their years. They'd had hard lives before they met each other, each having endured multiple marriages. Boone had seen Jack through several relationships since then, but he'd never seen his former partner, mentor, and boss truly in love. Until Margaret.

Jack could have passed for late forties, as could Margaret. Both took great care of themselves. Jack was a daily jogger and lifter, and while Boone didn't know Margaret's regimen, it wasn't common for a woman in her late fifties to look so fit and young. She was tall and lithe and tanned and freckled with long chestnut hair featuring attractive streaks of gray. Her pale azure eyes appeared both friendly and mischievous, and Boone could imagine her having been a hippie—before he was born.

He'd been amused when he first met her because she wore clothes too young and revealing for her, and he assumed that was what attracted Jack. After only a couple of brief conversations, however, Boone got an inkling of what had actually so enraptured his partner. Margaret was honest and direct yet also others-oriented. She seemed the type who would do anything for a friend.

Boone had to admit he had been surprised after knowing

Margaret awhile to learn she had a dimension he'd been wholly unaware of. Staying overnight with the couple once, he'd discovered a whole shelf of Christian books and Bibles. And when he cautiously broached the subject with her at breakfast, she scolded Jack for having told her about Boone's faith without telling Boone about hers.

She leveled those expressive eyes at Boone. "You didn't know I was raised like you? Church and Sunday school, VBS in the summers, Bible camp, the whole thing?"

"No kidding?"

"You're wondering what happened?"

"I didn't say that."

"But you're surprised?"

Boone had shrugged and nodded.

Jack had interrupted. "We don't have time for this right now. Let us get past our case, and you two can have a prayer meeting or whatever it is you types do."

Before the conversation was dropped, Margaret had said, "You're wondering how a Christian girl grows up to live in sin. Well, I want to talk about it, but I'm gettin' the evil eye from my man here, so another time."

Boone hoped that maybe now would be the time. He was more curious than ever, given that since that last conversation, Margaret had left Jack, insisting she would see him only if he joined her at church—Community Life, the same church Boone and Haeley attended.

Jack was clearly not interested in church. He hadn't been to one since Boone's first wife and son's funeral. But apparently he never lost interest in Margaret. He wasn't attending enough to put Margaret's mind at ease, but Boone and

Haeley had seen them there together often enough to know that Keller was making an effort. More than once Jack had confided to Boone, "I'm still not sure this is the right reason to go."

Haeley herself had a story similar to Margaret's, minus the marriages, and that was likely what Jack wanted to pursue today. Boone knew he would not find Haeley eager to talk about her past.

Boone and Haeley and Max were greeted in the lobby of Florence's modest apartment building by the ancient doorman, Willie. "Miz Quigley's expecting you," he said, quickly standing. "I'll buzz you up."

A minute later Haeley said, "Florence!" embracing the matronly, heavyset widow at her door. "It's been too long."

Florence cackled, gathering Max into her massive arms. "Too long is right. Y'all are still goin' to church somewhere, aren't you?"

"Of course; now stop that."

Florence peeked into the grease-stained bag Haeley had brought.

"I'll cook your burgers and dogs, but you don't shop where I shop. This boy needs to be 'sposed to pigs' knuckles, hocks, and trotters."

"Ewww!" Max said.

"Don't knock 'em till you try 'em, little one," Florence said. "I ever fed you somethin' you didn't like? I ever try to feed you chitlins?"

He shook his head.

"A'ight then. You trust Aunt Flo. Your mama and daddy

be getting regular barbecue. You be getting the real thing, just like Erastus used to make."

"We've got friends in the car," Boone said, "so we'd better scoot."

Florence seemed to be having none of it, apparently eager to chat. "You're goin' to your former boss's, you say? He a brother?"

Boone nodded.

"Then they ought to be serving the real thing too, but I bet they're tonin' it down for you."

"I hope so!" Boone said. "Pigs' knuckles?"

"I promise you, one of these days I'll get some down you, and you'll change your mind."

Boone drove, Jack sat next to him, and the women sat in the back.

As he pulled out of the parking lot, Boone noticed a navy four-door Buick sedan parked down the street. It would have made little impression on him but for its age—at least thirty years old—and the out-of-state plates. South Carolina. As he passed it he couldn't help memorizing the tag. DLJ 725.

"Erastus was her husband, Hael?" Boone said.

"Yes. Talks about him all the time. He was a CTA driver. Died way too young. Diabetes. Just coming up on retirement, and they had all kinds of plans."

"That's awful," Margaret said.

"Worse was that her two teenage boys fell in with gangs after that," Haeley said. "Both died in the streets."

"Such a wonderful person," Boone said, "She doesn't seem bitter. That's a tough life."

"Says it all drove her back to her faith," Haeley said. "She finally quit asking why and started asking what's next? Feels like she's supposed to serve people."

"So, speaking of *why*," Jack said, wrenching himself around to face Haeley, seatbelt straining, "can I jump right in?"

She laughed. "What if I say no?"

"Don't waste your breath," Margaret said.

"I just gotta know what you ever saw in that DeWayne Mannock character."

Boone glanced into the rearview mirror and saw Haeley blanch.

"Jack, no!" Margaret said. "Unfair. We've all got regrets. Just leave it alone."

"No, now I'm really curious. I mean, Haeley, you and I have worked together, been friends. You know I think you're special. But Mannock, really? I s'pose you've had this conversation with Boones, but did the guy have one redeeming quality? Looks, personality, brains, a soft spot for kids or dogs? Was he smart, funny, have a business sense? Anything?"

Boone noticed Margaret gaze out the window as if she wanted no more to do with this. Haeley appeared to be trying to fashion a response.

Jack said, "I read his deposition transcript. He's a sleazebag, a liar, a—"

"All right!" Haeley snapped. "Listen, this is all from a very brief period of my life I don't like to talk about. At church we like to say it's under the blood. Know what that means?"

Jack shrugged. "I wouldn't have if this one hadn't forced me to go with her, but yeah, I do. Seems a little convenient, sticking old mistakes under the blood, but if it works for you—"

"Jack!" Margaret said, suddenly engaged again. "Let her answer."

Jack raised his brows and gazed back at Haeley. "The floor is yours. Tell me what could have possibly attracted you to that white trash."

"All right," Margaret said, "now I need to let Haeley talk, but you happen to be in love with white trash."

"Oh, come on," Jack said. "You have a little redneck in you, but you're a far cry from white trash."

"He was convenient," Haeley said.

"Convenient?"

"Listen, Jack, you're one of my favorite people in the world. And though I don't owe you any explanations, and I'd like to think a true friend wouldn't ask for one, I'm going to talk about this one last time. Then if you ever ask me about it again, not only am I not going to answer, but I'm going to be angry with you. Understood?"

"Fair enough."

"Now, hear me, I'm not blaming what I did on anyone else. I could say my too-strict parents drove me to this, but no, I own it. Other people were raised the way I was, and they didn't rebel. They became better for it, and they're raising their kids healthier. That's what I want to do too, but that's not what I chose when I was young and stupid."

"Is that enough, Jack?" Boone said. "This is supposed to be a fun day."

"It's all right, Boone," Haeley said. "Let me get through this for Mr. Nosy Badge, and then I'll be forever done with it."

"Mr. Nosy Badge!" Jack said, chortling. "I need to get that onto my business card!"

"Maybe they can give you a nose pin for your uniform," Margaret said.

That made Boone laugh.

"So here's the bottom line," Haeley said. "DeWayne carried himself like an athlete, had some old sports stories. He wasn't what I would call handsome, but he looked okay in a rough sort of way. I didn't like his booze breath, his smoking, his personality, any of it. But before I found out what he was really like, I had already turned my back on everything I knew. He showed me attention, and he was everything I wasn't. No rules, no standards, did what he wanted, and didn't care what anybody else thought.

"Was that attractive? In a sick way, yeah. I was someone I had never been, so part of me hoped my parents would find out and be horrified. And they were. That God let a beautiful son come out of all that ugliness is just a miracle.

"As soon as DeWayne knew I was expecting, that's the last I heard from him or even about him until he was deposed for the case. Tell you the truth, I couldn't believe all it took was a pregnancy to get rid of that bum. Till that night, what was it, Boone, ten days ago or so?"

"So that's it?" Jack said.

"That's it. It wasn't about him; it was about me. And it seems like a million years ago, yet not long enough; know what I mean?"

"*I* do," Margaret said.

"Thanks for being a good sport," Jack said. "Sometimes I get curious and—"

"Tell me about it," Margaret said. "Now I'd love for you two to stay friends, so can you leave it alone now?"

"Forever?" Haeley said. "Please."

"Just one more question . . ."

"Jack!" Margaret said.

"You promised," Haeley said.

"I just gotta know. Am I really one of your favorite people in the world?"

"Well, you were, but now you're going to have to reapply, and the decision of the judges will be final."

As Boone neared the Galloways' modest bungalow, Margaret said, "I owe Boone a conversation too."

"You don't owe me anything."

"'Course I do. I know you're curious, and I promised. Trouble is, I need permission to do it in private. I mean, not private private, but just the two of us, maybe just sittin' apart from everybody else later this afternoon. Jack, you or Haeley got any problem with that?"

"Fine with me," Jack said. "I've heard it all before and didn't like it then. You sure you want to bore him with this?"

"It won't bore him, Jack, 'cause he'll understand it."

"I understand it. I just—"

"Don't like it; yeah, we got that. You don't like it because you lost something you liked. Now you've got to play your cards right."

"I'm curious too," Haeley said, "but Boone can tell me later, if it's all right with you."

"I'd never tell a spouse to keep anything from the other," Margaret said.

4

★★★★

SURPRISE

"WILL YOU WATCH this with me, Aunt Flo?" Max said.

"Sure, honey. Everything's in the oven and will be for a coupla hours. What you watching?"

"*SpongeBob*," he said.

"We watched that before, haven't we?"

"Yeah! I like it."

"Me too. It's silly, but I like it."

Florence had just settled in next to Max when her intercom buzzed. She rocked her way off the couch and waddled over to it.

"I'll pause it," Max said.

"No, no, I seen this part. You go ahead. I'll just be a second." Florence mashed the button. "Yes?"

"Yes, ma'am, young fella down here in the lobby to see you."

"Who is it?"

"Says it's a surprise."

"I'm not 'specting no surprises, Willie. And I'm busy."

"That's why they're surprises, ma'am. 'Cause you're not expecting 'em. Should I let him up?"

"What'd I just say? Don't you be lettin' strangers up in here. What he look like? He from my church?"

She could hear the young man in the background. "No, sir, but tell Mrs. Quigley I got her name and address from her pastor."

"What's he want?"

"Maybe if you could just come down and talk to him . . ."

"All right, but it's got to be quick."

Florence made her way back to Max. "You be all right here for a minute? I'm gon' lock the door, and you don't open it to anybody, hear? I got my key, and I'll be right back."

In the lobby Florence found a sunburned young man with a buzz cut and wearing Army fatigues tucked into spit-shined boots. He approached smiling and held out his hand. She slowly offered hers but left it limp as he shook it.

"And who might you be?" she said.

"You don't see the resemblance, ma'am?"

"To who?"

"To my sister, ma'am. I'm Alfonso Lamonica, but you may call me Al."

Florence cocked her head and studied him. "Haeley never told me 'bout no brother."

Alfonso laughed. "She wasn't supposed to, ma'am. I was on a classified assignment. Did she ever ask prayer for an 'unspoken request'?"

"Many times! That was for you?"

"Reckon it was, ma'am."

"I'll be! Now stop with the *ma'am* stuff, will ya? Making me sound old. I'm Florence, but you can call me Aunt Flo if you want to."

"I'll stick with Florence, ma'am, for now. I just wanted to tell you that Haeley does not know I'm back from Afghanistan, and—"

"Now just hold on. Maybe you're who you say you are, and maybe you ain't. You got any proof a who you are?"

"Of course, ma'am—Florence."

Alfonso produced a South Carolina driver's license and a military ID. Florence took the ID and held it next to his face. He smiled.

"You wasn't smiling when this was taken."

"I wasn't too happy," he said, and appeared to force a comical frown. It matched the picture.

"Well, welcome home," Florence said. "And thank you for your service. What can I do for you?"

"Tell you what I'd like more than anything else in the world, ma'am. I'd like to meet my first and only nephew, and I'd like you to shoot a picture of him and me I can send to Haeley. Then, just about the time she's getting it, I'll be at her door."

Florence grinned. "That sounds like a wonderful surprise. You know where she lives?"

"Oh, yes. I went by there, hoping to surprise everybody at once and meet her husband, but they were gone. She'd written me about her church, so I tried there and met the pastor, Reverend Waters. He told me where to find you."

"How much time you got? We're gonna eat here in a little while, and I'd love you to join us."

"That'd be wonderful, ma'am. Florence. When will Haeley and Boone come and get Max?"

"Tomorrow. Mid-mornin', I believe."

"That would be even a better time for me to surprise her!"

"I'd love to see that."

As they headed toward the elevator, Alfonso nodded to Willie. "Nice to meet you, sir, and thanks so much for your assistance."

"Yes, sir," Willie said, saluting.

Max didn't seem to have moved a muscle when Florence entered her apartment again, Alfonso hidden behind her ample frame. "You ever see a real army man, Max?" she said.

"Huh-uh," he said, eyes still on the screen.

"Well, pause that thing and c'mere."

"Do I have to?"

"Obey orders, young man," Alfonso said, and Max jumped. The soldier laughed.

Max paused the video and slowly approached as Alfonso emerged from behind Aunt Flo. The little boy's eyes were wide. "You're a real army man?"

"I'm a Ranger, sir," Alfonso said. "You know what that means?"

Max shook his head.

"Well, you will in a while. Aunt Flo has invited me to dinner, and at dinner I'm going to tell you lots of stuff you never knew. Do I look like anybody you know?"

"No."

"No, what?"

"No, you don't."

"No, *sir*."

"No, sir, you don't."

"Are you sure?"

"You don't look like Daddy."

"How about Mommy?" Florence said.

Max kept staring. "Maybe a little."

"Well, your mom is my big sister," Alfonso said. "You know what that makes me?"

"Her brother?"

Alfonso and Florence threw their heads back and roared.

"It makes me your uncle, little buddy. Do you have any other uncles?"

Max squinted. "Yes! My new dad has two brothers. He told me I'm a forever Drake and they're my forever uncles."

"Well, there you go. I'm your third uncle then. Put her there." Alfonso thrust out his hand, and Max shook it. "You need a firmer grip there, soldier. Let me feel it!" Max squinted and seemed to be working at it. Alfonso dropped to one knee. "Oh, now you've done it! You're too strong!"

Max beamed. "You want to watch *SpongeBob*?"

"Do I! And maybe after dinner we can all go play. Is there a park nearby?"

"There is!" Florence said. "You wanna do that, Max?"

"Do I!"

5

★★★★

FEAST

BOONE HAD ALWAYS been impressed by how regal Fletcher Galloway looked in a suit or in uniform. A big black man with a good-size middle, he knew how to camouflage it, and he carried himself with solemnity and grace.

That was a contrast to the host who greeted the two couples from the grill across the tiny, fenced-in backyard. Today Fletch wore a sun-faded Cubs cap too small for his head and hair longer than he had ever worn it on the job. A cooking apron covered his polo shirt, his retirement belly testing the limits of both. The ensemble was completed with plaid Bermuda shorts that looked as if they could apply for statehood and flip-flops tucked between the toes of black dress socks.

"Don't laugh!" he called out, waving a spatula. "Had her way, I'd be wearin' a big ol' chef's hat. Feel fool enough as it is."

Dorothy, a handsome woman in her late sixties wearing fashionable shorts and a plain white top, opened the gate at the end of the driveway that led into the yard. The women embraced her, but when Boone approached, she shot up an open palm and said, "Uh-uh, you 'member what I said. I'm talking only to the women. You can talk to the hand."

Then she burst into laughter and gathered Boone in. "I can't stay mad at you!" As she drew close to his ear, she whispered, "But you know exposin' one of his best friends in the department liked to break his heart."

"I know."

She backed away and glared at Jack. "Now *you* I can stay mad at, mm-hm." But she quickly dissolved again and hugged him. "Y'all get out there and keep Chef Boyardee company."

"One stip-a-lation," Fletcher said as he greeted everyone. "Nobody be telling me how to cook meat. If there's one thing I know . . ."

Dorothy showed the women her flower and vegetable gardens while the men huddled around the grill. "You been to Stateville at all?" Jack said.

"To see Pete? You kiddin'? Hard enough knowing he's there, much as he deserves to be. Don't know if I could take seeing it with my own eyes. Plus, what would I be saying by going? He spit on everything both of us built our careers around."

The three men stood nodding sadly until Jack mimicked what friends would ask him Monday. "So, how was it seeing your old boss? What'd you talk about? Have a good time?"

That made them all chuckle. "Yeah," Fletcher said, "enough with the doom and gloom. Looks at these brats."

"Everything smells great," Boone said. "Can't wait."

"Ain't seen you since you became all high and mighty," Fletcher said. "I ever congratulate you?"

"Yes, sir, you sent a nice card. Appreciated it."

"Well deserved. Two of my best guys top cops now. Feels good. Almost makes up for Pete. Still can't figure that one out. But hey, we were trying to change the subject. Tell me about the new squad."

"Well, we handle certain cases of aggravated assault, burglary, murder, rape, robbery, and—my favorite, 'cause it gives us so much latitude—any other crime that constitutes a threat to the city."

"How do you stay out of Homicide's way?"

"We don't. They resent us."

"Doesn't surprise me."

"That's not true, actually," Jack said. "Boone's being modest. Yeah, things started rocky, but he took the bull by the horns."

"Yeah, and I found out there was more bull than horn."

"Fletch," Jack said, "Boone pulled together the two squads and told 'em that he knew Homicide had all the experience and the authority and the jurisdiction. He said Major Case would take only those murders assigned from the superintendent's office, and even then, he would work closely with Homicide's best people. It really calmed things down."

"Smart," Fletcher said.

"It's not perfect," Boone said. "There are still turf wars and squabbling over who gets the credit. But I don't care about that stuff. Get the bad guys off the street, I say. Who gets the collar doesn't make that much difference."

"My man."

When it came time to eat, the six sat at a picnic table situated on a slab of concrete that served as a patio. The table was more suited to four, and with the men on one side and their partners on the other, Fletcher said, "Don't one side be gettin' up without the other. Whoever's left is gonna tip over and have all the food in their laps."

"That's not all bad," Jack said.

"Hope y'all don't mind if I say grace," Fletcher said.

Everyone nodded, but Boone was stunned. He hadn't ever come to any conclusions about Fletch's spiritual life, but he had certainly never heard the man pray.

"I jes' like this little poem," Fletch said. "Dear Lord, 'For food that stays our hunger, for rest that brings us ease, for homes where memories linger, we give our thanks for these.' Lord, make us truly thankful for these and all other blessings. I ask this in Jesus Christ's name; amen."

Margaret added her own loud amen and reached to take Fletcher's hand. "Thank you, sir. That was wonderful."

"You know," Dorothy said, reaching for a huge bowl, "when I made my joke about y'all's cholesterol, I wasn't kidding. So if you have a problem with it, you probably don't want much of this potato salad. I even looked it up, and a couple of scoops of this stuff will add up to about a hundred grams of cholesterol. If I wasn't on my pills, I couldn't have any of it. And if Fletch hadn't behaved all week lookin' forward to this, he couldn't either."

"This is why I work out," Jack said.

"Me too," Boone said.

It didn't seem much later that Boone was stuffed to where he could hardly breathe. The potato salad, greens, fruit salad, and especially the charcoal-grilled meats were irresistible. "Jack, we're going to have to work out two hours a day for a month."

"Or jog to Colorado."

"This is how we keep you here longer than you planned," Dorothy said. "I know you want to run off soon, but you can't."

"Because we can't move?" Boone said.

"Well, that and you've got to wait a while before you can enjoy my pie. Rhubarb and apple today, and there'll be no doggie bags leavin' this establishment. And you can say all you want that you couldn't eat another bite, but you don't want to offend me that bad. Give it a few hours, and you'll find your appetites again."

6

★★★★

RANGER

FLORENCE BEGAN SETTING serving bowls on the table in her tiny kitchen, smiling at the laughter coming from the next room. Haeley's brother sure seemed to be enjoying *SpongeBob*, or Max, or both. "Time to shut that down now, you two!" she called out. "Dinner in two minutes."

"C'mon, little buddy," she heard Alfonso say. "Let me show you how Rangers wash up for chow."

When they joined her at the table, Alfonso's eyes were wide. "Whoa, man! Look at this feast. We never saw anything like this overseas, and I haven't been back long enough for my mama to feed me."

"You haven't seen your mama?" Florence said.

"Just for a minute. I came back through Fort Benning in Georgia, then hitched my way home to pick up my car. Drove all night to get here." He grabbed Max's shoulder and rocked him in his seat. "Didn't want to wait another minute to meet this guy. Didn't it surprise you a dark-haired girl like Hael would have a blond kid? You can see where he gets it."

"I sure can!"

"And Haeley doesn't even know I'm stateside, let alone here, so Mama and Daddy are sworn to secrecy."

"I assume you're a believin' man like your sister," Florence said.

"Yes, ma'am, washed under the same blood you are."

"Then would you mind askin' the blessing?"

"Honored." He reached out and the three of them held hands. "God is great, God is good, now we thank Thee for our food. Amen."

"Amen!" Max shouted. "I got to learn that prayer!"

"I can teach you," Alfonso said as they passed bowls and dug in. "But first I want to teach you the Ranger creed. Know what that is?"

Max shook his head.

"Well, it might take me a while, because I'm going to be eating at the same time, but I'll get through it." He cut himself a large bite slathered in sweet red sauce and filled his mouth. Florence cut Max's meat while Alfonso chewed.

"What is this, by the way, ma'am?" he said, reaching for his iced tea.

"Pigs' knuckles."

Alfonso laughed. "I'm glad I tried it before I knew that! It's good! I like it."

Florence beamed. "I'm tickled. I had a feelin' they'd be new to you. And how about you, little one? You like pigs' knuckles?"

Max nodded and said with his mouth full, "But I didn't even know pigs had fingers."

After helping clear the picnic table and schlepping things into the kitchen, Fletcher Galloway suggested everyone congregate in the basement rec room, "where it's cooler and the Cubs game in LA will be coming on."

"Okay if Boone and I join you in a few, Mr. Galloway?" Margaret said. "We just need to chat."

"Suit yourself," he said. "We got no agenda."

"Still okay with you, Haeley?" Margaret said.

"Sure," she said with a sigh. "I think I'd better lie down awhile anyway."

"You okay, hon?" Boone said. "Eat too much?"

"She hardly ate at all," Dorothy said. "Don't think I wasn't watchin'."

"Sorry, Mrs. Galloway," Haeley said. "Everything was delicious. I'm a little under the weather is all."

"Just teasin'," Dorothy said. "You take a load off. You don't have to watch the Cubs."

"Oh, I'm a fan, but I'm afraid I need a little peace and quiet, just for a little while."

"You do look pale."

"Do I?"

"You do, babe," Boone said. "Would you rather I take you home?"

"Oh, no! If I can only rest a bit."

"Let me show you to the guest bedroom," Dorothy said.

"Is right here all right for us, Boone?" Margaret said, nodding at the picnic table.

They sat across from each other, the sun toasting Boone's head, shining off Margaret's hair, and baking the concrete.

"You know I'm more'n twenty years older than you, right?" she began.

"Never thought about it, but yeah, I guess."

"Sweet. C'mon, you know I'm an old lady."

"You don't play old; I'll say that."

"Old enough to be your mama."

Boone shrugged. "Where you going with this?"

"Just sayin'. I'm going to tell you about my mistakes. I knew better, and I take full responsibility, but I need you to give me the respect due your elder. Can you?"

"I told you once; you're not going to get any judging from me. I'm not about to tell anybody how they should live."

"But you can't deny you were surprised to find out I was a Christian. There I was, livin' with your boss, carrying on, and I tell you I was raised just like you. Made you curious, didn't it?"

Boone cocked his head. "That's fair."

"Well, my story's a lot like Haeley's, only I went further and stayed in the muck longer. Plus I've got former husbands."

"Why do you feel you need to tell me all this?"

"I want to tell you what happened 'cause I consider you a brother in Christ."

"I am that."

"Then let me."

"The Ranger creed is an acronym," Alfonso said, "Know what that is, little buddy?"

Max shook his head.

"Well, 'course you don't. It just means that every line of the creed starts with a different letter, and all the letters spell Ranger. Understand?"

"We don't do spelling yet."

"Well, let me run 'em down for you anyway. Someday you can memorize the creed like I did." He glanced up at Florence. "He'll understand some of this, won't he?"

"I 'spect he will. He's a smart boy."

Alfonso continued to eat throughout his recitation. "Okay, the first one, which starts with *R* because *Ranger* starts with *R*, is: 'Recognizing that I volunteered as a Ranger, fully knowing the hazards of my chosen profession, I will always endeavor to uphold the prestige, honor, and high esprit de corps of the Rangers.'"

Florence saw Max's eyes glaze over before he looked away. She said, "That jes' means he signed up for that job of being a Army man, so he's gon' do it with all his might."

Max nodded.

"That's right, ma'am. Then, 'Acknowledging the fact that a Ranger is a more elite soldier who arrives at the cutting edge of battle by land, sea, or air, I accept the fact that as a Ranger my country expects me to move farther, faster, and fight harder than any other soldier.' Can you make that one simple for him?"

"Rangers are the best, so he's got to be faster and tougher."

Alfonso was beaming as he chewed, and Florence could see Max was following now.

"'Never shall I fail my comrades,'" Alfonso said. "'I will always keep myself mentally alert, physically strong, and morally straight, and I will shoulder more than my share of the task, whatever it may be, one hundred percent and then some.'"

"That means the other Army men can count on him."

"'Gallantly will I show the world that I am a specially selected and well-trained soldier. My courtesy to superior officers, neatness of dress, and care of equipment shall set the example for others to follow.'"

"He'll never forget to act like a gentleman."

"'Energetically will I meet the enemies of my country. I shall defeat them on the field of battle, for I am better trained and will fight with all my might. *Surrender* is not a Ranger word. I will never leave a fallen comrade to fall into the hands of the enemy, and under no circumstances will I ever embarrass my country.'"

"Your Uncle Alfonso will always do his best and never give up."

"'Readily will I display the intestinal fortitude required to fight on to the Ranger objective and complete the mission, though I be the lone survivor.'"

"Even if he's the last one alive, he'll show guts."

"Couldn't have said it better myself, Aunt Flo," Alfonso said. "Great job. And great barbeque."

"I want to be a Ranger!" Max said.

"Everybody should, little man."

7

★★★★

REVELATION

The sun was so unrelenting that Boone made a visor of his hand, despite that he was already wearing sunglasses. Margaret was doing the same, her pale skin reddening and her freckles darkening before his eyes.

"I'm gonna keep this short for both our sakes," she said. "What turned me was abuse. Both my first husbands knocked me around, and to tell you the truth, I never did understand that. Thought it was my fault at first. I was raised in a good, Christian family. My daddy was a little standoffish, but he was the real deal. Maybe I didn't get enough hugging and I-love-yous, but I never doubted he loved me, and he was good to my mama and all of us. Problem was my first husband only pretended to be a Christian, and by the time I found out I'd been hornswoggled, we were already on the skids. He was drinking and beatin' on me, wouldn't go to counseling, and I wouldn't take any more, so that was that."

"Sorry," Boone said. "That's rough."

"Not as rough as how my family treated me after that."

"Blamed it on you?"

"Divorce is wrong and a sin—bam, done."

"Like it was your fault."

"They thought I coulda done more, and maybe I could have. But I wasn't gonna live with anybody that hurt me. Guess I coulda just separated and got his attention and made him do what was right, but I didn't. All of a sudden I'm more alone than I could imagine. Divorced *and* without a family."

"They abandoned you?"

"Wouldn't even speak to me. Still won't. 'Course, brilliant me, I jump right into another romance. Found me a man who didn't pretend nothin'. Wasn't even a churchgoer, but nice, quiet, gentle, showed me lots of attention. And he didn't drink."

"But you say he hit you too?"

"Says I drove him to it. Maybe I did. Bunch of stuff worked together to kill that marriage. He proved to be boring. Didn't want to do anything. Didn't even wanna talk much. I was still young, wanted to go out, see people. He thought I was a flirt. Maybe I was. I've always been friendly, look you in the eye, smile. And when your husband pays you no mind, maybe you do look for other connections. I wasn't looking to cheat on him, but he thought I was. Only thing I got out that marriage, 'sides a fat lip and a black eye, was my daughter."

Boone looked up and squinted. "I didn't know you had kids."

"Just the one. She's in heaven."

"Sorry."

"The one thing I did right. Told her about Jesus. Took her to church. Got her saved before she got sick and died on me. Spinal meningitis when she was eleven. I gotta tell ya, Boone, that put me in the dumper. I was no good to anybody for years, except the guys I persuaded to keep me warm at night. Drugs, booze, and more men than I care to count."

She paused as if for a response, but Boone found himself speechless. Margaret seemed such a precious woman. Friendly, outgoing, selfless. Yet wounded. He shifted position and found the exposed wood of the picnic table blistering.

"Still listenin', son?"

"You know I am."

"Curious 'bout what brought me to where I am today?"

"Right again."

"One more marriage. I was in a bad, bad spot, totally away from the Lord, goin' to AA but still smoking dope. We were unfaithful to each other almost from the beginning, and it didn't last long. That brings me up to just a few years ago, before I met Jack. Somehow I got my act together except for me and God. Decided I didn't want to grow old alone. Kicked my addictions, got me a job—"

"You were working in an old-age home when you met Jack, weren't you?"

She nodded, digging a floppy hat out of her bag and plopping it on. "Stop grinning, child. You know you're jealous. You want to find a cap?"

"I'm all right, but you do look goofy."

"'Least I won't have a sunburned scalp. At least slap some sunscreen on yours."

She rustled in her bag again and squirted a dollop into his palm. He rubbed it onto his head with both hands as if washing his hair.

"Now who looks goofy? Anyway, one thing I always knew: a girl didn't ever have to be out of job if she was willin' to work. Just do what nobody else wants to do, and the money will follow."

"That's what you found at the—?"

"You betcha. Lotsa people want to push the old-timers around in their wheelchairs, but not many'll bathe them and change their diapers."

"You liked that?"

"I know it sounds weird. Part of me did, yes. I mean, that stuff wasn't on my bucket list, but the Lord put something in me—empathy, I guess—that made me want to live out the Golden Rule with these people. They deserve dignity, and they deserve dry clothes and a clean body."

"That's what Jack loves about you."

"That's not all he loves," she said with a wink. "Aw, look at you, Boone. You're the only man I know can blush through sunburn."

"I'm not blushing."

"You are too."

"Well, that was too much information."

"Sorry. You know he and I are behaving ourselves now."

"That's what I want to hear about."

"I'm getting there. Jack was investigating something, questioning one of the old men about something, and passed me coming out of a room with an armful of soiled sheets. We chatted, and I saw that look. 'Course he's a beautiful man, but I couldn't imagine him taking an interest in a woman over a mess of smelly laundry. But he did. We started seeing each other, and—"

"You moved in."

"I did. And it wasn't long before I was in love."

"Now, see," Boone said, "that's interesting. That's the first time you've mentioned love, and you've talked about a lot of men."

"I loved everything about Jack. Still do. Besides that he's true blue as a Boy Scout, takes care of himself, is smart and funny, he's just so drop-dead honest. No games. No puzzles. You know exactly what he thinks every minute, whether you like it or not. And I happen to like it."

"That's the thing," Boone said. "Over the years I've seen Jack with his former wives and more than a few girlfriends. And I never saw him in love before either."

Margaret fell silent and shook her head.

"He really cares for you," Boone said. "You know that, right?"

She nodded. "The difference is, I love him too much to stay with him. I care for his soul."

"How'd that happen?"

"I'd become a different person, but not different enough. It was like I had pulled myself up by my own bootstraps, whatever that old saw means. Cleaned up my act, grew up a little, quit making such horrible decisions—except moving in with him. I fell so hard for Jack, it scared me. I waited till the shine wore off and finally realized it was the real thing."

"And that made you run?"

"Hardest thing I've ever done."

"But why?"

"Thought you'd never ask."

Florence pushed her chair back from the table in her tiny kitchen and folded her hands over her belly. "Whoo-whee!" she said. "I did me some damage with all o' that!"

"So did I," Alfonso Lamonica said. "And how 'bout you, Max?"

"I didn't do anything!"

Florence and Alfonso laughed. "But you filled yourself right up," she said, "didn't you, little man?"

"Uh-huh, but I still want munch-a-politan."

"He wants what?" Alfonso said.

"He can't say Neapolitan, that three-flavors ice cream."

"One of my favorites," Alfonso said.

"His absolute favorite, but I couldn't force down another bite of anything right now; could you?"

"No!"

"Yes!" Max said. "Ice cream!"

"We need to let this settle, soldier," Alfonso said. "How 'bout we help Aunt Flo clear the table like good Rangers. Then maybe we can play in the park before we come back for dessert, hm?"

"Okay."

"Okay what?"

"Okay what you said."

"'Okay, sir!' And let me teach you to salute."

Max didn't quite master the salute, but he seemed pleased to be helping his uncle clear the table.

"I need to sit a spell," Florence said. "Catch my breath. Maybe watch me some Cubs."

"You've earned that, ma'am. We're going to wash the dishes for you—"

"Oh, just leave 'em. I'll git 'em later."

"Not on your life, Aunt Flo. You've done your part. It's time for us to do ours. You just relax."

Florence settled onto the couch and used the remote to eject *SpongeBob* and switch to WGN. With one out in the top of the fourth, she lost the battle to keep her eyes open.

What an intriguing person. Boone Drake studied the handsome, aging southern belle as she recited her story. Margaret was a little old for his taste, so it wasn't like he was attracted to her in the conventional sense. But he could sure see why she had drawn so much attention in her prime. It was her personality as much as her earthy sensuality.

"I got the impression Jack was getting ready to pop the question," she said. "And I was feeling pretty good about that. Did I want to be married for the fourth time, and to a man with the same record? No. But I'm a romantic. I believe there's someone for everyone and that sometimes it takes a lifetime to find your soul mate. I know it's starry-eyed thinking, but that's where I was.

"Strangest thing, though. One night Jack was workin' late—with you, I think—and I stayed in, turned off the TV, and just sat thinking about our future. I liked what I had to look forward to and decided I'd say yes. Give it one more shot, this time going for broke. Don't ask me what that one means either.

"Anyway, for the first time in decades—in fact, since just after my daughter died—I found myself wanting to pray."

"Really."

"You believe that?"

"Sure. One of those life moments."

"But I'd been so far from God for so long, I had no business—"

"Yeah, but—"

"I know; I know. He was still there. I was the one who had moved. But still, when I found myself asking God if I was doing the right thing, I honestly expected him to say, 'What're you askin' me for? You haven't cared up to now.' Don't imagine God talks that way, but that's what I was expecting."

"And what *did* he say?"

"Well, 'course he didn't say anything. He never has—to me, anyway. I guess he talks to some people, if you can believe 'em. He just sorta impresses stuff on me, you know?"

"I do."

"He pretty much just opened my eyes. He wasn't telling me I didn't deserve to be happy or be in love. But it was like truth just washed all over me. I sat there knowing that I had been rationalizing, justifying living for me, doing what I wanted to do, the heck with what I knew God would want. It was my true love for Jack that opened my eyes. All of a sudden I just knew that if I married Jack, we wouldn't be equally yoked and I wouldn't have done a thing about the way I was living."

"So that's when you gave Jack all those conditions?"

"Was that how it came off?"

"Well, to him, sure. And that's how it was, wasn't it?"

Margaret leaned forward and rested her elbows on the table, supporting her chin with her fists. "First I went back to church, started listening to Christian radio, brought home some Christian books, and—"

"Quit sleeping with Jack."

"He told you that too?"

"He wasn't happy."

"I know I made things difficult for him, but I tried to explain. I wasn't too happy with him either, that he had told me all about you being a Christian but never mentioned my faith to you. I mean, I was what they call backslidden, living in sin, all that, but I knew better. I was a believer. I worried I was too far gone and that God wouldn't forgive me and take me back. My parents were both gone by then, so it was already too late to reconcile with them. I had to figure this out on my own."

"Jack has some church background."

"True," she said, "but not a good one. I guess when he was a teenager he went with friends for a year or so, but it was one of those churches that was all about working to try to be good. He liked booze and girls, so he never felt worthy. 'Course, you and I know nobody can earn salvation anyway. But the whole rules thing turned him off."

"And so did your leaving him and telling him that if he wanted to see you it had to be at church."

"It worked."

"I know, but he still says he's not comfortable and that it doesn't feel right to go only so he can see you."

"I told him it's not a date and that he has to go without me sometimes too."

Boone sighed. "Guess he doesn't think it's fair."

"And maybe it isn't. But I know it's right. I can't be marrying him, and certainly I can't be living with him, the way things stand."

"But you still love each other."

"We sure do. And that makes it tough."

8

★★★★

CHAOS

Florence's eyes were shut, the Cubs' announcers droned on, and her body felt leaden. She was vaguely aware that Haeley's brother and Max had finished up in the kitchen and were tiptoeing and whispering as they came into the living room.

"You know what my name means?" Alfonso said quietly.

"Nope. I don't even know what *Max* means. Are names s'posed to mean something?"

"Most people don't think about it, but your mom's and my parents did. *Alfonso* means 'noble and ready.'"

"Like a Ranger."

"Exactly."

"What does my mom's name mean?"

Alfonso laughed. "You won't believe it," he whispered. "You ready?"

Max nodded.

"It means 'hay meadow.'"

"*Hay* meadow?"

"Yup. Guess they just liked the name."

That almost brought Florence to life. "I've always loved her name," she slurred, eyes still shut.

"Me too," Alfonso said. "Sorry to wake you, ma'am. How're the Cubs doing?"

"Haven't been watchin'. Got a little shut-eye."

"Want to get some more? I can take Max to the park, and we'll be back within the hour."

"Oh, no, no. I'll go. Just give me a minute."

"Would you rather watch the Cubs, Max?" Alfonso said.

"Baseball? No! Boring!"

"Only because you don't understand it," Florence said, sitting up. "You'll like it someday." She found herself wishing she'd taken Alfonso up on his offer to take Max for a while. She could use a little more time on the couch. If he offered again, she decided, she'd say yes.

"I hope you don't feel I wasted your time, Boone," Margaret said, reaching for her handbag, still looking silly in her floppy hat.

"Not at all. A lot of that was new to me."

"Basically, I just want you to pray for Jack. And for me. I feel like I've learned a lot and come a long way the last several months. But I've got a long way to go. And you know Jack does."

Boone started at the sound of the back door and looked up to see Haeley slowly step into the light. "You guys about done?" she said, her voice faint and shaky.

He looked at his watch. "Did you get some rest?"

"Not really. I think I'd better get home."

"Sure," Boone said, rising quickly. But as he did, the table rose a few inches on his side and Margaret's purse slid off, hit the bench, and then the concrete. Her stuff scattered, and Boone hurried to help her gather it.

Margaret scooped most of the contents back into the bag, then held it open and told Boone to just drop in his handfuls. Haeley approached and found a lipstick tube at the edge of the patio. As she bent to pick it up, she stayed down for a second. When she rose slowly and brought it to Margaret, Boone was alarmed at how pale and weak Haeley looked in the sun.

"You'd better sit down, hon," he said, but the words were barely out of his mouth when she stopped about six feet away and dropped the tube. Her head fell back as if she were studying the sky. Then her eyes rolled up.

Boone moved to get to her just as Margaret did, stepping directly into his path. As he tried to shove the older woman out of the way, Haeley began to sway.

To Boone's horror, he could tell she was unconscious as she spun. Her knees appeared to lock and she toppled, as if in slow motion. As he reached in vain to try to block her fall, the back of Haeley's head hit the concrete with a crack so resounding that Boone feared it had killed her.

Margaret screamed for Jack and Boone bellowed, "Call 911!" as he knelt over Haeley. Her body lay rigid, pupils fixed and dilated. Boone pressed his head against her chest and heard her heart thudding. But when he gently felt the back of her head he found her skull had shattered like an eggshell. A black pool expanded around her in the merciless sun.

"Happy to take him for a little while, ma'am," Alfonso said. "We can have our ice cream when we get back."

"Actually, that sounds good," Florence said. "Would you like that, Max?"

"Like what? Ice cream?"

"Going to the park with your uncle."

"No!"

"No?"

"I want *you* to come, Aunt Flo."

"I'll be fixin' your Neapolitan."

"No! You come!"

"Let's let Aunt Flo rest, eh, little buddy?"

"No!"

"Be a good soldier."

"He's a little shy of you yet," Florence said. "It's all right. I'll get myself together here."

Boone fought with everything in him to stay on task. How was one supposed to stanch bleeding from the skull? "Margaret, get me some towels!"

Margaret stood whimpering as the back door flew open and everyone burst out. "What happened?" Fletcher Galloway said, rushing to the other end of the yard, where he found an old canvas umbrella lying near a stack of chopped wood.

"She fell!" Margaret said as she hurried inside. "Dorothy, we need towels!"

Jack Keller was on his cell phone, barking the address

and ordering an ambulance. With his free hand he helped Fletcher wrestle the umbrella open and situate it so Haeley was shaded. "Jack," Fletcher said, "switch places with Drake. She doesn't look good. Lord, help the girl."

Boone was awash in a tidal wave of emotion, frantic to keep terror from overwhelming him. Could he again be losing the love of his life? Had God not taught him enough by allowing one catastrophe?

As Margaret reappeared with towels, Jack pulled Boone away from Haeley. "Let me," he said. "Closest trauma center is Mount Sinai at Ogden and California. Call the ER there and tell 'em what to expect."

Boone felt helpless, anger now invading. He was trained in every emergency situation, yet all he wanted was to drive his fist through something.

"Do it, Boones!" Jack said. He hit a button on his own cell and said, "Chicago Police. Connect me with the ER at Mount Sinai in Douglas Park." He handed Boone the phone and carefully placed the towels under Haeley's head.

Boone felt as if time were racing, every second taking his beloved closer to the point of no return. He wanted nothing more than to hear a screaming siren. As Margaret and Dorothy held hands and prayed over Haeley and Fletcher stood grim sentinel with the umbrella, the ER answered.

Boone was somehow able to recite what had happened and answer questions, finally hearing the ambulance in the distance. He switched to his own phone and called Dr. Murari Sarangan, catching him at home. After Boone filled him in and pleaded with him to meet them at Mount Sinai, Dr. Sarangan said, "My whole family will be praying, sir. And

I am on my way. The EMTs are professionals and will know this, but remind them to be very careful how they secure and move your wife. That is the absolute most crucially important thing right now."

"Can she survive this?"

"It sounds very serious, sir. Are her eyes still open?"

"Yes."

"Still fixed and dilated?"

"Yes."

"Still getting a pulse?"

"Jack! Pulse?"

Keller held his thumb and forefinger on either side of Haeley's neck at the carotid artery. "Faint," he mouthed.

"Weak," Boone reported.

"Any tremors, extremities quivering?"

"I see nothing."

"The body is protecting her; she may already be in a coma."

"A coma?"

"That's not all bad, Boone. But how the EMTs deal with the injury while monitoring her vital signs will make all the difference. They must be very careful with the neck. I'm getting in my car. When they arrive, would you give them my number?"

Florence was perspiring by the time she and Max and Alfonso reached the lobby. Alfonso was texting on his phone. "Keeping Mom and Dad up to date. They want to know how Haeley reacts when she sees me. I might even record it."

Willie had a tiny TV going with the Cubs game on, but he

was dozing. He roused when they reached his desk. "Where we goin'?" he said.

"To play!" Max said.

"Good for you! Hot out there."

"Only a little while," Alfonso said.

"Ain't gonna be too hot for you, soldier. Nothing like over there, I bet."

"You're right. But I know better than to keep anyone else in the sun for long."

As soon as they reached the sidewalk, Florence felt her baggy top cling to her back. "Oh, my," she said. "I'm not gonna be able to stand much of this."

"Can we swing?" Max said.

"Long as there's a place for me to sit in the shade," she said.

"First I want to show you my car," Alfonso said. "It's just down here."

He walked briskly ahead, and Max ran to keep up. "Don't be gettin' too far ahead now," Florence said.

"Sorry!" Alfonso said, slowing and reaching for Max's hand. "Let's wait for Aunt Flo. We can run a little later."

When they reached the old blue Buick at the curb, Florence was struck that Alfonso had left the front windows open. "This's no neighborhood to be doin' that in," she said.

"It's insured," he said, chuckling. "Anyway, nobody wants to steal an ancient beast like this. It's older'n I am. Dad could never let it go. Haeley and I pretend drove it in the garage when we were little."

"It's nice," Florence said. "I 'member those. Mr. Quigley always wanted one."

"I like it too," Max said. "Can I have a ride?"

"Maybe later," Alfonso said. "We can all go somewhere."

"For ice cream?"

"You got ice cream at my place," Florence said. "Let's just get your swingin' in and get back, hmm?"

She found a wood bench under a tree near the swings and sat fanning her face with both hands. Max ran toward the swings, but Alfonso called him back. "Let's get some pictures for your mom," he said, pulling out his cell phone. "Sit next to Aunt Flo."

Florence chortled. "There is no 'next to Aunt Flo.' You want the boy to disappear?" She opened her arms, and Max climbed into her fleshy lap.

"You're all hot and sweaty," Max said.

"I am that," she said, wrapping her arms around him and hoping he would disguise how wide she was. Cameras were not her friends, especially phone cameras. "Now, Alfonso, I'm as dark as he is white. Can your phone handle that?"

"We'll see. Smile."

Alfonso showed it to her as Max wriggled for a view. Florence was stunned. She actually loved the picture. Max had pressed his head back against her chest at the last instant and looked as comfortable as a boy could be. They looked happy together. A sliver of sunlight through the branches made his hair look shiny white.

"You got to send that to me. Can you do that?"

Alfonso handed her the phone. "Sure. Just punch your cell phone number in there, and I'll show you how to send the picture to your phone."

It took a few tries and some coaching from Alfonso. He leaned close and pointed to the keypad. "View pictures, select, share, text, send." He looked up. "Done! Now you shoot one of Max and me."

"All right, if I don't have to move."

Max joined Alfonso in front of Florence, and she shot a slightly crooked picture of them.

"Haeley'll love this!" he said, pushing a bunch of buttons. "And I'm copying you on it too, ma'am. Hey, Max, you want to see your mom and me just before I shipped out?" He pushed a few buttons and sat on the bench next to Florence. Max climbed in his lap and stared into the phone. One of the pictures stored in his phone was of him shoulder to shoulder with Haeley, and if Florence had to guess, she would have said their smiles hid the fear of what his overseas assignment could mean.

Soon Alfonso was lifting the boy into a swing. He pushed Max higher and higher. "You be careful now, soldier!" Florence called out. "I got to answer for this boy, you know."

"I'd no more hurt him than you, ma'am! Max, you want to play tag?"

"Sure! How?"

Alfonso caught the swing in midair and brought it to a slow stop. "I tag you—like this—and run away. That makes you *it*. Then you catch me and tag me, and I'm it. Trees and my car are safe."

"You gonna be runnin' all around?" Florence said. "I need to keep sittin'."

"We'll stay in sight," Alfonso said. "Won't we, Max?"

"Yeah!"

"A'ight then."

But when Max and his uncle began scampering around

the park, laughing and squealing and chasing each other, Max racing from tree to tree for safety, Florence worked herself up off the bench. The boy was getting redder by the minute and looked to be sweating more than she was. It was time to get back to the cool apartment and some Neapolitan. You're never cooler, she told herself, than when you've been hot.

"I'm not leaving her," Boone told Jack as two EMTs, a man and a woman about his age, flew into the yard.

"That's fine; you go with her. We'll meet you at the hospital."

"Can Margaret come with me?"

"We don't want to crowd the back of the bus," the male EMT said.

Jack flashed his badge. "You're going to have the patient and two riders," he said. "Let's not spend one more second arguing."

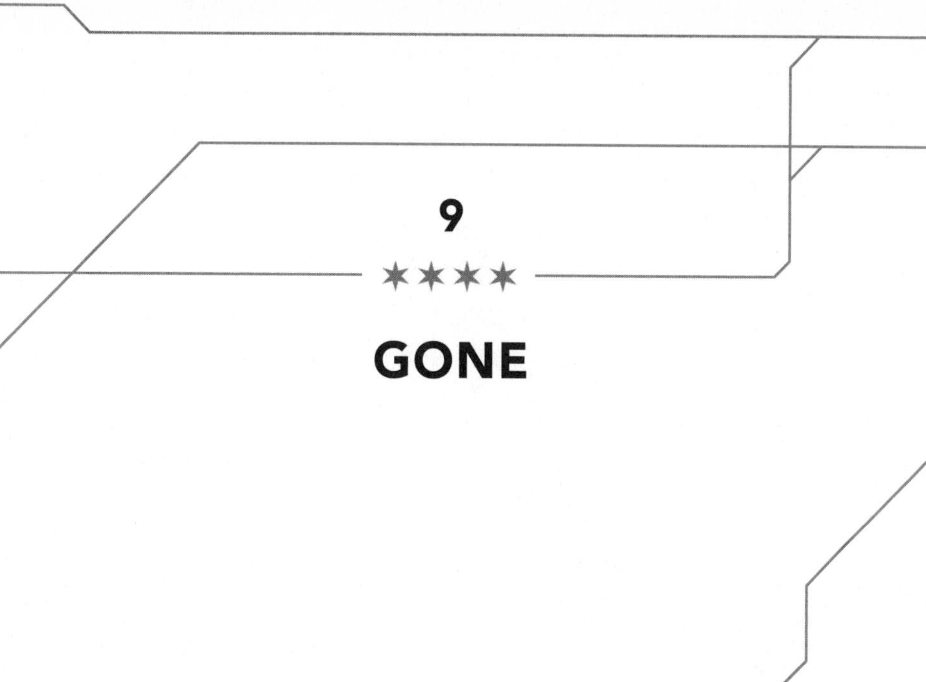

9

GONE

FLORENCE TRIED TO stay in the shade as she shuffled along, working to keep Max in sight. He appeared to be having the time of his life, and she could hear his high-pitched laugh from way across the park. Apparently Alfonso was *it*, and Florence could tell he was running slowly after Max on purpose. He could have easily run the boy down with his strong, athletic stride. How nice for Max to have another uncle, especially one like Alfonso.

The boy had bolted from the last safe tree and was running in the open now—heading toward Alfonso's car. Florence was glad it sat on the park side of the street, but still she hoped Alfonso would know better than to let Max get too close to traffic. As soon as his uncle caught him, she was going to signal them it was time to head back.

But it seemed the more she hurried, the farther away they got. *Must be nice to be young.*

Now Max was cackling, looking back, pumping his little arms and legs, and heading straight for the Buick. "Not my car!" Alfonso cried out in mock fear. "The car is safe and you'll have foiled me again!"

Max proved he had a sense of humor too, because when he reached the Buick, he didn't touch it for safety but stood near it, seeming to tease his uncle.

"You rascal!" Alfonso called out. "Be careful or I'll tag you!"

Just as he reached the boy, Max touched the car. Alfonso collapsed to the sidewalk as if spent and defeated, and they both laughed and laughed. Alfonso stood and opened his arms and Max went to him. The Ranger lifted him and twirled him, making Max hoot even more.

"But you know what?" Alfonso said, setting the boy down. "You're it!"

"No fair!" Max said and charged his uncle. Alfonso ducked out of the way at the last second, then deftly dove through the window of the car. Max followed, and as he got his torso in the window and pushed off the door handle with his foot—disappearing from sight—Florence heard Alfonso yell, "I'm safe in here! I'm safe!"

Florence was within fifty feet of them now. She hated to interrupt their fun, but it was time for at least Max and her to get inside and cool off with some ice cream. Maybe a Ranger could keep running around in this heat, but not them.

Then she heard the car start. "Hey!" she hollered. "No time for joy ridin'! Let's go!"

"I'll just run him around the block!" Alfonso said. "Be right back!"

"Make sure he's buckled!"

As the big old sedan eased away from the curb, Alfonso called out, "Buckled in good!"

"He shouldn't be in the front seat!"

"I'll be careful! Have our ice cream ready!"

Boys.

Boone kept enough of his wits about him to know how important it was to stay on the good side of the EMTs. Haeley's life was in their hands.

"We need to tend to the victim," the man told him when Boone tried to pass along Dr. Sarangan's number. "I can't really talk to a doctor until we've got her on board."

"Let me put him on speaker then," Boone said, dialing.

As the doctor tried to walk them through the best procedure for keeping Haeley alive in transit, both EMTs kept saying, "Yes, sir; yes, doctor, we know; we know. Let us work."

"I have full confidence in you," Sarangan said. "I'll meet you at Sinai."

Boone found himself hovering, staring, straining to see any sign of life. Haeley looked ghastly. She had gone from pale to nearly translucent, and her lips were bluing. Her unseeing eyes never moved; she never blinked.

Boone also watched for the responses of the EMTs as they grimly squatted beside her, the man checking her vitals while the woman traded out the blood-logged towels for sterile pads. Both seemed to be trying to appear merely focused, but Boone could tell they were as sobered and shaken as everyone else. He saw them catch each other's eyes, and he could tell they were not optimistic.

"You may not want to watch this, sir," the woman said, as the other EMT brought a neck brace from the ambulance. "It will look strange."

"Don't worry about him," Jack said. "He's a cop."

But the young woman was right. It did look weird for them to gingerly stabilize Haeley's head while painstakingly applying the brace to keep her neck straight. The man took her long dark hair, now black and caked with blood, and held it free of the brace. He had to then change out even the latest supply of sterile pads collecting the blood.

"Hurry, please," Boone said, trying to mask his dread.

"We need to get her to the ER fast," the man said. "But we must not move her in any way that could make things worse."

He jogged to the ambulance for the wood board and straps that would convey her to the gurney inside the vehicle. Readying her for transfer to the board seemed to take forever, but finally they seemed satisfied. "We'll need some help," the man said. "We'll handle her from the shoulders up, but could you and you"—he pointed at Boone and Jack—"keep her legs absolutely in line with her body as we move her."

The woman EMT cradled Haeley's devastated head, gloved hands dripping, while the other worked his arm all the way under her shoulders. They directed Boone and Jack to each support her with one hand on her lower back and the other just below the knee. On a three count they moved her from the concrete to the board.

"Now please give us room."

With one EMT at each end of the board, they lifted her to waist level and smoothly moved her through the back gate to the boxy truck, its back doors yawning. They slid the board directly onto a fixed gurney, and then the man climbed out, peeling off his gloves. He reached back in and deposited the gloves in a contaminated-waste receptacle.

"I'll pull out when I hear these doors shut," he said, heading for the cab.

"Whoever's going, let's go now," the woman said, and Boone and Margaret clambered aboard. The EMT pointed to a narrow bench on one side of the gurney. Boone sat near Haeley's head and Margaret slipped in behind him and draped an arm across his shoulders. "I'm praying," she said.

"Can I hold her hand?" Boone said as the woman reached to slam the doors.

"As lightly as you can," she said, deftly attaching monitors, an IV, and an oxygen mask. "If we sway or jostle, let her move naturally."

Boone took Haeley's hand and lightly enfolded it in both of his. If not for the beeps from the monitor, he would have been hard pressed to believe she was still with him. "Is she going to make it?"

Boone's heart sank when the young woman hesitated and wouldn't meet his eye. Finally the EMT sighed. "If you're a cop, you don't want any bull. Truth is, I don't know, but we're going to get her to where she'll have every chance."

Margaret whispered urgently into her cell phone. When she was finished, she asked Boone for the number of Max's sitter. "Better see if she can keep him a few days. I can pick up some things from your house and get them to her."

Boone showed her Florence's number from his phone and turned back to Haeley.

"I'm not getting an answer, Boone. What was the name of her building? I'll leave a message with the desk."

It wasn't like Boone to have to rack his brain for such details. He closed his eyes. "Something Arms. Bethune, that's it. Bethune Arms."

As Margaret punched in 411, Boone couldn't keep himself from wondering what the odds were of a man losing two wives within years of each other.

Life had been too good.

He hadn't deserved it.

The other shoe had dropped.

Florence was on meds for blood pressure and sugar, and as she stood shaking her head at the idea of Max's uncle taking him for a ride around the block, she couldn't remember whether she had taken her pills that morning. Her breath came in short puffs, and her heart raced. "Gettin' the dehydration, I bet," she muttered. "Got to get me a drink."

Though she knew it was dangerous to wait and that water was more important than getting off her feet, she was about to drop where she stood. Florence looked for another bench. If she could only take a few minutes to slow her heart and get her breath, she'd find the energy to get back to her apartment.

The closest bench was the cement one at the bus stop outside her building. That became her goal. It wasn't a bad spot, either, for seeing when Alfonso got back with Max. She knew his uncle would take good care of him, but

Florence was also prepared to scold that boy—veteran or not—*for usurpin' my authority.*

Suddenly the rotund old woman found herself sweating profusely. Perspiration dripped from her hair into her eyes and down her cheeks. Her arms sent rivulets into her hands. Well, that was good, wasn't it? At least she wasn't clammy and shaking like when her sugar was low. And if she was dehydrated, her body's cooling system would have shut down; she knew that much.

Still, Florence had to get off her feet and regroup, then get back to her lobby. If she was in trouble, Willie could help. But that bus bench, like Max and his uncle had done, seemed to get farther away the more she moved toward it. Florence wiped her eyes and her mouth with both hands, then stopped and rested her fists at her sides, arms akimbo. *Breathe,* she told herself. *Just slow yourself down and breathe.*

"You okay, Big Mama?" A slender man in sagging pants with a bottle-shaped paper bag in his hand leaned close to stare into her face.

He was one of the local alkies. "Hey, Scooter," she said. "No, I don't feel so good. Jes' trying to get to the bus bench."

"Don't you live right there? Where you goin'?"

"Need to rest 'fore I go back up."

"I kin get you to that bench, Mama. You got any change on you?"

"I ain't payin' you to walk me, Scooter."

"Come on now, I'm just sayin' . . ."

"Do I look like I got my purse with me?"

"Just remember me next time you're out."

"I'll give you a couple when I see you. Now, you gonna help me or what?"

"Calm yourself down and come on."

Scooter slipped a bony hand under Florence's elbow and let her lean on him till he delivered her to the bench. "You gon' be all right now?"

"Mm-hm. Thank you, Scooter."

"You won't forget me now . . ."

"I'll whip your tail you remind me again. I told you I would; now get on outta here."

"Kill a guy for helpin'," he said, lurching away.

Florence was relieved to be off her feet, but then she chastised herself for thinking it made any sense to still be in the sun. She should have just let Scooter get her to the building. But then he would have wanted five bucks. Now her pulse felt funny. Fast, then fluttery. Her breathing should have slowed from sitting, but because of what her heart was doing, she was huffing. Suddenly her priority became getting herself inside.

Boone was desperate for any sign of hope. He didn't want to distract the EMT, and Margaret was sitting there with her phone calls made and her head bowed. Boone took a modicum of comfort in that the sounds from the equipment were steady and regular. He'd been in enough traumatic situations to recognize when respiration or pulse were erratic. That was never good.

Sarangan was probably right; Haeley was in a coma. She was going to need blood; that was sure. Boone started when the EMT tried to close her eyes. "Just don't want them to get drier and more irritated," the woman said. When she had trouble keeping the lids closed, she sprayed something into the eyes, and Boone was sure he saw Haeley flinch.

"That's good, isn't it?"

"Yes, sir, it is. She's not conscious, but she's not entirely comatose, either."

The driver slowed almost to a stop before swinging into the ER port at Mount Sinai. A dip in the pavement made the ambulance sway, and the young EMT braced herself and held both sides of the gurney. "Let go your wife's hand, sir, and you and your friend stay put until we get her out."

Boone and Margaret gripped the edge of the bench to stay upright until the vehicle settled. Boone was warmed to see medical personnel huddled under the overhang. As soon as the ambulance stopped, they rushed the back and swung the doors open.

Several men and women in scrubs grabbed the gurney and waited while the EMT released the fasteners and arranged for the equipment to go with Haeley. As soon as they rolled her out, a woman with a clipboard began scribbling as the EMT called out pulse, BP, pulse-ox, and tried to describe the trauma. Boone heard neutral words like *Caucasian*, *female*, and *twenty-nine*. Then *severe*, *cranial*, *hemorrhaging*, *nonresponsive*, and *grave*—not one of those hopeful.

By the time Boone and Margaret exited the ambulance, the ER team was far ahead, running with the gurney through doors held open by their colleagues. "You go ahead, Boone," Margaret said. "Stay with her. I'll find you."

But as Boone ran to catch up, an ER nurse stopped him in the corridor. "She's going straight to the OR, sir."

"I'm going with her."

"She has the best chance if the room remains sterile. You don't want to get in the way of this, Mr. Drake."

Of course the nurse was right. But the last thing Boone wanted was to sit in some waiting room for the same news he'd heard too few years before—news that had obliterated life as he had known it. The nurse pointed to a room. "Your friends, your pastor, and your doctor are on their way. I'll send them to you as soon as they get here."

Margaret reached him and put her hands on his shoulders, steering him down the hall. "There's nothing we can do but pray," she said.

He knew that was true too, and he hated it with all that was in him.

10

★★★★

LIMBO

By the time Florence reached her building, she was afraid she was going to faint. She grabbed the handle of the glass doors leading into the lobby and forced herself to stay upright, despite how light her head felt. She just knew Willie was snoring in front of the TV.

But no, here he came. *Thank God.*

"Miz Quigley!" he said. "What'sa matter?"

"Dizzy."

He was a wiry man, older than Florence, but she felt much better supported with his arm around her waist than she had with Scooter. "Let's get you in here. You're burnin' up."

"Need water."

"Where's the boy and the soldier?"

"Out for a ride. They'll be back soon."

Willie situated her in a saggy easy chair near the counter and made sure she wouldn't pitch onto the floor before he rushed to the washroom. He emerged with two plastic cups of water in one hand and a bunch of soaked paper towels in the other.

Florence took a cup in each hand as the man dabbed her forehead and face with the towels. "Just sip," he said. "Don't overdo it."

"You're a dear," she said. "Can you do me one more favor?"

"Anything, ma'am. You know that."

"Could you get my pills from my flat? I think I forgot this mornin'."

"That's no good."

"I know. I keep them on the counter in the kitchen, next to the sink. Just bring the whole dispenser box. You need my key?"

"My master'll work, ma'am. Can you get to the phone if it rings while I'm gone?"

"Oh, go on, Willie. You told me yourself nobody ever calls here."

"Got a call for you just a few minutes ago. Woman said the boy's mother was in some sorta accident and could you keep him a few days if necessary."

"Oh no! What happened? Car wreck?"

"That's all I know, ma'am. Lady seemed in a hurry. Said she would bring you more clothes and such for him if you could do it."

"Well, 'course I can. I just hope Haeley's all right."

No surprise, when Jack arrived with the Galloways, he took charge. "Listen, Boones, we've got the logistics all figured out. Here's what's going to happen. We brought your car. It's in valet parking; here's the ticket. Fletch and Dorothy will run Margaret and me back to our cars at your place, and I'll bring back whatever you tell me to bring for you. Margaret will take stuff to the sitter's for Max."

"You got in touch with Florence?" Boone said, fishing his house key out of his pocket for Margaret. "She can keep him a few days?"

"You know she will. Margaret talked to someone at her building."

"We wanna be here for you, Boone," Fletcher Galloway said, "but we'd best be on our way and get Jack and Margaret back to their cars. We'll keep in touch and we'll be praying."

"Yes," Dorothy said, embracing Boone. "We will."

"Let's not leave till someone shows up to be with him," Margaret said.

"I'm all right," Boone said. "You can go."

"Nonsense," she said. "Not till your doctor friend or your pastor get here."

As if on cue, they entered together. As the others left, Boone shook hands with Dr. Sarangan and Francisco Sosa. "We've got to quit meeting like this," he said, and he wasn't kidding. Sitting in the waiting room of a trauma center with these two brought back memories he had fought to whip into submission.

"They're allowing me to assist," the doctor said, "so let me scrub up and get in there. I'll tell you everything as soon we get her stabilized."

"Don't let them give up on her, please!"

"Giving up is not on the agenda, Boone," Dr. Sarangan said as he hurried out.

"Let's sit," Pastor Sosa said, worry and compassion in his eyes.

"I can't, Francisco. And don't think you and I need to pray together either. I'm praying every second, and I don't know what else to say or ask. If I sound bitter, I am. I don't know how much of this I can take. I barely survived last time."

"This isn't about you, Boone."

"You think I don't know that? But who's it going to be about if I lose her? What am I going to tell Max?"

Boone broke down and Francisco embraced him. "I don't pretend to know what to say, Boone," he whispered. "Just know that everybody who stood by you before is with you again, come what may."

Boone pulled away and paced. "Come what may? They're going to be a big help if I wind up a single father to a boy who just took my name. And you! What was with that last Bible verse you sent me?"

"What was it?"

"*You* don't remember?"

"Sorry. I send those to people when the Lord prompts me. Just remind me what it was about or where it was—"

"Job! Job, Francisco! I couldn't imagine encouragement coming from that godforsaken book, and I was right. Something about man being born to trouble. Well, you were right; I sure was. Am I Job now? Does God have to strip everything from me again? Why?"

Boone read the pain in Sosa's face. "I'm sorry, Pastor. This isn't your fault."

"I can take it. Fire away. Just don't take it out on God."

"Who else is there?" Boone said.

"Exactly."

"Don't get cute. But tell me, what was the Job passage all about?"

"You missed it, that's all."

"Missed what?"

"The passage in its entirety."

"Enlighten me."

Francisco pulled out his phone and seemed to be scrolling. "Found it," he said. "You missed the little *ff* after the reference. My fault. I should have been clearer. The *ff* means 'and following.'"

"I know what it means, Pastor, but I wasn't reading that closely."

"Well, I can see how that one verse, about man being born to trouble as surely as sparks fly upward, would be a head scratcher. What follows makes it make sense. I can read it to you if you're at a place where you can concentrate."

"Not sure I am."

"I totally understand."

The door cracked open and the ER nurse said, "Pastor Sosa, a moment?"

Boone had to fight the urge to tackle Francisco. What could it mean that she wanted to see him alone? Had Haeley already died, and did Francisco need to be briefed so he could break the news?

Boone slid onto a leather couch and buried his head in his hands. Was he ready for this? The same dark feeling came over him that had when he lost Nikki. The only difference was that he had no son to worry about then, as Josh had died in the fire too. The only light at the end of this tunnel was that Max would need his adopted dad as never before. What kind of shape would he be in to raise that boy alone?

Alone and helpless and pleading with God, Boone felt at the end of himself. What was he to do right now? Nothing? Wallow in hopelessness? This had to be what a death row inmate felt during his last hours.

Boone pulled out his cell phone and brought up his mobile Bible. He scrolled to Job 5, this time to see that sobering passage in its full context.

For affliction does not come from the dust,
nor does trouble sprout from the ground,
but man is born to trouble
as the sparks fly upward.

As for me, I would seek God,
and to God would I commit my cause,
who does great things and unsearchable,
marvelous things without number:
He gives rain on the earth
and sends waters on the fields;
He sets on high those who are lowly,
and those who mourn are lifted to safety.
He frustrates the devices of the crafty,
so that their hands achieve no success.
He catches the wise in their own craftiness,
and the schemes of the wily are brought to a quick end.
They meet with darkness in the daytime
and grope at noonday as in the night.
But he saves the needy from the sword of their mouth

and from the hand of the mighty.
So the poor have hope,
and injustice shuts her mouth.

Behold, blessed is the one whom God reproves;
therefore despise not the discipline of the Almighty.
For he wounds, but he binds up;
he shatters, but his hands heal.
He will deliver you from six troubles;
in seven no evil shall touch you.

Well, that made a little more sense, but just then it didn't offer more comfort, and Boone knew it was a passage that would take a long time to digest. *"Despise not the discipline of the Almighty"?* What was he being disciplined for?

Right now all he wanted was for Francisco to return with anything but bad news.

"Well, now that's somethin'," Florence said, squinting as she studied her plastic pill box. "Looks like I did take my pills this morning. I hate getting old. Don't you, Willie?"

"I quit getting old years ago, Miz Quigley. I'm what you call levitatin'."

She shook her head. "Now where are those boys?"

"I 'spect they'll be along directly," he said. "You feeling at all better?"

"Getting there."

"You want to try to get yourself upstairs?"

"No. I'll wait for 'em here. Least they can do is walk me up after what they put me through."

11

★★★★

NEWS

Francisco Sosa must have seen the fear in Boone's eyes, as he quickly disabused him of the notion of dreaded news. "Just the church wondering why I was ignoring my cell phone," he said. "I told 'em no more calls until they heard from me."

Boone let out a huge breath.

"You okay?" Sosa said. "I mean, considering?"

Boone nodded. "Trying to talk myself out of 'despising discipline.'"

"Not easy, is it? Just remember the beauty of the next four lines."

"Yeah, well, we'll see."

"And remember, if it turns out you are being reproved, you're also blessed."

"Sorry, not feeling it right now. Just hanging on."

Florence may not have been educated, but she was anything but stupid. Something wasn't right. Too much time had passed. She searched her mind. It would be just like Max to beg for a longer ride, and from what little she knew of his uncle, it might be like him to give in. Maybe he had tried to call her and let her know, but did he even have her number?

"Willie, can I ask one more favor?"

"I done told you, Miz Quigley, I'm just here to serve."

"My cell phone's on the couch up there, and—"

"Say no more. I saw it and shoulda thought to bring it down."

Murari Sarangan arrived with his surgical cap and mask in his hand, and Boone leapt to his feet, frantically searching the doctor's face. The doctor looked him in the eye—which was encouraging, and while he wasn't smiling, he didn't appear defeated either.

"She's not out of the woods yet, Boone, but we do not believe we're going to lose her."

Boone dropped to his knees, and Francisco and Dr. Sarangan had to help him to the couch. He shook his head, nearly unable to speak. "Thank you," he managed.

Sarangan pulled up a chair and sat before him. "I'm not telling you anything you don't know when I say she suffered a severe injury. We're not even certain how severe yet, but we were able to stabilize her."

"Is she conscious? When can I see her?"

"Let's not get ahead of ourselves. There must be much progress before she will be conscious. It could be days."

"Days?"

"She's very lucky in many ways. The specialist said that if she had fallen from any higher than her own height or had landed an inch or two to her right or left, it's unlikely she would have survived the ride here."

While Boone was silently thanking God, he was also reeling. "How bad is it? Can she fully recover?"

Again Boone hated the hesitation.

The doctor rose, tossed his mask in the trash, tucked his cap in a pocket, and sat again. "Let me be frank, Boone. I confess that remaining professionally objective in this case is not easy for me. I forced myself to stay focused in the OR, but when Haeley was being wheeled into the recovery room, I was perhaps more optimistic than was warranted."

"What are you saying?"

The doctor raised his brows and straightened. "I'm afraid that while asking Sam—that's the specialist, the neurosurgeon—what I could tell you, he immediately noticed that I appeared unrealistically positive."

"Meaning?"

"I couldn't hide that I thought things went as well as could be expected. He made me promise not to get your hopes up."

Boone recoiled. "You already have! What do you mean?"

"Just that he reminded me it's way too early to determine what brain functions may have been affected, let alone which might be completely restored."

"You mean memory, speech—?"

"Boone, really, it could be a long time before we know what may have been affected, how seriously, and whether we can expect progress."

"Then what are you telling me? Should I be preparing for a vegetative state, in-home care, rehab, what?"

"There's no need to jump to conclusions. Our sole goal at this stage was to save Haeley's life. That we were able to stabilize her was a major accomplishment, and I'm just thrilled to tell you that we expect her to survive."

Boone sat back. "Whoa. For now I'll take what I can get. Do you have a few more minutes?"

"I do. I'm planning on being here for about four more hours to monitor her."

"I appreciate that. Listen, Francisco here will tell you that I can be a little detail oriented."

Dr. Sarangan appeared to fight a smile. "I don't need our pastor to tell me that. What do you want to know?"

"Just everything. What am I dealing with here? Can you give it to me in layman's terms?"

"Sure. Haeley's in a coma caused by blunt force trauma to the brain. A coma can be caused by bleeding, swelling, or not enough oxygen or blood sugar to the brain. Are you familiar with the RAS—the reticular activating system?"

"Uh, no."

"It's like your body's on-off switch for automatic reflexes like respiration, heartbeat, even blood pressure. When someone slips into a coma, the first thing we have to determine is whether the RAS has stopped or both hemispheres of the brain have shut down for some reason. The specialist thinks Haeley's RAS malfunctioned because of the fall."

"I'm still trying to figure out why she fainted. Do you think she's pregnant?"

"We should know that in a matter of minutes. We sent

blood to the lab. Frankly, I hope she is, because otherwise we need to diagnose what else might have caused her symptoms."

"But wouldn't pregnancy be bad while she's trying to recover?"

"It would certainly add an element of risk for her and for a baby. But comatose women have delivered healthy babies before."

Boone stood. The relief that Haeley was still alive was one thing, but the prospect that she might be pregnant was almost too much. "So what exactly happened to her brain when she hit the ground? What does blunt force trauma mean?"

"The brain is fragile, not intended to absorb a lot of force. That's why it's protected by six layers of tissue, including bone. With nothing apparently blocking her fall, Haeley's impact with the concrete effectively penetrated all those layers. I hate to use this medical term, but the neurosurgeon called it a 'pre-death event.' Ironically, the best thing that happened, all things considered, is that the shattering of the skull allowed the injured brain to swell without pushing down on the stem, where the RAS is headquartered. Had this occurred without anywhere for all the blood and fluid to go, we would have had to reduce the pressure by drilling a hole. Otherwise the swelling could push down on the stem enough to result in permanent shutting down of the RAS."

"The on-off switch. So, death."

"Correct."

"Never thought I'd be thankful for a cracked skull."

Sarangan nodded. "A minor blow to the head can knock someone out, but in most cases the brain is able to turn itself back on. In this case, the impact rendered Haeley unable to respond. Fortunately we don't have to worry about edema because of the damage to the posterior skull."

"English?"

"Edema is the swelling, and because the back of her head is open for now, the additional fluid has somewhere to escape rather than compressing the brain against the skull. Of course, she lost a lot of blood, and we had to replenish that."

Boone nodded. "So, how long till you can get her out of her coma?"

"Oh, we must not do that yet. In fact, the specialist gave her meds that will keep her in an induced coma that will allow us to treat every affected area. If she were to regain consciousness now, there's no telling what damage the body might do in an attempt to heal itself."

"We don't want the body to heal itself?"

"Not yet. Sometimes the body will perform a sort of triage and shut off blood to damaged areas. We don't want that. There will be swelling, and the more swelling, the deeper the coma, but because the injury has helped us with the extra fluid, she's stable. And the best part about moving her from a trauma-induced coma to a medically induced one is that it is reversible when Sam decides it's time."

"So you didn't repair the fracture? It felt pretty bad."

"The skull will be reconstructed eventually, but for now it's left more elastic for our purposes. She won't be able to rest on the back of her head, and she won't look her best for a while, but for now, she's right where we want her to be."

"I can't ask for more than that."

"And we have no idea how far back she can come functionally."

"If at all?"

"Oh, I think she'll return to the person you knew, but it could be a long, slow process, and she may never be 100 percent. On the other hand, some patients completely recover. But I am making no promises."

Florence quickly scrolled through her phone messages and found only the one from Margaret about her keeping Max a few more days. She wanted to call Margaret back and let her know she was more than happy to keep Max and also to find out what had happened to Haeley. But she had a sick feeling in the pit of her stomach. She wanted to know where Alfonso had taken Max, and she wanted to know right now.

"Willie, you put on some sort of recordin' for when you have to be away from the desk, don't you?"

"Yes, ma'am, but management doesn't like me to use it much, and neither do I."

"Well, it's time to turn it on. I got a job for ya and no time to argue about it."

"But, Miz—"

"Willie, you know me! Now set it up and do what I tell ya. I wouldn't ask lightly, and you said you'd do anything for me. This is an emergency."

He fiddled with the buttons on the phone at the desk while Florence worked herself out of the easy chair.

"You ought not to be standin', ma'am," Willie said.

"Jes' come with me. We gon' find my Max."

As Willie helped her outside, Florence felt much better. She didn't know if it was the water and the rest and the evidence that she had indeed taken her meds that morning, or whether it was because her need to lay eyes on that boy made her forget her ailments. She got herself shuffling down the sidewalk to where Willie had to hustle to keep up.

And there was Scooter again. "You got a couple for me like you said?"

"I got ten for you by tomorrow if you help us."

"Ten? I'll help you knock over a bank for that!"

"I'm looking for Max, little white boy, blond hair. White tennies, blue shorts, red shirt. He's with a Army Ranger in a camouflage outfit. Drives a big old dark-blue Buick with South Carolina tags on it. You go that way; Willie and me'll go this way. You find 'em, Scooter, and we're talkin' twenty."

"Twenty! I'm on it!"

"What you're telling me," Boone said, "is that when I do get to see her, she won't even know I'm there."

"Not likely for at least a week," Dr. Sarangan said. "That's not to say there isn't value in touching her, talking to her, sitting with her. It certainly can't hurt. There's a lot we don't know about the comatose patient. When she's out of the recovery room, she'll be in neuro-ICU. I'll let you know as soon as she's settled in."

The Mount Sinai PA system came alive, and Dr. Sarangan was summoned to the lab. "That's going to be the pregnancy-test results," he said, rising.

"Any reason I can't come with you?" Boone said. "I'm going to be jumping out of my skin in here."

12

★★★★

NIGHTMARE

"WILLIE, GO THAT way and ask ever'body you see. Somebody had to see that car."

"You don't want me to stay with you, make sure you're all right?"

"I don't find that boy, I'll never be all right again. And if something happened to him, I'm gon' be killing me somebody."

"Don't talk like that. We'll find 'im."

"Go on, now. I'll go this way, but you won't have any trouble finding me."

Florence soon developed the same symptoms she'd had last time she was out. Sweating, gasping, pains in her hips, knees, ankles, feet. Her heart raced, but there was no time to rest, to catch her breath. This wasn't the heat. This was trouble. Trouble she had caused by letting it happen. What was she going to do?

She couldn't call the cops, couldn't tell Mr. Drake she'd lost track of his boy, not with his wife in the hospital.

"Lord, help me. Help me, please."

"It doesn't sound like there's much more I can do here, Boone," Pastor Francisco Sosa said as they waited for Dr. Sarangan outside the lab. "Unless you need me to stay. Happy to do it."

"No. Just ask everybody to pray."

"You know I will. Keep me posted, and let me know as soon as I can see Haeley."

"Don't leave till we get these results."

The doctor emerged with a printout, which he waved at Boone. "Your wife is with child."

"Seriously?"

"No question. I need to call Dr. Fabrie."

"She's on vacation."

"I know, but she should have the right to decide whether Haeley's condition warrants an early return."

The doctor scrolled through his contacts.

"Can they tell if it's a boy or girl?" Boone said.

"No," Dr. Sarangan said. "Too early by several weeks."

He held up a finger as he put the phone to his ear and talked softly, urgently. Boone heard many of the same terms he'd heard from the woman EMT when Haeley was delivered to the ER team.

Pastor Sosa congratulated him. "Can I share this news too?"

"Haeley probably wouldn't want you to under normal circumstances, but I guess I have to decide now, so I say yes. I want people to be able to pray specifically."

"You've got it," Sosa said. And he was gone.

"Dr. Fabrie would like to speak with you, Boone," the doctor said, handing him the phone.

"Yes, ma'am?"

"I've been looking forward to meeting you, Chief. Sorry it has to be this way. I'll book the first flight out of here and meet up with you there as soon as possible."

"So sorry to interrupt your vacation. . . ."

"I was getting squirrelly anyway, if you want to know the truth. I've never been much for sitting around doing nothing."

"I sure appreciate this. Haeley thinks the world of you."

"Here's how this works. Dr. Sarangan will inform the neurologist of the pregnancy and get me on the team. So you'll have the specialist who operated on Haeley, plus Murari, who will serve as her GP—general practitioner—and me as the ob-gyn. That's one for her brain, one for her overall health, and one for the baby. And it sounds like we all have a lot of work ahead of us."

Florence found herself only more panicky as she confronted everybody she saw, pleading for information. A few had seen the soldier and the boy playing in the park. One said he noticed "an old Buick heading that way." But she knew all that. Had no one seen them or the car since she had?

Florence finally headed back to the steps in front of her building, clenching and unclenching her fists. She would sit in the shade and plead with God as she waited—about to explode—for Willie and Scooter. Odds were bad that either of them would have had any more luck than she had.

Florence would rather die herself than see something happen to that precious child.

Just as she was wearily situating herself on the cement steps, her cell phone chirped. "Mrs. Quigley, this is Margaret, the Drakes' friend?"

"Yes, ma'am. I—"

"I hope you got my message. I'm on my way to your place from theirs with some clothes and other things for Max. Is that all right? Can you keep him a few more days?"

"Yes, ma'am, but I—"

"I know you're curious about what happened to Haeley. She wasn't feeling well and fainted. Took a terrible tumble on a concrete patio. I'm afraid she really hurt her head and may be in the hospital for some time."

"Oh, Lord, no!"

"Boone is with her, and he wants you to know how much he appreciates—"

"That's all right, but ma'am, how soon will you be here?"

"Just a few minutes—maybe ten."

"'Cause I need to talk to you right away."

"Of course. What is it, Florence?"

"I need to talk to you face-to-face, ma'am."

Boone sat in a coffee shop with Dr. Sarangan, waiting for Haeley to be moved to ICU. "I know this wasn't how you expected to spend your Saturday," Boone said. "You get back to your family as soon as you can."

"I will, but you know, they understand. What I do is a calling, Boone. It is what I was created to do. God blessed me with opportunities that few people enjoy. My parents were able to provide me with a good pre-med education in Delhi, and I came to the States on a scholarship. I promised God that I would devote myself 100 percent to my studies and then serve people—and him in the process—with all that I had learned. My wife and I are determined that I not neglect the family. Aside from emergencies like this, I am highly regimented, and the kids see me a lot. But when emergencies arise, they must be seen as opportunities, privileges. I am glad I can be here for you today."

Boone just sat shaking his head, wanting to remember every word of that. He too had been blessed in his career and believed he was doing what he was meant to do. He wanted to be a father like Murari was, making his family a priority while also giving himself wholly to serving.

The doctor's phone buzzed. "She's been moved," he said, rising. "We can go."

On the way Boone asked if there was someplace for him to stay overnight.

"Actually, there is. ICU can bring a cot into her room for you. You simply have to agree to follow all their rules and stay out of the way. You can store your things in one of the drawers, and you may use the bathroom when it's available. In Haeley's case, they will not be taking her to the facilities as long as she is in a coma. You will be tempted to assist them in their care for her, but refrain. There are all kinds of reasons—insurance and medical—for their restrictions against that, so just comply. That you can stay with her at all is a major development just in the last several years."

They stopped at the ICU nurses' station, where Dr. Sarangan asked for Haeley's chart and introduced Boone to the head nurse—a compact, short-haired blonde of about fifty who wore no makeup and didn't seem to need any. Her name badge read CHAZ CILANO, RN.

"You know she is entirely noncognitive and unresponsive, correct?" Ms. Cilano said.

"I know."

"She will not know you're here."

"Got it."

Dr. Sarangan asked for a cot for Boone and informed her that he would be staying.

"Suit yourself," she said, "but I'm telling you that you would be more comfortable in a hotel and certainly more comfortable at home. We would be happy to keep you informed—"

"Thank you, ma'am, but I've decided."

Nurse Cilano squinted at him. "Aren't you the sweetest thing? If my first husband had been like you, I wouldn't be referring to him in the past tense."

"She's my life," Boone said.

"Don't hear enough of that anymore. But listen, you're gonna get bored, and my staff won't have time to entertain you, so—"

"So stipulated."

"Just so we understand each other."

"And may I call you Chaz?"

"I hope that's the worst you call me, Mr. Drake."

Dr. Sarangan whispered to her.

"Oh," she said. "Sorry, Chief Drake."

"I go by Boone."

"One more thing, Boone. Take and make all your cell calls out here. Cell phones wreak havoc with our machines in the rooms. In fact, it's best if you just leave yours with us while you're in there."

"I don't know what I'm gon' do, Willie," Florence said when the doorman returned, having told her he struck out. "Their friend is coming with Max's clothes, and I got to tell her."

"No way around it, ma'am."

"They're gonna kill me. And they should."

"Don't be saying that, ma'am. We'll find that boy."

"His uncle's got some answering to do."

"If he *is* his uncle," Willie said. "That's what scares me."

Florence lurched as if pierced and buried her face in her hands. "Oh, no, no! Willie, you don't think—"

"I don't wanna think anything, ma'am. I'm hoping they just come cruising right back here with a story of fun and losing track of the time. I don't wanna think that soldier boy played you. Here come Scooter, but he ain't in no hurry."

"Anything?" Florence called out, as soon as Scooter was within range.

"Didn't see those boys," he said. "But I found that car."

Florence leapt to her feet, in a manner of speaking. "Blue Buick?"

"Yep. Parked in a alley 'bout three blocks up."

"They're close by! Show me! Take me!"

"I ain't walkin' all that way agin', and you owe me twenty."

"Ten. You didn't find 'em."

"Whatever. I want it now."

"I told you, tomorrow. Now where do I find that car?"

He told her the cross streets and described the alley. "But that car got no South Carolina tags on it. Got no tags at all."

"Give me just a moment with her," Dr. Sarangan said. "I want to check all the lines and readouts; then I'll be out of your way."

Boone waited down the hall, watching an orderly follow the doctor into Haeley's room. He was rolling a cot topped by a pillow and a stack of bedding. Boone heard him set it up before he hurried away.

When Dr. Sarangan emerged, Boone was excited. It hadn't been that long since he had seen Haeley, but he had wondered whether he would ever see her alive again.

The doctor finished making his notes on the metal clipboard, then gave his full attention to Boone. "She's presentable," he said, "and everything is as expected. But her face was covered during emergency surgery, so I was unaware how much discoloration had occurred. How did she look in the ambulance?"

"Pale with blue lips."

"She does not look that way anymore, so be prepared for that. And the swelling of the head is normal. Remember that the surgeon is keeping the fracture open to prevent internal edema."

Boone nodded. And suddenly he was alone in the corridor.

As he approached Haeley's compact chamber, Boone decided to consider this a new beginning. A long road may lie ahead, he told himself, but he was prepared for every step, regardless how arduous. *Whatever it takes.*

He hesitated at the door. Haeley lay on her side facing him. Her face was swollen, deep purple with yellow blotches. Her eyelids were puffy. Her head was wrapped completely, covering her ears, and it appeared the size of a basketball.

From beneath the gauze came a dozen wires that apparently

monitored her brain waves. A tube ran from the back of her head into a drain bubble. A pulse-oxygen monitor was attached to her index finger, an IV line dug into the back of her hand, and two other sets of lines ran from her, one from a vein in the crook of her elbow and the other from her middle to an elimination container.

Boone pulled a chair close, unable to stop the tears. Haeley's free hand, so delicate, lay open on the bed, palm up. Soft and precious, it was the only part of her he recognized.

Boone placed his hand gently over hers, expecting and receiving no response.

"Oh, Haeley," he rasped.

As he sat there, realizing that this could be his lot for days, Boone suddenly realized how bone weary he was. Why would that be? It was his day off. He had enjoyed sleeping in, then meeting with friends, dropping Max off, chatting with dear Florence. He rehearsed in his mind the conversation in the car when Jack had playfully pestered Haeley.

Then the barbeque with Fletch and Dorothy had been so relaxing and fun. And he had stuffed himself. He found the chat with Margaret enlightening, and while it had been beastly hot, all he had done was sit.

Boone chastised himself as Haeley's fall played itself again in his mind's eye. Why couldn't he get to her, catch her, at least break her fall?

There was no future in that kind of thinking, but neither was there anyone to blame but himself. He should have rushed to her as soon as she had come out of the house, but how could he have known?

The only explanation for his fatigue was the crash from his

adrenaline rush. From the instant Haeley's skull had slammed into the concrete, Boone had been on high alert, scared to death of losing her and doing everything in his power to get her here.

Boone lay his head on the bed rail, and while it was anything but comfortable, he felt his body shutting down. The pressure was off his back, and he was content to sit there, Haeley's hand under his, until she came back to him.

Boone heard footsteps tiptoe behind him and a hand on his back. "I'll be here another couple of hours," Dr. Sarangan said. "If she's still stable, I will feel more confident leaving her until morning. If you need me or have any questions . . ."

"Thank you."

"You're all right?"

Boone snorted. "Better than I deserve."

"Are you hungry?"

"Ugh. I ate enough at lunch to last me a week."

"Just don't forget about your own health while you're here. Know where you can get snacks and meals, and stay on a regular meal schedule. I called Chief Keller and suggested he bring you something. There's a waiting room down the hall where you can eat."

"Not sure I can yet."

"It doesn't have to be much, but you must. Your system will fool you; you need your fuel."

13

CONFESSION

FLORENCE FORCED HERSELF to ignore her discomfort as she hurried down the street, grateful that Willie had rushed to catch up with her. As he held her hand and tried to support her, she knew she must be a sight. Her clothes were soaked through and sweat poured from her. She limped, but she would not stop.

"I can't be away from the desk too long, ma'am. If we don't find those boys here, we can't go lookin' around for 'em."

"You go back if you have to. And keep an eye out for Miz Margaret. I don't know what she looks like, but she'll be asking for me."

Sure enough, Florence spied the Buick parked in the alley, just as Scooter had said. "No tags, but this is the car," she said. The front windows were still open. "Oh, Willie, what can this mean? Why would he take the plates off?"

Willie just shook his head as Florence peered down the alley deep into the shadows cast by the buildings on either side. "I'm of a mind to knock on them doors," she said. "I just wish I had a pistol with me."

"Miz Quigley," Willie said, and she shivered at his tone, "it's time to call the police."

Florence's phone rang. It was Margaret. "Can you buzz me up?" she said. "There's no one at the desk."

"I'm down the street," Florence said, "but I'm coming. Just wait there."

Florence slapped her phone shut and said, "Willie go on ahead and let Margaret into my apartment. I'm gonna hafta be sitting down when I tell her what's going on."

"She's going to ask me where you are, ma'am."

"Just tell her I'm on my way."

Boone could hear Jack talking with Nurse Cilano. "Can't take food down there, and only one visitor at a time anyway. Since you're not blood, you really shouldn't be in there at all."

Jack must have shown her his badge. "Oh, sorry," she said. "But you know you won't be able to talk to her for several days."

Boone hurried out, and his aversion to eating vanished when he saw the grease-stained bag and smelled the burgers and fries. "Just what we need after that barbeque, eh?" Boone said.

"From the same place we used to lunch at when we were on the street," Jack said.

The nurse pointed them down the hall to the waiting room. "Anything new?" Jack said, handing Boone a huge grocery bag full of clothes and toiletries.

"That's something I'd appreciate if you wouldn't ask," he said. "There's going to be nothing new until she's out of the coma, and that's not going to be soon."

"Got it," Jack said as he laid out their food in the empty room. "Now, listen. I've already talked to the super. I'm going to keep tabs on Major Case for the time being. Just leave everything to me and don't even check in. If there's anything you need to know, I'll tell you."

"But we've got two investigations going right now that—"

Jack held up a hand. "I know, all right? You may think you're indispensable, but I'm pretty sure . . ."

"Thanks, Jack."

"You've got plenty of personal and vacation time, and the big boss says you've been through enough to have earned special consideration. So just take care of business."

Florence marched up the steps to the foyer of her building and found Willie's gaze. He looked grave. "Miz Margaret's up there."

"She know something's wrong?"

"I don't think she does. She kept talking about how nice it was that you were out having fun with Max. I just nodded and tried to look busy."

"I wish I could disappear, Willie. I feel like I'm goin' to the gas chamber."

"Just worry about finding that boy, Miz Quigley. Nobody gonna blame you."

"'Course they are! And they should! It's my fault."

"Pardon me for sayin', it, ma'am, but time's a-wastin'. Sooner you get help searching, the sooner you get that boy back where he belongs."

Florence went to the elevator and wished that for once it would be as slow as it used to be. She found her apartment door ajar, and when she entered Margaret turned from unpacking a suitcase on the couch. The woman had an expectant look, like she was trying to force herself to be cheerful and not worry Max about his mama yet.

"Mrs. Quigley!" Margaret said. "Are you all right? You look like you've been running a marathon. Where's Max?"

"Oh, Miz Margaret, we got trouble—bad trouble!"

ICU head nurse Chaz Cilano poked her head into the waiting room. "Your phone just buzzed," she said, handing it to Boone. "Didn't know if it was important."

He thanked her, and as she left, Boone became aware that he had smiled for the first time since Haeley had fallen. "Look at this, Jack. Another verse from Francisco."

Jack looked glum. "I got to tell you, Boones, I don't know how you guys do it. I hear this guy preaching every weekend now when I can get there, and he's good. I'm learning a lot. But I don't know how you explain stuff like, you know, this that you're going through now."

Boone shook his head as he looked up the verse. "I quit trying to explain it a long time ago. All the answers sound trite. We live in a fallen world. Know what that means?"

"Sin, yeah. Got that part. But haven't you had enough? I mean, seeing how you came out the other side of that from a few years ago impressed me; it really did. But here we are again, same song, second verse. I'm not tellin' you anything you don't know. Doesn't seem fair, and don't tell me life's not fair. I know that. So, what's Francisco say?"

Boone read it silently, then handed the phone to Jack.

"'Not by might nor by power, but by my Spirit,' says the Lord of hosts." (Zechariah 4:6)

Jack handed the phone back. "Nice, but I'm not sure what it means. Some kind of promise or encouragement?"

"To me it means that when there's nothing I can do, when I can't use my strength, God's Spirit is with me."

"That make you feel better?"

"A little, yeah. Nice to be reminded of sometimes."

"Well, you can't ask for more than that, I guess."

"What do you mean you don't know?" Margaret said. "Don't take this the wrong way, Mrs. Quigley, but this is no neighborhood for a little boy to be alone in!"

"That's the problem, ma'am," Florence said, sobbing now. "Max's not alone."

"Tell me exactly what's going on, Florence, and don't leave one thing out."

Boone found himself eager to get back to Haeley, though he knew she was unaware of his presence. He missed her, wanted to be with her. She needed him whether she knew it or not. And he needed her.

As Jack started picking up their trash, he said, "Margaret will tell Max his mom got hurt, but she won't tell him enough to scare him. She'll let you know when it would be good for him to hear from you."

Dr. Sarangan slipped into the waiting room. "Hope that was a healthy meal."

"Well," Jack said, "we hit a lot of the food groups, if that's what you're asking. Listen, gents, I'm going to go. I'll keep in touch, Boones."

Boone was thanking him as Jack's phone rang. "Oh, it's Margaret."

"Let me know when I can talk to Max," Boone whispered.

"Yeah," Jack said, "he's right here. You want to—oh!"

Jack blanched and hurried into the hall.

"What is it?" Boone said, following him.

Jack covered the phone. "Ah, just something downtown I've got to get to. I'll call you, Boones."

"What did Margaret want with me?"

"Uh, she was just making sure I could leave you for a while so I can call my people."

"I'm fine."

But it appeared to Boone that Jack gave Dr. Sarangan a look. And as Boone delivered his own phone back to the nurses' station, the doctor was following Jack down the hall.

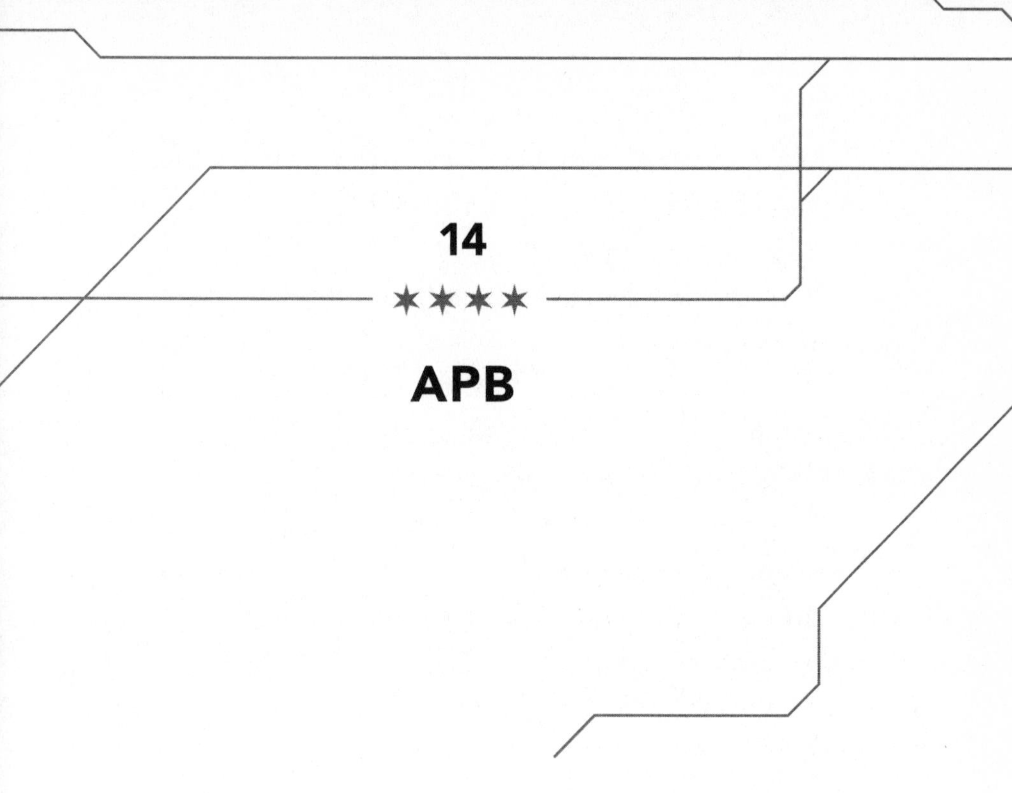

14

★★★★

APB

By the time Jack Keller slid to a stop in front of the Bethune Arms apartment building, his all-points bulletin had been in effect for more than half an hour. Eight squads, two of them unmarked, were already there. Uniformed officers had fanned out through the neighborhood, and he could see them talking with everyone on the street and entering various establishments.

Antoine Johnson, a stocky, cocoa-colored member of Boone's Major Case Squad, awaited Jack at the front door. He looked much different in a natty suit, athletic neck and shoulders squirming under a white shirt and tie, than he had in uniform the last time Jack had seen him.

Johnson thrust out his hand. "Remember me?"

"'Course," Jack said. "We can catch up later. What've we got? How long has he been gone?"

Johnson gushed everything they had learned from Florence Quigley, including the abandoned Buick.

"Crime scene guys on that?"

"On their way. You need to talk to this woman, chief. She's got a heckuva story."

Jack and Antoine flashed their badges at Willie as they headed for the elevator, and the old man said, "I'm here till five today if y'all need to talk to me."

Jack stopped. "Why would we need to talk with you, sir? You know something we need to know?"

"I met the young man that's got the little boy is all. I can only tell you my impressions."

"I appreciate that, sir. I'll want to hear everything you can remember, okay?"

"Yes, sir."

On the elevator, Jack said, "Get someone set up at Drake's home to take ransom calls."

"Will do."

Jack scribbled on a sheet of paper. "Here's the combination for the spare key lockbox."

"Let me have all the numbers besides the home phone too. Boone's cell, his wife's, the sitter's."

Jack found chaos in Florence's apartment. A man and a woman detective sat on either side of the big woman, who appeared to be hyperventilating. Margaret was massaging Florence's shoulders from behind the couch.

The detectives stood as soon as they saw Keller. The woman read from her notepad everything they had extracted from Florence since Antoine had been briefed.

"Alfonso Lamonica," Jack said quietly, letting the syllables roll on his tongue. "Her little brother. Maybe I'm gettin' old, but I don't remember a brother. Sisters, I think."

"It's all my fault!" Florence wailed. "I know better! I always been careful with Maxie!"

"Give me a minute with her," Jack said, and the detectives moved into the kitchen with Margaret. Antoine stayed by the door, speaking urgently into his phone.

Keller knelt in front of Florence and waited until she wiped her eyes and face. She whimpered, "Anything happens to that boy . . ." Jack reached for her hands, and she reluctantly took his. "You're Margaret's boyfriend," she said, "*and* you work with Mr. Drake?"

"Yes, ma'am. Now hear me. I can only imagine how you feel."

"No, you can't! You never lost no one's child!"

"Listen, every second counts, and we don't have time for you to lose focus. I know you feel bad. We all do. And yes, I won't sugarcoat it: you screwed up."

"I wish you'd just shoot me dead!"

Jack dropped her hands and cradled her sweaty, tearstained face in his palms. "Mrs. Quigley, listen to me. Do you want to sit here feeling guilty and—"

"I *am* guilty!"

"—and feeling sorry for yourself, or do you want to do whatever it takes to get Max back?"

"I'll do anything. *Anything.*"

"You are the single best chance we've got. You've got to focus and remember. Now, I'm going to make a quick phone call, and then I'm going to need every detail you can give me about this man. Start from the beginning, and tell me absolutely everything you can remember."

"I been through all that."

"I need to hear it straight from you. I can't even initiate an AMBER Alert until we know for sure this is an abduction, a kidnapping. And we have to know whether someone is going to demand a ransom or if they have something else in mind."

"What's an AMBER Alert anyway?"

"It stands for America's Missing: Broadcast Emergency Response. It's a very powerful tool, and we want to be able to use it. It'll inform law enforcement agencies all over the country and get Max's picture to them. Everybody will be on the lookout for him."

"Well, do it!"

"Ma'am, hear me; we don't even know if this is a kidnapping yet."

"Well, 'course it is!"

"I agree it probably is, but to put all the information into the National Crime Information Center system, we have to rule out that this was just a misunderstanding or that this guy really is Haeley's brother."

Florence's eyes widened. "I got a picture of him. He sent it to me on my phone."

She dug into her pocket, hands shaking as she poked at the screen, bringing up her texts. "There's his name! With a picture!"

"May I?" Jack said, taking the phone. He clicked on a message to Florence from "Lamonica, Alfonso" with the subject line "a picture for you."

"This will be too good to be true," Jack muttered. "If he's a kidnapper, he's not too bright."

The photo showed Florence on a park bench with Max in her lap, smiling contentedly as he leaned back on her.

"You say there's one with this Alfonso in it too?"

"Yes, sir."

"I don't see it. There's just the one, and this is it." He showed her.

Seeing Max made Florence break down again. "I took the picture myself with his phone! It was of him and Max. He said he was sending it."

"Maybe he's not as stupid as I thought," Jack said. "Ma'am, we're going to have to take your phone for a while."

"You are?"

"We might be able to glean something from what he sent you."

"Sure, if it'll help."

Jack turned and beckoned Antoine with a nod. He scribbled on a notepad and ripped the page off. "This is the home number of the director of the crime lab. You know him?"

"Just *of* him. Everybody calls him Dr. Scandinavian."

"Tell him it's an emergency and that I need him as soon as he can get here." Jack turned back to Florence. "Now let me make a quick call, and then we're going to go through it all again, okay?"

"Anything, Mr. Keller."

Jack dialed Boone's phone, but after three rings it went to voice mail. "Call me right away," he said. But when Boone had not called back after a few minutes, he remembered that Boone's phone was at the nurses' station. If they told him it rang and he saw it was Jack who had called, he'd call right back. But if the nurses were busy or didn't hear it . . .

Jack waited another minute, during which Antoine told him, "Dr. Waldemarr is on his way but none too happy. Says you owe him one."

"I owe him more than one," Jack said. He called Information and asked for a direct number to the neuro-ICU nurses' station at Mount Sinai, and he was put through.

"ICU, Cilano."

"Hey, Chaz, Jack Keller here. I need to speak with Boone right away."

"I'll have him call you, sir. I don't want to tie up this phone."

"Understood. Thanks."

Florence sat up. "You're not gonna make me talk to him, are you?"

"No, ma'am. I'm not even going to tell him what's going on yet. He's got enough on his plate."

When his phone chirped a few minutes later, Jack rose and moved to the corner of the room.

"Jack, what's up?" Boone said. "Can I talk to Max?"

"Not yet. I just thought of something. Do you need me to call Haeley's siblings, her brother, anyone in her family?"

"No, I've talked to everybody, told 'em what happened, that she couldn't have visitors, and that I was staying here. So for now, they just want to be kept informed."

"Good, okay. Her brother and sister up to date?"

"That's the second time you've mentioned a brother, Jack. You met her only two siblings at the wedding: twin sisters about eight years older than her."

"Oh, that's right. There's no brother."

"No, that's me. I've got the two."

"Yeah, that must have been what mixed me up."

"Let me know when I can talk to Max. Has Margaret told him anything yet?"

"Waiting for the right time. I'll let you know."

"And your emergency, Jack? How'd that turn out."

"Ah, nothing to speak of. People get excited when the chief's away, you know."

As Jack put his phone away, he hoped Boone was preoccupied enough with Haeley to have missed his gaffe. Pretending to have mixed Boone's brothers with Haeley's sisters simply wouldn't fly, especially with Boone. Jack was legendary for getting details right, and while it might have made sense for him to not remember that Haeley had no brother, there was no way he would bollix up the whole family tree like that.

Half an hour later Jack had wrung everything out of Florence he could think to ask. "If it makes you feel any better, ma'am, this guy sounds like a pro. Not too many people would have been able to see through him."

"He's not Haeley's brother, is he?"

"No, ma'am."

"Then where'd he get that picture of him and Haeley?"

"People can do anything with computers these days."

"Trick photography?" she said.

"Trick something," Jack said.

"You gonna talk to Willie now?"

"Willie?"

"The man downstairs."

"Yes, we are."

On the way down, Jack briefed Antoine on the AMBER Alert. "I've never initiated a modified one," he said, "but this has to be for law enforcement agencies only. No media yet."

"But isn't that the most important, Chief? You want to get the boy's picture on the news, get the public involved."

"Not until Boone knows. I can't have him seeing it on TV or on his phone."

"He's got to know, Chief."

"And I've got to be the one to tell him."

Jack's mind and notebook were full of details telling him that whoever pulled this off had done a ton of research and planning. Nuances. They're what set apart good con artists from amateurs. The story of why he was keeping his presence a secret from his "sister." The account of coming home through Georgia and then South Carolina for his car, the out-of-state tags, the supposed picture of him with Max's mother. All the Ranger stuff. But where had he gotten all the details? And why the grand production? Why not just nab the kid? This guy had gone to a lot of trouble to charm Max away from his sitter.

As Jack and Antoine reached the lobby, Willie was gathering his stuff, and a young woman was waiting to take his place at the desk.

"Have a few more minutes, sir?" Jack said.

"All the time you need, Detective. Let's go over here, and you ask me anything you want."

They sat on a padded bench by a window with Antoine standing behind Jack. Keller sped through his notes, seeing how much of Florence's account Willie could corroborate. "That's pretty much the way I remember it."

"Take me back to when this Alfonso first arrived. Did he say how he knew where to come?"

"Yes, sir. He said he'd gone to Haeley's house first and then to her church."

"North Beach Fellowship."

"I wouldn't know that, but Miz Quigley could tell you. Anyway, he said he told the pastor about the big surprise, and the pastor gave him her address."

Jack turned to Antoine. "Get that pastor's name. And send Margaret down, would you? Tell Mrs. Quigley that when the rest of the detectives leave, she should stay put. Tell her to talk to no one except CPD about this and that she should call me if she remembers any details she forgot to tell me."

Dr. Ragnar Waldemarr came through the front door and headed straight for Jack, looking none too pleased. Jack held up a finger so he could finish with Willie, and the crime lab director stayed back. It was nice to work with professionals, Jack decided.

He left his card with Willie and thanked him for his time.

"I'll be prayin' you find that boy," the old man said. "For his daddy and mama's sake, and for Miz Quigley's too. She's feelin' awful bad."

15

★★★★

HAIRCUT

Boone took seriously his vow to be faithful to Haeley in sickness and in health, and it struck him that this was the first time he'd had to fulfill that part of his promise. She'd had not so much as a sniffle since he had known her, until these last few weeks when her pregnancy had resulted in morning sickness and whatever led to her fall.

But sitting there watching her breathe was not easy. He was willing to do anything for her, of course. But he could do nothing to help. He tried whispering to her, caressing her, gently squeezing her hand. But there was not a hint that anything had changed. The monitors droned on, her pulse and oxygen and pressure and respiration reading the same, the same, the same, the same.

He wandered the halls, noticing others in ICU. A man down

the hall, looking no more than forty, lay glumly staring, one leg elevated, the foot gone from just above the ankle. Boone stole a peek at a sheet on the wall next to the door. Something about his diet. Sugar. Clearly the ravages of diabetes.

At intervals Boone would mosey to the nurses' station, but he knew better than to bother them. Once when he approached, it was as if Chaz Cilano could read his mind. She handed him his phone, and he drifted to a quiet corner to check for messages. When he delivered it back, he whispered to Chaz, "I'm waiting for a message that I can talk to my son. He doesn't know yet."

"I gathered that. Got a picture?"

Boone found one on his phone and showed her. "Precious," she said. "Raised three of those myself."

"You did not."

"Can't believe I'm even old enough to have been married, right, Chief?"

"Exactly."

"Didn't know cops were liars. Well, I can't promise we'll hear your phone, but if we do, we'll find you. You don't look so good, by the way. You all right?"

"Exhausted for some reason."

"You can't imagine why? What you've been through emotionally alone would put some people in our unit."

"Plus it's boring in there."

"Don't say I didn't tell you you'd be more comfortable in a hotel or—"

"I know. But I'm not leaving her. She wouldn't leave me. I just wish there was something to do. Watch TV, listen to the radio."

"Don't even have 'em on this floor," the nurse said. "Can't have them in the rooms, as I told you. Used to have one in the waiting room, but people waiting on this floor usually can't concentrate on TV anyway. We lost it due to lack of use. There's TVs in the waiting rooms on all three floors below us."

Boone shook his head. "Where can I find a book or magazine or something?"

"Gift shop, first floor." She looked at her watch. "Closing soon, though."

Boone hurried down, surprised to notice the sun was sinking. Nothing in the magazine racks appealed. His mind kept going to Haeley and Max. He chastised himself for not taking his phone with him. What if Jack or Margaret called while he was away from ICU?

One corner of the gift shop's book display included classics. It had been years since he'd read *To Kill a Mockingbird.* He ferried his find back up to ICU, hoping there would be news. Boone raised his eyebrows at Nurse Cilano as he approached. She pressed her lips together and shook her head. "Sorry," she said. "Find something?"

He showed her.

"Nice."

Boone settled into the chair in Haeley's room but found it uncomfortable. He didn't want to turn the light brighter over her bed, either, though he knew it wouldn't bother her. Finally he sat on his cot. It was hard but also lumpy, and he could feel the wire mesh beneath the thin mattress.

Boone squirmed as he opened his book and followed his normal custom—reading every word, skipping nothing, not even the copyright page. By the time he got to the first chapter he'd been in three different positions. Finally he stretched out on his stomach and read from the light above the door. Within minutes he found himself mired in one of the first paragraphs. The words swam as he fought to concentrate.

Dr. Ragnar Waldemarr, sixtyish and thin with wisps of white hair, sat glaring at Jack in the corner of the lobby of Florence's building.

"C'mon, Rags. You know I wouldn't do this to you on a Saturday evening unless it was important."

"I had the grandkids over, Jack."

"Then you'll know how we're all feeling when I tell you this is about Drake's boy."

"The one he just adopted."

"That's the one."

The doctor leaned forward, suddenly animated. "What've you got and what do you need?"

Jack ran down the whole story—including what had happened to Haeley—as Waldemarr winced and scribbled. Finally the older man held up a hand and said, "Let me check with Crime Scene about the Buick."

A few minutes later he slapped his phone shut. "Interesting," he said. "That car never had South Carolina plates, at least not valid ones. The VIN shows it's registered to a Mr. Shane Loggyn of East Chicago, Indiana, but it's supposed to have Illinois plates."

"How's that work?"

"It's close enough to the border that the owner could have residences in both states. Or maybe just moved."

"Excuse me a minute, Doc," Jack said.

He moved to another corner, where Antoine and Margaret chatted in hushed tones. Jack handed the detective a slip of paper with the car owner's name on it. "Get me everything you can on him."

"Done," Detective Johnson said, and excused himself.

"I'm going home for supplies, Jack," Margaret said.

"For what?"

"You know I'm going to be taking over for Boone. He's not going to want her left alone, but he's not going to sit there for a second once he knows Max is gone."

"I'm trying to keep that from him."

"And how long do you think you can do that?"

Jack shrugged. When she was right, she was right. "Maybe you can stall him a little. Go see him, check in on her, but don't let him know you've got your stuff in the car."

"He's gonna ask me, Jack. What do I say when he asks what I told Max?"

"Tell him I said we shouldn't tell Max yet and that I'll be along in a little while to talk about it."

Margaret shook her head. "You think you're dealing with a junior higher? He's gonna know something's up."

"Blame it on me. Tell him I said I've got my reasons but that I'll let it be his call once I've talked to him."

Margaret gazed at the ceiling. "I don't know if I can pull it off. I'll feel like a complete fraud, chatting him up and making up stories, knowing the whole time that he's gonna flip out when you tell him what's going on."

"I need you to do this, Margaret. Buy me some time. I need to be able to follow some leads here without an emotionally invested father in the mix."

"There's no way you can leave him out of it. Would you stand by and let everybody else do the work if it was your son?"

"'Course not. But I want to keep him out of it as long as I possibly can."

"No promises," she said. "I'll do my best, but don't leave me hanging there too long."

When Jack returned to Waldemarr, the forensics expert was studying Florence's cell phone. "This guy may not be as coy as you think he is, Jack."

"Why's that? He made her think he was transmitting a picture of himself with Max, but he didn't."

"But he did send the one of her and Max," Waldemarr said, "and that could prove a huge error."

"I'm listening."

"It's just that some people know how to turn off all the tracking devices on their phones, and others don't. You make him sound like a pretty slick guy, but if he left us any breadcrumbs with the shot he transmitted, we may be able to keep tabs on his phone."

"Here's hoping."

"Crime Scene is having the Buick hauled downtown to be dusted and evaluated with a fine-tooth comb. And officers are still canvassing, looking for those South Carolina plates. What else do you need from me?"

"Just access, Doc. There's gonna be no time for red tape and bureaucracy."

"I'm all yours till this is over, Jack. You know that."

Margaret found herself lifting a strange prayer as she threw clothes and other necessities into a bag and stored it in the trunk of her car. "Lord, you know I want you to help us find Max and bring him home safe and sound. And I want you to heal Haeley and keep her new baby healthy too. But most of all, I want this whole thing to somehow reach Jack. Show off. Show him what you can do."

At the hospital she approached the nurses' station and introduced herself to Chaz Cilano. "Let me get this straight," the nurse said. "You're Chief Keller's girlfriend?"

"Yes, ma'am."

"I'm getting to meet the whole extended family, family doctor, pastor, everybody."

"Yeah, sorry."

"Not a problem, 'cept my shift is over. I'll be back tomorrow. We've got Chief Drake's phone here, and you can't go down the hall while he's in there. I assume you want to see Mrs. Drake."

"I do."

"Then you two will have to trade places. I'll go get him."

Margaret went over and over in her mind how to tell Boone why she was there without mentioning Max. To her great relief, the nurse came back alone.

"Ma'am," she said, "I'm sorry to have wasted your time, but Mr. Drake is dead to the world. I put his book aside and pulled a blanket over him."

"I'll wait."

"Wait for what? Wouldn't surprise me if he slept through the night."

"Oh, he'll wake up wanting to talk to his son soon enough."

"Max?"

"He told you?"

"Loves that boy, doesn't he?"

Margaret nodded.

"By the time he wakes up," Nurse Cilano said, "it'll be too late, right? The boy will be in bed."

"Ms. Cilano, there's something I think you should know. Can we sit a minute?"

"Rather than hurry home to an empty condo? Sure, we can sit."

"Can I buy you a cup of coffee?"

"That sounds good too. First floor." Nurse Cilano left instructions for the next shift.

"Oh," Margaret said, "would you mind also tellin' them that if he wakes up, they should tell him I'm on my way up to talk to him?"

Jack was on his way to Mount Sinai when Ragnar Waldemarr called. "Coupla uniforms from the 11th found the South Carolina plates in a dumpster about three blocks from the car. They're on the way to the lab to be dusted. The dumpster was next to a barbershop, and get this: The barber says an Army Ranger brought in a little blond kid who wanted a buzz cut just like his. Said it had been a long time since he cut a white person's hair, so he was glad it was a buzz."

"When was this?"

"They figure it was just minutes from when they left Mrs. Quigley in the park. Guy was nervous and kept telling the barber to hurry, paid him with a hundred, and told him to keep the change."

"I'm going to want to talk to that barber."

"No need. He's got a camera in his shop. We've got a visual on the Ranger."

"That's a start. Transmit it to me as soon as you can. Did the barber see where they went after that?"

"Said they ran down the street. A few people in the neighborhood saw them, thought it was strange for them to be looking like they were having so much fun. They were laughing and playing tag, and the boy kept running his hands over his fuzzy scalp. They jumped into a white van."

"Make, model, year, tags?"

"Nobody even paid attention. White or light-colored is all they said."

"Quick and planned," Jack muttered. "This is not good, Rags."

"It's more than we had when you and I talked."

"And what about Florence Quigley's phone?"

"Being examined now. You'll be the first to know."

Jack phoned Margaret. She told him where she was and with whom and that Boone was asleep.

"That's a relief. Greet Chaz for me. I'll be there soon."

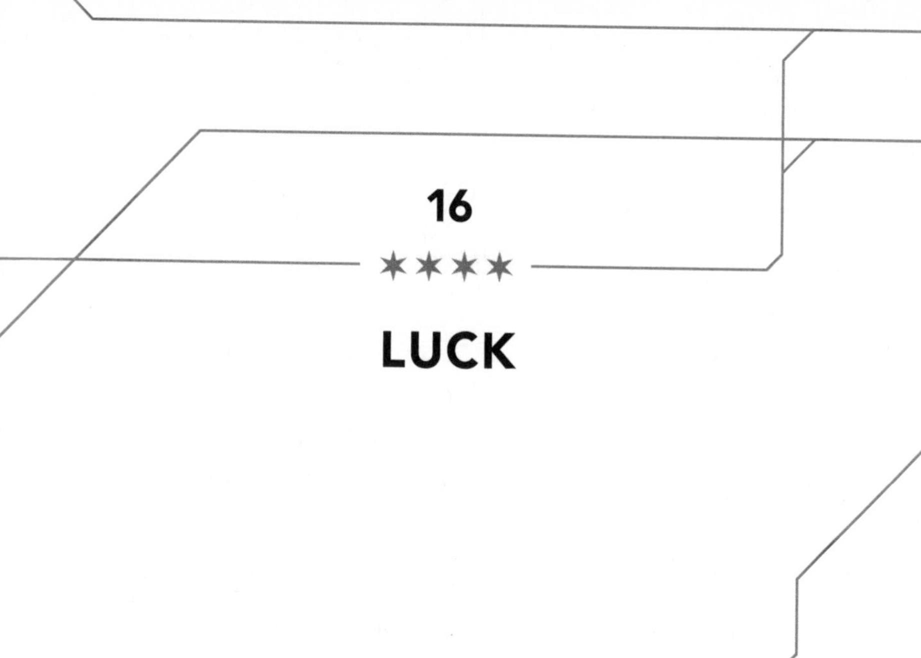

16

★★★★

LUCK

MARGARET SAT WITH a suddenly sober Nurse Chaz Cilano in the coffee shop at Mount Sinai.

The nurse sipped her coffee and seemed to be mulling what to say. "You know, Margaret, I get to meet all kinds of people in this job. Usually they're in distress—like your friend Boone—because someone they care about is in ICU, the last place you want to be besides a morgue. You all seem like good friends, and it's neat to see you supporting him, but I've got to tell you, you're making a mistake here."

"Keep talking."

"That man needs to know what's going on. You ought to send me up there to wake him so you can tell him."

"Oh, I don't know, Chaz. That's not my call, and he's got more than enough to deal with right now."

"Wouldn't you want to know? He's a cop. He can take it."

"That'd be like kicking him when he's down."

"You're not doing him any favors. You can tell him you were just trying to protect him, but withholding something like that? I don't like it."

Margaret wrung her hands. "I know you're right," she said. "But it's not up to me. Jack thinks Boone being asleep gives them a chance to gather as many leads as they can before they have to add him—and however he'll be feeling about this—to the mix."

Chaz shrugged. "He wakes in the meantime, he's not going to let you up about this. You can lie to him, tell him you didn't want to wake him, and now that he's up, Max is asleep. But that's just another whopper you're going to have to answer for."

"I'm prayin' Jack gets here before I have to face that."

Jack took successive calls from Antoine Johnson and Ragnar Waldemarr as he drove toward the hospital. Antoine told him the ransom team was set up and were sure they had entered the Drake house without being noticed—ready to monitor calls on all the likely phone numbers.

"And I texted you the contact information for Mrs. Quigley's pastor. Rev. Warren Waters, age 53. He's what they call bi-vocational. Works somewhere else during the week."

"You still with me, Antoine? I may need you the rest of the night."

"The wife understands."

"You didn't tell her . . . ?"

"I just said we're on a case that involves my boss. I did tell her what happened to his wife. She knows I'm staying on this till we see it through."

"You know what we need from Pastor Waters."

"Every detail. How much can I tell him?"

"Whatever's necessary to get all we need."

"He's going to feel terrible, Chief."

"I hope so. Getting talked into giving up information on one of his own parishioners . . . and look what came of it."

"I hope he wasn't involved," Antoine said.

"You and me both."

"I'm on it."

Waldemarr transmitted a grainy still from the barbershop video camera, and bad as the quality was, Jack could see clearly that the man in the photo was not DeWayne Mannock. Doc also told Jack the South Carolina license plates his people had found in a dumpster, DLJ 725, were traced to a minivan that had been totaled in a wreck four months before. The car had been dismantled for parts at a junkyard in Aiken, South Carolina.

"So, we've got a car owned by a guy in East Chicago, Indiana, that's supposed to have Illinois plates, and plates off a wrecked car in South Carolina. Any report of that Buick being stolen?"

"Nothing. The owner, this Shane Loggyn, is a black male, 57, a poker dealer at the Lucky Day Casino in Hammond. No record."

Jack got that shiver cops get when things start to come together.

"Anything new with Florence Quigley's phone?"

"That's going to take a while, Jack. I gave it to one of the snot-nosed kids on our staff who knows all that stuff. He tells me he wishes he had the sending phone. Well, duh. If we had that, we'd have our guy."

Jack called the poker room at the Lucky Day. "Is Shane Loggyn working tonight?"

"He is," the floor man said. "Till midnight."

"Does he have a break between now and then? I want to talk to him for a minute."

"I don't think he does."

"How about DeWayne Mannock?"

"DeWayne is no longer with us."

"Since when?"

"Last week. Hit the lottery or something."

"Really?"

"Well, he came into money somehow. Probably not the lottery. He's been around, flashing his money, showing off his new clothes. Was he one of your favorites, sir?"

"Yeah, in a way he was."

"Well, you were in the minority."

"That so? You weren't sorry to lose him?"

"Players either loved him or hated him. An acquired taste, if you know what I mean. Geez, I hope you're not related or something."

"Just an acquaintance."

"Now, Shane *is* everybody's favorite. No complaints about him. This is a busy night. Can I put you on a list for a game?"

"No, I just want to talk to Shane for a minute."

"Like I say, he probably won't be available till midnight."

Jack called Margaret. "You still with Nurse Cilano?"

"No, she left."

"Shoot. I was going to ask if there was something we could slip Boone to keep him sleeping till daybreak. I've got to follow another lead."

"So you want Haeley *and* Boone in induced comas? What's the matter with you, Jack? You know, Chaz thinks we ought to tell him right away."

"Yeah? Well, I don't tell her how to do her work."

"She's right, you know."

"Of course. But I also know Boone."

"You think he'll overreact?"

"Well, I would. But he can also be corralled and his passion focused. But I need more time. I need to follow a lead in Hammond, and I've got somebody talking to Florence's pastor. Then I'll be ready to involve Boone."

"And what am I supposed to do in the meantime?"

"Be there for him. Be ready. He wakes up now, tell him you just want to relieve him for a while. He'll know it's too late to talk to Max tonight."

"I'm not going to lie to him, Jack. If he makes me tell him what's going on, I'm likely to do it."

"You don't want to do that without me there."

"No, I don't. And if you're here, you can do it. I'm just telling you—"

"You're going to have to deal with the fallout, Margaret. Now you can do this. You don't have to lie. Just be creative. I'll see you on the way back from Hammond."

"Any idea when?"

"You know better than to ask that, Margaret. I've never been able to guess how long these things take."

"That's for sure."

17

★★★★

INTERVIEWS

Detective Antoine Johnson knew that even in this day and age, a black man couldn't just show up at the door of a white man and his family in Chicago and expect to be invited in—especially after dark—even if he's in a suit and flashes a badge. Johnson called the 11th district stationhouse and reached the desk sergeant.

Antoine told him the name of the man he was going to see, in case Waters called for verification—as he should.

The sergeant laughed. "I'll tell him we have no record of you on the force and that your badge number is bogus."

"You're a laugh a minute, Sarge."

Johnson was within a mile of the Waterses' when he called their home.

"He's putting the kids down," Mrs. Waters said. "May I have him call you?"

"Sorry, no. Chicago Police Department, ma'am. I just need permission to pay him a visit this evening."

"Tonight? What's this about?"

"I'm not at liberty to say, ma'am. Can I just have a minute with him?"

Antoine heard the muffled sounds of Mrs. Waters fetching her husband and telling him the police were on the phone.

"This is Pastor Waters," he said, wariness in his voice.

Johnson introduced himself and read off his badge number. "You'll need that to verify me."

"That shouldn't be necessary. How can I help you?"

Antoine was tempted to lecture the man. Yes, it *was* necessary to check out someone who wants to visit you in the middle of the evening, claiming to be a cop. That same naiveté had made the pastor reveal exactly who was babysitting Max Lamonica Drake and where she lived.

"Just need to chat about one of your parishioners. Shouldn't take long."

"We can't do this by phone? I'm putting the kids down and—"

"I do need to talk to you in person, sir."

"Is it about Ray-Ray, because his parole officer tells me—"

"I'm not familiar with a Ray-Ray, sir."

"Oh, sorry. He's been coming to church since he was moved to a halfway house, and I think he's doing well. But you never know."

"I should be there momentarily, Pastor. I'm sorry to interrupt your evening, but it *is* important."

Antoine exited his unmarked squad in an alley behind the three-flat house where the Waterses lived on the first floor. He transferred his wallet badge to his outside breast pocket so it would be visible in the light over the back entrance. The pastor was waiting for him at the door.

"Thanks for making time to see me. I hope you checked me out."

"I wasn't going to," the squat redhead said, looking embarrassed. "But the wife insisted." He wore a sleeveless T-shirt over suit pants and was barefooted.

"Good for her. That's wise."

"You checked out," the pastor said, leading the detective through a narrow hallway into a tiny kitchen.

"Good for me."

Pastor Waters laughed a little too loud at this. He introduced his wife, who shook Antoine's hand, looking concerned, but excused herself to finish getting the children down.

"If you don't mind my saying," Johnson said, sitting across Waters at a Formica-topped table, "you seem a little—"

"Old to have young kids? They ought to be my grandkids, shouldn't they?"

Johnson shrugged. "Just curious."

"We married late is all. Three kids ten and under. Wish we could afford a bigger place, but this is what the Lord called us to."

"Mm-hm," Antoine said, pulling out his palm-size leather notebook and studying a page. "And you're, uh, bi-vocational?"

"Yes, sir. I work at Big Box in the electronics department during the week—salesman. Trying to make ends meet and keep too much of a salary burden off the congregation. You a churchgoing man, detective?"

"Not as much as I used to be or as much as I should, but yeah, I go when I can. Still visit my mama's church. She goes all the time."

"Good, good."

"Let me get down to business, if it's all right, as this is urgent." Johnson busily thumbed through his notes. "You didn't work today?"

"I work every day."

"I mean at the store."

"Yes, no, I work there only Monday through Friday. Saturday I spend at the church, getting ready for Sunday. I was at the church all day today. North Beach Fellowship. You know it?"

"No, sir. Sorry."

Pastor Waters tried to tell Antoine where it was, something about a strip mall near a KFC. "I know the area," Antoine said. "Now, did you have a visitor this morning?"

"Several. We're a small congregation, but the people know I'm there Saturdays, so that's when they come to see me, for counseling and the like. This morning our outreach team leader met with me, and also our food-drive chairwoman. Oh, and the head of our women's missionary society."

"This concerns a visitor from outside your congregation."

"Oh, yes! The soldier! The brother of one of our former parishioners. She's married to a policeman. Do you know him? Boone Drake."

"I work for him."

"Wonderful! How did the surprise go?"

"The surprise?"

"Her brother just got home from Afghanistan or Pakistan or wherever they're fighting now, and he had planned a big surprise for her."

"Yet he didn't know where she lived?"

"He did, but the Drakes weren't home, and a neighbor or someone told him they were gone for the day. He was just wondering if I knew where they were."

"Hold on a second. Excuse me." Antoine rose and moved to the back door, where he whispered into his cell phone to the leader of the ransom team stationed at the Drake home. "How many homes near the Drakes'? . . . Cul-de-sac? . . . Six? Get someone to canvass 'em. . . . Yes, tonight. C'mon, man, there's a kid missing! I need to know if anyone saw a blue Buick in the area or if a guy in Army fatigues was asking where the Drakes were."

When Antoine returned to the kitchen, Pastor Waters looked puzzled. "I'd sure like to know what's going on."

"Back to your story, sir. How did this Alfonso know where to find you?"

"He said his sister told him all about the church and me and everything. I just happened to know that little Max—that's her son from a previous relationship; Boone Drake recently adopted him. Oh, but you'd know that. I'm saying too much. . . ."

"No, go on."

"I knew they were at some party—I don't know where—but that Florence Quigley would be watching him. She's a member of our church and the Drakes' regular sitter."

"And you thought it was wise to tell a stranger who she was and where she lived?"

"Oh, he wasn't really a stranger."

"You knew him?"

"Well, no, but I'm a pretty good judge of character. And the brother of a dear friend isn't a stranger long with me."

"You accepted without question that he was Haeley Drake's brother?"

"Well, sure. Why else would he want to surprise her? He showed me a picture of them together before he shipped out. And you know what else? I told him I bet he was her unspoken prayer request. You know what that is?"

"I do."

"I told him she did that often. She would ask prayer for her son or something else in her life, and she would almost always add, 'And one unspoken request.' Well, it's never polite to ask what that is. People need to be able to keep private things private. But Alfonso agreed that he had to be that unspoken request, because he'd been on a classified assignment. And she didn't even know he was back. He was so excited to finally meet his nephew."

"Pastor Waters, I need you to tell me everything you can remember about what this man looked like, what else he said, anything at all."

"One thing. I always like to get a reading of where a person stands, spiritually I mean. With Alfonso I asked if he shared his sister's faith. He said he was washed in the same blood I was. You know what that means?"

"Sure, the blood of Christ."

"You have to admit, that's an inside term. People outside the church wouldn't say that."

"Mm-hm." Antoine Johnson set his notebook and pen aside and massaged his face with his palms. "Pastor Waters, it gives me no pleasure to tell you this, but I think it's fair to say that this man purporting to be Alfonso Lamonica is a long way from being an insider."

If it was possible, the pale man grew paler. The light seemed to fade from his eyes, and his smile froze. "Why? What has happened? Did I do the wrong thing?"

"Yes, sir. I'm afraid you did."

Jack Keller was not a gambling man, but his work had taken him into establishments like the Lucky Day. He found himself amused at the casino rats who frequented such places. People of all socioeconomic levels—judging from their apparel—crowded the acres of gaming floor, playing table games, slot machines, craps, roulette, you name it. And this was one of the last remaining venues where one could smoke indoors.

Besides what looked to Jack like barely twenty-one-year-old gangbangers, he saw adults of all vintages, including the elderly and infirm, some in wheelchairs, many using canes, and others pulling oxygen tanks as they searched for hungry machines into which they slid plastic cards tethered to their belt loops by curly stretch cords.

Ironically, Jack found the poker room a strange oasis from the blue clouds, as for some reason it had been decreed smoke free. He approached a reception desk under a bank of TV monitors listing available games and waiting lists.

"I called and talked to a floor man a little while ago," he told a young woman.

"That would be Goose," she said, pointing over her shoulder without looking.

Across the massive poker room lay an elevated area with a podium, behind which stood a big man in a natty sport coat with the Lucky Day logo on his pocket.

Jack shook the man's hand.

"We've got a waiting list," Goose said. "You on it?"

"I'm the one who called about talking to Mr. Shane Loggyn."

Goose's eyes narrowed. "And I'm the one who told you he's on till midnight."

"Which one is he, by the way?"

"Right behind you, but don't bother him."

Jack turned to see a dealer in the customary Lucky Day outfit—ruffled shirt, sleeve garters, gaming badge dangling from a lanyard around his neck. Shane Loggyn proved distinguished looking, with a dark-chocolate complexion, close-cropped salt-and-pepper hair, wearing a gaudy watch, and displaying manicured fingers. He appeared to have impeccable posture, sitting straight with his lower back tucked in, making him appear taller than the players. He had large, expressive eyes and maintained a steady, lighthearted patter. The players at his table looked happy to be there.

"You say he's popular?"

Goose nodded. "And has seniority. Everybody knows him."

"Do people ask for him?"

"They would, but that's not how it works. We assign you to a table, and our dealers move every half hour. You play long enough, you'll get Shane your share of times."

"So they rotate to a break occasionally?"

"Occasionally, but as I told you, Shane's next break is when he's finished for the night."

"So you have other dealers currently on break?"

Goose hesitated. "Why?"

"Because someone will need to sit in for Shane while I chat with him for a few minutes."

"You got a hearing problem? I've made it clear that—"

"Don't make me show my badge right here on the floor, Goose. That wouldn't be good for business, would it?"

Goose sighed. "Who you with?"

"Chicago PD."

"You realize you're in Indiana, right?"

"Do you really want to do this the hard way, Goose? Chicago and Hammond, we reciprocate. You need to see if I'm legit, I can give you the personal phone number of Lieutenant Tidwell, but I don't think he'd appreciate being bothered after hours."

"I know Lefty Tidwell."

"I thought you might."

"He's good people."

"So am I, if I get a little cooperation."

"Shane in trouble?"

"Just—"

"Need to talk to him. Yeah, I know the drill." Goose whispered to a passing woman. When she responded, he said, "Have Kenny do it and tell him I'll make it up to him."

Jack said, "And do you have a private place Shane and I can—"

"Nobody's in the high-limit room, but we've got a game scheduled in there in about thirty minutes."

"That'll be more than enough time."

Goose pointed him toward the room.

Jack sat at an empty table, gazing back out through smoked-glass doors. Goose approached Shane Loggyn with a young dealer in tow. Shane finished a hand, shoved the chips to the winner, moved the dealer button, and was gathering the cards. When Goose whispered in his ear, Loggyn raised his eyebrows and spread his fingers on the table to show the overhead cameras his hands were empty. He lifted his chip tray from a hole in the table and followed Goose to the high-limit room as Kenny slid in behind him and set his own tray into the table.

Goose introduced Shane and shut the door on his way out. Shane tucked his tray under one arm and shook Jack's hand with the other.

"You know I work on tips," he said in a sonorous baritone. He sounded like a professor.

"Sorry?"

"I get a few dollars an hour for showing up in costume, but I live on tips. The longer I'm away from those tables, the less I make."

"I'll be brief."

Shane set his tray down and sat across from Jack. Suddenly he was slouching, as if his entire demeanor in the other room had been an act.

"Beat," he said. "But a couple of hours to go. What do you

need? I can tell you I have a nephew serving time in California on a weapons charge and that I have never been arrested. Other than that, I have no idea what you want with me."

"Fair enough. You still own a blue Buick?"

"I do, sir, and I love that car."

"You drive it to work today?"

"No, I drove the wife's car. Lent the Buick to a friend."

Jack pulled out his notebook. "May I ask who that was?"

"A friend of a friend."

Jack looked up. "I need a name."

"I believe the last name is Bertalay. Something like that."

Jack cocked his head. "Someone is using your vintage car and you don't know his name?"

"His name's John. I'm guessing at the last name, but I think that's it."

"Did he tell you what he wanted it for?"

"A date, I think—oh, don't tell me. Was my car used in a crime?"

"I'll get to that. For now—"

Loggyn cursed under his breath. "I should have known."

"Should have known?"

"I didn't worry about it because my friend asked, and he gave me like a security deposit."

"How much?"

"Two large."

"Thousand?"

"No!" Loggyn chuckled. "In our business a hundred is large. Two hundred."

"So your friend gave you two hundred dollars to make you feel better about letting *his* friend use your car. For how long?"

"He promised I'd get it back in time to drive to work tomorrow morning."

"And this Bertalay took it when?"

"Last night."

"Did you meet him?"

"Briefly. Seemed like an okay kid. Just back from the service."

"Wearing fatigues? Buzz cut? Sunburned?"

"That's him. Well spoken. Polite. Grateful."

"I'll bet. And who's the mutual friend?"

"Former employee. And I may have overstated the *friend* part. I can't say DeWayne's actually my friend."

"DeWayne Mannock?"

Shane grinned and shook his head. "Why doesn't it surprise me a Chicago cop knows that name?"

"So, not really a friend but a coworker?"

"Well, former coworker. DeWayne and I don't have much in common. He's a lot younger. I never liked his attitude, his work ethic."

"But you let a friend of his borrow your car."

"I've let DeWayne use it a time or two as well. But this time it was only because of the two hundred and that his friend seemed like a good kid. And I'm a veteran myself, so maybe I've got a soft spot. Am I getting my car back?"

"Eventually."

"It wasn't wrecked, was it?"

"It's evidence, but no."

18

★★★★

DEALING

DETECTIVE ANTOINE JOHNSON felt as if he were watching a man disintegrate. Pastor Warren Waters sat with his head in hands, the bald spot separating what was left of his rim of red hair shining under the dingy fluorescent bulbs in the kitchen.

"I'm such a fool," he moaned, causing his wife to tiptoe in.

"What is it, Warren? What's happened?"

"You remember I told you about that brother of Haeley Lamonica's?"

"Wanting to surprise her, yes."

"He wasn't who he said he was."

"Mr. Loggyn," Jack Keller said, sliding his business card across the felt, "I appreciate your cooperation. Now I'm going to ask you a few more questions, and of course I'm going to check you out. If you remember anything else, call me, and if I need your help to apprehend either Mr. Mannock or his friend, can I count on you?"

Shane Loggyn squinted. "If they've committed some kind of a crime, especially with my car, yes, you can."

"Excuse me," Jack said, fishing out his phone. He was punching in the number for Lieutenant Tidwell of the Hammond PD when he noticed Loggyn checking his watch. "I'll get you back out there as soon as I can."

The number rang twice, then: "You know how many people I answer the phone for this time of night?"

"Only the ones you love, Lefty."

"So I made an exception for you. What's up, Jack?"

"Kidnapping and possibly GTA."

"If it was only grand theft auto, it coulda waited till Monday; am I right?"

"Right, but a CPD cop's kid was taken, Tid. Little boy."

"Who'm I rounding up?"

"DeWayne Mannock."

"Get out. That scumbag isn't smart enough to kidnap a cat."

"Don't know how deep he's into this, but he had help."

"If he's in Indiana, we'll get him for ya."

"Thanks, Tid—"

But the lieutenant had already hung up.

"Mr. Loggyn," Jack said, "what do you know about Mannock coming into some money?"

"Well, he's got some—I know that. I remember when he used to beg me for loans so he could play when he was off duty; he was that poor. I put the kibosh on that because it took him so long to pay me back. That's why he had to give me the two hundred for the car up front. He dealt mostly tournaments, and there you're depending on the winners to be generous. In cash games you get a buck or so every hand. That's where the money is."

"And you get more cash games because of your seniority?"

"That's only part of it. Mannock had been here long enough to get his choice too, but he had a lot of points on his record."

"Points?"

"You get demerits if you're late, get complaints, take too many days off, that kind of stuff. He was broke and dealing almost only tournaments, and getting fewer and fewer shifts as it was. All of a sudden he's flashing wads of cash and telling us he may never have to work again. Then a week or so ago he up and quits. But he still comes around. I don't know if he knocked over a bank or won the lottery, but he's dressing nice, got himself some jewelry, talks about buying a new car—wants an Escalade."

"That's a lot of car. Yet he needs his friend to borrow yours."

"Yeah. Curious."

"Why'd you mention the lottery?"

"'Cause that's what he claims. But a guy from Gaming—the state gaming commission—said that was easy to check online. So we did. Mannock hasn't won any of the big ones, certainly nothing big enough to change his life."

"Sir, I don't know if it'll come to this, but would you be willing to have your phone rigged so we can record your conversations with DeWayne when he comes back here without your Buick?"

"Are you kidding?" Shane said. "He comes back here without my car, I'm willing to wear a gun."

"We can make it so we can monitor phone conversations and regular conversations."

"Whatever you have to do. I want that car back."

On his way to Mount Sinai, Jack answered a call from Antoine Johnson. "Didn't get much more out of the pastor, but he was duped, all right. He virtually handed Max to this Alfonso character on a silver platter. Feels awful. I told him not to mention it tomorrow at church. These guys like to get everybody praying about stuff like this."

"I know," Jack said. "And I wish he could, but the fewer who know about this right now, the better."

"Downtown tells me Mrs. Quigley has been begging to talk with Chief Drake and Pastor Waters. They put the fear of God in her and told her not to talk to anybody till she hears back from us. She wanted to go to church tomorrow too, but we talked her out of that. No way she could keep quiet."

"Anything from the ransom team?"

"I asked 'em to canvass the cul-de-sac because this Alfonso guy told the pastor some neighbor told him the Drakes were away for the day. Come to find out, no one in the neighborhood saw the car or talked to the soldier. He got his information somewhere else."

"So, obviously no ransom calls."

"No. Everything's quiet. No calls to Mrs. Quigley's phone, and they stop monitoring any calls to Boone's, Haeley's, or the home phone as soon as they determine the caller is not the kidnapper."

"I don't like it."

"Sir?"

"Bad as a ransom demand would be, if someone did call, we'd know what we're dealing with. Whoever took Max can't think a Chicago cop has means. It's likely someone who knows Haeley got that settlement or someone who has other ideas for the boy."

"I don't even want to think about that," Antoine said.

"Neither do I, but if we don't hear from anyone by morning, it's the only thing we'll be thinking about."

Jack told Antoine about the DeWayne Mannock connection.

"I don't know that name."

"Haeley's old boyfriend. Max's real father."

"Well, there you go. And he wasn't the impostor, pretending to be the brother?"

"Nah. Doesn't look anything like him. And the way Florence Quigley and the doorman described him, this guy was way too slick and glib to be Mannock."

"But if we find him, we find the kid, right?"

"Not so sure," Jack said. "Mannock has already been paid, which I can't make sense of."

"Well, it's more than revenge or the act of a jilted lover. He took a fee to give the kid up to someone else. But why?"

"And how did he get the money in advance?"

Jack pulled into the parking lot at Mount Sinai having told Detective Johnson to take the rest of the night off, "in case I need you tomorrow."

He found Margaret dozing in the ICU waiting room and gently touched her shoulder, startling her.

"I'm so glad you're here," she said. "I just know I was gonna blab everything if Boone woke up and asked what was going on."

"I hope he sleeps till morning."

"You know better than that," she said. "He's got to be like a mother with a newborn. Part of him is listening for any stirring from Haeley, and part of him is aware he hasn't talked to Max since we dropped him off. No matter how exhausted he is, one of those things is going to wake him."

Jack sat next to Margaret. "You staying here all night," he said, "even if Boone sleeps through?"

She nodded. "You know he'll be out of here as soon as he finds out about Max."

"I'm gonna check in on him."

"Jack, no. Let him sleep."

"Just for a second."

Jack headed out to the nurses' station and told Chaz Cilano's replacement where he was going.

"Sorry, one visitor at a time, sir."

"I won't leave the hall," he said. "I just need to know if Mr. Drake is still asleep."

"I can find out for you," she said, rising.

"No need," he said, heading down the corridor. When she stood as if ready to forbid him, he said, "Promise," and kept going.

Jack was grateful to find Boone dead to the world. But Margaret was right. It wasn't likely he would sleep in. Too much was whirring, even in Boone's subconscious. If only

Jack could buy another hour or two so he'd have a handle on what they were dealing with before he had to inform him . . .

Jack's priority would be to corral Boone, focus him, turn his fear, his rage into fuel for his passion. Jack had never seen a cop so obsessed with details. Boone could become a laser for the truth. He just needed to be persuaded, not to set aside the personal part of this equation—that would be impossible—but to invest his entire professional self into becoming the perfect tool for solving this crime.

Haeley lay there as if she had simply crawled into bed for a nap, though the prodigious ball of gauze encasing her head and the deep purple and yellow face assaulted Jack with the truth.

He had felt himself softening toward these people of faith—Boone, Haeley, Margaret, Francisco, and many others he had met at Community Life. But he had to admit, seeing Boone go through this again, with Haeley on the brink, and with a wholly innocent child who-knows-where . . . somebody was going to have a lot of explaining to do—starting with God himself.

Jack's phone chirped, and he remembered he was supposed to have left it with the nurses. He hurried back down the hall, waving an apology to the nurse heading his way. He slipped into the waiting room to take a call from Lieutenant Tidwell.

"Here's everything I got, Jack, and at the end of it, tell me what you want to do, because I gotta get to bed. Mannock lives in the attic of a house on the west side of Hammond. Even though his old Nissan Sentra was parked out front and all the lights were on in his dung heap of a room, he wasn't there. Landlord who showed me the room lives downstairs.

Says DeWayne went out about an hour before with a package under his arm."

"Can you keep that landlord from telling Mannock you were asking?"

"Already swore him to secrecy. He's got so many violations—'fact, I don't think he's even eligible to be renting here—that he'll cooperate."

"DeWayne left on foot?"

"Took a cab, of all things. Landlord remembered the color, so we knew the company, called them, found out Mannock was taken to the north side of Chicago, originally as a one-way fare."

"Bet the cabbie loved that."

"Well, while we're on the phone with them, the cabbie radios in that he's bringing the fare back to Hammond after all. We wait out of sight, then pull the cab over a few blocks away after he's dropped Mannock off. Cabbie had an interesting story. Says he tried to get out of the job when the rider told him it was one-way, told Mannock there was no way he'd find somebody in Chicago who wanted a ride to Hammond, especially this time of night. Mannock told him he'd pay him double, but he had his own way back."

"He went to the north side, eh?" Jack said. He read off the address of the Bethune Arms apartments, Florence Quigley's building.

"That's the street but not the address. First stop was three blocks or so from there."

"*First* stop?"

"We caught a break, Jack."

"Tell me."

"Cabbie says Mannock had him pull into an alley, said it

must not be the right one, and had him pull into a couple more. He was pretty exercised about not finding what he was looking for. He gets out at the last alley and goes deeper into it, looks both ways at an intersection. Comes back looking disgusted. Makes a few phone calls, apparently not reaching anybody, claps his phone shut, does a lot of cussing, then tells the guy to drive him back home. Pays him in hundreds, including a big tip. Funny thing, though. Cabbie says all the guy wants to talk about is the new Caddy SUV he's gettin' next week, but then the driver gets a peek at what DeWayne's carrying. Illinois license plates."

"So now DeWayne's home?"

"Yep, and we'd be happy to roust him out for you."

"Not yet," Jack said and briefed Tidwell on his conversation with Shane Loggyn. "I'm guessing Mannock went to Chicago to put the original plates on that Buick so he could get it back to Shane tomorrow morning."

"You don't want us to collar him?"

"No. I want you to let the air out of a couple of his tires. I'm going to get Loggyn to rattle his cage in the morning, and when Mannock tries to either appease him or make a break for it, I want his car out of commission."

"Police work the way we used to do it. Love it, Jack."

"Got anybody who can rig Loggyn's cell phone so we can hear both sides when he calls Mannock?"

"This time of night?"

"Remember, Lefty, we're talking about a cop's kid."

"Consider it done. Where do I find this Loggyn?"

Jack told him and also advised him what to tell Shane to say when he called Mannock.

"Jack, you look terrible," Margaret said. "You've got to get some sleep."

"So do you."

"I can sleep right here," she said, laying her palm on the sofa in the waiting room. "I've done it before. You need to stretch out."

"I know. I've got to be ready in the morning. And I have an idea. I'm going to have a squad sent to my place to pick me up some clothes."

Jack found the nurse in charge. "I see you've got a couple of empty rooms down the hall. I need one."

"I'm not authorized—"

"I don't have time to argue with you about this. Now, I'll take the heat, but I'm going to sleep in one of those beds, and I'm going to use the bathroom in there for a shower and a shave in the morning."

"Chief Keller, I really—"

"Do you have anything to help me sleep?"

"We've got a supply of Ambien, but—"

"You gonna make this happen, or are you going to keep telling me why you can't? I'm on a major case and I have no choice, so you don't either. What's the worst that could happen?"

"I lose my job."

"I guarantee that's not going to happen. I'll bring the full force of the city down on anyone who threatens that."

The nurse produced a container of Ambien from her own purse. Jack told her that when a uniformed officer brought his stuff, she should just deliver it to the room. She insisted he take the last room in the corridor and pull the privacy curtains. And she posted a quarantine card on the door.

As Jack lay on his back in the darkness, his mind swirled with every detail of the case. He knew from experience that Ambien worked quickly for him. As he felt himself drifting, he was imagining Tidwell's conversation with Shane Loggyn and Loggyn's recorded conversation with Mannock in the morning. The veteran poker dealer would tell Mannock that if he didn't have his car delivered to his home by 9 a.m., he'd be calling the cops.

If that didn't get this ball rolling, nothing would. Jack faded with the warm feeling that at the very least, he would have Boone with him on the job shortly after he awoke.

19

★★★★

DAWN

JULY 1

Boone Drake awoke as a rim of orange peeked over the buildings in the distance. Medicinal smells told him where he was, and the sight of his beloved—her ravaged face an even darker purple now—reminded him why.

Boone checked his watch. Way too early to call Florence and try to talk to Max. He couldn't imagine anyone had told the boy the truth about his mother. When Boone went to relieve himself and caught a glimpse of himself in the mirror, he decided to shower and shave. Who knew when Jack might come by?

Boone was grateful to feel rested. His emotions were a jumble, naturally, but he was on a mission. He wanted to study everything there was to know about Haeley's kind of trauma and prepare himself—and in the process, prepare Max—for whatever had to happen from here on to restore his wife to full health. He wanted to be a model at the hospital, staying atop things, of course, but also staying out of the way of medical personnel.

When he emerged from the bathroom, refreshed and more optimistic than the night before, Boone started straightening his cot.

"Morning, sir," Chaz Cilano said. "Leave that. I'll have someone make your bed."

"Were you here all night?" he said.

"Yeah, I'm here 24/7. Drugs keep me from having to sleep. Are you nuts? I just got in. Working double shifts this week. Your friends up yet?"

"My friends?"

"I got to know Margaret a little last night. She slept in the waiting room. Chief Keller intimidated one of my girls into giving him a room down the hall."

"That's nice of them," Boone said. "But they shouldn't have felt obligated."

"They care about you."

"Where's Jack?"

She nodded toward the end of the hall. "He was given a sleep aid, so I'm guessing he's still out."

Boone hurried down the corridor. "This one?" he said.

"The quarantine, yes."

Boone knocked lightly and pushed the door open a few inches. Jack was snoring. Boone pulled the door shut and headed past Chaz toward the waiting room. "Margaret doped up too?"

"Not that I know of."

Boone went to the waiting room, where Margaret leaned up on one elbow and squinted at him. "Everything all right?"

"You tell me."

"You talked to Jack?"

"Why? What's up?"

She sighed deeply. "Police stuff. I don't know. He can tell you."

"He told me not to even think about what's going on in the office. Should I wake him? Does he need me?"

"Oh, please don't, Boone. He was up late last night."

"Doing what?"

"I told you. The usual. He'll be up soon. Get yourself somethin' to eat while I get myself together, huh?"

Boone *was* hungry. "If he's not up when I get back, I'm waking him."

"Well, don't tell him it was my idea."

As Boone headed for the elevator, he saw a look in Chaz Cilano's eyes. It didn't take a trained observer to know something was going on.

Downstairs, he waited in a long line for a toasted bagel and a large cup of black coffee. He ate and drank on the way back to the ICU, having convinced himself that Haeley had taken a turn for the worse in the night and that everyone had conspired to make Jack be the one to break the news.

Back at the nurses' station, Boone beckoned Chaz with a nod. "You and I are going to become friends," he said.

"Okay . . ." she said, suspicion in her voice.

"But I need you to shoot straight with me. Have you heard from Dr. Sarangan since I talked to you last night?"

She nodded.

"I knew it. What's up? I don't need Jack to tell me."

"The doctor called just after I got here and said to tell you he'd drop in after church."

"Why?"

"To do what good doctors do, check on his patient. He asked if there'd been any change in her vitals. I assured him there had not, so he said to look for him sometime early afternoon."

"No changes?"

"No, sir, and that's good news."

"Well, 'course, yeah."

"This is the diciest time for her. The coma is designed to keep her in stasis. You know what that means."

Boone nodded, puzzled. "Makes no sense that Jack and Margaret stayed the night."

"It doesn't make much more sense that *you* stayed. Except you're that kind of a husband. Aren't they that kind of friends? You could be more grateful."

"Just stressed, I guess," he said.

"Understandable. Why don't you relax until Chief Keller gets up."

"Relax? Yeah, that's not going to happen. I need my phone please."

Boone found an empty waiting room one floor below and checked his messages. Except for a Scripture reference from Francisco, nothing. Not even a call from Florence. You would have thought . . .

What was so important that Jack had to work late? Boone called Antoine Johnson. His wife, Rebekah, told Boone he was still sleeping. "So sorry to hear about your wife, Chief. I pray she's on the mend."

"As well as can be expected right now, thanks. Was Antoine working late last night too?"

"Yes, sir. You know he'll never let up."

"What are he and Jack working on?" Her pause was too long. "Rebekah?"

"You know he never tells me anything. You taught him that."

"I'd like to hear from him when he's up."

"I'll tell him."

Boone thanked her and rang off, idly looking at Pastor Sosa's text. Mark 4:22. He looked it up on his mobile Bible: "For nothing is hidden except to be made manifest; nor is anything secret except to come to light."

It was time to find out what was going on.

Boone returned to ICU to find that both Jack and Margaret were up and showering. When they finally joined him in the waiting room, he noticed that Margaret had straightened up the area where she had slept and that she had two duffel bags. "Staying?" he said.

She glanced at Jack and nodded.

"You don't need to do that," Boone said.

"I want to."

"Jack," Boone said, "they keep telling me there's nothing I can do here, but I'm not leaving Haeley. At least not for long. But I need to tell Max what happened, and I should do that in person, don't you think?"

He caught the look between Jack and Margaret. "You need to sit down, Boones," Jack said.

"Just tell me."

"Sit."

When Boone reluctantly sat, Jack dragged a coffee table over and sat facing him. Margaret quietly left the room. *What in the world?*

"Boone, there's no easy way to say this. Max was abducted yesterday."

Boone leapt to his feet, reaching for the snub-nosed .38 in his pocket. What he was going to do with that he had no idea. Shoot himself? A strange feeling washed over him, leaving him cold, and he found it hard to breathe. Even learning of the death of his son Josh—devastating as it was—did not compare with this. There was a horrible finality to that, but now all his senses were engaged, and he had to know everything at once. He wanted to be able to hear it, see it, touch it, taste it, smell it.

Boone collapsed back onto the sofa and beckoned to Jack with both hands, as if to say, "Give me everything."

And Jack did. He used his notes and his legendary memory for detail to paint the entire picture, from Alfonso's visit to the pastor to the afternoon spent with Florence, and from the Buick to DeWayne Mannock.

"Now, you won't think you need or want to hear this," Jack said, "but you're going to listen anyway. I know you. I know what you want to do right this instant."

"No, you don't."

"Don't insult me, Boones. If I guess right, will you hear me out?"

Boone nodded.

"You want to go on the stakeout to Shane Loggyn's and blow DeWayne Mannock's head off the instant you see him."

"Okay, so you know me. What are we doing?"

"If I were you, I'd feel such rage and fear right now that I'd worry whether I could be trusted to have any part in this. And the fact is, few superiors would let you anywhere near it. But as lead investigator on this, I want my best man involved. And despite that you're the father and standing vigil at your wife's sickbed, if you can force yourself to focus, I need you."

"You couldn't keep me away."

"I could, and I will if I have to. If you can't digest this and get that analytical mind of yours around it, you'll be no good to me—or to Max."

Boone nodded.

"Tell me you get it."

"I do."

"Do you need to vent first? Kick something, hit something, throw something?"

"All of the above, but there's no time. Why are we sitting here?"

"You're not going on the Mannock stakeout. You know what happens now. You have to immerse yourself in every detail of the investigation."

"What haven't you told me?"

"I've told you everything, but you need to get all this firsthand, starting with Florence. She's a mess, feeling terrible, guilty, miserable. But you need to get the whole story from her and go from there. Meanwhile, we'll bring DeWayne in. You'll get your chance to talk to him."

"I want to torture him till he tells us where Max is. But you're right; I wouldn't trust myself at the stakeout."

"It wouldn't surprise me if he doesn't know where Max

is. Why would whoever's behind this trust him with that information?"

"No way *he* could have masterminded this," Boone said. "So who are we dealing with?"

"That's the thinking path I want you on. Can you stay there?"

"I don't know."

"Just keep me up to date on where your head is. You'll know if it's too close to home for you to be effective."

"I said you can't keep me off this, Jack."

"No way you'll be able to concentrate the way you need to if you leave Haeley here alone."

"Exactly."

"Margaret is setting up camp where you were last night, and she's in this for the long haul."

"I hope Haeley understands," Boone said. "I mean, someday she's going to know."

"She will. Now, I'm going to Hammond. You're going to see Florence. And I've told everybody—from Antoine to Dr. Waldemarr—to give you access to everything and everyone. By the end of today, I want you as up to speed on this as I am."

Chaz Cilano accompanied Boone and Jack to Haeley's room, explaining that she could allow three visitors at once provided she was there. As soon as they entered, Margaret stood and embraced Boone.

"Thanks for doing this," he whispered.

"I'll do anything, Boone."

"But should I leave her?" he said. "What'll she say when she finds out?"

"She's going to appreciate that she wasn't left alone."

"But doesn't she want *me* to stay," Boone said, "*me* to be with her?"

"You want to know what she'd say right now if she knew what was going on?"

"I do!"

Margaret grabbed Boone's shirt at his chest, bunching the material in both hands and drawing him to where they were nose to nose. Her eyes were moist and her voice emotion-choked. "Here's what she'd tell you, Boone: 'Go find our son!'"

Boone wrapped his arms around her again, then pulled away and leaned over Haeley. He laid a hand lightly on her swollen head and gently kissed her warm cheek. "I'll find him," he said. "I'll get him back."

20

★★★★

WIRETAPS

Jack walked Boone to his car, advising him to go through the doorman at Bethune Arms to see Florence. "You call her to let her know you're coming, she's liable to do nothing but blubber. Just have Willie let her know."

Boone slid behind the wheel of the car that had been a gift from Haeley, docked his cell phone, and dialed the Bethune Arms.

"Oh, Mr. Drake," Willie said. "Have they found your boy?"

Boone filled him in, asking him to let Florence know he was coming. "And I'd also like to talk to you and the young man on the street who found the car."

"Scooter's not always easy to find."

"If you could just try."

"I surely will."

When Boone was within a few blocks of Florence's place, Willie called him. "Two things, sir. First, Miz Quigley is all upset worryin' you're mad at her."

"I'm not. I just need to get the story firsthand."

"I got her to agree to see you. And I found Scooter. He's here in the lobby wondering if he can talk to you first."

"Sure, I guess."

"He says he'll tell you the same story he told everybody else."

Jack Keller met Hammond PD Lieutenant Lefty Tidwell about six blocks from the apartment complex where Shane Loggyn, the casino dealer, lived. They climbed into the back of a nondescript brown van with tinted windows. It was outfitted with surveillance devices. Two other plainclothesmen nodded, then turned back to their screens and keyboards.

Lefty Tidwell was about Jack's age but, unlike Jack, looked it. Jack assumed the man hadn't seen a workout room in twenty years. He limped on a bad knee, had worn the same broken-down shoes for as long as Jack had known him, and still sported a 1970s moustache—now gray except for nicotine stains—which grew untrimmed over his lip.

But he was all cop.

He pointed to a map on one of the screens and showed Jack where they were in relation to Loggyn's apartment a few blocks away. "He lives with his wife on the top floor of a six-story brick building. The area's rundown, but the complex is tidy and fenced. We've got perfect reception from here.

"Lucky for us, Loggyn has one of the newer, fancier phones my techies tell me are easy. I wouldn't know from

Adam's housecat. I'm still lookin' for a cell with a rotary dial, know what I mean?"

"Yeah."

"Am I right?"

It was Tidwell's favorite question, as if he feared losing your attention if he didn't keep you engaged.

"You're right," Jack said. "Now what do we know?"

"We put a chip in Loggyn's phone that'll transmit, so we can record calls in or out, but it also will record live conversations." Tidwell nudged one of his guys, who dutifully pointed to a toggle switch. "And play for Chief Keller that one we already got."

The techie hit another couple of switches and handed Jack a set of earphones. The fidelity made it sound as if Loggyn and DeWayne Mannock were right in front of him.

"Hey, DeWayne," Loggyn said.

"Shane! My man!"

"Everything work out with the car?"

"Far as I know."

"Your friend have a good time?"

"Yup."

"You bringing it this morning? The wife's already gone, and I'm on ten to six today."

"Oh, you need it today?"

"Don't start with me, DeWayne. That was the agreement from day one. You don't have the car back yet?"

"Oh, no, I got it. It's just, ah, I had something else to do this morning. My bad, man. Hey, take a cab and I'll pay you back, all right? I can bring the car to the casino this afternoon."

"And then how will you get home?"

"*I'll* take a cab."

"C'mon, man, the deal was I get the car back by nine this morning, so make it happen."

"I can't, Shane. What if I throw in another fifty?"

"Forget the money. If I don't have that car by nine, I'm calling the cops."

"What're you, serious?"

"As an undertaker. Do what you've got to do."

"If I can't get the car to you, I'll come by and drive you to work myself, how's that?"

"What are you talking about? You just said you had the car!"

"Well, not exactly. But I know he's bringing it later."

"So you lied to me."

"Sorry, dude. But you can trust me."

"Be here by nine or I'm reporting the car stolen, and I'm not kidding."

"You got it, man."

Jack slid off the earphones. "We could use someone like Loggyn on our team."

"I know, right?" Tidwell said. "Listen, we did like you asked and let the air out of two of Mannock's tires last night. He'll find out as soon as he tries to pull away from the curb."

"Then what?"

"Either he gets 'em fixed fast or he has to call Loggyn again, and we've told Shane what to say."

"It's almost nine now. You got guys watching Mannock?"

Tidwell nodded.

"We ought to just bring him in. We've got enough on him already. Time's wasting."

"Yeah, but Jack, don't you want to see if Loggyn can get

him to say where he's getting his money? If it's you or me badgerin' him, he can lawyer up."

Jack nodded.

"Am I right?" Tidwell said. "Huh?"

Boone Drake found Scooter sleeping near a radiator in the lobby at Bethune Arms. Willie immediately rose and greeted Boone, whispering, "He wasn't hard to find after all. He was sleeping outside on the steps."

Boone was antsy, wanting to get on with this. The sooner he had the entire picture in his mind, the sooner he could get to finding Max. Boone kicked the bottom of Scooter's foot, making the young drunk hold tighter to his bag-wrapped bottle. "I'm your first appointment, man."

As Scooter sat up, his stench nearly bowled Boone over. "I done told my story twice. Now what you want to know?"

"Same thing. Everything."

"I never seen the boy or the soldier. Only the car."

"Then how'd you know he was a soldier?"

"Miz Quigley was describin' 'em both to everybody. I ain't deaf."

"That's all you've got for me? You went looking when Mrs. Quigley asked you, and you found the car."

"I told you that's all I got. But when you talk to her, remind her she owes me."

"Owes you what?"

"She told me she'd give me a ten to help her look and she'd double it if I found the boy."

"We haven't found him yet, and you're worried about getting yours?"

"Fair's fair."

Boone ripped a twenty out of his wallet, wadded it, and threw it at the man. It hit him in the chest and rolled to the floor. Immediately Scooter was on his knees after it. "Now get out of here," Boone said, "before I run your tail downtown!"

Scooter had proved a waste of time, but Willie was helpful. He had a good memory of just about everything Alfonso had said. "I got to tell you, officer, I didn't suspect him for a second. It didn't hit me till they didn't come back and didn't come back. I just kinda went cold, you know, and had to wonder."

Whoever Alfonso was, the way Willie quoted him made him sound like a pro—believable, nuanced, charming. Tempted as he was to scold Florence and demand to know how she could let a little boy out of her sight for even an instant, Boone wondered if he himself would have seen through the con.

Boone found Florence's door ajar, held open by the chain on her security lock. He knocked and she called out, "Jes' come on in!"

Boone hadn't thought it possible that a woman Florence's size could tuck her feet up under her, but there she sat, all folded in on herself. Soggy tissues lay about, and a nearly empty box sat in her lap.

"Oh, Mr. Drake, I been cryin' all night. Prayin' for that boy. Begging Jesus to forgive me. Can you ever forgive me?"

"Florence," Boone said, sitting across from her, "you really must stop this. No one's blaming you."

"Miss Haeley will! No mama gon' put up with something like this."

"She doesn't know Max is missing, ma'am. I want him back safe and sound before she even knows he was gone. I know that's what you want too."

"With all my heart!"

"It's okay to feel bad. We all do. And we're scared for Max. But that doesn't help us get him back, does it?"

"Tell me what I can do."

He walked her through every detail, and the more she remembered, the more she wailed. But as he kept reminding her that the best thing she could do was to help with information, she gradually controlled herself.

Boone felt the clock ticking, knowing every second counted. The absolute best leads were found the quickest, and the longer you went without information, the worse it was for the victim. Still, before he left, Boone took the time to help Florence up off the couch so he could hug her.

The old lady shook on legs that seemed to have fallen asleep, but she held tight. "You know I love that boy," she sobbed.

"We know. Believe me, we know."

"You're not making assumptions about Mannock, are you, Lefty? There's no guarantee he shows up to see Loggyn."

"No, no. He makes a run for it, we've got him."

"Loggyn's phone," one of the techies said.

Lefty leaned forward. "Put it on speaker. And see what you can get on Mannock's phone. We want to be able to tap into that, too."

"This better be good news, DeWayne," Loggyn said. "It's after nine."

"I know, man, but my car got vandalized. Two flats."

"Mine or yours?"

"Mine. My guy musta got hung up or thought it was tomorrow too, so I was comin' to take you to work."

"Never mind; I'll just call the cops. It's obvious he stole my car and he's probably giving you half of whatever he gets for it."

"No! No way, Shane! I'd never do that to you. I'm getting my new Caddy this afternoon, so you can have the Sentra. I'll get the tires fixed."

"You think that's a fair trade for a vintage Buick? You're out of your—"

"No! I'm saying you can have that *and* I'll get your Buick back."

"What're you, paying cash for the Escalade too?"

A pause. "Matter of fact, I am."

"So did you really win the lottery or what?"

"Better than that."

"Anything you can cut me in on?"

"Ah, I don't know, Shane. I don't think you'd be willing to do what I'm doing."

"What, pushing dope? Knocking over businesses? I'm too old for that."

"It's a lot easier than that. I'm a consultant."

"You don't even know what the word means."

"Well, for bein' that stupid, I'm paying cash for a car today."

"How much?"

"About half of what I've earned so far."

"Those suckers cost over sixty grand, Mannock."

"Over seventy, actually."

"And you're a consultant. For who?"

"Okay, not really a consultant. More like a finder."

"A finder. You've made a hundred and a half in the last month for finding what?"

"I don't know how much I should tell you unless you're really interested."

Shane Loggyn paused—so he would sound intrigued, Boone hoped. "Tell me how dirty I've got to get."

"Nothing can be traced to you. All you got to do is point these guys in the right direction, and they pay up front. Only thing is, if they don't succeed, you owe 'em the money back."

"Succeed at what?"

"The less you know about that, the better. Like I found somebody for 'em, they handled everything from there, and I got lots of cash. That's all I know."

"Some*body*? You found somebody? . . . DeWayne, you there?"

"I'm here."

"What are you talking about? Human trafficking?"

"I don't ask questions. They tell me what they're looking for, and if I give 'em the right lead, they pay. I don't know and I don't wanna know what happens after that. But, uh, Shane, you might not be right for this. They're looking for white people."

21

★★★★

ANAGRAMS

Boone Drake knew he wouldn't be able to handle all the questions and good wishes at the 11th, so he had Antoine Johnson meet him in a grocery store parking lot a few blocks from the stationhouse. The big detective ran through all his notes, most of it a repeat of what Boone had already heard, though Boone found it valuable to get firsthand the details of the Warren Waters interview.

"Guess I'm jaded," Boone said, "but I don't get how anybody can be so naive. I know he's a good guy. I've heard him, met him. But does being nice mean you have to be stupid, too? Guy tells you he's Haeley's brother, and you send him right to Max and his babysitter?"

Boone went directly from meeting with Antoine to the crime lab, where Dr. Ragnar Waldemarr was the only one working on a Sunday morning.

"Good timing," the director said. "One of my guys just called me from home. He broke the encryption code on the phone that transmitted the picture of Mrs. Quigley and your son to her phone."

"That's good news, right? You can trace the con man's phone?"

"We ought to be able to detect it if it's pinging off any of the towers in the Chicago area. So far it's been quiet. Hold on a second."

Waldemarr reported in to Jack Keller, then showed Boone the navy Buick and everything that had been removed from the glove box and trunk. "No surprises," Waldemarr said. "All this stuff traces back to the real owner, Shane Loggyn."

Boone nodded. "So it really was borrowed for this job, fake plates put on, then removed. And the car was abandoned."

"Not really."

"No?"

"It was clearly left for someone else to pick up, Boone. Keys were under the visor. We'd have done better to leave it there and see who came for it."

"We've got a lead on him," Boone said.

"I heard. But it would have been easier my way. Nobody ever listens to me. I've got more contacts and more ways to get things done than most people dream of."

"I know, Doc. Jack's told me about your military background and all your international contacts. You don't always follow regulations, either."

"I skirt protocol for the greater good? Guilty. But you know I couldn't—or at least I wouldn't—ever doctor evidence."

"I do know that."

"Boone, listen. You need anything for this case—and I mean anything—you come to me first. Got it?"

"White people for what?" Shane Loggyn said.

"I told you," DeWayne said, "I don't know and I don't care. All I know is, the whiter the better."

"What's that mean?"

"It means not just Caucasian. Light hair and pale skin."

"What's this for, the sex trade?"

"I told you, I don't ask questions."

"I don't know if I could be involved in anything like that, DeWayne."

"What if that wasn't what it was?"

"What are you saying?"

"I'm saying I don't know what it is, 'cept I've never heard of anybody paying as much as they paid me just for one person to be in the sex trade."

"You got experience in that?"

"Ha! No. I'm just sayin' . . ."

"DeWayne, I've got to get to work. How'm I supposed to do that?"

"Call a cab and keep track of how much. I'll add fifty to it besides the two hundred when I deliver your car. And you can still have the Sentra."

"You know what?" Loggyn said. "I'm going to take you up on all of that, because you owe me."

"Do it!"

"But only one thing is going to keep me from calling the cops about my Buick."

"Name it. Last thing I need is heat."

"You've got to meet me and tell me all about whatever it is you're into."

"The money sounds good, doesn't it?"

"You know what I can make at Lucky Day, even on my best night. I'm not against a little extra—"

"A lot extra, Shane!"

"—as long as all I have to do is find people. I know plenty of white people."

They agreed to meet in the cavernous parking garage at the casino at six fifteen that evening. "I'll have my new car, man. And if the Buick isn't ready yet, I'll take you to my Nissan, and it'll be all yours, no matter what happens after that."

"DeWayne, listen. If anything's happened to my Buick, you're buying it."

"Wow. How much would that be?"

"The Blue Book on it is probably under five grand, but you know I've kept that car in cherry condition. I wouldn't take less than ten for it, and it should be more."

"That's a promise, Shane. If I don't get the Buick back for you, I'll give you ten grand."

Jack whispered to Tidwell, "Give me Loggyn's cell number."

Lefty slid him a sheet of paper. Jack texted, "Ask him where he's getting his new car."

"I'll tell you, DeWayne, truth is I'd rather have the car back than the money, know what I mean?"

"I just want to do the right thing."

"Yeah, that's you."

"You got that right, Shane." It was clear Mannock had missed the sarcasm.

"So, where you getting your Caddy?" Shane said.

"Manley."

"Manley Motors? Seriously? That's not far from me."

"I know."

When the call was over, Loggyn called Tidwell. "How'd I do?" came his voice over the speaker.

"You should get an Oscar, friend," Lefty said. "Let me have you talk to Keller."

"Yeah, you were great," Jack said. "And we owe you a ride to work." He turned to Tidwell. "We can work that out, can't we?"

Lefty nodded.

Shane said, "As long as it's not in the back of a marked car."

Tidwell called the Hammond PD motor pool and asked for an unmarked squad to deliver Shane to the Lucky Day. Jack said, "Were we able to get enough on Mannock's phone?"

One of the techies slid off his earphones, smiling. "If he'd stayed on any longer, we'd have been able to tell you what he had for breakfast."

"Can we hear who he calls?"

The techie flipped another switch, and Jack heard ringing.

"This is Jammer." The voice sounded older and exhausted. "Do you know what time it is here, DeWayne? What do you need?"

Mannock ran down the conversation he'd just had with Loggyn.

"I know him," Jammer said. "He's dealt to me at the casino. You borrowed his car for this?"

"Yeah, and I think Bertalay took it."

"You're dumb as dirt, Mannock. That would have been the last thing Johnnie would do. Why would he want to be cruising around in a boat like that, that ties him to the kid?"

While Mannock was saying, "All I know is it's not where he left it, and he's not answering his phone," Jack noticed Lefty Tidwell shoot a double take at one of the techies.

"Not a nice neighborhood, correct?" Jammer was saying. Tidwell was whispering urgently to the tech, then leaned over his shoulder and started tapping at his keyboard.

"True," Mannock said.

"Somebody stole it, then, or the cops have it. That's your mess. You clean it up. I don't need to even be involved in that."

"You got another number on Bertalay? I've called him half a dozen times and it goes straight to voice mail."

"Well, didn't he use the phone on the job, DeWayne? Didn't you give him some picture of the mother?"

"That's what he was going to use that for?"

"Duh! Now he's probably already ditched the phone. You think this guy's an amateur? He's been around the block a time or two."

"Then how'm I supposed to get hold of him? I gotta have that car."

"C'mon, DeWayne, I told you. If he deep-sixes a phone, you know good and well he's not riding around in a hot car. Somebody else jacked it. Let it go."

"That's easy for you to say. I got to get it back to this guy."

Jammer sighed. "I'll tell you one more time. That's not my problem."

"If you hear from him, could you at least have him call me?"

"I'll tell him you're looking for him, but I don't tell him who to call. I'm not his secretary. Now you're lying low, right? Not letting anybody know you don't still need your job, not flashing your money around."

"I quit my job," Mannock said as Tidwell hit Print and sheets began spilling from the portable printer.

Jammer paused. "Why would you do that? It was the perfect cover."

"I hated it, and they weren't happy with me anyway."

"Just don't do anything to bring attention to yourself."

"Oh, I won't," Mannock said. "Listen, you need other finders?"

"Always, but my assistant and I handpick 'em."

"How about Loggyn?"

"What? Nah. He's not cut out for this. Frankly, we look for people who really need it."

"He's interested."

All Jack could hear was heavy breathing. Jammer sounded furious. "Could I have made it plainer, DeWayne, that you were to tell no one, absolutely no one, about this?"

"I didn't tell him. I just hinted at it."

"You're an idiot."

"I thought you'd be happy if I got you another finder."

"No, I don't need your help with that part of it. Recruiting is all about getting a read on somebody. It took me six months to decide on you, and I should have taken longer, apparently. If I'd wanted Loggyn I would have started with him. He's about the furthest thing I can think of from what we're looking for."

"But wouldn't you want to talk to him if he really wants to get involved?"

"No! Do you hear me? No! He brings it up again, you tell him you were mistaken and there are no openings. Got it?"

"I think he'd be good."

"Quit thinking. If his car turns up, get it back to him."

"What if it doesn't?"

"Do I really have to say it again, DeWayne? That's on you."

"Okay," Mannock muttered. "I'm buying a new car today."

"Good for you. I gotta go."

"Big Caddy. The Escalade SUV."

Jammer hyperventilated again. "That's your idea of keeping a low profile? Where you gonna park it? It's going to be more valuable than any house on your street."

"I've been thinking about getting my own place."

"You're hopeless, DeWayne. You know all that money is coming right back to me if anything happens to this deal. I explained that. Where are you going to get it if you need it?"

"Ah, you'll get it done."

"Listen, DeWayne. You get another good lead for us, let me know. Otherwise don't call me again."

Tidwell had been reading the printout and now sat with the pages crunched in one palm.

Keller raised his eyebrows. "You look like that cat that—"

"He did say *Bertalay*, didn't he, Jack?"

Keller fished out his notebook and thumbed through a few pages. "Yeah, John Bertalay. Didn't I tell you that last night?"

"If you did, it flew right past me." Both techies were engaged now, facing the two veteran detectives, earphones dangling. "We call John Bertalay 'AKA,'" Tidwell said gravely, handing Jack a mug shot.

Jack pressed his lips together as he squinted at the pale young man with long dark hair, sharp features, and aquiline nose. "Also known as?"

"Exactly. He's got a rap sheet as long as your arm—a half dozen semesters in Michigan City and he's not even thirty yet."

"Hold this up to the light, would you, Tid?" Jack shot a picture of the mug shot with his cell phone. "And you call him AKA because he uses aliases?"

"Bingo. And he thinks he's cute. He uses anagrams for names."

"Anagrams?"

"Yeah, you know. C'mon, Jack, you're smarter'n I am. Words made of the same letters of other words. Like *Bertalay*. Think about it."

"I'd love to, Tid, but this case is time sensitive. Spare me the puzzle."

"*Betrayal.* He's used that one before. If you arrested him this morning, he'd be somebody else."

"What's his real name?"

"Kenleigh," Tidwell said. "First name Kevin." He consulted the printout. "Middle name Samuel. His real friends call him Knives."

"Knives?"

"Another anagram. Comes from his first name and middle initial."

"So where did he get Alfonso?" Jack said. "Any clue there?"

One of the techies was scribbling. "That's an easy one," he said. "Son of Al. Who's Al?"

Jack sat shaking his head. "Kenleigh does this just to rile you?"

"Yeah," Tidwell said. "Like I said, thinks he's cute. It's been three, four years since we've nailed him on anything. Always just out of reach, you know?"

"We get anything on this Jammer's phone?"

"Too sophisticated," a techie said. "Untraceable so far, but it's clear he was outside the country."

"He knows Loggyn," Jack said, pulling out his own phone. "I'm going to see if Shane can give me anything on him."

As Loggyn's phone was ringing, Jack articulated softly, "Alfonso Lamonica," letting the sound play on his tongue. "Son of Al. What's cute about that?"

And then it hit him. As soon as he got off with Loggyn he had to call Boone.

"I hope you're calling to tell me my ride is here," Loggyn said.

"Shouldn't be long. Sure appreciate your help."

"I'll be glad when this is over. I'm not looking for more excitement."

"What do you know about a guy named Jammer?"

"Not much. He's a regular. Mannock knows him better."

"What's he look like?"

"Big. Heavy. Old. Keeps to himself mostly, but when he does talk seems to know a lot about a lot of stuff. One of those, you know?"

"How old?"

"Late sixties maybe? Dresses plain. Comes in a couple of times a month, but when he does he must stay here or close by because he plays two, three days in a row. Pretty good player. Plays position well, knows when to bluff."

"Describe him more."

"Thinning hair, which I think he dyes kind of yellow. Heavy jowls. Glasses. Nice enough guy."

"Jammer can't be his real name."

"No, it's Jasper something. Goose knows him. I've heard him call him Mr.-something. Wait, I know this. I clock him in all the time. Pitts! Name's Pitts."

"Jasper Jammer Pitts," Jack said. "Thanks again, Mr. Loggyn."

"Just get me my car back, would you?"

"Pretty sure you can count on that. Another call coming in. See ya."

"This is Boone, Jack. Where to next? I'm just leaving the lab."

"Head for the Lucky Day Casino in Hammond. We're gonna set up there for a meeting tonight between Mannock and the owner of the Buick."

"Jack, tell me that no matter what goes down there, we take DeWayne."

"That's the plan. And Boones, what's your father-in-law's name?"

"My father-in-law? Al Lamonica. Why?"

22

★★★★

PROGRESS

Boone didn't like the idea of sitting in a surveillance van when he had no idea where Max might be. And clearly DeWayne Mannock was the best source of information. Maybe Mannock had merely given the abductors enough information to find Max and had been left out of the rest of the details. But Boone would have loved to get him alone and beat him to within an inch of his life if necessary until Mannock coughed up what he knew.

As Boone drove toward Hammond, he called Mount Sinai ICU and reached Nurse Chaz Cilano. "No change here," she told him. "The neurosurgeon and your doctor are encouraged."

"What's to be encouraged about?"

"No news is good news, sir. All they're hoping for right now is to lose no ground. They don't want her to deteriorate."

"Any idea how the baby is doing?"

"Dr. Fabrie is expected tonight. If the fetus is more than three weeks along, they should be able to detect a pulse."

"Fetus?"

"That's just nursespeak, chief. I'm as pro-life as you are, and I know that's a baby in there."

"How's Margaret doing?"

"Seems fine. Let me get her."

When Margaret came on, she sounded tired.

"You going to be able to get some sleep tonight?" Boone said.

"That cot isn't much to speak of, but it's got to be better than the sofa in the waiting room. Feels like I didn't sleep at all."

"If you need to go home—"

"Boone, listen to me. I'm not going anywhere. I'm staying with Haeley until you bring Max back. I don't want to hear another word about it."

"But you shouldn't feel obligated."

"I said, not another word! I *am* obligated. She's my friend. You're my friend. Max is my little buddy. I want you to be able to concentrate out there, so just know I'm here and always will be. You don't even need to call. I'll text you every few hours to keep you up to date, all right?

Boone suddenly found it hard to speak. "Margaret, you have no idea how much—"

"You'd do it for me, wouldn't you? For Jack?"

"I would."

"Then shut up and get back to work."

As Boone pulled into the massive parking garage at the Lucky Day, he wondered if the concrete floors and walls would interfere with the bugging devices. Jack had given him a description of the van and the plate number and advised that he locate it, then park a couple of floors above.

While the garage was open-sided on all floors, drawing in a hot breeze, the near-triple-digit temperatures were somewhat mitigated by the shade. Still, the cops couldn't sit there all day in a closed-up van with the air running without drawing suspicion.

Boone was impressed that someone had thought to park the van near one end of the fourth level where little foot traffic would intrude. The cops could peer out the tinted windows without being seen and know when they could steal into the building for bathroom breaks or food runs.

Boone parked on six, took the lift down, and left the elevator bank as if he were leaving the casino and heading to his car. He slowed when a group of young men piled out of a sedan and noisily made their way in. Then he slipped behind a wall and entered the van through the front passenger door.

Ingenious. Both front side windows were open, allowing air into the back. But a thin film between the front seat and the equipment in the back made it impossible to see the surveillance setup. Boone had to look twice to realize he could squeeze through a small opening in the film and disappear into the back. The film bore an image of an empty van, so anyone nosy enough to stick their head in would see what looked like open space.

Yet in the back, Boone was greeted by Jack and Lefty and introduced to the two techies. There certainly wasn't room to stand or move much, but everyone had a seat and a view.

"I've put Antoine Johnson on the John Bertalay phone. Nothing so far, but if AKA uses it, we'll know where he is."

"We'll know where the phone is, anyway," Boone said. "Can't imagine he's still carrying it."

"Well, yeah. I need to let Antoine know that we've got Bertalay's real name. Alfonso isn't John. And Lamonica isn't Bertalay. Can't tell the players without a scorecard." Jack turned to Tidwell. "While I'm doin' that, can these guys play for Boone the call we just heard?"

Boone watched Jack make his way out of the van and walk through the parking garage, whispering into his phone.

"You know Mannock," Tidwell said. "The other voice is Kevin S. Kenleigh, slash Johnnie Bertalay, slash Alfonso Lamonica. Listen. . . ."

"We're not even s'posed to be talking, Mannock."

"That's why you haven't been answering your phone?"

"That phone is long gone, dim wad. What do you think, I carry around evidence that'll connect me to the job?"

"I need the Buick."

"I left you the Buick, just like we planned. You can't find that beast, you're blind. Both front windows open, keys behind the visor. If it's not there, it ought to be easy to find."

DeWayne swore.

"What'sa matter, man? You got paid, and way earlier than you should have. You know why, right?"

"What?"

"I told you, man. Jammer got paid in cash for his last placement, and he couldn't deposit that much without questions. He laundered a bunch of it by paying you up front. Just don't spend all of it, in case the thing falls through on the other end. But at least give that old black guy a few bucks and make up a yarn. Car got totaled, everyone's fine, end of story."

"What if the cops got it? The sitter saw the car, right?"

"You think I didn't wipe it down? You're why I don't like working with amateurs. That car is going to be traced back to the owner. He gives you up, you can give me up. Thing is, they'll never find me. I'm in the wind. Then it'll be on you."

"Loggyn won't give me up."

"When he finds out what the Buick was used for? Why not? I would. His car is gone because he trusted you."

Mannock sighed. "It wouldn't take 'em long to connect me with the boy."

"You think? He's only your flesh and blood, man. Hope the money was worth it. Enjoy it while it lasts."

"Yeah, but I got other leads for you guys."

"Don't say 'you guys,' man. I'm a freelancer. I don't do much repeat business. It's hit and run—do the job, take the money, disappear. It's what you should have done."

"I'm new at this."

"Tell me about it. You'd just better pray Jammer never finds out the kid is connected to the highest-profile cop in Chicago. And your former girlfriend hasn't exactly been anonymous either."

"You didn't tell him, did you?"

"Are you serious, Mannock? Make him think I'm as clueless as you? I enjoyed the danger. You're the one who's going to have to answer to Jammer when the full force of the Chicago PD comes down on this."

Boone sat shaking his head. "I knew Mannock was a

lowlife, and he's never acted like Max's father. But how could a person stoop this low, Lieutenant?"

Tidwell studied the ceiling of the van, as if searching his mind. "People do crazy things for money. Question is, why so much? No ransom call, so they're not looking for cash from you or your wife. What makes your son so valuable, and to who?"

The inside speaker came alive. "Mannock dialing," a techie said.

"Who's he calling?" Tidwell said.

"Looks like a business number. Hang on."

"You've reached Manley Motors. We're open Monday through Saturday, 10 a.m. to 10 p.m. If you'd like to leave a message—"

DeWayne Mannock cursed loudly, and the line went dead. He immediately dialed Shane Loggyn's cell. It went to voice mail. He dialed the Lucky Day poker room and reached Goose.

"Shane's working, DeWayne," Goose told him. "I'll tell him you called."

"No! This is an emergency. I need to talk to him right now."

Boone cringed when Goose said, "Is this about that—?" hoping against hope he wouldn't tell Mannock a Chicago cop had been in to talk to Loggyn. Fortunately, Mannock interrupted him.

"Tell him to call me on his next break. When is that?"

"About ten minutes, but you know he likes to just sit."

"I told you, it's an emergency."

Loggyn called Mannock a few minutes later.

"I don't think I can come see you tonight after all, Shane."

"Why not?"

"I can't get my new car till tomorrow. Why wouldn't Manley be open today?"

"You never heard of blue laws? You can't buy booze and you can't buy cars on Sunday."

"That doesn't even make sense. And by the time I get my Sentra tires fixed, it'll be too late."

"Not too late for me, DeWayne. You've got me thinking about this extra income."

"Yeah, about that. I talked to my people, and they're not looking for any more help right now. Sorry."

"I was getting pretty excited, DeWayne."

"My fault."

Loggyn paused. Finally, "So what're we going to do about my car?"

"I'm still on that. And like I promised, you don't get it back, I'll pay you for it."

"I'd better just call the police."

"Please don't, Shane. Give me a couple of days, okay? It's got to be somewhere."

"Let me tell you something, buddy. If I don't have that Buick by the time I leave for work tomorrow morning, you'd better be nowhere near Indiana. 'Cause if the cops don't find you, I will."

"Thanks, Shane. You won't regret this."

"I already do."

Boone was sitting glumly in the van when Keller returned. "Jack, what's stopping us from picking up Mannock right now? We've got plenty on him. We know he's connected. He's got a lot of cash, maybe with Jammer's prints on it."

"He'll lawyer up, and that'll just cost us more time," Jack said. "Let's go slow and see if he'll lead us to Jammer."

"That just went out the window," Boone said. "If he'd kept the appointment to tell Loggyn more about the operation, we might have gotten something. But that's off the table. Give me ten minutes with him and—"

"Threats aren't going to do it, Boones. He's such a lowlife that we should be able to get everything we need by making a deal."

"A deal? For a guy who would sell his own son?"

"He's still gonna serve time, and a lot of it. He's an accessory to kidnapping, and if Max is taken across state lines, that's a federal felony."

"I don't even want to think about Max being taken that far, Jack. How will we ever find him?"

Boone's phone chirped, and he found a text from Margaret: Dr. Fabrie is here and wants to talk to you in person. Any chance, or should I just have her call you?

Boone sighed. "Jack, I've got to defer to you on this. Everything in me says to take Mannock now. What am I missing?"

"You're too close to it, Boones. Sometimes things aren't what they seem. I promise we'll take Mannock into custody tomorrow."

"You don't think he's going to make a run for it?"

"Lefty's guys have him under constant surveillance. He's going nowhere."

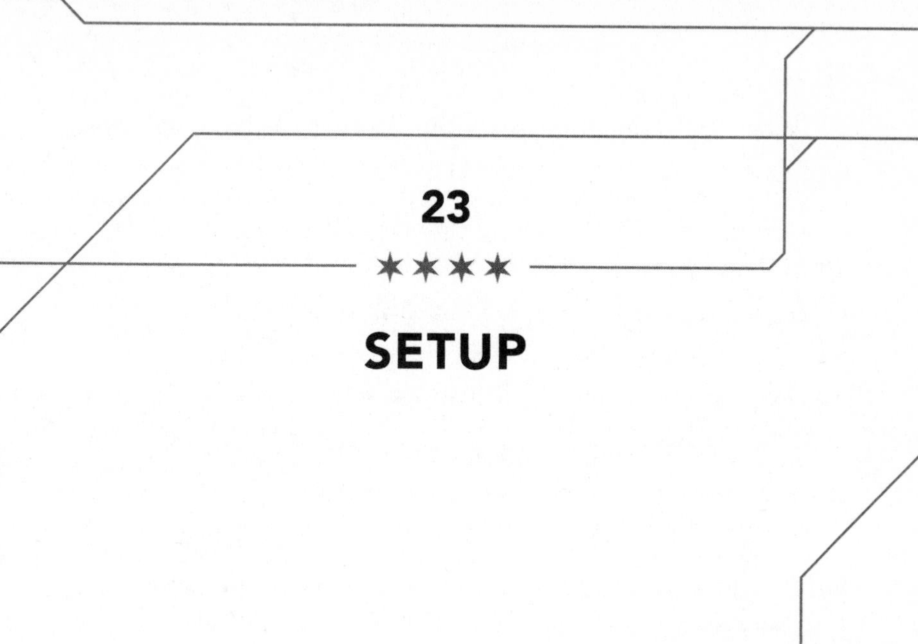

23

SETUP

Dr. Kristin Fabrie, a striking brunette, was chatting with Dr. Sarangan when Boone arrived at the ICU.

"Thank you for coming, under the circumstances," she said, shaking his hand. "Murari has brought me up to date. We both feel that unless it's absolutely impossible, you need to sleep in your own bed tonight. Can you do that?"

"I'd rather not, but—"

"Doctor's orders," Dr. Sarangan said. "Boone, I understand you're deep into this investigation, and nothing is more important. But Dr. Fabrie assures me the baby seems in no danger, as long as we can keep Haeley stable. Can I impress upon you the importance of taking care of yourself?"

"Frankly, I'd rather not be alone."

"Then can you stay with Chief Keller? Or have him stay with you?"

"I could live with that, but I still can't imagine sleeping, knowing every second counts."

"I understand," Dr. Sarangan said. "I can give you something that will put you out. Safely."

"Jack says they gave him Ambien last night," Boone said.

"This is stronger than that. This will shut you down so you won't be fretting even subconsciously."

"I need to be able to think through this case." The doctors looked at each other. "Not while you're sleeping, you don't," Dr. Fabrie said.

Dr. Sarangan pulled a small bag from his pocket. "I took the liberty of having this filled here at the hospital pharmacy. Trust me, Boone. You'll be better for your task if you're really rested."

On the way to Boone's house, Jack phoned the head of the ransom team and told them to clear out, as he and Boone were spending the night there. "You can still monitor all those numbers from elsewhere, right?"

"We can, Chief, but you know as well as I do, the longer we go hearing nothing, the more likely it is that we'll never hear from anybody."

"Just like old times, Boones," Jack said a few minutes later as he unpacked his duffel bag. "Except you were bunking with me in those days, not the other way around."

"I appreciated that—as low as I was—and I hope you know I'm grateful now. Someday we're going to have to enjoy some time when I'm not just this far from the abyss."

"Whoa, Boones. Sit down. Let me be the doubter here, okay? You've always been the strong one, keeping your blind faith in the face of—"

"Oh, Jack, don't even start. It's not blind faith. I believe with everything that's in me. I just don't understand God sometimes."

"I don't understand him anytime," Jack said. "Margaret does, and Haeley's right there with you two."

"True."

"I guess we all need something, Boones. I don't want you to lose hold on whatever it is that gets you through."

Boone snorted. "You make it sound like some lucky charm. That's my problem, Jack. I want the faith to believe God will bring Haeley back to me the way she was and protect Max until he's back with us too."

"If I were you," Jack said, "I'd want God to give me a clean shot at whoever's behind this."

"Well, that too. I don't know what he's trying to teach me. He already knocked everything out from under me the first time I went through something like this, and I learned—or thought I did—that he's there when no one or nothing else is. Do I have to prove I learned it again? I'm willing. But why should the people I love have to suffer for it?"

"You're personalizing this too much, don't you think?"

"It's my wife and son, Jack. It doesn't get more personal than that."

Keller sat there nodding. "This has me rattled too. I was starting to halfway admire y'all's beliefs, you know? But I wouldn't blame you if this made it all seem like just theory."

Boone sighed and shook his head. "God is real. I know he

can be trusted. But that doesn't mean everything turns out perfectly. Nikki and Josh are still gone, and that's what it cost for me to really rely on God. But can I really go through this again? And if I can't, does that mean God loses you, too?"

"Wanna know the truth, Boones? God better help us solve this one. I don't see the point of believing otherwise. And frankly, we need his help."

Boone raised a brow. "We do, don't we?"

"This is a tough one. I'm not telling you anything you don't know, but time is everything. With no ransom demands, who knows what their intentions are? That scares me more than anything. I don't know if God lets you pray if you're not even sure you believe in him, so I'm trying something different. I'm just telling him that if he's really there, and if he really cares, would he prove it to me? Lettin' us find Max would be a good start."

"You've been praying, Jack?"

Keller shrugged. "Can't hurt, can it?"

"That means a lot to me."

"It would mean a lot to me if you were well rested for tomorrow. Take that dope and get to bed."

"It's hard to believe anything will put me to sleep when everything in this place reminds me of Haeley and Max."

"The docs swear by the stuff," Jack said.

Boone took the pills and was gone in fifteen minutes.

JULY 2

The next morning they raced in Jack's unmarked squad to a drive-thru for breakfast, then rendezvoused with Lieutenant Tidwell and his tech experts in the van behind a precinct stationhouse in Hammond. One of the techies borrowed their cell phones, fiddled with them for a few minutes, and gave them back, along with small earpieces. "If Mannock has his cell on him, you'll be able to hear everything, even live conversations. His phone becomes the transmitter, even if it's not on."

"I've heard of this," Jack said. "How do you do it?"

"You'd be amazed. A phone can be rigged to bug a person from halfway around the world, and they'll never know it."

Right at ten that morning, they listened in on Mannock's phone conversation.

"Manley Motors, how may I direct your call?"

"New car sales."

"One moment."

"This is Phil."

"Phil, it's DeWayne Mannock."

"Well, hello there! Ready to take ownership of your new chariot?"

"I sure am."

"Your financing all in place, or do you want us to handle that?"

"Paying cash, Phil."

"Sorry?"

"This is a cash deal."

"Cashier's check, right? Make it out to—"

"No. *Cash* cash."

"I'm not following."

Mannock laughed. "What? My money's no good? I'm bringing it in cold, hard cash. Dollar bills."

"Surely not."

"Well, not dollar bills. Hundreds."

There was a rustling of papers. "Mr. Mannock, the total out-the-door price of this vehicle is seventy-one thousand four hundred thirty-two dollars and sixty-nine cents."

"I know. I'm looking at the same sheet you are. If I give you seventy-one thousand, four hundred and thirty-three, you can keep the change. How 'bout that?"

Phil laughed. "I don't think we've done a cash transaction here—outside the used car lot, I mean—in decades. You seriously bringing in that much in cash?"

"Seriously."

"You know we have to report that."

"What do you mean?"

"Anything over ten grand in cash, we've got to let the authorities know about it. It's just routine, but—"

"I don't need that. What should I do, take the cash to the bank and bring a check?"

"Yes, a cashier's check. But you know the bank reports any cash transaction over ten grand too."

"They do?"

"Yeah, something about preventing money laundering, you know, like drug pushers do, that kind of a thing."

"Well, I want the car today."

"And we want to see you in it today. How're we going to manage this?"

"So you report the cash, but that doesn't keep me from taking the car, right?"

"Right. But within a few days you'll be hearing from the state or the feds or whoever cares about these things. They're going to want to confirm the money was yours and that you didn't get it through nefarious means."

"Nefarious—?"

"A crime, Mr. Mannock. They're going to have to establish—well *you're* going to have to establish—where you got that kind of money and that you're not a criminal. You're not, are you, sir? . . . I'm just joshing you."

"Ha! No! Not a criminal!"

"Well, if you're seriously bringing that kind of cash, I need to let my boss know, and we're going to have to get someone from security in here. They won't want to keep it on the premises long."

"You don't have a safe?"

"Sure, but we're not in the habit of holding large sums of money overnight."

"Whatever."

"Anyway, the car is ready, and she's a beauty. When should we expect you?"

"Taking a cab. See you soon."

Boone turned to Jack and Lefty. "If DeWayne were smart, he'd disappear in his new ride and stand up Loggyn. Then we won't be any closer to Kenleigh or this Jammer, and I think we all know Jammer is the key."

"No question," Tidwell said. "So what do you want to do?"

"We've got to take DeWayne and all that money at the dealership," Boone said. "Once we get Mannock downtown, we'll for sure get a lead on Kenleigh, maybe even Jammer. The sales guy already told him they'd have a security guy there. Let me be that guy. As soon as DeWayne sees me, he'll know he's been had."

"You kiddin'?" Jack said. "First thing through that thick

skull of his will be wondering what the odds are of you showing up at the same car dealer on the same day."

"Not the sharpest bulb in the woods?" Tidwell said, and even Boone had to smile.

"You're likely to shoot him," Jack said.

"Security guys don't carry," Boone said. "All I need is a suit coat." He pointed to one of the techies. "His would fit me. You guys back me up."

"You can play that role, Boones, but you know as well as I do that you can't be the officer of record on the arrest. How would that look in court? Father of the kidnapped kid makes the collar. I'll give you the satisfaction of gettin' the cuffs on him, but—"

"Fine, Jack. We need to go. He'll be on his way soon."

Just then the surveillance tap on Mannock's phone picked up his call to the cab company. The dispatcher told him someone would be there for him in twenty-five minutes.

"That means an hour, most likely," Tidwell said, "but let's assume they're efficient today. If we're going to do this, we've got to do it now."

"Let me set it up with the car dealer," Jack said as he and Boone exited the van for his squad. "This is sort of my thing." He reached Phil at Manley Motors, knowing the other cops were listening in the van as it pulled out.

"Phil, this is Jack Keller, chief of the Organized Crime Division of the Chicago Police Department."

"C'mon, who is this really? Biff, is that you?"

"Phil, I'm going to read off to you my badge number so you can call the Chicago PD and verify my identity. You ready?"

A pause. "Sure."

Jack recited it and continued. "I need you to listen carefully. My colleagues at the Hammond Police Department and I just monitored a call between you and a DeWayne Mannock."

"I knew he was a crook!"

"Are you listening, Phil? We need your complete cooperation, and we appreciate it."

"Is this guy dangerous? Will he be packing?"

Jack glanced at Boone and rolled his eyes.

"We don't believe he's dangerous, but we do plan to apprehend him inside your establishment. Can you help with that?"

"Whatever you want me to do. You know my uncle was a cop, and he—"

"And I'd love to hear all about that, but we need to get there before Mr. Mannock does, all right?"

"Yes, sir."

Jack outlined how Phil was to welcome DeWayne as he would any new buyer, then ask to see the money. As soon as DeWayne showed it, Phil was to remind him that he needed security present. "At that point, the chief of our Major Case Squad will assume that role, and I'll make the arrest."

As they sped toward Manley Motors in East Chicago, Indiana, Jack called Tidwell in the van. "Lefty, we haven't talked about jurisdiction."

"You know me better'n that, Jack. I wouldn't mind a little credit. You send a note to my chief, that kind of a thing. Looks good in my file, am I right? Huh?"

"Done."

"But the abduction happened in Chicago," Lefty said, "and I don't need all the paperwork, the interrogating, all that."

"We're set, then," Jack said. "Drake and I will transport Mannock and the money to Chicago, and if you could tie up the loose ends with Shane Loggyn, I'll owe you."

"Well, he's getting his car back, isn't he?"

"He is."

"Loggyn's the only one who's gonna come out of this unscathed."

"Unscathed," Jack said. "Nice word choice there, Tid."

"I know, right? You like that? Every once in a while, you know? Am I right?"

As the Hammond PD surveillance van pulled in behind Jack in the shadow of the service bay at the far end of Manley Motors's used car lot, Boone picked up the conversation between DeWayne Mannock and the cabbie. He could see that everyone else had a finger pressed to their ear jack too as they entered the new car showroom from the back.

"New car, huh?" the new voice was saying. "Whatcha gettin'?"

"The big Caddy. Escalade."

"No way!"

"Yup. First new car."

"Your first and it's one of those? What'd you do, win the lottery?"

"Matter of fact, I did."

"Don't think I ever met anybody who won the big one. One of my buddies won a grand or so once."

"Can't buy much with that."

"Nope. Well, good for you."

"Hey, you got change for a hundred?"

The cabbie laughed. "High roller now, huh? Nah. Can't break bigger'n a twenty. Sorry."

"Man, all I got is hundreds."

"I can wait while you get change."

"Ah, it's okay. Let's make it an even hundred."

"Oh, you don't have to do that, man. We've only got about another mile. Meter's gonna say less than thirty bucks."

"I insist."

"Wow, thanks, dude."

As the cops took positions inside, Tidwell and the techies hid their guns in their pockets and strolled around the showroom. They split up and told the salespeople they were just looking. When one salesman tried to show Tidwell "a ride that looks like it was built just for you," Boone saw Lefty flash his badge and say, "Looking. Got it?"

Jack and Boone met with Phil, a fiftyish string bean, impeccably dressed and well spoken. "Do you always sweat this much?" Jack said.

"AC's not that great in here. The customers sweat too."

"As long as it's not just nerves."

"Well, I *am* nervous, but no. Sales is like acting, chief. I'll play my part. You watch."

Jack and Boone waited in the office of the sales manager—the aforementioned Biff—near the back of the showroom, sitting with their backs to the window but able to monitor the front door in the reflection behind Biff's desk. They would be able to see when Mannock came in and watch what was happening in Phil's office.

Biff, a young man in a dark suit, sat at his desk, fidgeting with a pen. "Haven't had excitement like this in here for years," he said. "Selling the Escalade was going to be the highlight of our week, but we're not going to see that money, are we?"

"No, sir," Jack said. "You're not. But we sure thank you for your cooperation."

"As if I had a choice."

Boone shot Biff a look and saw his smile.

"Happy to help, really," the sales manager said. "You're not expecting trouble, are you? Fighting, shooting, hostages?"

Jack shook his head. "This is a bad guy, sir. But we won't have any trouble with him."

"Sort of a low-level crook?" Biff said.

"That's for sure," Boone said. "We will have to take him out of here in cuffs, though. We'll try not to make a scene."

"Would you mind taking him out through the back then, in case we have customers? I mean, Monday mornings aren't usually busy, but you never know."

"Back door it is."

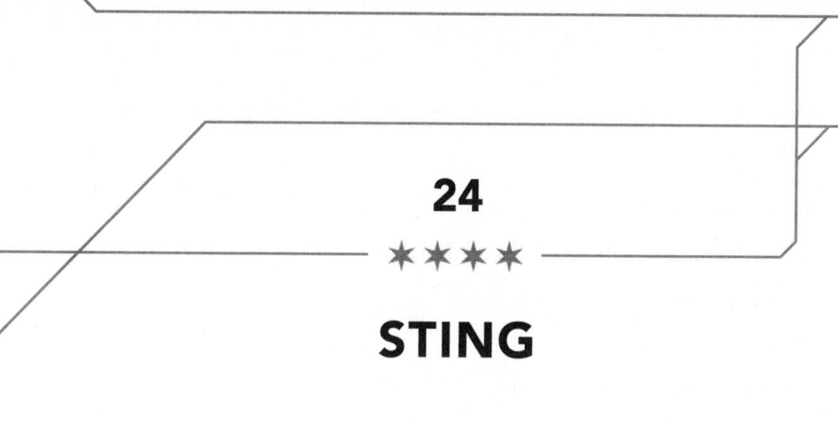

24

★★★★

STING

"I'M SERIOUS ABOUT waiting if you want to get change," the cabbie said.

"And I'm serious about you keeping the change, my man," Mannock said.

Boone hoped DeWayne was enjoying his last minute on top of the world. He glanced at Jack. "If he'd give me one reason to—"

"You gonna be able to deal with this, Boones?"

"I got it."

In the reflection, Boone watched Mannock stride in, grinning like he owned the place, a heavy canvas satchel at his side. Phil immediately rose and left his glassed-in cubicle, meeting Mannock with a hearty handshake. "You look like a man who just bought a new car!"

"It's gonna be sweet!" DeWayne said. "All prepped and everything?"

"Absolutely."

"Can I see it?"

"Before we do the paperwork?"

"Yeah, that okay?"

Phil's bravado seemed to have suddenly failed him. "Let me check with the guys in the back. Come into my office."

"It's always something," Boone said. He leaned forward and whispered to the sales manager. "The car was prepped, right?"

"Yes, but after we heard from you guys we put it back in stock. I didn't think the sale was supposed to get that far."

"Neither did we."

Biff peeked at his ringing desk phone. "That's Phil," he said.

"Make up a story. Stall."

"Yes, Phil."

"Hello, Service?" Boone heard Phil's side of the conversation through Mannock's phone.

"Yes, Phil. I'm with you."

"Yeah, Service, is Mr. Mannock's car ready for him to see? He'd just like to take a peek before we complete the transaction."

"Well, Phil, as your *boss* has told you, that's not customary. Mr. Mannock saw it when he was shopping, and we like to make a big presentation when we hand him the keys."

"Okay, Service, I'll tell him." Phil covered the phone. "Mr. Mannock, they've, uh, they're just, um, drying it now. Want to make it really nice for when we give you the keys."

Mannock swore. "Well, what's another couple minutes, eh? Let's get this done."

"Okay, Service," Phil said. "Take your time." He hung up and turned back to DeWayne Mannock. "This still a cash deal? I don't need to get our finance guy in here?"

"Cash on the barrel," DeWayne said, hefting the bag onto the desk. "You wanna see it?"

"Well, not only have I never seen that much cash before, but someone here is going to have to count it. That may take a while."

"I know. It took *me* a while." Mannock laughed loudly.

"As I mentioned, sir, I'm going to ask a security guard to take the money to our accountant while I'm printing out all the documents."

"Sounds good."

Phil dialed the sales manager's office again. "Could you send security to my office for a cash delivery? Thank you!"

"Stay here," Jack told Biff. "Boone, follow me."

They headed toward Phil's office, where Jack introduced himself as the sales manager. "Congratulations, Mr. Mannock!"

"Thank you!" DeWayne reached up to shake his hand.

"You are DeWayne Mannock, right?"

"Yes, sir."

"You're going to be very happy with your purchase."

"I already am!"

"Before we have security take custody of the cash, could I see some identification?"

"You betcha."

Mannock rocked forward to reach his wallet and showed Jack his Indiana driver's license.

"Security," Jack said, and Boone stepped out from behind him with a pair of handcuffs.

"DeWayne Mannock, please stand and turn around with your hands behind your back."

"What the—?"

"You're under arrest for the kidnapping of Max Lamonica Drake—"

"Kidnapping! No way! I—"

Boone yanked Mannock up out of his chair and twisted him around, reaching for his hands. "Get 'em behind you, DeWayne!"

"C'mon, Drake! You know I—"

"You have the right to remain silent," Jack said as Boone applied the cuffs and turned Mannock around. He dropped him back into the chair.

"I don't need to remain silent. I didn't kidnap anybody!"

So much the better, Boone thought.

"Anything you say can and will be used against you in a court of law," Jack continued.

"Once you let me explain, there won't be any court! C'mon!"

"You have the right to an attorney."

"I don't need one! Just listen to me!"

"If you cannot afford an attorney, one will be provided for you."

"Don't provide me nothin'! Just hear me out!"

"Do you understand the rights I have just read to you?"

Mannock gritted his teeth, and shook his head.

"Come now, DeWayne. You know you have to answer these two questions. Do you understand the rights I have just read to you?"

"I understand 'em! I just don't need 'em!"

"With these rights in mind, do you wish to speak to me? . . . DeWayne? Silence is not an acceptable response to that question. You told me you understood your rights. With those rights in mind, do you wish to speak to me?"

"Will you listen?"

"Do you wish to speak to me?"

"Yes! Yes! Yes, I wish to speak to you."

"That's going to happen in Chicago," Jack said.

"Oh no! Now, I'm buyin' a car here! I got all this money."

Boone leaned into Mannock's face. "You're riding into the city with us, DeWayne. Your money is evidence. The car stays here."

"I'm not leaving without my car!"

"You won't need it in Stateville, DeWayne. You know that."

"Drake, listen to me. When you hear how little I had to do with any of this, how little I even knew, you're gonna bring me right back here and let me buy my car."

"We have to do the interrogation properly. Don't start talking till we get to Chicago."

"I'll be talking all the way."

"We won't be listening."

"Didn't I just say that? I knew you wouldn't listen!"

"When we get downtown, you can talk all you want, and we'll record every word."

"Well, you're going to feel like idiots once you know everything."

"Telling us everything is the best idea you've ever had, DeWayne."

25

★★★★

RASPBERRY

On the ride back to Chicago, when Boone could think over DeWayne Mannock's incessant badgering, he allowed himself hope that finally, finally they had made some progress. With no ransom demand, the mystery deepened over what had become of Max. Boone had to push from his mind thoughts of the boy's fear. He didn't allow himself to think of injury—or worse—to Max, because Mannock had been paid as much as he had simply to be a finder, the boy was a ridiculously valuable commodity. But why? And to whom?

Boone's phone vibrated, and he looked down at a text from Lefty Tidwell. Mannock's phone still transmitting. Mind if we listen in?

Suit yourself, he texted back. You guys must not get out much.

Not half the fun of you big city cops.

Sitting on his cuffed hands in the back of the squad, Mannock whined and cried and moaned. "C'mon! You can take the cuffs off! They're killin' me."

"You think I want you comfortable?" Boone said. "Is Max comfortable?"

"Listen, here's all I know about that. I—"

"Not now, Mannock!" Jack barked. "I told you. Downtown. You have the right to remain silent, and I suggest you exercise it."

"Drake, *you* wanna hear, don't you?"

"Put a sock in it, DeWayne," Boone said, desperate as he was for any news. How a man could be involved in the kidnapping of his own biological son was beyond him. But the more they frustrated Mannock, the more they forced him to wait to be heard, the more they'd likely get from him. Hopefully he'd gush everything he knew. Plus they wanted the first interview in this case air tight, recorded, and with witnesses watching on the other side of the two-way mirror.

"I'm tellin' you guys! You're gonna be apologizing to me. I was nothing in this, a pawn. None of it really traces to me."

"Good one, DeWayne," Boone said. "Tell you what: if you're right and we're wrong and we misunderstood everything we overheard you say the last eighteen hours, I guarantee I'll personally apologize and beg your pardon."

"You will?"

"I'll do better than that. I'll personally see that you get to keep your money."

"And buy my car?"

"It'll be yours to do with as you please."

"You serious?"

"Absolutely."

"'Cause that's gonna be how it goes down. You'll see I'm innocent. A hundred percent."

Boone rested his hand on the butt of his Beretta, wishing DeWayne would give him reason to whirl and put one between his eyes. They already had more than enough on him to put him away for years. Proclamations of innocence were nothing new, but Boone was intrigued about what they'd hear once Mannock had been assigned an interrogation room.

"I'm tellin' you guys, you're gonna feel like fools."

"I need to tell you something, Mannock," Jack Keller said.

"What?"

"Are you listening?"

"I said 'What?'!"

"I need to know you're hearing me, so you don't get hurt."

"What're you talkin' about?"

"I've never been charged with police brutality."

"Well, I'll charge you with it if you try something on me!"

"See? You're not listening. What I should have said is that I've been *accused* of brutality many times—which goes with the job, doesn't it, Chief Drake?"

"It does," Boone said, wondering where Jack was going with this.

"But I've never had it stick. You know why?"

"I don't give a—"

"Yes, you do, Mannock. Because today it may be your turn. You follow?"

"No! What're you saying?"

"Just that if I hear another word out of you before we get to Chicago, you're gonna feel like you've been abused."

"You threatening me?"

"Yes. So you're listening?"

"I am now."

"It won't be anything you can get a handle on. Maybe I squeeze your arm too tight when I pull you out of the car. Maybe I'm not careful enough to keep from banging your head on the way out. Maybe before I get the cuffs off you for fingerprinting, I mistakenly tighten them more first."

"They're already too tight!"

"Well, see?"

"You better not—"

"Have you heard about our famous garage elevator door, DeWayne?"

"What about it?"

"It's the old-fashioned kind that doesn't stop automatically when a light beam is tripped. It was made with one of those old rubber coated vertical bars that's supposed to push the door back if it hits anything. But you know what? Some pranksters, maybe some colleagues of Drake's and mine from the 11th, they removed that thing several years ago. Now when we take someone from the parking garage to the booking room, we have to be very careful to get them in the elevator before that door starts to close. It can leave a real bruise. Some guys have even been caught in there until we can find the Open button."

"I'll sue! You'll lose your job!"

"For being careless? I don't think so, DeWayne. Like I say,

I've been accused a lot of times, but there's never been enough to make anything stick. Wonder why? Because I've had such an illustrious career? Is it my reputation, DeWayne? Or is it because the accusations always come from lowlifes like you?"

"Maybe you just know how to get around the system and not make it obvious."

"Bingo! You win the prize, DeWayne! So here's what you do to make sure I'm extra considerate while we're getting you to booking—listening?"

"Yeah."

"You keep your mouth shut the rest of the way. If I'm tired of hearing you, I know Chief Drake is. Am I right, Chief Drake?"

"You're right, Chief Keller."

"So, not another word. If I hear one, even one, I can't promise you'll be as comfortable in the interrogation room as you are now. And you're not really that comfortable now, are you?"

Mannock sucked in a breath through his teeth, as if preparing to say something.

"Ah-ah-ah, DeWayne," Jack said. "Not another word."

Octavia Frazier sat in her office in Calona, Michigan, putting the finishing touches on her monthly report for the city council that night. Two of her four police officers were on duty, and the civilian dispatcher-receptionist-assistant Madge poked her head in the door.

"Fed Ex for you, Chief," she said. "You order something?"

Ms. Frazier held out an open palm without looking up. "Back to your desk, Madge. I'll let you know if it concerns you."

The small box was light, and the sending information had

been blacked out. The chief tore it open to find what looked like a brand-new cell phone and a note that appeared to have been written by a child, or by an adult with his opposite hand.

Free phone just for you, Chief. All charged up and ready to go. Just use it to call Lieutenant Tidwell of the Hammond, Indiana PD, and it's all yours. User manual available on line. Love ya. J.B.

"Madge!"

"Yes, ma'am."

"How much is a phone call to Hammond?"

"Indiana? Can't be that much. Why?"

"Darndest thing. C'mere and look at this."

"You just banished me back to my desk, Chief!"

"Get in here."

The women studied the phone and the letter. "On this kinda phone, it's probably free," Madge said.

Octavia turned on the phone and colorful icons appeared. "This is like a mystery, Madge. We haven't had a mystery since that guy in County killed himself."

"See whose it is."

"How do I do that?"

"Give me that," Madge muttered. "I shoulda been chief; don't even know how to use a phone. Here, see? Oh, it's blank."

"Well, 'course it's blank, Mrs. Smarty-pants. If they wanted me to know who J.B. was, they woulda signed their whole name."

"You gonna call the number?"

"They didn't give me a number."

"They gave you a name, silly! You want me to get the number?"

"Okay, but let me make the call."

Madge dialed information and asked for the Hammond, Indiana, Police Department. "No thanks," she told the operator, "we'll dial it ourselves."

Lefty Tidwell sat in the passenger seat of the surveillance van on the way back to headquarters while one of his techies drove and the other monitored the equipment in the back. They had all enjoyed listening in on the conversation between DeWayne Mannock and the two Chicago cops. Tidwell had been hooting over Jack's threats.

"Keller's a piece a work, ain't he? Huh? Am I right or am I right? Huh?"

"Whoa!" That came from the techie in the back.

Tidwell whirled in his seat. "What's up?"

"Just got a ping on the phone used to send the picture to Mrs. Quigley."

"AKA's?"

"It's on; that's all I know. Pinging off a tower in northern Michigan. Way up there. Western side of the state. Now here's a call. Hang on." He turned on the speaker and heard a woman ask for the number for the Hammond PD."

"Curious," Tidwell said.

Two minutes later, Lefty's cell chirped.

"Tidwell."

"Got a call for you, Lieutenant. A police chief in Michigan."

"Put it through." *Click.* "This is Tidwell."

"Yes, hello, sir. Chief Frazier here in Calona, Michigan."

"Yes, ma'am."

She told him the story of the phone. ". . . and that's everything I know."

"Have you touched it, Chief?"

"I'm afraid I have. It's in my hand."

"It's evidence in an open investigation. Could you do me a favor and overnight it to the name and address I give you?"

"Absolutely. Um, we're on a real small budget here, Lieutenant. There's only six full-time people—"

"Just pop an invoice in there, Chief. Chicago PD will be glad to reimburse you." He gave her Jack Keller's name and address. "Now, Ms. Frazier, I'm going to read you off a list of names. If any one of them sounds at all familiar, stop me, okay?"

"Sure."

"John or Johnnie Bertalay. DeWayne Mannock. Alfonso Lamonica. Florence Quigley. Kevin Kenleigh, that's K-E-N-L-E-I-G-H. Jasper or Jammer Pitts."

"Nothing, Lieutenant. Sorry."

"Just trying to get a bead on why that phone would have found its way to you."

"I haven't the foggiest. I'm sorry."

"But you'll box it up for us?"

"And get it to Chief Keller in Chicago, yes, sir."

"Anyone else touch it?"

"My dispatcher, yes."

"Do both of you have your fingerprints on file there?"

"Only sworn officers, sir. Mine, not hers. You want me to fingerprint her?"

"That won't be necessary. Pop a copy of yours in there, and we'll know whose the others are. We'll be hoping for one more, one that fits our suspect."

While Tidwell was thanking her and hanging up, the techie in the back appeared between the front seats.

"What?"

"He's playing us again, Lieutenant."

"Who is?"

"AKA, or whoever he is this week. Take a look at this."

Tidwell accepted a printout bearing the location of the cell tower that had picked up the phone signal. It read, "Calona, MI."

"We already know that," Lefty said.

"Read it closely, Lieutenant. He sent that phone all the way there, just because of the anagram. C-A-L-O-N-A-M-I. A little verbal raspberry right in our faces."

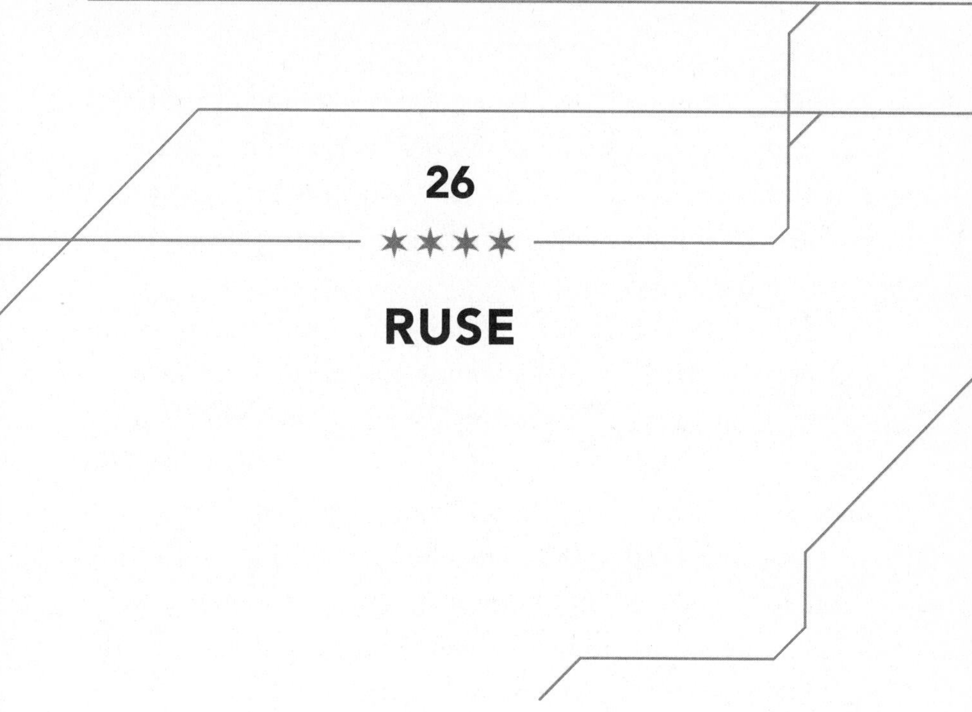

26

RUSE

"THANKS FOR BEHAVING yourself, Mr. Mannock," Jack said as he helped DeWayne out of the backseat in the underground garage at the 11th.

Mannock looked wary to Boone, who assumed the man was both struggling to adjust to the low light and keeping an eye out for shenanigans from Keller. He was still quiet when they reached the elevator, Keller on his left, Boone on his right. When it opened, Mannock mince-stepped aboard, careful to avoid the door.

"Can I talk now?" DeWayne said. "'Cause I—"

"I wouldn't," Boone said, nodding toward Jack as if the last thing he wanted to do was get that man riled. DeWayne shook his head and puffed out his cheeks.

Boone himself was in crisis mode. It was all he could do to

keep from slamming Mannock against the wall of the elevator and demanding to know where Max was. If he was sure of anything, though, it was that DeWayne did not likely know. Who in their right mind would trust a scumbag like him with that kind of information?

Still, Boone imagined holding the cold muzzle of his Beretta against Mannock's temple and demanding to know how he slept at night, knowing he had put his own offspring in danger. Up till now, Boone had assumed Mannock had never even seen Max. But somebody had been staking out the boy and Haeley and even Florence. And it hadn't been that long since Boone himself had accosted DeWayne in the cul-de-sac in front of his own house and endured the cockamamie reason Mannock had used for wanting to talk with Haeley.

DeWayne was uncuffed and taken to be fingerprinted. "How many times you guys gotta do this?" he said. "I mean, I been fingerprinted a half-dozen times, at least in Indiana. I'm not in your system?"

"Didja hear that, Chief Drake?" Keller said. "This upstanding citizen has an idea how we can improve our efficiency."

"Impressive, Chief Keller. Maybe we should give him a form he can put in our suggestion box."

"Just tired of gettin' ink all over me."

"Well, then, welcome to the twenty-first century, DeWayne," Keller said, sidling close to Mannock. "Guess you Hoosiers haven't caught up, but here we scan. No ink." At first it appeared DeWayne was trying to stare Jack down, but when Keller leaned close and said, "Boo!" the prisoner flinched.

"I'm kinda scared of this guy, Chief Drake," Keller said. "Aren't you?"

"Shaking, Chief Keller."

"Yeah," Jack said, taking Mannock by the arm. "Tough customer. Think we ought to cuff him again for transport to interrogation?"

"Nah, let's take our chances."

"Yeah, and hope he tries something."

As they led DeWayne into the interview room upstairs, Boone and Jack were met by 11th District Commander Heathcliff Jones, who had always reminded Boone of Fletcher Galloway. Not all commanders dressed in uniform every day, but Jones did. A big man with a deep voice, he always looked the part.

"Everybody's in place," he said. "Detective Johnson is on his way. We'll watch from out here, and sound and video are rolling. Drake, we're all here for you, man."

Boone appreciated that, but it went without saying. The brotherhood under the blue had each other's backs, as the cliché went. Anytime one suffered, the others were there. But all Boone wanted to hear just then was that someone had a solid lead. Something. Anything.

Boone was too antsy to sit, so he stationed himself standing in a corner, thinking it would put him behind Mannock.

But DeWayne had to know he was on stage, that this case was a big deal to the 11th. He also must have felt safe, knowing that Chief Keller was being watched as closely as he was. DeWayne quickly lost his mousy tentativeness, immediately strode to the chair usually reserved for the interrogator, flipped it around, and straddled it as he sat, facing Boone and resting his elbows on the table.

"That's my chair," Keller said. "You're over there."

Mannock sighed as if disgusted, rose slowly, and sauntered to the other side of the table. When he started to flip that chair around, Keller said, "Just leave it the way it is. This is my house, not yours."

Mannock lifted the chair and let it bang on the floor, then flopped into it and slouched, arms folded, his back to Boone.

"You're gonna give me attitude, really?" Jack said, leaning over the chair Mannock had left and resting his palms on the table, putting himself face to face with DeWayne. "Sit up and act like you care about what's going to happen to you, because I know you do."

"You don't know what I care about," Mannock said.

"Well, there's truth in that," Keller said. "You don't seem to care about much, not even your own progeny."

"My own what?"

"Your own kid, DeWayne. You may not be a dad, but biologically you're a father."

"What, you and Drake gonna play good cop, bad cop with me now? Like I haven't been through this before?"

"You worry only about me, Mannock," Jack said. "I'm your good and bad cop rolled into one today. State your full name for the record, please."

"DeWayne William Mannock."

"And will you stipulate that your rights have been read to you, that you understand them, and that you're choosing to waive them for this interview?"

"Yeah."

"Yeah, what?"

"Yeah on all three of those."

"Just so we're crystal clear. You acknowledge that you have the right to an attorney and to have that attorney present while you are being questioned, and that if you can't afford one—

"I said yeah! Can we get on with this?"

Jack straightened up and looked into the two-way mirror. "We're rolling and you got all that?"

A red light appeared above a squawk box near the ceiling, and Boone heard a staticky woman's voice: "Yes." That had to be Ronette, the attractive young uniform in charge of audiovisual at the 11th.

Boone wondered how stupid Mannock could be. Any lawyer would be able to see within sixty seconds that he was into this thing up to his neck and his only prayer was to trade a little of what he knew for a modicum of consideration. But no . . .

"All the way here, you were dying to tell your side of this, DeWayne," Jack said, finally sitting. "Here's your chance."

"Yeah, and now I'm hungry. I didn't have breakfast."

"You think this is a restaurant?"

"You want me to talk, give me something to eat."

"I thought *you* wanted to talk. You're not going to like what I've got to say."

"You got nothing to say," Mannock said, "because you got nothing on me."

"*Nothing* that connects you to this case, DeWayne?"

"Well, I didn't kidnap anybody, and you can't prove I did, so you gotta let me go."

"You really need me to walk you through this? You introduced a friend to a former coworker. You borrowed a car from that coworker for that friend. That friend used that car and was the last person seen with a child now missing and unaccounted for. That makes you an accessory to kidnapping, and depending on where that child is taken and what happens to him, your prospects can only get worse. Do I need to go on? Should we go straight to central booking? Or would you like to plead your case now?"

"Not on an empty stomach."

"You're seriously going to clam up without food?"

Mannock nodded. "I could do worse, you know. I could lawyer up."

"I gave you half a dozen chances to do that. *Now* you want to?"

"I want to eat."

"We haven't got much. What do you want?"

"I'm easy. A sandwich?"

"I've had them out of the machines here, DeWayne. I wouldn't want one."

"You might if you were hungry."

Keller turned to the mirror again. "Somebody get Einstein a sandwich."

Through the squawk box, Ronette said, "Vendor hasn't been in for a week. The ones still in there are old."

Mannock shrugged.

"Bring one anyway!" Keller said.

"And a Coke!" Mannock said.

"Sure you don't want a glass of wine?"

Mannock sat defiantly, as if he had won. When the food

and drink were delivered, Keller slid them across the table. DeWayne took his time opening the sandwich and smelling it. From where Boone stood it looked hard and stale, and it took Mannock a while to chew. But if he didn't like it, he didn't let on. When he was finished with the sandwich, he finally popped open the Coke, guzzled half of it in one gulp, then belched.

"Your turn," Keller said.

"I got nothin' to say."

"Really. So you just want to sit in County for who knows how long, then be tried as an accessory to kidnapping, and wind up in Stateville or, worse, a federal pen?"

"Won't happen. I know the law."

"Do you? Then tell me what's gonna keep you out of prison?"

"Lack of evidence."

"DeWayne, you're not much of a criminal, but you're a worse lawyer. Your former coworker will testify he lent your friend the car and that you even paid him a security deposit. Two hundred ring a bell? Your friend was seen in the car with the child. The car was abandoned and still hasn't been returned to the lender. And it just so happens that the kidnapped child is your biological son."

"Circumstantial, or whatever they call it."

"You're willing to bet your freedom on a word you don't even understand?"

"I know enough to know that all I did was be like a, what do you call it . . . broker, I guess. My friend wanted to borrow a car. My other friend had one to loan. I put them together. What happened after that is not on me. I didn't have nothin' to do with any kidnapping."

"We've recorded conversations between you and the kidnapper, talking about the car, talking about the kid."

"I don't remember that."

"You don't have to. The prosecutor will refresh your memory when the recordings are played at your trial."

"Trial for what?"

"We're not going down this road again, DeWayne. You don't have to play stupid with me, because I'm already convinced."

A knock came at the door and Detective Antoine Johnson leaned in. "Chief Keller, a word."

Keller left and Mannock turned to face Boone. "So, what do y'all want from me besides what I told you? You've got no evidence that ties me to any of this. I'm innocent—just tried to help a friend. What that friend did is on him. Right?"

Antoine Johnson briefed Jack Keller on the phone Kevin Kenleigh had sent to Michigan.

Jack shook his head. "He's a dandy. Any leads on his whereabouts?"

"Nothing."

"We'll find him soon enough," Jack said. "I'm looking forward to collaring that guy."

"He's got a record in DuPage County. When he was a teenager he got students to pay him to take their college entrance exams. Phonied up IDs, got C students big numbers on their ACTs and SATs. That's become a big thing now, but he was a pioneer."

"He may be the smartest one in this little hole-in-the-wall gang," Jack said, "but he's in over his head."

"Think Mannock's gonna crack, Chief?"

Jack shrugged and peered through the window at DeWayne and Boone.

Boone had intended to leave the interrogation alone and let Keller handle it, but he couldn't resist. "DeWayne, you need to do yourself a favor here. When Chief Keller gets back, you'd better tell him everything you know. We've got you with an unexplained pile of cash, conversations with people connected with a kidn—"

"I won the lottery, man!"

"Will you stop? You know how easy that was to rule out? We know where you got your sack of cash."

For the first time, Mannock looked beat, at least on that point. "Well, that money had nothing to do with this."

"Then what were you trying to pitch Shane Loggyn on? You told him you were paid to be a finder. What was it you found, DeWayne?"

"I should have said I was a pointer, not a finder. I'm like a bird dog. Bird dogs don't really find. They point."

"You pointed at what?"

"I'm done talking."

Keller returned, and Boone could tell from Jack's look that he had been listening in and was content to let them keep going.

"If you're done talking," Boone said, "there's nothing more we can do for you."

"Nothing *more*? What have you done for me now?"

"Given you a chance to tell your side. But you've failed, DeWayne. You could have helped yourself. You know the penalty for being an accessory to kidnapping? It's the same as if you'd kidnapped Max yourself. And you rarely hear of a kidnapper getting anything less than life."

"I didn't touch anybody, so that doesn't—I'm not—you can't . . ."

"Life in prison, DeWayne."

"That'll never happen."

"It's as good as done," Boone said.

"It *is* done," Keller said, and Mannock twisted back to face him.

"Cops in Michigan just picked up Johnnie Bertalay, and he's singing like a canary."

"No kidding?" Boone said, strolling toward the door. "Guess we're done here. What'd he do, blame it on DeWayne?"

"All of it," Jack said, his hand on the doorknob. "You had your chance, Mannock."

"Wait! What're you talking about?"

"You begged us to hear you out, and then you gave us nothing. We're getting all we needed from Johnnie. Some friend."

"He's not my friend! I hardly know him. I saw him only a few times. *He* did it! It's all on him!"

Boone shook his head. "Should have started with that, DeWayne. Sounds like Johnnie's out ahead of this, working his own deal. He's gonna wind up serving less time that you."

"Hold on! I can tell you things about him!"

"No need," Jack said. "We're getting the whole story from him. How different can your accounts be?"

"Way different if he's saying this was my idea! The idea came from Pitts. He's the one who introduced me to Bertalay. Johnnie works for him."

"Well, Chief Drake," Jack said, turning back to the table, "maybe we're being a little hasty."

Boone returned to the corner behind Mannock, who kept stealing urgent glances at him over his shoulder. Jack turned his chair around and sat facing DeWayne with his legs crossed, as if he had all day. "Johnnie never said a word about anybody but you. Says you were the mastermind. Who's Pitts, anyway? Tell us about him, and maybe *you'll* get a little consideration."

"I ought to get a lot of consideration, because Pitts is the guy."

"Okay, slow down and take it from the top. Where did you meet this Pitts?"

27

★★★★

SINGING

DeWayne Mannock suddenly sat up, leaned forward, and seemed to be boring in on Jack Keller. "Pitts is a regular—well, sort of—at the Lucky Day."

"Full name, and what's 'sort of regular' mean?"

"His player's card just reads J. Pitts. I think his real name is Jasper, but he goes by Jammer."

Boone turned to the mirror. "Johnson, you on that?"

"He says yes, Chief," Ronette transmitted.

"What's he look like?"

"Big old fat guy, funny-colored hair—like dyed orange or yellow—and not much of it. Smart guy. Knows a lot of stuff. Good player."

"Regular or not?"

"Couple of times a month for two or three days at a time, but that's it. Seems he likes to play and plays when he can, but he's a world traveler."

"Yeah? Where?"

Mannock shrugged. "Everywhere. Always talking about other countries."

"What's he do?"

"I always thought he was like an importer/exporter or something like that. In a way, I guess he is."

"I'm going to quit asking questions here, DeWayne. I want you to tell me everything you know about this man, why you say the kidnapping was his idea, his relationship with you and Johnnie Bertalay, all of it. It's your only chance to get a year or two off your sentence."

"I shouldn't have any sentence! I hardly did anything!"

"Convince us. And help us get Max back. Otherwise, you're going to prison for a long, long time."

"I don't know where Max is! I swear. If I did, I'd tell you."

"Tell us everything you do know. And make it fast."

"You sure I don't need a lawyer?"

Boone caught Jack's eye. *Please, no.* This was the last thing they needed right then. Jack gave Boone a nod, as if he should trust him. Boone did trust him, but he didn't like the way Jack started.

"Truthfully, DeWayne, I do think you need a lawyer. I've told you that from minute one. And you know too that the second you tell us to get you one is the instant this interview ends. We walk out, and the next person in here will be whoever the court appoints as your public defender. That's your right, and of course, at some point you're going to have to be defended.

"Now here's the thing. You don't know if Johnnie's lawyered up yet or not. Neither do I. All we know is that if you don't get on with your story, his is going to be the only one out there. And that's not looking good for you. So, you want your lawyer right this minute, or when you need him for the court case? We can't be listening to your side of this, even if you've decided to finally come clean and tell us everything, if you'd rather be represented now. It's totally your call."

"I want to talk."

"Then talk."

"Okay, I've known Jammer for a few years, just from the casino, you know. I used to get a kick out of hearing him talk. He wasn't one of those loud ones who brag about where they play and how much they win and all that. He's just one of those guys who knows a lot about a lot of stuff and enjoys answering questions. People just figure he knows best, you know? They'll be talkin' sports or politics or famous people or anything, and pretty soon they get around to seeing what Jammer thinks. And he says it so smooth and smart-like, nobody argues with him.

"Well, about two years ago he seems to take a liking to me. Starts asking me about myself, my prospects, my plans. I didn't even know what prospects were. I was kinda faking it, telling him I hoped to be a floor man someday, like Goose. Those guys don't live on tips. They have actual salaries. Not big ones, but any salary sounds good to me. Something regular with benefits the company pays for, all that.

"So Jammer's kinda pushin' me. He's saying, 'Really, that's what you want to do with your life? Spend it in a casino in a blazer making a chump's salary?' I told him no, that what

I really wanted to do was win the lottery, and he says, 'Now you're talkin'.'

"I thought he meant he knew a way to do that, but he just meant that that kind of money was what he was talking about. He said everything else is chump change. He asked me did I know how much he was worth, and 'course I said no, how would I know that? And he said, 'Would you believe eight figures?'

"I was embarrassed, 'cause I didn't even know what that meant. I knew seven figures was a million, but I couldn't have told you what eight was, not off the top of my head." "At least ten million," Boone said.

"Yeah, exactly, I know that now. So a guy tells me that, he's gotta know I'm gonna wanna know where he gets that kind of money. He tells me he's in the international people business. I have no idea what that means. I've heard of people who find executives for companies—"

"Headhunters," Boone said, trying to move Mannock along.

"Yeah, like that, so that's what I'm thinking for a long time. Every time Jammer comes in to play, we get a little time to talk. One day he says, kind of like out of nowhere, 'Do you know there are people willing to pay a million dollars for the right child?'

"Like a dummy, I say, 'For what?' He tells me he's heard of people who want a certain kind of kid. They know exactly what they want. They can't have their own, and they're rich, of course, and they decide they want a kid a certain age, a certain skin color, hair color even, nationality, all that. And you know, we're standing there talking about this, and I have no idea he's talking about his own business. I don't know why. I just never put it together. I'm like, 'No way!' and he's like, 'Really.' And I'm still thinking it's just smart Jammer talking about stuff most people don't know about.

"Then, later, like maybe a year, he asks me have I been thinking about what we talked about. And the thing is, I hadn't. Not really. It was strange and all that, and I thought about it for a few days, but million-dollar kids is not the kind of thing I think about for long, you know?"

"We're still with you, DeWayne," Jack said. "You're doin' good. Keep going."

"Well, one night he asks me what am I doing on break, and it's perfect timing because somehow I got a double break, an hour right at dinnertime. He takes me to the buffet, buys my dinner, and starts right in. He tells me, 'You know I pay a 15 percent finder's fee when I provide a child.' I almost wet my pants; I really did. It all kinda hit me at once. He's in the people business. Rich people pay a million bucks for the right kid. And he provides 'em!

"I couldn't hardly eat my food 'cause, besides finally putting this together in my head, you know what's the only thing I can think about then."

"The 15 percent," Boone said, his stomach churning at where Max could be right now. The only silver lining in this story is that if Max was worth that much to someone, he was likely safe and not bound for the sex trade.

"The 15 percent!" DeWayne said, pointing at him. "I didn't know what eight figures was right off the top of my head, but I dang well know what 15 percent of a million bucks is. And I wanted it. He had me, hook, line, and sinker, whatever that means."

"Lured you in."

"Sure did. And he was pretty smart about it, because once he got me interested, you know, he sort of backed off. Every time he came in I asked him about it, and he said he wasn't sure he should keep talking to me about it, because keeping things totally quiet was everything in his business.

"I told him I'd swear on my mother's grave—"

And sell your own son, Boone thought.

"—to get in on action like that. And maybe the third or fourth time I saw him after that, when I asked how could I get in on this deal, he said, 'I doubt you even know the type of a person I'm looking for.' So I asked him; I says, 'What kind?'

"Well, he told me he had a lot of calls for American boys, preferably blond."

"Hold on," Boone said. "You're telling me he knew you had a son who fit that description?"

"No! That's just it! I think it was just one of those, ah . . ."

"Some coincidence."

"Yeah, one of those."

"Go on."

Detective Antoine Johnson introduced himself to Hammond Lieutenant Lefty Tidwell over the phone.

"Tell me the brilliant DeWayne Mannock has already sung for his supper," Lefty said.

"Oh, you know Keller. He and Drake are scraping it off him an ounce of flesh at a time. Slow but sure. Hey, we need all we can get on this Jasper 'Jammer' Pitts."

"Way ahead of ya. One of my guys was listening over all the stuff we recorded when Keller and Drake were here, and we knew you'd eventually need that guy. He's not listed in any phone books or online, but we got an address from the Lucky Day. I can fax you the sheet we got on him."

Antoine gave him the number. Within minutes he knocked on the interrogation room door and handed the printout to Jack.

Jack glanced at the sheet and handed it to Boone as DeWayne Mannock continued.

"Jammer told me there was a big, um, he called it a market, a market for fair-skinned Caucasian boys, especially blonds, from America, Canada, and Scandinavia."

"Hold on a second, DeWayne," Boone said. "Take five."

"C'mon, man," Mannock said. "I'm tryin' to be cooperative here so I can get goin'. They're holding that car for me, ya know."

Boone held up a hand as he speed-read the printout to himself.

Jasper Manchester Pitts

DOB: January 23, 1943

Height: 6'2"

Weight: 265

Hair: Auburn

Eyes: Gray

Sales manager, Jade Fortune Import/Export Enterprises, Bangkok, Thailand, 1991–1999

Current: Founder/CEO/President

Chu-Hua Children of the Globe Placement Services, 1999–present

Home & business address: 1 Willow Circle, Clarendon Hills, Illinois (DuPage County) 60514

No record, no priors, no warrants

Boone stuck his head out the door. "Antoine, let's get him in here and get a warrant to search his home."

As Boone returned to his station behind Mannock, DeWayne squinted at him. "Who? Whose home?"

"Everybody's throwing you under the bus today, DeWayne. You say you were just the pawn, but we're getting a whole different picture. Let's wrap this up so we can get you into something a little more comfortable and a lot more orange."

"I'm not going to County! Unless you make up somethin' to pin on me, I'll be back to that dealership before dinner."

"Then you'd better get to the point and start putting your finger on the bad guys. Somebody's going down for this, DeWayne, and right now the smart money is on you."

"All right, listen; so Jammer, he keeps putting me off, you know? Even though I tell him I got the perfect kid for him. I'm askin' him is he serious about somebody goin' a million bucks for these kids and would there really be a rock and a half in it for me, and he's saying, 'No, no, DeWayne, you don't really want to get mixed up in this.' I tell him I do, that I'd do anything for a hundred and a half, and he says, 'Including giving us everything we need and then keeping your mouth shut?' and I'm saying, 'You know it, man.'"

Boone moved next to DeWayne, towering over him. "Just curious. Did you tell him this was your own son?"

"Not then. That came later. Actually Johnnie figured that out."

"And Pitts had no problem with that?"

Mannock shook his head. "He just said he wanted someone not too many people would care about. You know, if the kid is well-known—"

Boone slowly closed his eyes and was glad his sidearm was not allowed in the interrogation room. *Someone not too many people would care about?*

"You're getting ahead of yourself," Jack said. "You said Jammer introduced you to Bertalay. Walk us through that."

"Well, Jammer is still putting me off. I can't believe it. I'm no smart guy, but pretty soon I catch on that he's just making sure about me. He wanted me to point him to a kid he could deal, but he wanted me to understand that this was serious business and to convince him I was trustworthy. I musta finally done that, 'cause finally, after months and months of dancin' around it, he tells me he can cut me in on a deal. He's got a live request for just the kind of kid we've been talking about; he's got what he called an, uh, extraction specialist—that's what he called Johnnie—and we've got to all meet and talk this through so he can decide if it's doable."

"So, where did you meet?" Boone said.

"At a coffee shop in Burr Ridge, right off the expressway."

"Here in Illinois, in DuPage?"

"I don't keep track of which county I'm in, but yeah, I guess. Jarvis's Cafe. I remember because I missed it a couple of times and had to keep gettin' back on the expressway and trying different exits."

"We need everything you can remember about that meeting," Keller said.

"And then I can go?"

Boone stepped back to where DeWayne would have to wrench around to see him. Boone had a perfect view of Mannock's face in the mirror and studied him for tics and tells that would indicate when he was lying or rattled.

Jack leaned forward again, hands flat on the table, his face inches from Mannock's. "DeWayne, you've been doing okay up to now, but you need to hurry. You don't want the other guys' stories on the record before yours; you know why?"

Mannock shook his head.

"Because we tend to believe what we hear first."

"Well," DeWayne said slowly, "this is all on the record, isn't it?"

"Yeah, but are you going to give us the whole story first? Or second? Or last? Who are we going to believe?"

"You can believe me 'cause I'm not lyin'!"

"Fine, but you need a reality check, and I've got to ask you again, are you listening?"

"Yeah, sure, what?"

"DeWayne, you're giving yourself the best chance you can here, telling us every detail. If everything you say checks out, we're going to tell that to the prosecutor, and he's probably going to ask you to repeat it in court."

"Rattin' on these guys?"

"It's your only hope. What do you think they're doing to you right now? This is your only chance."

"Only chance for what? Gettin' out of here today?"

"Now, see, DeWayne? That's what I'm talking about.

You're in la-la land if you think you're going to be a free man for the next several decades."

"Well, I think you're wrong, and I think you're bluffing. I'm going to tell you everything, and when you see I didn't—"

"What? Do anything except put these guys onto Max and then take money for it?"

"Right."

"I've got to be honest with you, Mannock. I don't want you to be confused or misled when it comes to what's going to happen to you. Now I'm no lawyer, and neither are you. Still, one thing I know from decades in this business: you're going to prison for a long time. Now don't give me that look, and don't interrupt me. I'm not promising you anything but a long prison term. But I'm telling you that if you quickly give us everything on Pitts and the man you know as Bertalay, you might earn some consideration."

"Like what?"

"Like maybe ten to twenty instead of life. Maybe something this side of maximum security. Maybe segregation to protect you from other inmates. You're not a big guy, DeWayne, and there is a pecking order in prison. You know what that means?"

"I know they don't like child molesters and stuff."

"Well, this qualifies as *stuff*. You haven't molested a child, but do you think it's going to be a secret inside that you sold your own son?"

"I didn't sell him! Jammer sold him!"

"And you took a commission. You've got to wake up, DeWayne. What you're doing now is catastrophe control. The damage has been done. You're not getting out of here except on a bus to central booking, then straight to County, eventually to trial, and then to prison. I'd love to pretend otherwise to get you to tell us all we need to know. But you need to do that anyway, unless you want to live the rest of your life in general population in a facility full of murderers with nothing to lose and a hatred for people who victimize children. Am I getting through, DeWayne?"

"I need a lawyer."

"I've been telling you that. But just so we're clear, are we done here? You want to lawyer up before you tell us about the meeting with you and Pitts and Bertalay?"

"What should I do?"

"I can't advise you, DeWayne. All I can tell you again is that you have the right to stop this right here and have us get you a lawyer."

DeWayne twisted in his chair. "What do you think I should do, Drake?"

Boone shook his head. How he wished kidnapping were a capital offense. "It's entirely up to you," he said, fighting to control his breathing. "We're not going to screw this up by standing in the way of your getting representation."

"A lawyer would probably tell me to tell about the meeting anyway because it'll prove this was their thing, not mine. Right?"

Boone shrugged, hoping, praying Mannock would not lawyer up. Not yet. "We can't give you legal advice, DeWayne."

"I'll get assigned a public defender once I go to County, right?"

"As soon as you're booked. Right."

"'Cause I can't afford one. Not without my cash. And I don't suppose—"

"No, that cash is evidence. You can't use it for—"

"I got the other half of it at my place."

"Not anymore you don't. Hammond PD has turned your room inside out, and all that is being processed and delivered."

Mannock seemed to be studying the floor. "You promise me a lawyer when I get to County?"

"You're entitled to a lawyer at any time, even now," Jack said. "I have made that crystal clear."

"I think I want to keep going."

"What's that mean, DeWayne?" Boone said. "It has to be clear on the record if you're still waiving your right to counsel at this stage and want to keep talking."

"That's what I'm saying," he said. "I don't guess it makes much difference now. But I want everybody to know that, yeah, I helped and I took money, but this wasn't my deal. It was Jammer's. And Bertalay was his guy."

28

★★★★

DESTINATION

For the next hour, DeWayne Mannock, clearly convinced that Jammer Pitts and Johnnie Bertalay were ratting him out, did his best to turn the tables. Boone believed DeWayne was not smart enough to be making this up. Nuance was not his gift.

The meeting had taken place on a Tuesday night in the spring when DeWayne was off work. Pitts had told him where to meet him and Bertalay. They were already there when he arrived. Pitts had told him he was late and that that was not a good sign. Mannock had told him he had trouble finding the place, and Pitts said, "Yeah, you can only see it from the expressway. Can't imagine how you finally located it."

"He always talk to you that way?" Boone said.

"Mostly. Sort of mean and like I'm beneath him, but always

like he's just kidding. I didn't care. Kinda money I was gonna make, he could have ridden me down the street like a donkey."

He did, Boone thought.

"So tell us about Bertalay."

"He looked a lot like a stoner."

"Seriously?"

"Yeah, I've done my share of weed, and he didn't look high or anything, but he was wearing an olive drab coat, way too warm for the weather and way too big for him. He was swimmin' in it, and kinda slouched there."

"So what made him look like a stoner?"

"The hair. You ever see that funny guy on TV, 'Weird Al' something?"

"Yankovic, yeah."

"Long and black and curly like that."

"To his shoulders?"

"Yeah. And he was real pale, like he stayed indoors all the time. Thing was, he got up once to use the bathroom, and his coat kinda pulled open as he slid out of the booth, and I could tell he was cut. Almost like a bodybuilder. I mean, he wasn't huge. More my size, but hard."

"Interesting. Keep going."

"Everybody seemed to know Jammer at this cafe," Mannock said. "But nobody called him that. It was always Mr. Pitts. Even though we were in the last booth by the wall, people were comin' by, saying hi to him and smiling, and two showed him pictures."

"Of what?"

"Their families. One woman showed him one, and he made a big deal over how the little girl was so darling and was getting so big. He showed Johnnie and me the picture, and it showed a bunch of kids that looked like the woman and one little girl from Japan or Korea or China or someplace. She really was cute. The woman gave Pitts a big hug and said she owed it all to him. When she left he says, 'One of the perks of my job. Helps me sleep at night.'"

"You're saying he had sold that woman an Asian child?" Boone said.

"That's what I asked him. I said, 'Where would she get a million bucks for a kid?' Jammer laughs and says, 'This is an affluent area, boys, but the money's on the other end. Here I arrange the adoption and I clear a little under twenty grand. Girls are cheap in China.'"

Boone let that sink in. "All right," he said slowly. "Then?"

"Then we eat. And I mean, we *eat*. I like a good meal, but I don't stuff myself. Jammer orders a gigantic meal, some kind of breakfast they serve all day. Pancakes, eggs, toast, sausage, hash browns. Enough to feed a family. Thing is, Bertalay does the same thing. Not breakfast, but I think meatloaf or something with rolls, mashed potatoes and gravy, beans, everything. And a big dessert."

"We don't really care what they ate, DeWayne," Jack said.

"Yeah, sorry, but he asked what happened next, and that was it. I ate and they gorged. I don't know how else to say it."

"Get to the deal," Boone said.

"Okay, so Jammer tells the waitress we're gonna be there a while and could she keep people from interrupting. He said he would make it worth her while, and she said something like, 'Oh, I know you will, Mr. Pitts. You always do.' While she's saying that he makes a show of setting four twenties on the table. This is for a meal for all three of us that probably didn't come to much more'n thirty."

"So everybody knows him and loves him and he's generous," Boone said. "He helps families in that area adopt Asian kids. Sounds like a model citizen."

"Looked like a big shot to me. So then he tells me how his business works. He says his organization is nonprofit and places Asian orphans in Western families. It's all girls because boys are preferred in China, and they've got this one-child policy. You only get one, so if you have a girl, a lot of them are happy to take a few thousand and be told a story about where she's going. Better life, more opportunity, all that.

"So then Jammer goes into this big explanation about the supply side of the stateside business being in poor villages where he gives the parents of baby girls a thousand or two and tells 'em he'll make sure their daughters live in luxury in America and all that. He said other outfits in the same business make the same promises, but they send the kids into other Asian countries and get about twice what they paid for 'em. And don't care if the kids wind up in the sex trade. Jammer said he works with a higher class of people and makes a good living at it. Says it makes people happy, gives kids a nice home, makes him feel good. I guess his town named him Charitable Somethin'-or-Other of the Year once. Says he gives a lot of money.

"I ask him, 'Where does the big money come in?' That's when he tells me that some very wealthy people in China want these blond boys to raise as their own. Maybe they can't have their own or don't want to. It's some kind of prestige thing among the rich there, at least some of them. Jammer says, 'They're wealthy enough to be discreet.' And I say, 'And wealthy enough to afford you?' He goes, 'Precisely.'

"Anyway, he tells me he only does these big transactions a few times a year, three or four at the most, and I'm thinking, why would you have to do it more than once for that money? Anyway, he says he's got a client in northern China who really wants an American boy, and when he describes what he wants, it sounds like Max."

"How do you know?" Boone said. "How many times have you seen Max?"

Mannock shrugged. "More than you know."

"You've watched him?"

"That's where my cut came in. I got paid to find out where you guys come and go, church, school, who watches him, all that."

It was all Boone could do to keep himself from strangling DeWayne where he sat. Through a set jaw, he said, "Are you telling me that Max is in China?"

Mannock shrugged again. "Probably was on his way by Saturday evening."

Boone went rigid and his face flushed, though he felt cold in the stifling room. He doubled his fists and slammed them back against the wall, making Mannock start. "Where, DeWayne?"

"No idea, I swear."

"You pointed Pitts and Kenleigh to Max, knowing he would wind up in China?"

"Who's Kenleigh?"

"Just tell me."

"I'm just guessing where he is because of what Jammer

said. The people who want these kids are in China. That's all I know."

Boone stormed from the room, yanking out his cell phone. He noticed texts from Francisco Sosa and Margaret but didn't have time to check them. He called the crime lab and asked for Ragnar Waldemarr. Boone moved past the colleagues who were huddled around the two-way mirror, listening in silence and plainly avoiding his glance. When Heathcliff Jones and Antoine Johnson peeled away and started to follow him, Boone waved them off with his phone to his ear and camped out on the landing in a stairwell, hyperventilating.

"Boone," Waldemarr said, "any news?"

"Doc, you said I could come to you."

"For anything. Name it."

"Contacts in China?"

"Whereabouts?"

"The north."

"So Beijing. Yes. Are you saying that's where—?"

"How long would it take me to get a visa?"

"Depends on who you want to be, Boone. That's an awfully tough place to find—"

"I want to be anyone but me."

"You'll need a visa, a passport, ID, credit cards—all that, all in a new name."

"Right."

"Transmit me a head shot and I can have that done in a matter of hours. But it'll probably run—"

"Cost is irrelevant. What do I do about getting around, communicating?"

"I've got a guy."

"Can I take a weapon?"

"No, that cannot be done."

"Access to one there?"

"Sure. Dangerous, but that can be arranged. Man, the last thing you want to do is fire a weapon in a country like that. We'd probably never see you again."

"Just in case."

"I've got here in the lab the very model you'd get over there, if you want to familiarize yourself—"

"I do. How do I get on a flight fast?"

"When do you want to go, Boone? American has direct flights every evening that get you in just before midnight the following night."

"And your guy can meet me?"

"For a price, sure."

"And bring me a weapon?"

"Well, not in the airport, but he can take you to it. You and I are going to need to meet, and I can give you more then. You got an alias you want to travel under?"

"I don't care, Doc. Just get it done and tell me where to meet you."

"Well, it can't be here. I had nothing to do with this, right?"

"I hear you."

"I'll text you a location. And I have to get moving on this if you want to make, let me see here . . ."

Boone heard him leafing through a book.

". . . the 7:55 out of O'Hare. They want you there early to clear security, so I'll get cracking."

"Doc," Boone said, as he located his own photo on his phone and set it to transmit, "you have no idea how much—"

"Save that, Boone. Not a word about it until you come back with your boy."

Boone rushed back to the interrogation room.

"Anything else?" he said.

"We were kind of waiting for you," Jack said.

"All right, DeWayne," Boone said, "give me the rest of it as fast as you can. What happened? How did you point them to Max?"

"Well, that night you saw me, I was hoping I'd get to see him. You know I made up that story about wanting some of Haeley's settlement for a business thing. I knew I wouldn't need that if I could make this happen. But you weren't buying it, so I borrowed Shane's car, and luckily it had Illinois plates on it, so no suspicion, you know."

"Get on with it."

"So I followed Haeley and Max to church. I didn't realize they don't even go there any more, except when you're busy or something. But I saw them talking to the black lady, Mrs. Quigley."

"And you were doing all this because Jammer told you to?"

"No, once he decided Max was going to be his next target—"

The word pierced Boone. He silently prayed for control. Killing Mannock right there would be the end of any hope of finding Max.

"—he turned me over to Johnnie. We met at this strip club in Merrillville, Gents or something like that. I gotta tell ya, I couldn't concentrate watchin' the show, so later we talked in his car in the parking lot. Johnnie told me how to follow 'em, how to find out things, and he wanted every detail I could remember about Haeley's family, the sitter, the church, all that. Truth is, Johnnie's a con man. It's what he does. But he's real smart and thorough and careful. That's what he told me."

"He came up with the GI returning home story?"

"Yup. Buzzed off his hair, worked out more, found the clothes. I'm not sure how he got himself sunburned, whether he just laid out in the sun or went to one of those tanning places, but he sure fooled me. He really looked the part."

"Yeah, we're all impressed by how he was able to fool everybody, DeWayne. How'd you get paid up front? That makes no sense."

"I was surprised too! I guess Jammer needed to hide some cash, so I was supposed to hold it for him. It wasn't really supposed to be mine until he got paid on the other end, but what was I gonna do, have that much cash around and not do anything with it?"

"Any idea how Johnnie got Max onto a flight?"

"I guess that was the easy part. After he left the car for me, he was gonna get Max's head shaved. Then he had stashed some van that had hair dye in it and clothes and stuff for Max. Visa and passport too in a different name. All Johnnie had to do was shoot a picture of Max with his new haircut and dye job. He dyed black what was left of Max's hair, in case his picture went out on the news or something. Then Johnnie gave him some kind of medicine, not the kind that puts you to sleep but the kind that makes you not want to talk and not remember anything."

"Are you kidding me?"

"They swore on a stack of Bibles it wouldn't hurt him.

Johnnie told Max it was some kind of a game and that his mom had called and wanted to see him at the airport and take a plane ride with him."

"So when she wasn't there?"

"Johnnie was supposed to tell Max he misunderstood, that Haeley was going to meet him at another airport he would fly to with a friend of hers. She would sit with him on the plane. By then he was supposed to be so mellow that this woman was just gonna tell the customs guys that it was past his bedtime and isn't he cute and he's going to see his mommy in China, that kind of thing."

"So who's the woman?"

Mannock shrugged. "Jammer's assistant. I guess she does a lot of deliveries for him on both ends. She's brought girls here, delivered boys there. Johnnie told me Jammer says she's the best he's ever worked with."

"So what was she supposed to tell Max?"

"Max wasn't supposed to kind of wake up until it was normally time for him to go to bed. Even then he would be all sleepy. The woman would tell him his mother was waiting for him, excited to see him, couldn't wait, all that. He'd have his dinner and ice cream and then sleep, and when he woke up they would soon be there to see Mommy."

"We need a name, DeWayne," Boone said, barely able to contain his rage. "Who is she?"

"I know nothing about her. Never even saw her. Johnnie would know."

"And do you know Max's fake name?"

"I don't. I swear."

"Any idea where we find Johnnie Bertalay?"

Mannock shrugged, as if he'd been asked what time dinner was. "I'm pretty sure he's from Indiana, but I don't know where. Hey! Wait a minute!" He whirled and glared at Jack. "You said Johnnie was already bein' questioned, blaming it all on me! You guys lied to me! None of this counts! I'll deny it all."

Boone knelt in front of Mannock, making the man recoil. "You know you're the scum of the earth, don't you, DeWayne?"

Mannock looked over Boone's shoulder to Keller. "Come on, man!"

"I'm not finished," Boone said. "You know you're a worthless excuse for a man, don't you?"

"I was just lookin' out for myself. I wouldn'ta done it if I thought anything would happen to Max!"

"You don't think anything's happened to him? Do you have no recollection what it was like to be a young boy?"

DeWayne shook his head. "When I was his age I was knocked around a lot. He's not being knocked around. He's gonna be living with multimillionaires, man! It's not like he's going to suffer."

Boone shook his head and rubbed his face with both hands. "He's been kidnapped, DeWayne! Ripped from his parents, from his home, from everything he knows! He's been sold!"

"I know."

"You know?"

"Yeah, but—"

Boone could control himself no longer. From his crouch he leapt at Mannock, grabbing his shirt in both hands at the chest and tipping his chair back. Mannock clamped onto Boone's wrists to keep from toppling, and Boone pulled him close to his face.

"Killing you right here and now would be too good for you," he growled.

The squawk box came alive, and Heathcliff Jones's voice came through. "Keller, stop him!"

From behind him, Boone heard Jack say casually, "Stop what, Commander? We're almost through here."

And with that the door burst open and officers poured in, big Antoine Johnson yanking Boone off DeWayne Mannock with Heathcliff Jones's help. Boone tried to wrestle free and wasn't sure what he would have done if Johnson had let him go.

Jones led DeWayne from the room, intoning in his deep voice, "I agree the time has finally come for you to lawyer up, son."

"Wait till my lawyer sees what he just did to me!" Mannock railed.

"What who just did to you?" the commander said.

"You saw it! You saw him!"

"I saw nothing, son. And I don't believe anyone else did either."

"You've been recording the whole thing! It'll be on the tape."

"Hmm," Jones said. "My guess is there ain't nothing on that tape after your last question and answer."

29

★★★★

RAGS

"Ronette!" Keller called out from the interrogation room. "A word, please?"

Ronette entered shyly, stealing a glance at Boone, who slouched in a chair, panting.

"Chief Drake and I will be chatting in here for a minute. All recordings off, please."

"Yes, sir."

"And as for that last . . . exchange?"

"Oh, we missed that, sir."

"Did you?"

"Yes, sir. My fault."

"Nothing past the last question and answer?"

"No, sir. I'll do better next time."

"See that you do. I'd hate to have to write you up."

"No, sir. Wouldn't want that in my file."

Ronette left, closing the door without a sound.

"So, Boones, I s'pose you think you're going to China."

"Don't ask questions you know the answer to."

"Can't let you do that, buddy."

"Jack, if you think there's a one-in-a-million chance you can keep me from it, you don't know me like I thought you did."

"I'd hate to have to write you up."

"Yeah, I wouldn't want that on my record."

"So, we're clear, right, Boones? You're telling me you're too close to this case, too emotionally invested, feel bad about what you almost did to the arrestee, and have decided to take a leave of absence and stand vigil by your wife for the time being."

"We're clear if you understand you won't be seeing me for a few days, or however long it takes to bring Max—"

"To see your wife start to rally. Sure, I understand. That could take a while, and no one—least of all me—would have a problem with that. You take the time you need. I'll manage the Major Case Squad and remain the lead on this investigation. And we'll keep in touch."

"What's your next move, Jack?"

"We'll get someone on the passenger logs out of O'Hare to Beijing Saturday night. Has to be a woman and a young boy together. We'll at least get their pictures and aliases from the database. Then I want to get a warrant to toss the Pitts place and round him up. And of course, Kevin Kenleigh is next."

"And you'll get me whatever you find?"

"So you can think about it and study it as you sit by your wife's bed in ICU, sure."

"Exactly."

"Got it."

"Jack, I need a car."

Keller hesitated, then leaned close. "Listen, Boones, we can be all cute and sly about this, but we both know that if I'm going to officially be under the impression that you're at Mount Sinai, you're going to have to be in your own car."

"Then run me to it right now because I've got to, you know, check in—"

"About Haeley."

"Right."

"Wait in my car," Jack said, handing him the keys. "I'm going to tell Heathcliff and Johnson you decided to stay away from all this for a few days."

As Jack drove him home to pick up his own car, Boone fell silent and checked his messages.

"Hope you're taking advantage of Rags," Jack said.

Boone looked up. "Hmm?"

"You heard me."

"Yes, I did."

The message from Margaret read, All quiet, all the same. Docs are encouraged. Praying. Stand firm.

The message from Sosa read, Deuteronomy 29:29.

"Francisco and his Old Testament verses," Boone muttered.

"What?"

"'The secret things belong to the Lord our God, but the things that are revealed belong to us and to our children forever, that we may do all the words of this law.'"

"Deep," Jack said. "Not sure I got it all, but he sure seems to know what you need when you need it."

"I just hope God will reveal to me whatever's secret."

The other message bore no sender name or number. It read merely, The Night Visitor, 4 p.m. Ask for Sven. It included an address on North Wells.

Jack followed Boone into the house and upstairs, where Boone grabbed a duffel bag and began filling it with everything he could imagine needing in Beijing. "You *will* keep in touch, right?" Jack said.

"Of course. I'm going to need to know everything."

"Believe me, I'll let you know. I hope to have messages waiting for you as soon as you get there. I assume Rags will be able to tell me how to contact you—securely, I mean."

"I imagine."

Boone lugged his bag down the stairs with Jack trailing. When he got to the back door he sensed Jack had something on his mind. "Anything else, Chief?"

"Yeah, uh, this is gonna sound strange, but before I chicken out—"

"What?"

"I was just wonderin' if you minded if I, ah, prayed for you."

Boone was momentarily speechless. "Well," he managed finally, "sure. If you want to."

"I kinda do."

"By all means."

Jack suddenly looked as if he had already thought better of the idea. "You know I don't do much of this."

"It's all right, Jack. I'll take all the help I can get."

"Okay, here goes." He intertwined his fingers before him,

bowed his head, and closed his eyes. Boone was so stunned by the gesture that he just stood there staring.

"Um, God, dear God, this is Jack. I just want to say, to pray, that, ah, you would help Boones. He's goin' into a country with a billion people looking for one little boy, a boy we all love and want back. Amen."

Boone's eyes filled and he turned away quickly, exiting the house and hurrying to his car. He couldn't remember having heard a sweeter prayer as long as he'd lived, and he couldn't even find the voice to thank Jack. He waved as he pulled away, and Jack waved back.

Boone flew past the Night Visitor but saw the sign in time to pull into the next alley and backtrack to park behind the tiny Middle Eastern eatery. He entered between two massive, smelly dumpsters, swinging open a heavy, bent, and dented metal door. He moved from the sickly sweet rotting cabbage stench of the alley to the rich aroma of cooked meat and spices. Boone hadn't eaten since breakfast.

A mustachioed man in a turban and apron grabbed the two-sided menu and said, "One?"

"Actually, is Sven here yet?"

"Right this way."

Boone followed the man from the back hallway to the dining area, which featured a black concrete floor, black-painted brick walls, and a black ceiling with the venting ducts exposed. Somehow it proved exotic and strangely inviting, though the ornate lamps seemed to be losing a war with the darkness. Boone could see just enough to make out the textures and avoid the pillars.

The man led him inside a curtain to a private booth that proved brighter than the main dining room—but not much. Garish, colorful fabric covered overstuffed seats. An Aladdin's lamp graced the table.

Dr. Waldemarr rose when Boone entered and uncharacteristically offered a fist, which Boone bumped, and they sat across from each other. A thin leather attaché lay next to the doctor.

"Scandinavian cuisine?" Boone quipped.

Waldemarr smiled. "I hope you're hungry. Can you eat?"

"Feel guilty about it," Boone said, "but I'd better."

"Yes. You'll get good food on the plane too, but you never know what you might get in Beijing. You'll need your strength. And your rest. Do you have anything for that?"

"Got some stuff last night that works." Boone showed him the bottle, and Waldemarr nodded as he read the name.

"We'll get to that, but let's not waste time. I recommend the falafel in a pita."

"Works for me," Boone said, and Waldemarr parted the curtain and signaled the man, whispering their order.

"The owner," Waldemarr said as the curtain closed. "An old friend. Well, anyway, I've been busy. Called in a few favors, shelled out a few bucks—"

"You're keeping track of every penny, I hope."

"Sure."

"I'm so grateful, Doc."

"I told you, stop that now. Some things are worth doing. This is one. Let's save the congratulatories for the other end."

Ragnar Waldemarr put the attaché in his lap and slid from it a thick manila envelope.

"Sure I'll even need the pills, Doc? I'm pretty wiped out."

"Use 'em anyway. As soon as you've eaten dinner, tell them you don't want to be awakened until the last meal before landing. Then stretch your bed out flat and—"

"I'm flying business class?"

"First; sorry. All they had."

"That's gonna cost me."

"Almost fifteen grand, but you said—"

"Price was no object. Of course it's not." Boone realized he was going to have to dip into Max's education fund. He couldn't imagine Haeley would hesitate for a second.

"Anyway, stretch out, wrap yourself in a blanket, strap yourself in with the belt showing so they don't have to wake you to make sure it's fastened when there's turbulence. There rarely is, but you don't want to be bothered. You're going to get to Beijing a little before midnight tomorrow, and strangely, you'll find yourself tired enough to sleep again a few hours later. Which is all right, because my guy is going to need that time to take you to a few places under cover of darkness."

"Such as?"

"Where you'll stay. To get your weapon. That kind of a thing."

"Where'm I staying?"

"I didn't ask. I assumed you didn't want to be conspicuous, so the big chain hotels are out. Feng will take care of you."

"Feng?"

"Feng Li. Former People's Liberation Army officer. Has your weapon."

"What's that look like?"

"I'll show you after we're served. Don't want anyone walking in on that."

Dr. Waldemarr casually flipped the envelope over when a waiter came in and poured tea.

As soon as they were alone again, Waldemarr pulled the Aladdin's lamp to the middle of the table and tipped the envelope until several more items slid into his hand. He spread them on the table. The passport and Illinois driver's license looked anything but new, and there was Boone's picture, his date of birth (off by one day), and a Chicago address he didn't recognize. The license was laminated but soiled and bent, set to expire in just over a year, so it looked appropriately used and abused. Same with the passport. It came with visa stamps in the back that showed the bearer had been out of the country six times in the past three years. Along with all that was an American Airlines ticket and a pristine Chinese visa, which Boone knew normally took weeks to acquire.

"Dean Booker?" Boone said. "How'd you arrive at that name?"

"Needs to be easy for you to remember. You see why it is?"

"I'd noodle it if I was in the mood."

"That's just me having a little fun with your anagramming nemesis," Waldemarr said.

"It's an anagram? Oh, I see it! Cute. And memorable."

"That's why the birthday is close too. The address is one we use in our database, and you, Mr. Booker, are listed in there now too." Waldemarr pointed out the visa stamps. "As you can see, you've been to Tel-Aviv, London, Rome, Bangkok, and Hong Kong, recruiting nationals to sell space in your sports catalogs."

"I know nothing about that kind of business."

"Neither will anyone who asks. Just sound bored and you'll be convincing."

"The craftsmanship is astounding, Doc. You must use—"

"You know better than to even wonder who I use."

"Expensive?"

"Enough, but nothing like the phone." Waldemarr pulled it from his pocket. "All this was done this afternoon, but it looks used too, doesn't it?"

Boone hefted it in his palm. "Heavier than it looks."

"Built from scratch today. My guy hacked into your cell, so all your old stuff, apps and all, is in there, but this one is wholly impenetrable, international, GPS equipped, has a mic and a transmitter—"

"When you say all my usual info, you know I'm tapped into Mannock's phone and the one Kenleigh used."

"Which is out of commission now. And all you're getting from Mannock's is whoever is leaving him messages. We still haven't been able to penetrate Pitts's, but we haven't given up. He's out of the country, but we don't think Kenleigh is."

"There's a guy I'd like to—"

"Leave stateside stuff to us, Boone. You know Jack and Antoine and everybody at the 11th are on this full-time."

"I want to see the gun."

"It's the model Feng will issue you, but I told you, this one stays with me. I just want you familiar with it. Again, after we've eaten. When you leave here don't forget to store in your trunk anything that identifies you—your gun, your credit cards, all that."

Waldemarr reached into his inside breast pocket and

produced a wad of currency and an 8.5×11 sheet folded vertically. "Chinese yuan," he said, "and here's a laminated card with the exchange rate. Don't want you getting ripped off."

As Boone slipped the cash into his pocket, the doctor slowly unfolded the sheet to reveal a photograph of a Chinese man. "Feng Li looks perhaps five years younger than you, Boone, but with Asians age is hard to determine. He's actually forty-one."

"Not in this picture he's not."

"That's a fairly recent shot, Boone."

"C'mon, Doc. This man is not over thirty, whether he's Chinese, Mongolian, or Canadian."

"I'm telling you, with Asians—"

"I'm not buying it."

"All right, he's had a little work done. He's AWOL from the People's Liberation Army, and despite that there are three million of them, he's hiding in plain sight. Had a long history with them before we started using him."

"For what?"

Waldemarr hesitated and a smile played at his lips. "He sells space in our sports catalogs."

"Where would he have had face work done?"

"At his home. By one of our people."

"Is there no limit to what you can provide?"

"If there is, I haven't found it. Now, you'll find Feng's English entertaining, but realize that he understands everything you say."

"Will he be armed?"

"Discreetly. But not in the airport. And he is a master of martial arts. But naturally he must abstain from anything that would bring attention to himself, so don't count on him to bail you out unless he's sure no authorities are watching."

"Got it."

"Now memorize that face and the name and let me have the picture."

Boone angled it fully toward the light and locked in on the young-looking visage. "What's his cover?"

"Tour guide. And though he's self-taught, he's good. Sometimes he has to give a tour of Tiananmen Square or the Forbidden City, even to people who would have him put to death if they knew who he was, and he pulls it off. Of course Feng Li is not his real name."

The owner of the Night Visitor cleared his throat and slowly opened the curtain, which gave both men time to tuck away their documents. He laid the steaming food on the table and bowed slightly. Ragnar whispered his request that the man stand guard for the next thirty minutes. "No servers until you hear from me—no one."

The owner pulled the curtains together as he backed out.

Boone wolfed down the delicacies, realizing that under any other circumstances he would have found them delicious. For now his mind was revving and food was merely fuel. He was also mindful of the clock, aware that he had to absorb everything Waldemarr had for him and get to O'Hare.

Both men finished eating inside of ten minutes. Waldemarr pushed the dishes aside and produced a small leatherette bag containing electrical socket modifiers Boone would need in China. "That's also where you'll find a cheat sheet of what to say to passport and customs agents. Memorize it."

"You think of everything, don't you?"

Waldemarr nodded. "There's even a pronunciation guide for simple words and phrases jammed in there, but I can't imagine you'll have time to study it. Feng should be all you need. Don't eat on the street, and make him take you to more Western-type places, just to be safe."

"I hope I'm not there long, Doc."

A female cleared her throat outside the curtain, and Dr. Waldemarr peeked out. Boone watched for an expression of annoyance, since he had clearly asked not to be interrupted. But Rags beckoned the newcomer in with a nod, and Boone instinctively stood.

Could it be?

30

★★★★

BEWILDERED

Boone would have been more confused only if Haeley herself had appeared. But it was, of all people, Brigita Velna, the Chicago Police Department counselor and caseworker Boone had twice been assigned to. The no-nonsense matron had proved warm and encouraging in the end, but she had been the bureaucrat in charge of his evaluations after both the loss of his family and his being shot in the line of duty.

So what was this? Had she been assigned him again, now that his wife had been injured and their son kidnapped? And how would she feel about his skirting department protocol? Had Dr. Waldemarr set him up? If the doc wasn't what he seemed, Boone could be in deep, deep trouble. But Waldemarr clearly acted as if he knew she was coming.

Boone slowly sat, imagining his trip being scuttled, the

case stalling, his career in jeopardy. Should he say anything? Call Fritz Zappolo? He opened his hands as if to inquire. Waldemarr smiled. Brigita Velna put a thin leather folder in her lap as she squeezed in next to Ragnar. "He didn't know I was coming?"

"Hadn't gotten to that yet."

Boone closed his eyes and shook his head, failing to make anything compute. "You invited Ms. Velna?"

"She's a colleague, Boone."

"I know who she is, Doc. We're well acquainted."

"No, we're not," Ms. Velna said quietly, and Boone thought her tone sounded sweet. "Doctor Waldemarr means that he and I are colleagues off the job, away from the office."

"Colleagues, meaning . . . ?"

"Meaning colleagues. His wife has become one of my best friends."

"Well, one of you is going to have to get real specific real soon. I'm lost."

"Brigita," Waldemarr began, "was attending an otherwise-innocuous social gathering when she happened to mention to my wife a bit of history with family members who have suffered at the hands of state officials. Not here, and not in China, but it has made her, ah, sympathetic to those who need, shall we say, extracurricular assistance. We have since collaborated on a number of extremely confidential tasks."

Boone sat trying to recollect whether he had detected an iota of that in his previous contacts with her. And slowly it came to him. Yes, he had. She had said all the right things, followed all the rules, and yet finally showed empathy and understanding and even put herself on the line for him.

"You may recall, Officer Drake," she said, "that I am an admirer of yours."

"I hope so."

She smiled. "Yes, I'm afraid that is critical to this mission."

"You know my mission?"

"Dr. Waldemarr has filled me in. While I delivered to him the documents he has already supplied you, I am not expert in manufacturing those. My role is slightly different. See me as a policy wonk."

Boone glanced at his watch. Ms. Velna had never been hasty, but he did have a plane to catch. She apparently noticed his discomfort. "I'm Ragnar's researcher. There are options I must ask you to consider and things you simply need to know so you're fully equipped before you leave."

"Seeing a version of the weapon I hope to use would be good."

Brigita raised a brow at Waldemarr. "You haven't even gotten that far yet?"

"It won't take long. He's a quick study."

"Still," she said, "I must get through this. You'll make your plane, Officer Drake—er, Chief Drake. The fact is, it won't leave without you."

"How did you manage that?"

"You've heard the expression, 'It's not what you know . . . ?'"

He nodded. "Well, I'm just feeling totally cared for. Fire away."

Ms. Velna showed more dispatch than he had ever experienced with her, pulling a sheaf of documents from her portfolio as Dr. Waldemarr moved the lamp yet again. She raised her glasses to her forehead, held the pages at arm's length, near the light, and used them as notes.

Boone's new phone vibrated. He peeked at a text from Jack. Call me when you can.

"That was automatically answered, by the way," Waldemarr said.

"No, it was a text from Chief Keller."

"He would have gotten an immediate response that you will get back to him as soon as you can."

"Which is true, but how—"

"Just something we had added to your phone to save you time. Seems to do your thinking for you. Now let's let Brigita get through her material."

"Okay," she said, "first we have decided to be very circumspect with the NCIC."

Boone nodded. Keeping Haeley's and his own name out of the database of the National Crime Information Center seemed prudent. "That's still my preference," he said, "though I know it goes against conventional wisdom. Everybody thinks that the more people who know about this, the better chance we have of—"

"Well," she said, "Max is listed as a missing person. And yet we're certain he's already in China. Tipping off his abductors on this end who you and your wife are would serve only to—"

"The one guy knows. Kenleigh, the one who uses all the fancy aliases, threatened to tell Pitts."

"He won't," she said. "Crafty as Kenleigh is, he doesn't need trouble from someone that powerful and connected. You understand why such news would be trouble for Kenleigh?"

"Because he should have told Pitts before the abduction, sure. And Pitts would have pulled the plug."

"Of course he would have. Pitts's whole livelihood is based on anonymity. He needs it to appear that these kids have just disappeared. No ransom demand, no evidence, no trail, no nothing."

Boone nodded.

"Now," Ms. Velna continued, "I assume you're aware that Alien/Fugitive Enforcement is one of the divisions of the US National Central Bureau."

"I couldn't pass a test on it, tell you how many divisions there are, but—"

"Six."

"—I'm aware of it, yes."

"Any interest in involving them?"

Boone shook his head. "What would they do with the knowledge that I'm on the case?"

"You know what they'd do with that. They'd report it."

"Then no," Boone said. "Plus, how slowly would that bureaucracy roll?"

"Almost as slow as Interpol. And of course Interpol relies way too much on national governments rather than local police agencies."

"Agreed," Boone said. "No on them too. And I'm almost afraid to ask whether we can expect any official cooperation in China."

"We can't," Brigita said. "Besides lack of professionalism—though they rarely show that side to the public—many Beijing police officers are corrupt. And the state publicly disavows any knowledge of human trafficking in country, so most US police agencies have to somehow act unilaterally over there."

"Which is what I'll be doing."

"You need to know that at the US–China summit in the late nineties, President Clinton and the Chinese president gave a lot of lip service to halting the spread of weapons of mass destruction and then got into human rights. The US offered judicial and legal training that got as far as a symposium on international human rights covenants. In '98 there was a memorandum of agreement that was to establish a law enforcement joint liaison group that would cooperate to combat narcotics, alien smuggling, and even organized crime."

"How's that gone?" Boone said, knowing the answer before Ms. Velna shook her head. "Then give me something I can use," he said.

"All right, just a couple more things," she said. "Lots of Americans like to adopt from China because the wait here is just too long. But the stories of Chinese orphans are largely just a ploy. Brokers buy those kids—mostly girls—cheap and sell them to Westerners. There's too much profit for it to be altruistic, as the adopting parents are led to believe."

"That's Pitts's business," Boone said, "but it doesn't concern Max. These big transactions going the other way, placing white males with wealthy Chinese—those are what line his pockets. The rest is just a cover, isn't it?"

"Ugly as it is, you're right. And Pitts is small-time in the adoptions that come this way. He's got lots of competition, and the whole one-child law and the anti-female sentiment impact every Chinese family."

"Forgive me, Ms. Velna, but right now I don't care about any family but my own."

"I understand, sir, but you need to know what you're walking into. Asian families have taken advantage of new technology, and as soon as they determine their unborn child is a girl, you know what happens. A hundred and sixty million abortions of female babies in Asia alone. Despite a Chinese proverb that says women hold up half the sky, thirty-five thousand girls are aborted in China every day. And five hundred women commit suicide."

Boone was stunned to silence. On the one hand, all he cared about was Max. On the other, he was on his way to an abortion mill that staggered the imagination.

"I want my son," he said, his voice thick. "And I want Pitts."

Ms. Velna put away her documents. "You know we have no extradition treaty with China. If you find Mr. Pitts, you'll have to deal with him yourself."

"Or administer justice on him there."

Dr. Waldemarr used a finger to part the curtains a sliver and seemed satisfied that the owner was still standing guard. He reached to the floor and dug deep in his case, pulling out a handgun that looked like a small Beretta. "Is that blue," Boone said, "or is it just this light?"

"It *is* blue."

Boone liked the weight and feel of it. "Loaded?"

Waldemarr nodded. "Fifteen-round magazine. It's called a QSZ-92, and it's manufactured in state arms factories over there. Feng Li has them in two styles. One takes 5.8mm ammo with a bottleneck case and pointed bullets. This one takes 9mm shells, more like a Luger. Locked breech, short recoil."

"Nice."

"It gets better. It's got an accessory rail there under the barrel for a laser sight or a flashlight."

"Hope he's got the laser sight."

"He does. And you can see the fixed sight even in this light because of the luminous insert."

Ms. Velna cleared her throat. "I understand that the official line on you, Chief Drake, is that you're separating yourself from this case to spend time at your wife's bedside."

Boone nodded miserably as he traded out his license and credit cards in his wallet and tucked everything else into the appropriate pockets. "Truth is, I'm not trying to deceive anyone except the bad guys. They used phony documents, so I'm fighting fire with fire. I don't care who knows within the CPD, because there's not a copper worth his star in this city who wouldn't do exactly what I'm doing. And I hope it goes without saying that if there's anybody I'm doing this for as much as me, it's Haeley."

"Not to mention your son," she said.

"I try not to even think about what's going through his little mind. Somebody's gonna pay for that."

The three decided to leave separately, the way they had come. Boone left first, feeling as if he were staggering to his car. Part of him was abjectly exhausted from stress and dread fear. Another part of him seemed limp with gratitude for the support system that had formed around him. His friends, his colleagues, everyone.

He tucked his real license and other docs between the spare tire and the floor of the trunk and lodged his Beretta deep in the wheel well. On the way to O'Hare he called Jack, his new phone coming to life as they talked, vibrating every few seconds. Boone noticed new messages coming in from Pastor Francisco Sosa and Margaret.

Jack quickly brought Boone up to date on what he'd found. "The most likely passengers matching the descriptions we got from Mannock were a woman using the name Virginia Tuttman and a little boy with a black buzz cut traveling under the name Mark Tuttman. I've attached photos from the passport database. That's definitely Max, isn't it?"

"Hold on," Boone said, fingers shaking as he accessed the photos. The woman looked in her midforties with short dark hair and glasses. And there was no question the little boy with the black buzz cut and panic in his eyes, despite a shy smile, was Max. Boone sucked in a breath. Oh, for powers that would allow him to rocket to Max in an instant!

"That's him," Boone told Jack.

"Counter personnel confirm he was sleepy to the point of nodding off during the boarding process and that the woman said he was her nephew and they were going to visit relatives vacationing in China. Their documents listed addresses in Palos Hills, Illinois, but the occupants of those residences have no knowledge of anyone by those names."

"How'm I supposed to find either one of them in Beijing? You realize how huge that place is?"

"Just hope they're still there, Boones. I mean, that's a monstrous city, but the rest of the country is just a bigger haystack. They've got lots of cities many times bigger than New York."

"You get into Pitts's place?"

"We did. A mansion. Lots of imported marble. Apparently

lives alone. No house staff, but there was a separate desk and phone and bunch of file cabinets in another room, like maybe somebody comes in and works for him. Humanitarian awards and pictures everywhere. If you didn't know—which apparently few do—you'd think he was God's gift to childless couples and needy children. Files are full of records of adoptions, but so far nothing incriminating. If you didn't know, you'd figure he was on the up-and-up."

"Any whereabouts on him?"

"He may already be in China, Boones. We didn't expect that, but we're trying to match something the techies found on his computer with flights out of Midway."

"Are you sure? I didn't even know you could get there from Midway."

"Not directly. Hang on a second. Let me check this message. Antoine again."

When Jack came back on, he said, "Bull's-eye. Flew under his own name but went Midway to Minneapolis to LA to Beijing. He's in country, Boones."

"So Tuttman is going to hold Max till he gets there?"

"Actually, I think he beat her there," Jack said. "Hang on, more coming in."

Boone allowed himself to hope that finding three people together would be easier than finding two.

"I don't know what to make of this yet," Jack said, "but Antoine just texted me that Ms. Tuttman is already back in the States. Took the first return flight. Alone."

"Find her, Jack."

"You think? I don't know who I want first, her or this Kevin Kenleigh character."

"I know who I want first. You tell Margaret where I'm going?"

"Been debating that," Jack said. "She can keep a secret; I know that."

"It's okay with me. I've got another text from her, so if it needs a response, I'll get back to her before takeoff."

When Boone parked at O'Hare and grabbed his duffel bag, he used his thumb to run through messages as he headed toward the international terminal. He had intended to save Pastor Sosa's until he boarded but found himself in the mood for encouragement.

Sosa's text directed him to Lamentations 3:22. Lamentations? Really? Was this going to be like the one from Job?

His mobile Bible brought up:

> The steadfast love of the Lord never ceases; his mercies never come to an end.

That, Boone thought, was Francisco—not to mention the Lord himself—at his best. As usual, it was just what Boone needed and just when he needed it.

The message from Margaret was just as good. *Don't know what this means or how it happens, but all three docs and the nurses keep telling me that Haeley's vitals are better. Heart rate, pulse ox, BP, all that. She's getting better, Boone. Chin up.*

31

★★★★

ABOARD

When Boone reached the first-class counter at American, he suddenly found himself treated like a king. It was no secret what a premium seat cost on an international flight, and apparently the entire staff was determined to treat him in kind. Once his ticket, passport, and visa had been confirmed, he was directed to the Admirals Club lounge.

"Don't think I'm a member," he said.

"You are tonight," he was told.

Boone wished he was hungry as he passed a buffet filled with delicacies, shrimp, and all kinds of other hors d'oeuvres. What fun it would have been to make a trip like this with Haeley, or even Max. What was he thinking? He was determined to make just such a trip with Max on the way home.

Boone dropped into an overstuffed leather easy chair and dialed Ragnar Waldemarr. "When I find Max," he said, "how do I get him home?"

"Way ahead of you, Boone. Jack briefed me on the alias they used for him. We'll just use it on the way back. Working with Feng Li on the docs now. Just need dates."

"The instant I can get him out of there."

"I hear you, Boone."

"And has Jack updated you on everything else?"

"He has. We're all in this thing together, Boone. And Ms. Velna asked if I would send along her good thoughts about the endeavor. We'll securely transmit any leads to Feng while you're in the air."

"Thought my new phone was secure."

"It is, but agents in the airport might want to turn it on. We don't want them seeing anything from us."

"I appreciate it."

"You know, we'll all be able to monitor your conversations from here, as long as you have your phone with you. Even if it's off."

"I'll keep you posted so you can all get together for a listening party."

"Don't put it past us."

Boone sighed. "Don't know why I'm so exhausted."

"You don't?"

"Well, sure, I guess I do."

"Don't fall asleep and miss your flight."

"Like that'll happen."

"And take that medication right after dinner."

"And do the seat belt thing; yeah, got it."

Jack Keller felt good about the momentum building in the case. As was true with homicides and kidnappings, the earliest leads were always the best and most crucial. Virginia Tuttman was no longer in China, but Jasper "Jammer" Pitts and Max were. That at least meant Boone's trip was no fool's errand.

Jack decided to drop in on Margaret at Mount Sinai and check on Haeley. Then he hoped to get some rest. But all those plans evaporated when he got a call from Lieutenant Lefty Tidwell of the Hammond PD. "Just got a big break, Jack. You're gonna love me."

"Talk to me, Tid."

"You've got this Mannock's cell phone in cold storage, and we've been monitoring every call to it and keeping the voice mail empty so we don't miss any. Everything so far has been from drinkin' buddies or collection agencies. Well, he just got a call from AKA."

"Kenleigh? Saying?"

"That if DeWayne didn't lay low and keep his nose clean, Knives was gonna tell Jammer what he'd gotten himself into."

"At least that tells us Pitts still doesn't know who Max is."

"Sounds like it. Thing is, Jack, AKA sounded drunk, and that's a good thing."

"Why's that?"

"'Cause he made a stupid mistake. It's not like him."

"Tell me you were able to trace the call."

"We were. He was just sober enough not to call with a cell phone, but he used a pay phone—"

"Who's still got pay phones?"

"—from a strip club called Gents in Merrillville."

"Was he still there? Did you get him?"

"I sent two guys in an unmarked squad, and they found a car registered to John Bertalay parked outside, so we think he's in there, Jack. I wanted you to have the pleasure."

"I owe you big time, Lefty. Give me the address."

Tidwell read it off.

"If he comes out before I get there, don't even let him get to the car."

As the time drew near for Boone's flight, he wandered to a huge plate-glass window overlooking the terminal. As was apparently usual in advance of nightly international flights, the place was full and buzzing. Lines led to every counter. Even the Admirals Club lounge was filling, and it was clear many were enjoying its comforts for the first time, as Boone was.

To his surprise, Boone was beckoned individually to come and board. "You look puzzled," the steward said. "You *are* in first, aren't you?"

"I am, but surely you don't offer this to anyone other than premium flyers."

"Full-fare first-class passengers are treated like our top frequent fliers. There are a bunch of you tonight, about half in first and the others in business."

The steward walked him all the way to the plane, asked where he wanted his bag, and helped him order his meal and something to drink. He told Boone what time to expect dinner and wished him a good flight.

Boone appreciated it and responded appropriately, but nothing could soothe the turmoil in his mind. This flight was taking him closer to Max, and all Boone could hope for was that the glacial thirteen hours of flying would give Jack and his team a chance to have more leads awaiting him, via Feng Li, when he hit the ground.

As Boone sat waiting for the plane to fill, he rehearsed in his mind everything that had happened from the moment he had heard that Max was missing. Jack had often complimented Boone on his ability to analyze mountains of complex data and come to sound conclusions. Right now this seemed a towering mountain.

As he sipped an orange juice, a senior couple began getting situated in the sleeper seats directly in front of him. *And they seem giddy. Terrific.*

Once they were settled and had ordered their drinks, the woman turned and greeted Boone. "What's taking you to China tonight?" she said.

"Going to get my son. He's . . . visiting there."

"How nice! We're celebrating our fortieth. Can't believe it. How the time flies."

"Good for you. That's great. Really."

"I know," she said. "Long marriages are so rare these days that when we tell people, they say, 'That long? To the same person?'" That made her laugh uproariously. She must have noticed Boone smiling only courteously. "Oh, I'm sorry," she said. "You're no longer married? Listen to me!"

"No, no, I am. She's just . . . under the weather, couldn't come along. Can't wait to reunite the whole family."

"I know what you mean," the woman said. "One of our kids is adopting from Thailand, and on our way home we're going to visit the orphanage and meet our new granddaughter, even before my daughter and her husband do. Isn't that something?"

"That's something," Boone said, unable to keep his dark thoughts from affecting his ability to sound interested. It *was* wonderful that a family was taking in an international child. And he had no reason to believe that everyone involved on both ends wasn't pursuing the thing with the purest of motives and the best interests of the child in mind.

But the flatness in Boone's tone must have given the woman whatever hint she needed to stop talking his ear off. She wished him a good flight and turned back around.

"All the best to you both on your anniversary and meeting your new grandchild," Boone said.

I'm off to rescue my son and do whatever damage I can do to the ones behind all this.

32

★★★★

UNCONSCIOUS

Boone's experience with sleep aids told him that even ones he found effective didn't work quite as well as their advertising claimed. In fact, they didn't affect him as strongly as they did Haeley. She was able to sleep a full eight hours when she occasionally took one. For Boone, the same medication gave him only about six good hours of sleep. Maybe it had to do with the differences in their sizes. Boone was nearly a hundred pounds heavier than his petite wife.

Did that mean he should take a heavier dose of what Dr. Sarangan had provided? One had certainly worked last night. Boone had heard bizarre stories—of sleepwalking, sleep-driving, refrigerator raiding—from people who had only slightly overdosed. The last thing he needed was to err with an even more powerful concoction.

With the announcement that cell phones were to be turned off in ten minutes, Boone called Dr. Waldemarr.

"Should I take one and a half of those pills I showed you, Doc?"

"No. That is way past even what a general practitioner would prescribe. You take more of this than you should and you'll have embarrassing consequences. You could sleep through touchdown, found you've wet yourself, stay groggy for another few hours, suffer amnesia. You could temporarily forget why you were flying to China."

"Not likely."

"I'm just telling you how powerful that stuff is, Boone. At least you'd forget everything we've discussed, forget your contact's name. What your doctor gave you is a hallucinogenic sedative. I'd guess your weight at a tick over two hundred pounds. Close enough?"

"About 210."

"Perfect. Have your dinner. They'll probably serve it during the first hour and a half."

"I'm stuffed, Doc."

"At least have the protein."

"I ordered the chicken."

"Eat as much of that as you can. Then relieve yourself and take one pill. It can take effect within twenty minutes, and you should sleep solid for at least nine hours. You know the rest of the drill."

"Glad I asked."

"Me too. The last thing we need is you stumbling about

in the new Beijing airport, smelling like a bed wetter, and wondering what the heck you're doing there."

In the moments before the doors of the plane were shut, Boone sat staring at the picture of Max. The haircut and color were strange, of course, but Max's sweet naiveté came through even his panicked expression, despite that Boone could read every bit of the tentativeness and curiosity in his eyes. By the time Max had had his hair cut and colored for the passport photo, Kevin Kenleigh had to have weaved a yarn so puzzling that all Max could hope for was to see his mother soon.

And about the time the story would unravel to the point of unbelievability, even for a child, whatever Kenleigh had given Max would have made him too loopy to ask questions.

Boone switched to the photo of Virginia Tuttman and found himself obsessing over how Max might have been drugged. He loved chocolate milk. Had Kenleigh asked what he wanted to drink? Slipped something into it?

Boone hardly knew what do with his swirling emotions. The detective part of him kept all angles bouncing off each other in his brain, while his heart burst with love for and worry over Max. Meanwhile he felt rage for Mannock, for Pitts, and especially for AKA. Why Kenleigh or Knives or Alfonso—or whatever he was going by these days—had taken center stage in Boone's gallery of targets, he didn't know. Maybe because the con had been so slick? To hear Florence tell it, "Alfonso" had won them both over. She and Max had quickly become enamored with him.

And all for what? The same motive as Max's biological father? Greed?

Pastor Sosa had spoken on that subject recently, and Boone had been struck by the fact that so many people misunderstood and misquoted the famous Scripture about it. People often said, "Money is the root of all evil." But Sosa had pointed out that money was merely a tool and could be used for magnificent purposes too. "The Bible does *not* say that money is the root of all evil. It says *the love* of money is. . . ."

Big difference. Pitts, AKA, Mannock, and probably this Tuttman woman, too, all seemed to have the same motive.

There was no sense burning the image of Ms. Tuttman into his consciousness if she was already stateside again. As he sat studying her short, cropped dark hair, hoping he'd see her in person one of these days, the rattling and colliding of all the elements seemed to coalesce. Could these evil ones' greed trip them up?

Boone had imagined somehow getting a bead on where Pitts was, busting in, and doing whatever he had to do to extricate Max. What happened to Pitts or any accomplices would be collateral damage in the strictest sense.

Needless to say, the worst collateral damage would be Max if anything went wrong. Much as Boone loved the idea of attacking, gun blazing if necessary, his priority—his primary goal—was to rescue Max unharmed. He knew the boy was already traumatized. He and Haeley could work through that, finding as much help as necessary. Boone just had to get Max home in one piece.

Sure, justice had to be served too, and Boone longed to have a part in that. People like Pitts and AKA and Mannock and Tuttman had to be stopped and, if not taught a lesson, certainly required to pay for their crimes. Getting those lowlifes off the street might have scant impact on the ugly world of human trafficking, but every little bit helped.

Boone's phone vibrated. A message from Sosa. No Bible reference this time. Just: Praying.

Boone immediately tapped back Enduring, then shut down his phone. He prayed silently, *God, keep me focused. Use whatever gifts you have given me. I'm yours. Be with Max, with Haeley. Somehow let me bring him home to her.*

Jack Keller pulled into the Gents parking lot and found Lefty Tidwell waiting in his unmarked squad next to another with two other Hammond detectives in it. The club sat in a dismal industrial park. As soon as Jack climbed in next to the veteran, Lefty pointed out AKA's car, the one registered to his Bertalay alias.

"Knows how to keep a low profile," Jack said. "I'll give him that." The car was a gray four-door sedan, something a family man might drive. "I see you've got backup."

Lefty nodded. "Need 'em?"

"I might. Do I look too much like a cop to wander in there and see if I can spot Kenleigh?"

Lefty seemed to study Jack. "Guy like AKA would probably make you, yeah."

"What do I need to do then? I don't want to sit here all night waiting for him to stagger out."

"No jacket, no tie, of course. Loosen your top two buttons, untuck your shirt."

"I need my piece. They don't have metal detectors in these places, do they?"

"You've never been?"

"Just on duty and only in Chicago."

"That so? What'sa matter with you, Jack?"

"Never appealed, that's all. I mean, I got nothing against good-looking women, but not at a place like this."

"Real Sunday school teacher."

"Hardly. But can I get in there with a gun in my pocket?"

Tidwell nodded. "Be discreet."

"You wanna come with me?"

Lefty laughed. "I wouldn't mind, but AKA knows me. And it wouldn't surprise me if a lot of the guys in there have been clients of Hammond PD. I'm not exactly anonymous 'round here."

Jack ran a hand through his hair, took off his jacket and tie, unbuttoned and untucked his shirt, and reached for the door handle.

"One more thing," Tidwell said. "No socks."

"Oh, man! I hate wearing shoes with no socks. I don't even like sneakers with no socks."

"Not one person in there will make you for the heat if you're not wearing socks."

Before he left the car, sockless, Jack studied the mug shot of Kevin Samuel Kenleigh stored in his cell phone. The only thing he knew for sure was that—unless Kenleigh had sprayed on his sunburn—he was not going to look pale.

"Have twenty bucks ready and don't look surprised."

"This is a new world for me, Tid."

"Cover charge. Show a receipt for at least three drinks on your way out and they'll give it back."

"I'm already outside my jurisdiction. Drinking on the job too? Good plan."

A little less than ninety minutes into the flight, dinner was served in first class. It was all Boone could do to force down about half the chicken breast with a few sips of water. He pulled out the sheet that told him what to say to passport and customs agents, locked that in, then tore it up. He took the scraps, plus his pill bottle, to the bathroom.

Boone threw his trash away, popped a pill, and checked his watch. Eleven more hours. If the med worked as long as it had the night before, he should awaken with a couple of hours and one meal to go. Back in his seat, he signaled the attendant to remove his tray, kicked off his shoes, untucked his shirt, loosened his belt, situated a pillow, and lowered the chair until he was flat from head to toe. He draped a blanket over himself, then fastened the seat belt around his middle. Boone intertwined his fingers behind his head and stared at the ceiling. He was so spent he wondered if he had really needed a thing to help him sleep. He considered grabbing something to read until he drifted off, but the idea of sitting up to find it did not appeal.

Jack Keller slipped the Gents doorman/bouncer a twenty and nodded as the man welcomed him. The place was crowded and hot, the music deafening. Everything lay in darkness except the stage, which was lit like noon in June.

He found a tiny round table near the back with a single chair and was immediately approached by a scantily clad waitress. When she started listing their beers and cocktails he said, "Diet Coke. Lime."

Her smile faded, and she narrowed her eyes at him. "That doesn't go against your cover charge. You gonna want some company?"

"I'm gonna want the soda and to be left alone."

She formed her mouth into an exaggerated pout and disappeared. Jack fought to adjust to the low light away from the stage, trying to casually scan the room. He saw more than one sunburned young man, but none who looked like Kevin Kenleigh.

Shortly after the girl returned with his Diet Coke and a bill for six dollars, the bouncer pulled up a chair. Jack had to quickly decide how to proceed. "Don't recall inviting you," he said, shouting over the din but careful not to sound threatening.

"C'mon," the man said, "you're not gonna be rude to me too, are you?"

"Too?"

"Weren't you rude to my girl?"

"Just want to be left alone. Waitin' for my buddy."

"Who's your buddy?"

"Goes by Knives."

The bouncer sat back and roared. "Where you know him from?"

"Here and there."

Chuckling now, the bouncer said, "He's already here, dude. In disguise tonight." Jack made a show of looking around. "Shaved his head about a week ago," the guy continued. "Musta got tired of it though. That's him up there with the locks."

Kenleigh sat nursing a beer with his back to the wall near the stage, dreadlocks to his shoulders.

"Want me to tell him you're here?"

Jack nodded, pulling out his cell phone and texting Tidwell. Back door. Dreadlocks.

The bouncer stood. "Name?"

"Alfonso."

"You got it."

As soon as the man headed toward the stage, Jack headed back to the front door and peeked out through the window. Tidwell's plainclothesmen were hurrying through the lot around to the back. Jack stood in the darkness, watching as the bouncer whispered in Kenleigh's ear. He appeared to ask where, and the bouncer jerked a thumb over his shoulder.

Kenleigh rose quickly and bolted for the back door. By the time Jack exited the front and got around the building, Hammond PD had the man on his face, his wig lying in the gravel. When the doorman appeared, Jack flashed his badge. "That'll be all for tonight, Igor. Just go back inside and mind your business, or I'm sure we can find reasons to shut you down."

About ten minutes into Boone's reverie, the shapes and patterns in the plane's ceiling began to swim. He knew it was the drug, but Boone was fascinated that it had begun to affect him even earlier than the night before. He decided to see how long he could resist the effects.

The attendant came by and said, "I assume you don't want to be awakened for the mid-flight snack."

In Boone's mind he was articulating, "That's correct," but he heard himself mumble and shook his head.

"Already out, are we?" she said, smiling. "Unless you tell me otherwise, I'm taking that as a no, you do not want to be awakened."

He nodded. And as he did the attendant leaned close and whispered in his ear. "I don't look like Jammer Pitts, do I?"

Boone tried to sit up, heart pounding. But he felt leaden. He was unarmed. What could he do? Pitts in disguise? A woman? He tried to speak, to protest, to threaten, but his lips would not part. He felt his jaw move, trying to open. His eyes bugged but began blinking slowly.

Somehow Boone forced himself onto his side, facing the aisle. His arm flopped as he reached for the attendant. He flailed at nothing. He wrenched his head to where he could look into business class. There she was, her back to him, attending to other customers. How could she have moved so quickly?

Someone must have asked for something, because she came hurrying past him again toward the front of the cabin. Boone's arm caught her at the knees.

"Excuse me, Mr. Booker! I'm sorry. Need anything?"

He motioned her close and managed, "Wha' d'you ask me?"

"Sorry?"

"You, um, axed a queshion."

"Did you take a sleeping pill, sir?"

He nodded.

"You probably won't remember any of this. I just asked if you wanted another blanket. You shook your head. You want one?"

He shook his head again, his eyes finally surrendering to the light. And as Boone felt himself cascading into a creamy, dreamy cocoon, he realized the flight attendant was no one in disguise. He had merely . . . he had just . . . he was just so, so . . . tired.

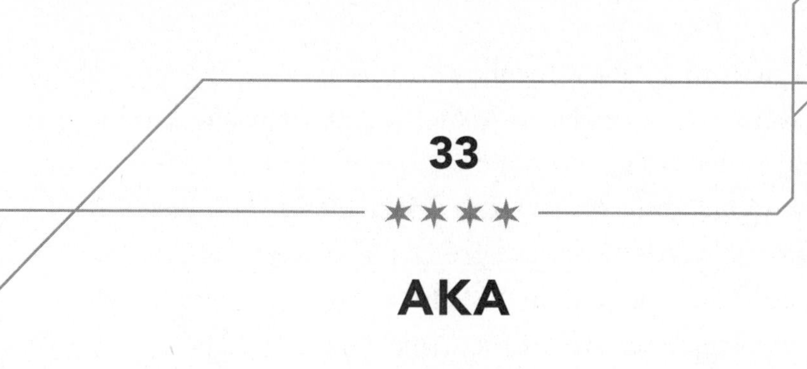

33

★★★★

AKA

"Wait, wait, wait, wait, wait!" Kevin Kenleigh said as Jack Keller helped pull him to his feet. "Don't arrest me, don't read me my rights, and I promise I'll tell you everything I know. I can't go back to prison, man; I just can't."

"Kevin Samuel Kenleigh?" Jack said.

"Yes! Now, please! Don't!"

"AKA Knives?"

"Yes!"

"AKA Johnnie Bertalay?"

"Yes, now don't—"

"AKA Alfonso Lamonica?"

Kenleigh sighed loudly. Keller grabbed his shirt and pulled him close. "You know I need a yes on that one, Kevin."

"Okay! Yes! But don't—"

"You're under arrest for the—"

"Why are you doing this? You Mirandize me and I'll lawyer up and you'll get nothing!"

"—kidnapping of Max Lamonica Drake. You have the right to—"

"See? Now you've done it! Why do you guys always have to be so stupid? I could have made a sweet deal with you, told you more than you need, even. Everything. Man, I got to stay out of the joint."

"Tempting as that is, you're not gonna con me, Kevin. Even if you told me everything from soup to nuts, if I can't say I properly arrested you and read you your rights, you wind up walkin'. I can't have that."

"Sure you can, 'cause I'm small-time. I know who you want, and I can give him to you."

As Tidwell's squad crunched its way around the building to the scene, Kenleigh stood there hands cuffed behind his back, chin tucked to his chest, vigorously shaking his head. Jack completed the Miranda warning and asked if he understood.

"Yes, I do, but you're going to regret this."

Keller asked Tidwell if the two plainclothesmen could deliver Kenleigh back to Hammond, where he and Lefty could interrogate him. The two veterans followed in their own cars, and half an hour later it was just the three of them in an interrogation room about half the size of the one at the 11th in Chicago.

"If I ask Lieutenant Tidwell to uncuff you, will you behave?"

"Yeah."

Tidwell freed him, and Kenleigh flopped loudly into a

chair. "Now we've got to wait for my lawyer. Is that what you wanted?"

"You know what I want, Kevin. The phone's right there. You know all you've got to do is pick it up and get your counsel in here before we can move another inch."

Kenleigh shook his head again. "You could have avoided this."

"C'mon, Knives. You think I'm new at this? I've got to cover my tail just like you do. Now are you calling your man or not?"

"Well, it's a woman, but no. Not yet."

"Are you waiving your right to counsel, and will you talk to us of your own accord?"

Kenleigh looked to the ceiling and appeared to be thinking about it. "I reserve the right to—"

"Stop this and call her at any time, of course," Jack said. "But you stipulate that anything you say in the meantime can and will be used against you in a court of law."

"I do."

"I don't know why, Kevin, but I'm gonna shoot straight with you. And I mean totally straight. I didn't do that with Mannock."

"What an idiot."

"The very reason we misled him. He was easy. We told him whatever we needed to to get him to—"

"Perfectly within your rights," Kenleigh said.

"But let me give you your props before we get too deep into this. I get it. I appreciate your gifts. You're too smart to be misled, to be played. That's why I didn't try to fool with you at the club. I knew as soon as you heard who I said I was, you'd know the jig was up."

Kenleigh nodded and his face softened. Maybe he was easier than Jack had thought. One thing his type loved was appreciation of his skills.

"Lieutenant Tidwell here and I are too old and too tired to play games with you. We're not gonna pull the good cop–bad cop routine, not gonna tell you that we've got everybody else ready to testify against you. But I need to be even straighter with you, Kevin. You want that, don't you?"

"We'll see."

"I'm not gonna blow smoke. You were going back to prison from the minute you took that boy out of the sight of his sitter, and you know it. You may have thought you could pull this off, and maybe now you think you can trade information for your freedom. Well, you can't. You *can* help yourself, and your lawyer would tell you the same. But whether we arrested you or read you your rights or not, nothing was going to be different."

"You don't know what I have to offer."

"I can only imagine. But I'm way past being bribed."

"You wouldn't have been way past the numbers I could have talked about. Think about that when I'm back in Michigan City and you're still covering your beat."

"I only want money I earn, Kevin. Now listen, here's what I'm prepared to offer you."

"I can tell already it doesn't sound like much."

"If you don't want to hear it, fine."

"I'm listening."

Jack signaled Tidwell to hand him a legal pad, and he pulled out a pen. "I'm prepared to put in my own handwriting a document you and your lawyer can present to any prosecutor or judge and even enter as evidence at trial. It will stipulate that you cooperated to the fullest extent and that you should be accorded every accommodation possible in your sentencing."

"What'll that get me?"

"I told you I wouldn't make empty promises, Kevin. But you know what I need. I'll tell you everything we know up to this point; you tell me everything you can about what's to happen next. If and when we get that boy back and have the perpetrator in custody, I sign this document."

"All those words and you still didn't answer my question," Kenleigh said.

"I can't answer it. I'm not a lawyer. You're a chronic, repeat offender. But kidnapping is the most serious rap on your sheet, and I'm not going to sit here and tell you that any judge worth his robe is going to let you plead down to probation on a charge like that. I'm gonna say this one more time, just so we're crystal clear: this is all predicated on your giving up Pitts and helping us get Max back. Then, if I was a betting man, I'd say that you might get your sentence reduced from life to something more akin to a slightly lesser offense."

"Like what?"

"Well, the abduction of a minor for reward constitutes aggravated kidnapping, a felony in the first degree. That's typically punishable by life in prison. We've got too much on you for you to credibly be able to say you voluntarily released the victim in a safe place, which might get your charge reduced to a second-degree felony.

"The problem is, we recorded you telling one of your accomplices that you knew where the victim was headed and what his predicament would be."

"Which is not dangerous to him, by the way."

"Because now he gets to live in luxury, is that it?"

"Just sayin'."

"That's not the kind of an attitude that's going to get a prosecutor, and certainly not a judge, to consider a lesser charge."

"Then what is?"

"Some show of remorse, but mostly cooperation that goes beyond our having to plead for it. Here's the deal, Kevin. You have come to realize the enormity of your crime. You can't believe what you have put this child through. You know you can't change your part in it, but you are now willing to do absolutely everything in your power to get that kid back where he belongs."

Jack let silence hang in the air. After a beat, during which Kenleigh appeared to seriously weigh his options, Jack said, "Listen, you know this has all been recorded. I'm willing to let your lawyer hear it and advise you. She's going to want to know what we have on you, and I'm happy to give her every detail. She'll agree with us, Kevin. She'll urge you to help yourself."

Kenleigh nodded, but that wasn't good enough for Jack. He didn't want Kenleigh to merely accede to this, be forced into it. He wanted the man to embrace it, to enthusiastically change his mind, to throw himself into giving Jack everything he needed.

"You know what happens when somebody kills a cop, don't you, Kevin? It brings us together like nothing else. Everybody responds; everybody rallies. Well, let me tell you, kidnapping a cop's kid is the same thing. You were never going to get away with this. There was nowhere to hide."

"Let me call my lawyer."

Jack turned the phone around and slid it in front of him.

Constance Wells proved to be a heavyset woman of about fifty, no makeup, no jewelry, and wearing a black sweat suit. "Give me a minute with my client," she said.

Jack and Lefty exited, but they could hear the conversation. "I'm just thrilled to be called away from home at this time of night, Kevin. What now?"

"Felony kidnapping, and I'm guilty. This is about damage control now."

"Have you said anything?"

"They got me, Connie. Thing is, they want more, and they're saying it's the only thing that'll help me."

"I smell liquor on you. I can get them for coercing a confession from an inebriated man."

"I think you'd better listen to how it went down."

Ms. Wells turned toward the two-way mirror and beckoned Keller and Tidwell. "Let me hear it," she said.

"Can I ask you something first?" Keller said.

"It depends."

"Are you a mother?"

"I'm not only a mother, Chief. I'm a grandmother. Why?"

"Just curious."

Tidwell brought her into the next room and issued her a set of earphones. She sat at a small desk and took notes. Jack camped out where he could watch Kenleigh—who seemed to be dozing—and his counsel, who seemed to be writing faster as the recording went on.

When she finally removed the buds from her ears, Constance Wells, Esq., sat writing some more. And shaking her head. Finally she rose and made her way across the hall. As she passed Jack she said, "You're a very lucky man."

"How so?"

"I'm not a religious woman," she said, "but I know that one verse from the Bible, the one the CIA has in its foyer, about truth. It says something about that you shall know the truth and the truth shall set you free. You're lucky because I was going to play the jurisdiction card on you."

"Kidnapping and crossing state lines, not to mention national borders—"

"Trumps that; yeah, I know. But I'm really good at throwing wrenches into the cogs of the legal system when it suits me. Making you claw your way out of a jurisdiction bag would have been fun to watch, but we clearly don't have time for that, do we?"

"Not if we want that kid back," Jack said.

"Give me another minute with Kevin."

He appeared to rouse when she opened the door. "We bothering you?"

"No. Just hammered."

"You ought to be."

"What?"

"Why did you come back to me, Kevin? I wasn't able to keep you out of prison the last two times. Isn't it time you gave up on me?"

"Nah. Those were my fault, not yours."

"Well, so's this one, and you know it, don't you?"

He nodded.

"Keller shot straight with you, and he's right. Best you can do now is cooperate. You ready to do that?"

"Yeah."

"Do this because it's right. And I'll help Keller draft that document he promised so it'll do you the best good. I don't know if I can get this down to second-degree, but that'll be my aim. Even that carries a whopper of a sentence."

"How long?"

She shrugged. "You may still serve twenty years."

"Wow."

"You deserve it."

"Hey, you're my lawyer! You supposed to say that?"

"It's something I've never told a client. Now do the right thing, and do it fast."

The cops joined them, and Jack pulled out all his notes. He had Kenleigh walk him through the kidnapping from the time he met Jasper "Jammer" Pitts to the afternoon he delivered Max Drake to the woman who called herself Virginia Tuttman.

As forthcoming as Kevin Samuel Kenleigh, AKA Knives, AKA Johnnie Bertalay, AKA Alfonso Lamonica was, Keller was frustrated to discover that even his knowledge of the Max Drake abduction virtually ended with his delivery of the boy to Ms. Tuttman at O'Hare.

"I hadn't met her before," Kenleigh said. "All I knew was that she worked for Jammer. I got the impression she was like his personal assistant, handled all the paperwork, and had done lots of deliveries of kids, overseas and back. Maybe she's like his office manager? One time, when Pitts was in a good mood and maybe a little lubricated—he wasn't much of a drinker as a rule—he said something about how he gets to Asia on his own for the big transactions and she accompanies the kids in case anybody's watching."

Jack narrowed his eyes at Kenleigh. "We found she came back on the next available flight. Are you saying Pitts got to

Beijing before she did and was waiting to pick Max up at the airport?"

Constance Wells interrupted. "He's telling you all he knows, Chief. How would he know what happened halfway around the world?"

"I've got to ask, counselor. I'm trying to make this make sense and see how many people are working with Pitts on the other end."

"You can ask," she said, "but you know Mr. Kenleigh is just guessing now."

"We're all just guessing now," Lefty Tidwell said, and Jack noticed that both Kenleigh and Wells looked up quickly, as Jack had, having nearly forgotten the old Hammond detective was there. Lefty wasn't one to say much, but he tended to nail the truth when he did. "Am I right?"

Jack nodded and looked at his watch. "We're thirteen hours behind China," he said. "I've got to talk with this Tuttman woman."

Wells interrupted only a few more times with minor legal clarifications. When it was over, she followed the cops out into the corridor and left Kenleigh at the table.

"I know what you guys think of defense attorneys," she said. "Some nights I feel the same about myself and my kind. We make you guys pay for your mistakes, and sometimes bad guys walk. But I'm going to sleep well tonight. I hope we just did something good in there."

34

★★★★

LORELEI

JULY 3

Boone awoke, at first unable to move or open his eyes. It was as if his lids had been glued shut. The more he tried to force them open, the more of an ordeal it became. He sensed the cabin was dark, but he wanted to look at his watch. Maybe if he raised his arm to his face he could make out the iridescent hands. But Boone couldn't even lift his arm.

This reminded him of the drug-induced haze following his shoulder surgery and how long he had taken to recover from the anesthetic. It was as if he was there but not there. Now Boone felt he could sleep another few hours. But if nine hours had passed, it was time to start getting himself together. Hunger made him believe it *was* time to rise, but clearly, he was going to have to take this in stages. That much sleep should have been invigorating, and perhaps it would eventually prove so. But now he felt merely thick and slow.

The smell of food finally roused him at least one level closer to full consciousness. Boone balled his fists, then straightened his fingers, rolled his ankles, and finally lifted his knees. It was as if he could feel his circulatory system come to life. He forced open his eyes. The flight attendants were tiptoeing about, asking people if they wanted the final meal before landing. Finally able to look at his watch, Boone found it was 10:30 p.m., China time. He found the controls on his seat and held the button until he was sitting up.

"How are we doing, Mr. Booker?" the attendant said.

Boone nodded.

"We had a strange conversation before you fell asleep."

"I remember. Sorry."

"Who's Haeley?"

"My wife."

"She in China?"

"No. Couldn't come."

"Well, you're eager to see her."

"Always."

"Sweet. And Max?"

"My son. In China. Eager to see him too."

"And Pitt? Or Pitts?"

Boone shrugged, alarmed. Doc hadn't told him he might give away his whole case on this drug. "Got me," he said.

The attendant chuckled. "You'd be surprised what people do on sleeping pills. Now how about a little food? Fresh fruit, cheese, crackers, and a warm chocolate chip cookie sound good?"

It sounded like heaven. But again, Boone felt guilty enjoying anything. Strange that the whole world hadn't stopped spinning when he and Haeley had lost Max.

After people had eaten and the trays were cleared, and before the final seat belt light had been illuminated, Boone tested his legs with another bathroom visit. It was a trek at first, and he had to steady himself on others' chairs on the way. But by the time he returned to his seat, forced his shoes back on—they seemed to have shrunk two sizes—and checked his duffel bag, Boone had begun to really awaken. He was eager to land, to get through customs, and to meet his contact. It was time to get this show out of the air and onto the road.

Kevin Kenleigh had been kept overnight in Hammond and transported to central booking in Chicago the next day. Jack left voice messages for Antoine Johnson and Ragnar Waldemarr to keep them fully informed.

At six the next morning in Chicago, Jack was awakened by a call from Detective Johnson. "Had me a brainstorm," Antoine said. "I'm going to that cafe in Burr Ridge where everybody seemed to know Pitts."

"Jarvis's?"

"Yeah. If she's been working with him, someone there might recognize her."

"Good idea. Remember she's probably wearing a wig in that passport photo, and the glasses could be phony."

Jack, at wit's end and not knowing what rock to turn over

next, headed toward the Burr Ridge/Clarendon Hills area. If Antoine got a lead on Virginia Tuttman, Jack didn't want to waste time getting there. He was twenty minutes from the Jarvis Cafe when he got a text from Johnson: Call me.

"Give me some good news," Jack said.

"Get this, Chief. I think I'm strikin' out, right? The place is hopping for breakfast, everybody busy and running. The waitresses seem really put out that I'm asking them to look at this picture. Finally the cook, who I think owns the place, comes stormin' out and demands to know what I want, am I gonna order breakfast, or can they all get back to work.

"I tell him I'm just looking for this woman, and if he doesn't recognize her, I'll get out of his hair. He gives me this frustrated, skeptical look like he just knows he's not going to have a clue, but as soon as he sees the picture he says, 'Wow, is her name Shearson?'

"I say, 'Could be. You know her?'

"He says, 'No, but she could be Lorelei Shearson's sister, maybe even her twin. 'Course, Lorelei don't wear glasses and has lighter hair, but these two got to be sisters.'

"So I ask him is Lorelei local, and he says, 'Yeah, lives about a mile from here. She works with adoptions, you know.'"

"You're kidding," Jack said.

"That's what he said, Chief. I go, 'Well, I'm really looking for this woman here.'

"He says, 'I never seen her I don't think, but Lorelei would get a kick outta seein' somebody that looks so much like her.'"

"You get a phone number or an address?"

"I didn't want to spook him or have him tell her someone was looking for her. I just called information. I'm sitting in the parking lot of her apartment building right now. Gotta tell ya, it's some complex. Real money lives here."

Antoine gave Jack directions, and a few minutes later they sat together in Johnson's unmarked squad, in the shadows of gleaming towers. "We've got to play this right," Jack said. "The last thing we want is to have her on the run or calling Pitts."

"What time is it in China?"

"Late at night."

Antoine sat nodding. "Trust me?"

"Trust you? You're good enough for Drake's team, you're good enough for me."

"Let me try something." He put his cell phone on speaker and punched in the number for Lorelei Shearson of Burr Ridge.

She answered, clearly in a hurry.

"Ms. Shearson?"

"Yes, who's this?"

"Name's Johnson. I got your number from someone at Jarvis's Cafe who said you might be able to help me."

"Could you call me in a half hour or so? I'm on my way out the door to work, and if this is about adopting—"

"It is."

"—well, you came to the right place. But I can be much more helpful at my desk, all right? Here's the number."

"Thank you, ma'am."

Antoine slapped his phone shut and looked to Jack. "She sound suspicious?"

"Not in the least."

"That her?" he said, nodding at a fortyish woman, short blonde hair, no glasses, laden with purse, attaché, and what looked like a box of printing paper. She tossed everything in the passenger seat of a late-model sports car.

Jack grabbed the microphone from Antoine's radio and asked dispatch to run the plate while the woman was sliding behind the wheel. Johnson threw the squad into Drive, but Jack held up a hand. "Let's be sure we're following the right car," he said. "No time to be wrong now."

The woman paused at a stop sign a block away, and just as the brake lights went out and she began to ease into traffic, the radio squawked with the year, make, and model of the car, registered to Shearson, Lorelei, then gave her address and date of birth.

Antoine Johnson followed her toward Clarendon Hills. "We tail her into Pitts's place, Chief, she's going to panic and try to get hold of him."

Jack nodded, pulled a portable, revolving blue light from the floor, fed the connector into the cigarette lighter, and set the light on the dash. "Light 'er up, Detective," he said, and Antoine floored the accelerator.

The unmarked squad was on the tail of the sports car in seconds, and Johnson flipped the siren switch on and off, causing it to emit one piercing whoop. The sports car immediately pulled over.

"I'll stall her," Jack said as he opened the door. "Call the DuPage County Sheriff's Office and tell them we need a matron fast. Anybody gives you any trouble, tell 'em we've worked with Deputy Harry Landmeir before."

"Landmeir, got it."

Jack stood slightly behind the driver's side window as the driver lowered it. "Good morning, ma'am. Officer Keller of the Chicago Police Department. May I see your license and registration please?"

"Sure," she said, digging in her purse, then in her glove box. "Was I speeding?"

"No, ma'am. Just noticed your taillight out and wanted to let you know before it caused you any problem."

"Well, thank you, but did you say Chicago?"

Jack moved next to her so he could see her face. "Yes, ma'am."

"What're you doing out this way?" she said, pleasantly.

"Just here on some routine business, but like I say, I noticed the light."

"I really appreciate this."

"Now, of course I'm not going to ticket you, but now that we've stopped you, I do have to make sure you are who you say you are and not an auto thief."

Ms. Shearson chuckled. "Whatever you need to do."

"Ma'am, may I see your cell phone too?"

"My phone? Whatever for?"

"Just need to check it. Make sure you weren't texting while driving."

She hesitated. "Am I out of order asking to see your badge?"

"Oh, not at all. In fact that's wise." Jack pulled out his badge wallet and also showed her his CPD identification card. "If you'd like to call and verify that I am who I say I am, you should certainly feel free to do that."

"No, I guess it's all right."

"When was the last time you were pulled over, ma'am?"

"Oh, it's been years," she said, handing him her phone. "And you'll see I wasn't using the phone. I'm a good girl."

"I'm sure you are. I'll be right back."

Antoine Johnson raised a brow when he saw her phone. "Couldn't risk her trying to get hold of Pitts," Jack said. "Matron coming?"

"Any second."

"Did you have to play the Landmeir card?"

"I did, but that was all it took."

Jack wanted to stall until the matron arrived. He didn't want one technicality jeopardizing this arrest. But neither did he want to further alarm Lorelei Shearson. He was already pushing the boundaries with the phone ruse.

Jack pulled down the passenger-side visor and checked the mirror for a DuPage County sheriff's car. Nothing. He approached Ms. Shearson's car again. "Are you still living at this address, ma'am?"

"Yes, now can I go? I really have to get to work."

Finally, Jack heard gravel crunching behind him. And Lorelei Shearson quickly looked in her rearview mirror. "What's this now?"

"Just another minute, ma'am. Sorry for the inconvenience."

Jack hurried back to the deep blue sheriff's squad as a stocky black woman slid out, inserting her nightstick through a ring hanging from her belt and pulling on her cap. "Female arrest?" she said.

"Yes, thank you. We're hoping to interrogate her in her own home."

"At your service for as long as you need me, sir."

Back with Ms. Shearson, Jack said, "Step out of the car, please, ma'am."

"What the—?"

"A female officer is here to pat you down."

"In public?" she said, getting out. "What for?"

"Face the vehicle, please," the woman officer said, "hands on the roof, feet back and spread 'em."

"I demand to know—"

"Lorelei Shearson," Jack began, "AKA Virginia Tuttman, you're under arrest for the kidnapping of . . ."

Shearson's knees buckled as soon as Jack had used her alias, and she began a slow slide down the side of her car. The sheriff's deputy grabbed under her arms and wrenched her back up, finishing the search as Jack finished the Miranda warning, then cuffed her.

"Do you understand these rights as I have read them to you?"

Ms. Shearson nodded, weeping.

"I need an audible yes, ma'am."

"Yes."

"Having these rights in mind, do you wish to talk with us now?"

"Yes, I do."

"I want to make this as easy on you as possible. Would you be most comfortable in your own home?"

"I can do that?"

"Absolutely. You'll ride with the deputy here, and we'll meet you there."

"Do I have to go inside in handcuffs?"

"No. There will be three of us with you, so we don't expect any trouble. I can't guarantee your neighbors won't notice you with the deputy, but, ma'am, I must tell you, it appears you have acted as an accessory to kidnapping that includes international travel and human trafficking. Embarrassment should be the least of your worries."

Jack was not surprised that Lorelei Shearson lived in a penthouse. "Just you here?" he said.

She nodded, pale and quivering.

He had her right where he wanted her. And he was going to be extremely careful not to talk her into calling a lawyer. Still, he had to cover his bases.

"Is there a table we could all sit at, ma'am?"

She led them to the kitchen, her gait unsure, as if she was aware she might never see this place again.

"Detective Johnson, could you see about a warrant? I don't want to toss this place, even with Ms. Shearson's permission, without legal cover."

"Please," she whined. "I keep no records here. Everything is at my office."

"Before we go on," Jack said, pulling out a legal pad, "I just want to clarify on the record that you acknowledge that I advised you of your rights, you stipulated that you understood those rights, and that I further asked if, with those rights in mind, you were willing to talk with us."

"Yes, sir."

Jack looked to the deputy and to Antoine, already on the phone, and they both nodded. He wasn't going to push her as he had DeWayne Mannock and Kevin Kenleigh. She was making a terrible mistake, sure, but it was on Jack only to make her fully cognizant of her rights, not to insist that she exercise them.

"Ms. Shearson, our records show that you have never been arrested before."

"Never. Not for anything."

"That's in your favor."

"Is it?"

"Yes, ma'am, but let me be straight with you. You are being charged with a serious crime, a first-degree felony. You have to know that we have solid evidence against you, and I think we all know that you're in this up to your neck. You're guilty. That this is a first offense isn't much help in light of such charges, but the more help you can be to us, the more help you can be to yourself. Understand?"

"I think so."

"Are you aware that the kidnapped child is the son of a Chicago police officer?"

She looked stricken, and she swore. "My boss must not know that either. He would never—"

"Ma'am, I'm going ask you to walk me through every detail of this abduction, and we'll eventually get to the rest of Mr. Pitts's activities. But I'm most concerned with the disposition of Max Lamonica Drake. I need to know where he is, who he's with, and what is supposed to become of him. If you give me anything less than what we need to bring that boy home safely, I will personally see to it that you spend the rest of your life in prison."

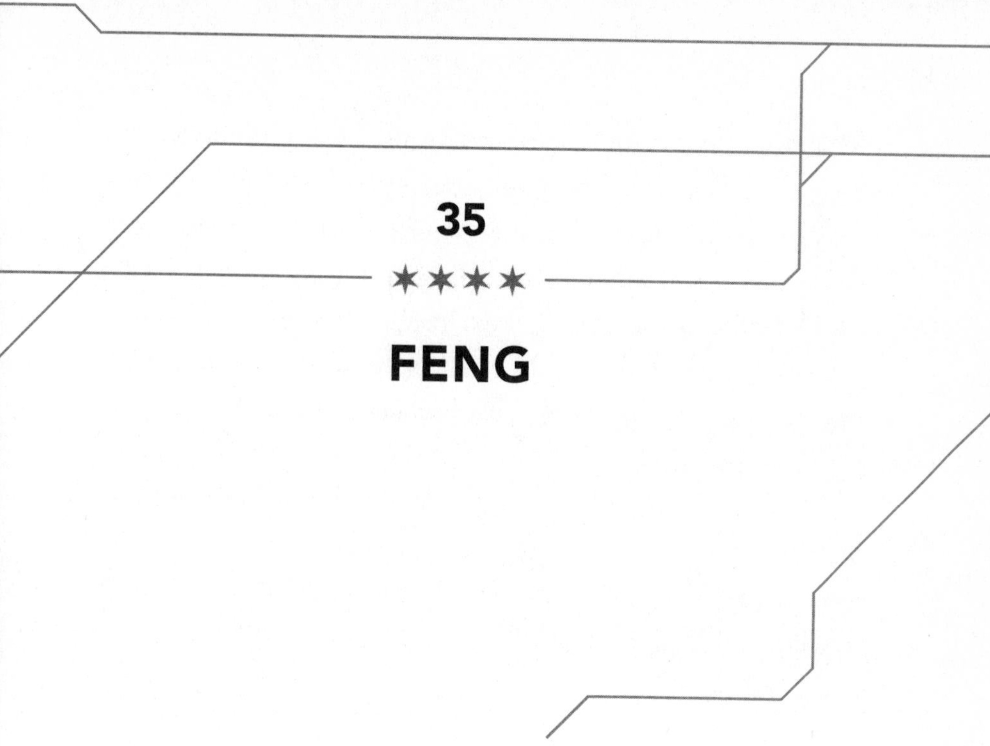

35

★★★★

FENG

Boone was certain he was among only a handful aboard who bore only one carry-on. Most passengers disembarked with a couple apiece and still headed toward baggage claim. Wanting a shower and a change of clothes, Boone was eager to get through the red tape.

While Boone had not been to as many countries as his passport indicated, he'd had experience with customs and passport agents in Canada, Mexico, England, Spain, and the United States and had noticed they seemed to share the bored gene. Maybe that was a cover for alertness, because surely they were closely monitored, and no one wanted to be responsible for allowing in a threat to their country.

By the time he reached the passport desk, Boone had seen

several dozen young men who could have convinced him they were Feng Li. The young women all seemed dramatically beautiful with almond eyes, perfect skin, gleaming teeth. And everyone seemed to have the same straight black hair.

The passport agent wore what appeared to be a tailored uniform, and while he sported the requisite detached air, Boone thought the young man looked like a twelve-year-old playing dress-up.

He deftly opened Boone's passport with one hand without looking at it and slid it into a scanner. He pulled it out and looked between the photo and Boone's face. "Welcome to the People's Republic of China, Mr. Booker. What brings you here?"

"Sightseeing."

"What is your business?"

"Sports catalog publishing. But not this trip."

"Pleasure?"

Merely nodding proved Boone's most difficult lie. Pleasure was the last thing on his mind, unless and until he came back through this airport with Max in hand.

"You have only the one bag?"

"Yes, sir."

"I see no return date."

"I can't stay long."

"And you're staying where?"

"With a friend."

"Name?"

"Mr. Feng Li."

"Occupation?"

"Tour guide."

"Address?"

"I know only his e-mail address. I expect I'll visit his home tonight."

"How will you get there if you don't know—"

"He's meeting me here."

"And if he does not arrive?"

Boone hadn't thought of that or been prepared to answer it. "Then I'll sample one of your many fine hotels. What would you recommend?"

"I am not permitted to suggest places of business, sir, but you are correct. There are many fine places to stay."

Because of having just the one bag, Boone was first in line, but now people were lining up behind him. The agent stamped a page in the back of his passport and pointed him to customs. "Enjoy your visit, Mr. Booker."

Because he was on his way into the country rather than on his way out, Boone's declaration form was just a formality. His bag would be scanned and searched anew, though this had been done in Chicago too. The customs agent noted Boone's single bag as the passport guy had. "You travel light. Not staying long?"

"Just a few days. First time. Can't wait."

Though the bag had not seemed to cause any concern to the employee peering through the monitor, the customs agent pulled it off the belt and dug through it. He looked up, clearly surprised, when he found Boone's phone.

"American, right?" he said, turning it on.

"Yes."

"Phone still off? Most Americans turn phone on right away."

"Don't even know if it works here," Boone said.

"It does!" the agent said, turning it so Boone could see his messages piling up. "Popular man."

Boone shrugged. He knew the messages would be either innocuous or refer only obliquely to info that had been forwarded to Feng Li. The agent flipped the phone shut, placed it back in Boone's carry-on, and closed the bag without another word. He left the duffel on the counter and walked away.

Boone waited a beat, then grabbed the bag and followed the exit signs. He pulled out the phone and scanned the list of messages. It was 10 a.m. the day before in Chicago, thirteen hours behind Beijing. By the time Boone was asleep, probably around 1 a.m., in China, it would be high noon in Chicago. He'd heard from all the usual suspects, but Boone also knew they were listening in, waiting until it was clear he was the only one with access to his phone.

After a few hundred more feet, Boone began scanning the crowd for Feng Li, but hundreds of young Chinese men around him looked like the picture he had committed to memory.

Boone's advantage was that he was distinctive even among all the Westerners getting off late-night flights. Feng Li shouldn't have trouble recognizing him by his height and build, and he, too, had been transmitted a photo.

Despite knowing he would soon have an aide who knew both the language and the locale—not to mention whatever leads Boone was to follow—he was suddenly nearly bowled over by a desolate loneliness. Boone had never been so far from home, from his loved ones, from his colleagues and friends. And there was a desperation about his mission he could barely get his mind around. How in the world was he supposed to find his son in this massive metropolis, fourteen times bigger than New York City and with two and half times the population?

As he strode through the cavernous, space-age terminal, feeling smaller and more insignificant with each step, Boone became aware of something peculiar. Any public announcement—and there seemed to be two or three every few minutes—was preceded by four musical tones over the loudspeaker system. The first few times the tones barely registered with Boone, and they were followed by announcements in Chinese, English, and he thought he also recognized French among a few others.

Waldemarr had told Boone he would find Feng Li's English entertaining, but Boone also found the PA translations unique. "Please to check in your oversized baggages." "Before you leave the terminal, make sure you have all your belongs."

The next time the tones sounded, a sense of peace flooded Boone and suddenly eradicated his feeling of isolation. What was it? Those tones sounded like the first four notes of a tune he recognized, something from home. From church! He hummed them to himself and found himself singing under his breath,

Under his wings I am safely abiding,
Though the night deepens and tempests are wild.
Still I can trust him; I know he will keep me.
He has redeemed me, and I am his child.

Finally Boone spotted a cadre of drivers and tour guides bunched along one wall. There, in front, with a crude, handwritten cardboard sign reading *Booker*, stood a young man who looked like a college student. He wore flip-flops, cargo shorts, and a red polo shirt and carried a forest-green backpack. The Feng Li of Dr. Waldemarr's photo greeted Boone with what looked like a shy smile. Boone stuck out his hand, but Feng ignored it and reached for his duffel bag.

"No problem, I've got it," Boone said.

"Sorry. Must take. Look strange. Custom."

Boone felt funny, letting a man half his size lug a heavy bag while he followed. Feng kept glancing back and smiling as he hurried out. "Sorry. You understand. Must not bring attention. Guides carry bags."

"No problem," Boone said.

"Car and driver wait down here," Feng said. "He work for tour company. You Booker unless we're privacy."

"Got it."

Boone found it strange, however, as they made their way through the crowds on this hot, humid night, that Feng did not introduce him to the driver of a tan minivan. He was a heavier, older man who looked half-asleep. "How ya doin'?" Boone said as Feng deposited his bag in the rear and Boone climbed into the air-conditioned backseat. The man nodded without looking at him.

Feng sat in the front passenger seat, and though he buckled himself in, he was able to turn almost completely around to face Boone. Boone nodded at the driver and said, "English?"

Feng shook his head and held up his thumb and forefinger, separated by a quarter inch. "You comfort, Mr. Booker?"

Boone assured him he was, and the minivan pulled into airport traffic that would surely dissipate once they were on their way into Beijing proper. But no; if anything, as the driver painstakingly merged onto the main thoroughfare, the traffic only intensified.

"Lots of cars for this time of night?" Boone said.

"No!" Feng said. "Traffical jams common all day."

"And all night?"

"Twenty-four hours. Wait till you see CBD. Central Business District has four millions cars, eight lanes traffics each direction."

As the minivan crawled along, Boone became concerned about the driver, who seemed to be nodding. Boone touched Feng's shoulder and mouthed, "He awake?"

"Sometimes I talk loud just to make sure!" Feng shouted, and the driver came to attention. Feng laughed heartily. "None accidents so far."

Boone muttered, "So far," and Feng erupted again.

"Where are we going?" Boone said.

Feng raised his brows and looked first at the driver, then at Boone, speaking quickly and quietly. "First part of *tour* is CBD, then release car and take short-distance walk."

"Your place?" Boone said.

Feng held a finger to his lips. "I will take you to where you stay, talk some more, arrange tomorrow." And again, as if to appease or reassure the driver that everything was normal, Feng said, "*Beijing* mean northern capital. Second-largest city in largest country. Only Shanghai largester."

Boone idly pulled a handkerchief from his pocket and held

it to his nose. He hesitated when Feng looked stricken. "Please! Not like United States. Bad taste to blow nose in public."

"Fair enough," Boone said, merely wiping his nose. "Thanks."

Just then the driver opened his window, loudly cleared his throat, and spat.

Boone winced. "But that's okay?"

Feng looked surprised that he had asked.

"How far are we going?" Boone said.

"Twenty-six kilometers," Feng said. "Uh, fifteen miles. One hour."

"An hour to go fifteen miles?"

"Yes! Lucky!"

As if to keep his cover in front of the driver, Feng continued his tour guide patter as they approached the city center. "Closer we get to CBD, rent is more the higher but not too much more tree." He pointed out a swimming pool outside a high-rise luxury hotel. "Not for enjoy the swim at noontime. Too much the hot. And never in winter. Drain water so none the freeze."

At a stoplight near the CBD, the minivan waited first in line in one of the lanes. Other cars inched forward, cheating into the intersection and making pedestrians walk around them. When one man stumbled getting around a taxi in the next lane, he steadied himself on the minivan before moving on. Feng's driver immediately laid on the horn, startling the man and making him brandish his fist and shout.

The driver rolled down his window and screamed as the man crossed the street.

"What was that about?" Boone said, as the driver closed

his window and seemed to be peeking sheepishly in the rear-view mirror.

Feng shrugged. "Japanese."

"That man was Japanese?"

Feng nodded. "You know, the Japanese people never did say the sorry for occupying."

"When was that?" Boone said.

"Fifteen years, from early of the 1930s to middles of the 1940s. Many millions killed."

"That guy looked about your age, Feng. Neither of you was even born then."

"Should still say the sorry."

At long last, at just after one in the morning, Feng spoke to the driver in Chinese, and he laboriously pulled off the main thoroughfare and onto a street crowded on both sides by parked cars. He continued to drive as if in what Feng referred to as a traffical jam, despite that the street was otherwise deserted.

"We get out here," Feng said. "We walk now."

Feng jumped out and opened Boone's door. Boone thanked the driver, who did not respond.

"Not a cheerful guy," Boone whispered as Feng fetched his bag out of the back and slammed the hatch.

"He finally go home now. Eighteen-hour shift."

"And we're going where?"

"My place first, then yours."

"Have you heard from Chicago?"

"Oh yes. Big news."

36

★★★★

HUTONG

Feng Li's mention of a short-distance walk had to have been for the benefit of the driver too, for it wasn't so short, and it wasn't all walking. As they brushed past many others in the street, Boone quickly checked his messages. Jack's and Margaret's both read: Refer to Doc's.

Waldemarr's said, FL will bring you up to date.

When they were alone, Feng spoke quickly in his personal brand of English, telling Boone that he had heard that the police detective had a "photographical memory" and that he was confident Boone would retain everything he was explaining.

"We will walk to the subway, then ride several kilometers to my stop, walk to my apartment, and I will give you the gun. You will stay about six kilometers' walk from me—"

Three and a half miles? Some short walk.

"—and we will meet in the middles of the morning for the train ride."

"Another train ride?"

"To Tianjin," Feng said. "A smaller city. Only ten to twelve of the millions."

"More like a village," Boone said.

Feng stopped and stared at him. "Much largers than a village."

"I was kidding," Boone said. "Much larger than any city in the US. What's there?"

"Your Chicago people say the transfer to happen at Astor Hotel there."

"Transfer?"

"Of the boy."

Boone felt gobsmacked. After all this, they knew where Max was to be transferred? He stood speechless.

"I show you messages at my place," Feng said. "Bullet train will take us only less than one hour. Hundreds kilometers per hour."

"And we'll get there how long before this transfer?"

"Many hours. Boy to be delivered just after dark. Maybe eight o'clock."

Feng said this so casually that Boone wondered if the man had any idea how monumental the news was. As Boone hurried to keep up with Feng, he wondered if he had misheard due to the language barrier. Just before they got to the subway stairs several miles away, Boone took Feng's arm and pulled him off the sidewalk into a shadowy area, tall shrubs blocking the street lamp. "Are you telling me my son is in Tianjin and is to be handed over to his new parents tomorrow evening?"

Feng nodded. "Wang and Bai Xing. You understand more when you read messages. Mother will not be there. Only Wang, the father. Very rich. Owns computer software company. Speak very good English."

"And where are they from?"

"Xi'an, over six hundred miles from here."

It was too much to take in. Feng was clearly not prepared to be more specific until he was safely in his own home. He bought Boone a subway ticket and used his own card for himself, and soon they were pushing into the shoulder-to-shoulder car. Some people were sitting, but Boone could hardly see how. He towered over the tiny Chinese, who rolled their eyes and seemed to look at him with amusement.

Forty minutes later he and Feng were deposited at a station where they climbed three flights of stairs and emerged into a brightly lit business area. Boone could scarcely believe it, but Dr. Waldemarr's prediction was coming true. He actually felt as if he could sleep again.

Feng led Boone on another long walk, this time through a *hutong*. "I've heard of these," Boone said.

"Very the famous," Feng said. "Especially in Beijing. Centuries old. Once were nice neighborhoods. Now mostly slums."

The narrow alleyways connected hovels that Feng explained had running water for public bathrooms only every one or two hundred meters. As they passed one tiny living space, Feng said, "Woman teach calligraphy to tour groups for pennies."

"How long is this?"

"Another one and a half kilometers."

"Feng, I need you to fill me in about tomorrow. Can we take a cab or—"

"Rickshaw," Feng said. "Much the faster. Avoid traffical jam."

They had their choice of bicycle-powered rickshaws at the next minuscule intersection. The bare-bones bench seat felt as if it might give way under Boone's weight, especially after Feng jumped in next to him. The ancient cyclist said something to Feng in Chinese.

"Want to know you want guided tour. I tell him no."

"Good. Is he taking us all the way to your place?"

"Almost. Not allowed outside hutong."

Boone nodded, hoping his silence alone would motivate the cyclist. But the man had his own plodding pace, and nothing seemed to affect that.

"Would he go faster if I gave him a tip?"

"Not the advised. Offensive."

So's his speed.

They climbed out at the edge of the hutong, and Feng said, "Half block now."

The miniature flats on that side of the street didn't look much different from what they had just walked and ridden through. "Is this another hutong?"

Feng shook his head. "Strange to think about. Hutong means water well, but hutong have very little water. This not hutong. Each apartment have the water."

"Is there a reason I'm not staying with you?"

"Too much the small."

Small didn't begin to describe Feng's place. His multi-locked door opened into a kitchen so tiny that two chairs and a table filled it. Every food item Feng owned appeared to have been crammed into a cupboard above a rudimentary icebox of no more than two feet square.

Feng pointed Boone to the shower, such as it was. The nozzle protruded from the wall between the sink and the toilet. There was no tub, no stall, and no curtain.

"Where does the water go?"

"Drain in floor," Feng said, pointing. "I visit America one time. Closets bigger than my bathroom. But luxury here."

A nail had been driven into the other side of the bathroom door. "For clothes," Feng said. "See bedroom?"

Feng's single bed pressed against one tall, narrow box of shelves that appeared to contain all his worldly goods. "No family?" Boone said.

"Long time ago."

Boone remembered that this collegiate-looking guy was forty-one.

"You want take shower? No shower at hotel."

"I'll just need one again in the morning. Can I come back then?"

"Okay! We talk now."

"Please."

Feng directed Boone into the bedroom, pointed to one end of the bed, and sat on the other. He handed Boone his phone.

All the lists and texts appeared in Chinese characters. Feng laughed. Boone shook his head. He didn't want to scold his host, but there was nothing funny about any of this.

Feng took back the phone and muttered as he punched buttons. "Translate and transmit."

Boone's phone vibrated, and he eagerly accessed the text from Waldemarr. It read:

> Success, success, success! Other side got sloppy. Knives made a call to Mannock, which gave Jack a location on him. Surrendered without a fight and Jack says he told all. Why and how later. Also found Tuttman. Never apprehended before. Told all about tomorrow in exchange for leniency. Feng has details. Be careful. We'll be listening.

Boone sat blinking. It sounded almost too easy, but he knew better. All that was just shorthand for heroic work stateside. How could he sleep now? Impossible without Dr. Sarangan's magic pills.

"So, you know this hotel in Tianjin, Feng? What did you call it?"

"Everyone knows, sir. The Astor. Hundred fifty years old. Oldest Western-style in China. Remodeled two years. Tomorrow we have the lunch nearby and you study."

"Case it."

"Yes, you case it."

"And you have a gun for me?"

Feng stood on his end of the bed and used a key to open a heavy metal door he said he himself had installed in the ceiling. As the strong box came open, everything in it tumbled into Feng's hands. He gingerly sat and sorted documents, ammunition, and two weapons. One was the replica of what Waldemarr had shown Boone, and the underslung laser sight was already attached.

"Perfect," Boone said, deftly checking the mechanism. Feng handed him two fifteen-round magazines, one of which Boone slammed into the handle from beneath.

"Mine almost same," Feng said, showing Boone. "You sharpshooter like me?"

Boone had no idea what Chinese targets or shot scoring looked like. He shrugged. "Top 2 percent of Chicago police."

"How many police?"

"More than thirteen thousand."

"Good as me, then," Feng said, beaming. "You protect me."

"I hope it doesn't come to that." Boone sighed heavily, stood, and stored the gun and ammo in his bag.

"Ready for short-distance walk to sleep?" Feng said.

Boone recalled that Feng's idea of short was six kilometers. He was exhausted by the time they reached a corner dive that rented rooms by the night. "Have toilet, sink, no tub, no shower."

After Feng gave instructions to the proprietor and told Boone how many yuan to give the man, they agreed on when to meet in the morning. "You come by for shower and I make morning pot sticker."

"*Morning* pot sticker?"

"You like. Fill you till lunch in Tianjin."

"Deal," Boone said, shaking Feng's hand. He recalled that they had not shaken hands when they met because Feng had immediately reached for his bag. Maybe tour guides and tourists weren't supposed to shake.

As he secured his door and laid out his toiletries, Boone could still feel the calloused impression of Feng's hand in his.

The man was a rock. Protect him, indeed. Feng needed no one's help in that department.

Boone's room was bigger than Feng's whole apartment. He undressed and lay on his back in the darkness. Knowing Doc was listening in on his phone, Boone said, "Do I dare take another pill? Have to be up in six hours. Just text me a yes or no. I'll be on the phone with Jack."

It was good to hear a familiar voice. "What time is it there?" Jack said.

"A little after two in the morning."

"Then you'd better get some sleep."

"Before hearing all the details? C'mon, Jack!"

"It would take a long time to give you all the details, and you and I both know you won't be satisfied with only a summary."

"Why do you think I called?"

"I know. But nothing is more important than tomorrow."

"Promise I'll get every scintilla of what went down."

"Boones, you bring your boy back, and I'll talk till you shut me up."

Waldemarr texted back, I assume you're wired?

Understatement.

Then by all means, take a pill. But set an alarm.

37

★★★★

MORNING

JULY 4

At eight the next morning Boone's watch beeped, and he endured the same ritual he had on the plane. Logy but anything but disoriented, he patiently waited until his body allowed him to stir. When he was finally mobile, he grabbed all his stuff, dressed in yesterday's clothes, and hurried back to Feng's.

Already the sun was high and insistent. Everything about this country was foreign except the weather. It reminded him of the extremes of Chicago. Somehow he hadn't expected the humidity, but that rivaled the Windy City too.

Was Max in Tianjin already? Boone didn't know or care, as long as he would be there that evening. Boone would not leave that city without Max. In fact, Boone would have to be shipped home in a box to leave the country by himself.

The walk back to Feng's, which—despite the heat—became a jog, seemed longer even than the night before. Boone decided it seemed that way only because every step he took this day got him closer to Max. He prayed the boy was only confused, not scared, but he knew better. Adults can fool kids for only so long. How many times had these scoundrels promised Max his mother would be waiting at the next destination?

Boone was dripping and could smell himself. The sooner he got under Feng's excuse for a shower, the better. He sped up as he neared Feng's place, then panicked, wondering if he would recognize it in the light of day. Everything began to look the same.

When he figured he was within a few blocks, Boone called Feng's cell. No answer. He texted him. Nothing. He soon realized that if he went any farther he would be past Feng's neighborhood. Boone stopped in the shade, which cut the sting of the sun but didn't seem to affect the temperature.

Time was getting away from him. He couldn't afford to miss the train to Tianjin, and he had to know what had become of his contact. Boone didn't want to even entertain the possibility that Feng Li had been made. Without him, everything was lost. Boone would be adrift on a trackless sea. In desperation, he pulled up the photo of Feng on his phone and showed it to passersby. "Feng Li?" he said.

The first few ignored him. A teenage girl stopped and studied the photo, then shook her head and said something in Chinese he assumed was an apology. Finally, an elderly woman carrying a baby boy scowled at the phone and barked something Boone could not make out.

"Sorry?" he said, realizing she wouldn't understand him either.

She shouted, as if angry, but he was able to recognize that she was simply repeating the name. "Feng Li!"

Boone nodded vigorously, and she broke into a beatific smile. She beckoned him to follow and hurried down the street into an alley that began to look familiar. She pointed to a door. Boone spread his arms and smiled. "Thank you!" The woman just giggled, and when he pulled some yuan from his pocket, she cackled and shook her head and hurried off with the baby.

Boone tried the door, then knocked. A neighbor's curtain opened and a grim man peeked out. Boone waved and smiled. *Nothing to see here. I'm harmless. Ignore me.*

He continued to check his phone, call, and text. The clock was his enemy.

At long last he heard running on the sidewalk. Boone's gun lay loaded in the bottom of his bag, but he wouldn't pull it in a crowded neighborhood in the light of day unless his life was in danger. He tensed and was ready to spring into a defensive position—or offensive as the need arose.

Flying around the corner came Feng, smiling and pulling his keys from his shoulder bag, a sheaf of rolled paper under his arm. "Sorry, sorry, sorry! Didn't expect to take so the long."

"I've been calling and texting, man!"

"I know! I was running. Better to just get here."

That's what you think.

He followed Feng inside, where the man leaned over the miniature kitchen table and spread the paper. It was a blueprint. "The Astor Hotel," he said, beaming. "Easier to, to, ah, case! By memory, memorize. Cannot take. Too obvious."

"Where'd you get this?"

Feng smiled shyly. "Have my places."

Boone noticed Feng needed a shave and was wearing the same clothes as the day before. "Have you slept?"

He shook his head. "All night for the documents."

"Documents?"

Feng dug in his bag and produced a passport and a driver's license bearing his photo under the name Wang Xing. He also pulled out a badge wallet and ID, identifying Feng Li as a detective with the Tianjin Police.

"I don't understand," Boone said.

Feng brought up a photo on his phone. "From Dr. W. in Chicago. Got from Jack Keller, who got from Pitts's assistant. Picture of Wang Xing."

The man in the picture wore glasses and had shorter hair than Feng, but they were roughly the same age and skin color. "Buy glasses, get haircut in Tianjin. Americans think we all look the like anyway."

"Okay, you're going to be Xing. Then what? And what's with the cop ID?"

"Cover at lunch in Tianjin. Now you shave, take shower, I cook, we eat, I shave, take shower, we go. But first . . ." Feng made a dramatic show of spreading on the table before Boone two American Airlines tickets for the early morning flight the next day—one labeled Dean Booker, Boone's alias, the other under Mark Tuttman. "Has to leave country with same identity he came with."

Boone cocked his head. "I don't know about this," he said. "You know the word *jinx*?"

Feng shook his head, and Boone read surprise on his face that Boone wasn't thrilled.

"It means that you can mess something up by being overconfident. How sure are you this is going to go the way we want it to?"

Feng picked up the tickets and waved them at Boone. "Not my idea. Chicago's idea. They believe in you."

Their lips to God's ears, Boone thought. Being home that soon was a dream, but he was resolute that he would not—could not—face Haeley without Max.

Boone backed into the tiny lav and stripped down, stuffing his dirties into his bag and pulling out his fresh clothes. He quickly shaved and brushed, then slid everything outside the door before he turned on the shower—such as it was.

While the stream was light, it sprayed all over the room. Boone wasn't surprised it started cold, but he didn't expect it to stay that way. He heard banging on the door.

"So sorry! Forgot wrench!"

"Wrench?"

"For the hotter. Okay?"

The door opened an inch, and what looked like an adjustable sink wrench appeared. Boone tried it on the Hot faucet, and while he felt very little more heat, the flow increased. Despite the tepid stream and his haste, he felt a lot better when he finished. Feng immediately thrust in a towel, and within minutes Boone was dressed and feeling like a new man.

He emerged to the pungent odor of fried meat and dumpling skin. Boone was used to American-style pot stickers little larger than an orange section, but Feng placed on each of their plates a steaming creation about the size of half a grapefruit.

Feng attacked his with chopsticks and was half finished when Boone asked if he had a fork.

"No fork! You know expression, 'When in Rome . . . '?"

"Sorry," Boone said. "If we want to make our train, I'm going to have to eat this with my hands while you're getting ready."

He found it delicious and filling.

On the way to the station Feng told Boone that the train to Tianjin used to go four hundred kilometers an hour. "Now just 350 because of accident last year. No wheels. Nothing touch track. Run on magnetism. But all bullet trains slower now while government study the braking."

"Slower?" Boone said. "Three-fifty is over two hundred miles an hour."

"Faster than US train?"

"Much."

Feng was moving fast but fortunately staying on the shaded side of the street, so Boone didn't feel so overheated. And there was no running.

The train station was crowded, but Feng quickly acquired their tickets and led the way through the terminal to their track. On the way, they passed a luxurious, high-end women's shop with a sign translated into English: *Lounging along with fashion, the elegance follows.*

Close enough, Boone thought.

On the train he saw a sign bearing another attempt at English: *Get on and off until the moving train is stabilized.* And they passed seats with handicap symbols on them labeled, *Only for the old and weak.*

Late in the evening in Chicago, Jack Keller, Antoine Johnson, and Ragnar Waldemarr sat in the first-floor coffee shop at Mount Sinai, waiting for Margaret. "You guys are like kids on Christmas Eve," she had told him by phone earlier. "You won't sleep till this is over."

"You got that right," Jack had said. "It's coming up on noon in China, and the thing isn't going to happen until sundown. That'll be like six thirty in the morning here, but we'll be tapped in."

"You might as well keep me company here, then. Chaz wants to tell you something anyway."

"We could do that," Jack said. "Beats sitting in the office or at some all-night restaurant."

Margaret finally arrived with Nurse Chaz Cilano in tow. The men all stood.

"My, my," Chaz said, "can't remember the last time that happened. Sit down."

"Never happens for me," Margaret said. "What do you want to drink?"

But before Chaz could answer, Ragnar Waldemarr said, "Miss Margaret, I don't know about these two louts, but I stood for the both of you."

"Why, thank you, Doctor."

"I'd say the same," Chaz said, "but I make it a point not to thank doctors. They should be thanking me."

Jack was impressed that Chaz waited until Margaret returned with coffee for the two of them before she brought the rest up to date. "This is just an observation," she said, "but it's based on a lot of experience. All three of Haeley's doctors were in today at the same time, and I don't think I'm violating any confidences when I say they seemed more than encouraged."

"What does that mean?" Jack said. "She's coming out of the coma?"

"No, not until they make that happen. Normally, with an injury like hers, that should be another week or ten days. But I think they're going to start adjusting her meds to see how she responds. Her vitals have been improving so steadily, it's like she's fighting to come back."

Jack's phone buzzed. "It's Francisco Sosa," he said. "Give me a minute.

"Hello, Pastor."

"About to head to bed, Chief. Any updates, anything I can pray about specifically?"

Jack shared the news about Haeley and added, "We've had major breaks in Max's case and hope to have good news by dawn."

"Praise God," Sosa said.

Jack chuckled. "From anyone but you, that would sound hokey. But I've been thinking the same thing. That doesn't mean things can't go wrong, though, so if you're praying, pray that Boone and his contact over there will be at their absolute best."

"I will," Sosa said, and it struck Jack that in nearly forty years of police work, he had never asked someone to pray over a case. "You know I occasionally text people Bible verses, right?"

"Do I!" Jack said. "Boone and Margaret show them to me all the time."

"Okay if I send you one?"

"I thought you'd never ask."

"On its way in a few minutes. Good night, Chief."

Jack sat listening to his friends and colleagues banter, all nervously awaiting action from the other side of the globe. He wished it wasn't too late to call Florence Quigley. How he hoped he would have good news for her the next day, which would be Independence Day in the US.

His phone vibrated, and Jack found the text from Pastor Sosa. "I need a Bible," Jack said, amused at the looks that elicited.

"I've got one on my phone," Margaret said, "but it's upstairs."

"Let's go get it," Jack said. "I'm curious about this reference. Jeremiah 29:13."

"Oh, I know that one by heart, Jack. It's a favorite. 'You will seek me and find me when you seek me with all your heart.'"

38

★★★★

MIDDAY

BOONE HAD NEVER been on a train that traveled by floating on a magnetic field. The bullet train proved smooth, eerily quiet, and lightning fast. It didn't take long to reach its maximum allowable speed, and Boone couldn't imagine that it used to travel nearly forty miles an hour faster. By the time it reached 215 miles an hour, the smaller towns and cities between Beijing and Tianjin were flying by. Boone found he missed the clackity cacophony of the Chicago L-trains, an experience that had never grown old for him. But silent swaying was interesting too.

He and Feng arrived at the gleaming Tianjin Railway Station—the one the locals called East Station—at about one in the afternoon. Not until they were on the streets and away from curious ears did Feng begin the conversation Boone knew would be the most important in his life to date.

"We will find place where you can study texts from your Chicago people," Feng said. "I will send to you from my phone everything, more pictures. Big problem is, uh, uh, *quán xiàn*. Understand?"

"No, Feng, sorry. I know no Chinese."

"Legal power?" Feng tried. "Authority?" He spotted a tour group on the street with British markings on their clothes and approached the Chinese female tour guide. "Speak English?" he said.

"Speak," she said.

"*Quán xiàn*?"

The young woman closed one eye and scrunched up her mouth. "Jurisdiction!"

"*Xie xie!*" Feng said, thanking her.

"*Méi shi!*" she said.

"Lucky she understand," Feng said. "Tianjin dialect different from Beijing."

"Will that be a problem at the Astor?"

"Should be okay," Feng said. "Staff trained for this."

This time what Feng described as a short walk really was—fewer than three miles. When they reached a street of fashionable shops, including one for men, he told Boone they were within half a kilometer of the Astor Hotel. "Must look rich," he said, working quickly on his cell phone. "You wait. Send you everything from Chicago. You read."

Feng disappeared into the store, and Boone found a wrought-iron bench in the shade. But once he sat he realized clouds were forming and intermittently blocking the sun. Did that mean rain? What might that do to their operation?

The long message, which included photographs, was addressed to Feng from Ragnar Waldemarr and included information from Jack, Antoine Johnson, and even some from Brigita Velna. A bracketed note read, Boone, when Feng transmits this to you, if time is an issue, I have summarized everything at the end, including Chief Keller's tactical suggestions.

Boone forced himself not to skip ahead. As was his custom, he wanted the progression, the flow, every detail. If there was something to decipher that no one else had noticed, that was the way he would find it.

The document began with everything they had learned about the kidnapping, the abductor, and the pass-off to "Virginia Tuttman" at O'Hare. Ms. Tuttman, who turned out to be Jasper Pitts's assistant, Lorelei Shearson, was the source for all the rest of the details. Boone read through the interrogation of AKA and Ms. Shearson and realized that the information she had provided—should it prove accurate—was a gold mine.

She began with her delivery of Max at the Beijing airport to a woman named Xui Shi, described as a "child protective matron for Chu-Hua Children of the Globe Placement Services." Shearson had delivered to and taken delivery from Ms. Shi on more than a dozen previous occasions. The accompanying photograph showed a stocky, slack-faced woman of about sixty dressed in old-fashioned Mao-style utilitarian garb. Lorelei Shearson had noted that Shi had the ability to blend into any crowd and not draw attention to herself. Interestingly, Lorelei had also added that she believed the woman was "wholly unaware of any unethical aspects of the work of Chu-Hua."

Lorelei had told Jack Keller and Antoine Johnson that

Jasper "Jammer" Pitts was booked at the J. W. Marriott in Beijing and would arrive in Tianjin that afternoon at six. She had hired a limo to take him the seven or so miles to the Astor. An accompanying picture showed a massive bespectacled man with sagging jowls, showing his age, with the thinning and unevenly dyed yellowish hair Shane Loggyn had described to Jack. Pitts was to meet Mr. Xing at the checkerboard table under the grand wood staircase in the History Lobby, and from there they would reconnoiter in Xing's Hai River diplomat suite.

According to Lorelei Shearson, each was to have a notebook computer on which they would engineer the transaction. Xing would arrange the transfer of 7 million Chinese yuan to Pitts's Swiss bank account, the equivalent of approximately 1.1 million U.S. dollars.

Ms. Shi was to bring "Mark Tuttman," the American orphan who matched Mr. and Mrs. Xing's preferences, to the suite. Once Xing took custody of the child, Ms. Shi would be excused, and Xing would trigger the deposit. When the new balance appeared in Mr. Pitts's account, the delivery would be considered complete, and Pitts would depart. His itinerary showed him traveling immediately to Beijing in time for his return flight to Midway Airport in Chicago, via Los Angeles and Minneapolis.

Dr. Ragnar Waldemarr had written, Boone, Chief Keller tells me to urge you to resist the impulse to exact justice from Pitts. You cannot arrest him, detain him, assault him, or threaten him. Whatever you do, he must keep to his itinerary so the FBI can apprehend him at customs in LA.

Terrific. How'm I supposed to pull that off?

Feng Li finally emerged from the men's store with a garment bag over his shoulder. "Are you hungry?" he said.

"I shouldn't be, but I am. Probably just excitement."

"Big job," Feng said. "Need energy."

"Let me get this straight," Boone said as they walked, the sky darkening. "This matron will have Max in a room, and when Pitts tells her, she brings him to Xing's suite?"

Feng nodded.

"Why don't I just find them and kidnap back my own son? We could be out of there and on our way back to Beijing before Pitts even gets here."

Feng shrugged. "What happens to Xui Shi?"

"Can't we protect her somehow?"

"From someone like Pitts or someone powerful and rich like Xing? She become new victim. Besides, cameras in hallways. You be seen. Anyway, if you think, you get better idea."

"I'm too close to this, Feng. It's hard to think. Believe me, I'm trying."

"I help? Give you hint? Clue?"

"Sure."

They had reached the Heping financial district, and Feng led Boone on a walk next to the Hai River. "Astor not far, on Taier Zhuang Road. Eat near there, then haircut and glasses."

"What's your idea, Feng?"

"When I remind you, it will be your idea."

"I'm listening."

"Whole meeting, delivery of child, everything happen when money transfer. How?"

"By computer."

"What Xing business?"

It was way too early to be so antsy. But Boone couldn't quit worrying about Max, how confused he had to be, wondering where Mom and Dad were and what was going on. Was he old enough to understand? No. All he would want by now were his parents, familiarity, home.

However this went down, Max must not be hurt.

Boone had never seen a menu like the one in the eatery within the shadow of the Astor Hotel. "What is 'eight great bowls'?"

"Meat dishes," Feng said. "Too much food. Maybe you like four great stews. You pick. Goose? Chicken?"

"Actually this snack looks good. *Mahua?*"

"Twisted dough sticks," Feng said. "You like."

"What in the world?" Boone said, pointing at menu pictures of dishes that didn't look bad but which were labeled *wild bamboo saliva* and *vinegar hibernation head.*

"Traditional Chinese food, wrong translation."

"'Five dirty, five factors'?" Boone pointed at the Chinese characters next to that line. "How would you translate that into English?"

"Five meat, five vegetable."

"Sounds good, but I wouldn't be able to get dirty factors out of my head." He stuck with the mahua, and it was plenty.

As they sat strategizing, Feng told Boone he believed Xing was like Mrs. Shi. "Does not know illegal."

"Seriously? He thinks a legitimate adoption would cost a million US?"

"Very special service. Choose type of child, even hair color."

"So what happens when he finds out?"

"Must avoid embarrassment, scandal. Protect business. If I scare, he cooperate."

Boone nodded slowly, gradually catching on to where Feng was headed. "You get to him early, scare him off, warn him not to tip off Pitts."

"Yes."

"Then you become Xing?"

Feng smiled. "Don't skip step."

"Xing will be angry."

"Right," Feng said. "Want revenge."

"You can get him to help sting Pitts."

"Sting?"

"Turn the tables? Betray?"

"Yes!"

"How?"

"Computer!" Feng said.

At long last, Boone had connected with Feng. He had found him fascinating, impressive, certainly. But for the next hour, as they traded ideas and suggestions, the language barrier seemed to fade. Boone had found a like mind, a kindred spirit. In, of all places, the most exotic land he had ever visited, with everything looking, sounding, smelling, and feeling foreign, it was as if he were just sitting with a fellow cop. And by the time they had memorized their next steps, Boone was as confident as he had been since he boarded the flight at O'Hare that this had a chance of working.

As they left the restaurant, a young woman at the counter stared at Boone. "American?" she said.

"Yes," he said, returning her smile.

"Try English?"

"Sure."

"Thank you and welcome for the next time."

"Very good."

Two blocks away Feng found a barbershop and pointed Boone to an optical shop. "Find frames like Xing in picture. Clear lenses."

"Feng, I speak no Chinese."

"Point to merchandise. Pay yuan listed on sign."

"You may have to rescue me."

For some reason, this made Feng laugh.

Half an hour later, when he added the new frames to his freshly cut hair, Feng at least looked like he could be Wang Xing's brother.

It was late in the afternoon when Boone and Feng came within sight of the Astor Hotel. Boone found it a stunning mixture of architectural styles. Situated on a corner rimmed with ornate double street lamps, it was surrounded by a wall topped with crisscrossing wood lattice patterns. A brick tower with square decorations and half-circle arch windows rose five stories on the corner, attached to a three-story building that covered half the block. This lower section carried the same motif as the tower but was adorned with light wood add-ons that served as patios for each room and repeated the latticework adornments.

"Just 153 rooms, three suites," Feng said.

"How do you know that?"

Feng smiled. "Tour guide."

The pure white lobby was graced by gentle sloping arches and a huge floral arrangement near the entrance. Boone and Feng each carried heavy bags over their shoulders, and Feng also had the garment bag, so it made sense when a man behind the counter said something in Chinese and quickly followed it with, "Checking in?"

"Just tourists," Feng said. "Looking."

"Make yourselves at home."

"Where is diplomat suite?"

The clerk told Feng, and added, "Occupied."

As they moseyed on, Feng whispered, "Only hotel in all of China with own museum. Too bad not enough time."

They passed several quaint eateries with names like O'Hara's, Cafe Majestic, and Victorian Lounge, some airy and modern, others heavily wooded and intimate. Boone imagined how interesting and fun such a place would be for him and Haeley and Max under any other circumstance.

The meeting place arranged for Pitts and Xing was a beautiful spot that must have seen many an interesting and romantic rendezvous in its time. But something told Boone that even if his and Feng's elaborate scheme worked perfectly and he was able to spirit Max out of the country, nothing could make him return to this hotel.

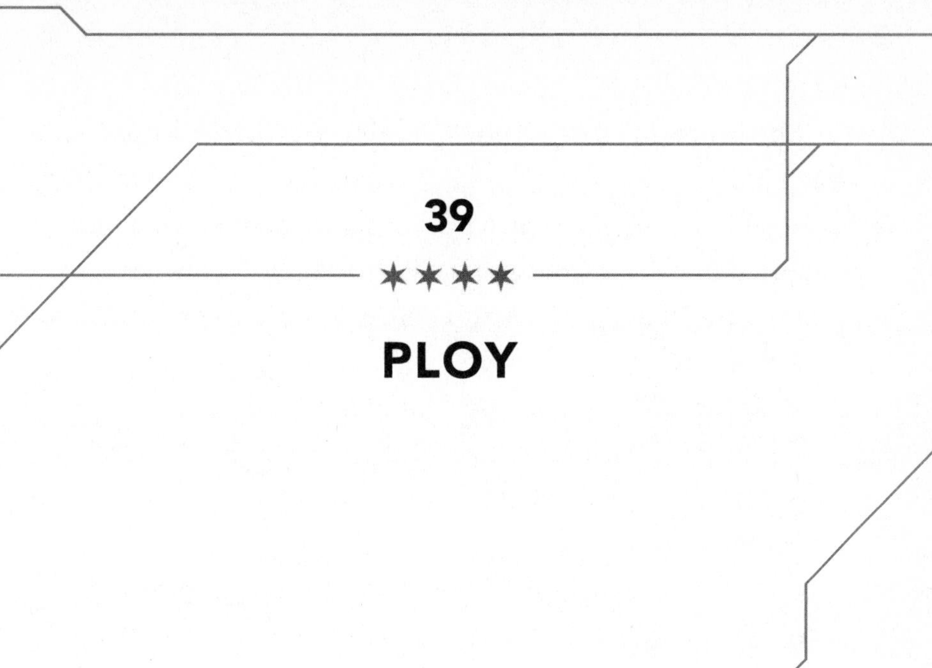

39

★★★★

PLOY

BOONE HEARD THE gentle rain begin as he and Feng made their way to the river-view side of the hotel and found the diplomat suite. They silently placed their heavy bags on either side of the doorframe. Feng tucked away his new glasses and ran a hand through his hair until it looked spiky, then folded the new garment bag over his forearm. Boone stepped a few feet down the hall and pressed himself against the wall.

Feng rapped smartly on the door and said, "Laundry!"

They heard movement in the room, but no one came to the door.

Feng repeated the knock and announcement. This time footsteps approached and a voice said, "Wrong room. No laundry order here."

"So sorry, sir!" Feng said. "Receipt says Mr. and Mrs. Wang Xing."

"Let me see that," the man said, quickly opening the door. He found himself staring at a badge. "What's this about?"

"Captain Feng Li, sir, Tianjin Police. Just need a moment."

"What for?"

"Please, sir. May I come in? Not long."

The fortyish businessman wore dress slacks, a silky black T-shirt, and black stockings. "I have a meeting soon and—"

"Promise not too long."

Scowling, Xing held the door open but looked surprised to see Boone follow Feng Li in, gathering up both shoulder bags as he came. Boone was struck that Xing's English was so good, much better than Feng's.

"What do you want?" Xing said, pulling out his business card. "I'm just visiting from Xi'an and—"

Feng set down the garment bag and took the card in both hands, making a show of reading it carefully. "I am familiar with your company, sir. A customer."

"Well, that's fine, but—"

"May we sit, sir?"

"I must start getting ready—"

"I will honor your time, Mr. Xing."

Pastel walls contrasted with brown and white drapes and an elegant chandelier in the contemporarily furnished suite. Boone draped the garment bag over his arm and dragged it and the other bags into the closet.

"What is he doing?" Xing said, rising.

"Please sit, Mr. Xing," Feng said. "This very important matter."

The man pressed his lips together, sat back down, folded his arms, and glared at Feng. "What is?"

Boone said, "It has come to our attention, sir, that you may have unwittingly involved yourself in a national investigation."

"What?"

"You *are* planning to adopt a son tonight, are you not?"

"I am. And my wife and I are quite excited about it. It is perfectly legal. I have gone through a wonderful American placement organization."

"I'm afraid, Mr. Xing, that you have been duped."

"Duped?"

"Fooled. Lied to."

"There is no child? No money is to change hands until the orphan has been delivered to me."

"There is a child, but he is not an orphan. He was abducted, and the organization that has promised him to you knowingly engages in human trafficking."

"I don't believe it!"

"The Chu-Hua Children of the Globe Placement Services, headquartered in Illinois?"

"Yes!"

"And you're dealing with the president?"

"Mr. Jasper Pitts, yes!"

"I'm sorry to have to tell you that Mr. Pitts is an international fugitive wanted by the United States Federal Bureau of Investigation."

Wang Xing turned ashen and covered his eyes with both hands. "Oh no! No! Bai will be devastated!"

"Your wife?"

Xing nodded, folded his hands, and stared at the ceiling. "How will I be able to tell her? We have had two other adoptions fall through at the last minute when the mothers changed their minds. She refused to come this time, unwilling to face another disappointment. I was so looking forward to taking home our son."

"I'm sorry, but I must ask. Did you not feel the price was exorbitant? Seven million yuan for an adoption? There are legitimate placement agencies, you know."

"No! I don't know! I thought this one was. Nothing in all our correspondence hinted at anything amiss! The boy was represented as an orphan from a top facility in the States."

"The truth is, sir, he has loving parents desperate to get him back."

"That is horrible!"

"I'm sorry for you and your wife," Boone said.

"Feel sorry for my workers, my company! I can't be mixed up in something like this! I'll be ruined!"

"That's why we're here, Mr. Xing," Boone said. "There is no need to publicize your involvement in this case."

"There isn't? How can that be?"

"If you're willing to help us . . ."

"Help you apprehend this man? I'd like to kill him. I will do whatever it takes to see him pay."

Boone rose and moved to sit closer to Xing. "If you are willing to do this, you will be free to go. I am sorry that you will have to bear bad news to your wife, but surely neither of you would have wanted a kidnapped child."

"Of course not!"

"You can leave immediately for Xi'an, and no one will ever know what you were doing here."

Xing looked back and forth between Boone and Feng. "Tell me how I can help."

"Tell me, sir," Boone said, "are you primarily a businessman-entrepreneur, or are you a computer-software expert?"

"I am both. I have been called the Steve Jobs of China."

"Perfect. Our understanding is that you were to set up the transfer of funds on your notebook computer and trigger it once you had taken delivery of the child."

"Yes, and then when the monies showed up in Mr. Pitts's account, the deal would be done."

"Tell me, Mr. Xing," Boone said, "is there a way that you could make it appear that the money has gone to Mr. Pitts's account, so he would be satisfied and leave, but it would never actually be deposited?"

Xing covered his mouth and appeared to be thinking. His head bobbed as he seemed to consider options. "It would be very complicated."

"We want him to board his plane this evening, satisfied that he has the money in his account. He'll be none the wiser until he lands in Los Angeles and the FBI can break the news."

Xing thought more. "That would be too perfect. And I think I can do it."

"Yes?"

"It's complicated, and I would have to do some careful programming, but I believe I can. Do you have a computer with you?"

"I do," Feng said.

"I will do the work on mine. Then, if I can successfully

transmit it to you, I'll know immediately whether it works. If it does, do you want me to go through the whole transfer with Mr. Pitts, take the boy, and then hand him over to you?"

"No," Boone said. "There is no need for you to stay, if you can set this up and show us how to do it, you can be on your way."

"How will you get the child?"

Feng went to the closet and put on his new jacket and the glasses. He smoothed his hair and returned.

"Astounding," Mr. Xing said.

The man fetched his computer and immediately set to work. Feng completed his outfit with dress slacks and expensive shoes, and Boone planted his new sidearm deep in the cargo pocket of his own pants.

About forty minutes later, Wang Xing was ready to try his creation. Feng Li gave him his e-mail address, and the man transmitted a mountain of data. It worked perfectly, so he showed Feng how to do it. Soon he was packed and ready to go.

"I am deeply saddened and yet grateful for your every kindness," he said. "Can you somehow let me know when the child has been safely returned to his parents?"

"I let you know," Feng Li said.

"You might want to leave the back way," Boone said, "in case Mr. Pitts arrives early."

"I had some gifts for the boy. Perhaps he would still like them."

Xing set two electronic games on the table, gave his room key to Feng, shook hands with both men, and was gone.

Boone was drained already, praying he could keep his wits about him for another hour. "Knowing Max is here is driving me crazy," he said. "I still want to just go get him."

"No, no. Spoil everything. Stay with plan."

"You know I'm only going to be pretending to know what you're saying when you speak to me in Chinese."

"You smart man. Can do this."

40

★★★★

PAYOFF

AT A LITTLE after 6 a.m. in Chicago, Jack Keller and his cohorts sat bleary-eyed in the coffee shop on the first floor of Mount Sinai Hospital, shaking their heads at what they'd overheard on their phones from halfway around the world. "As soon as this is over," Jack said, "I'm gonna sleep through Independence Day."

Ragnar Waldemarr looked grave. "I just hope Boone won't have to use the gun."

"If this works, he won't need it," Jack said. "We'd have a tough time getting him out of there if he opens fire. Especially with all the cameras in that hotel."

"I just wish I could be there," Antoine said. "And I'd give anything to be in LA when the FBI busts Pitts."

Boone had worked undercover before, but never had the stakes been so high. Not only was he determined to pull this off, but he was also committed to not throttling Jammer Pitts where he stood. It would be all he could do to control his rage. Part of him wished the man would give him a reason to use deadly force.

Feng Li exuded wealth and class as they strolled down to the History Lobby and sat on a small couch. "Let me do acting," Feng said. "You just interpreter."

Boone nodded. Was it possible he would have Max in his arms within the hour? He heard thunder and hoped the storm would not stall Pitts.

The man of the hour arrived a few minutes later in all his splendor, a mushy mountain carrying only a computer bag and brushing rain off his arms. Boone thought he saw a flash of hesitation when Pitts noticed him, but he focused on Feng and said, "Mr. Xing at last! What a pleasure to meet you!"

Feng leapt to his feet and shook Pitts's hand, looking every bit the sophisticated multimillionaire trying to keep his emotions in check. "You make my wife and me very, very happy," Feng said.

"Well, that's what we do, sir." And he turned questioningly to Boone, who extended his hand.

"American friend," Feng said, "Dean Booker. My English not so the good. He help."

"Nice to meet you, Mr. Booker. Happy Fourth of July."

"Same to you, Mr. Pitts. I've heard a lot about you and your work."

"Thank you! Are you a parent?"

"Yes, sir. Two boys. One in heaven."

"Sorry to hear that. If you're ever thinking about adding a child, you know whom to call." Pitts pulled out his wallet and handed Boone his card. "I've got the best job in the world. I put kids who need parents with parents who need kids."

"What could be nobler than that?" Boone said. "I imagine it's very gratifying."

"Now, Mr. Xing, before we repair to your suite and make the joyous transfer, I just need to see some ID so I know you're who you say you are. You understand."

"No," Feng said.

"Sorry?" Pitts said, glancing at Boone.

Feng whispered urgently to Boone in Chinese. Boone turned to Pitts. "I'm afraid he's slightly offended. Everyone here knows who he is, and he's wondering if this is entirely necessary."

"Oh, merely routine!" Pitts said. "Just have to cover my bases. I'd like to see your ID too, Mr. Booker. Maybe that'll set his mind at ease."

"Good idea." Boone pulled out his passport.

Pitts glanced at it and immediately turned to Feng. "See, that's all. This is a mighty important day for both of us. The future of a child. A business transaction."

Feng looked appropriately cloudy and glumly produced his ID.

"There, see?" Pitts said. "That's all I need. Shall we go do some business?"

Pitts allowed Feng and Boone to board the elevator first, which meant that Boone wound up directly behind the big man. He was breathing on Pitts, his gun two feet away.

In the suite Pitts plugged in his notebook. While it was

booting up, Feng beckoned him to the table, where he showed him the screen on his computer and mumbled in Chinese to Boone.

"He wants to know if everything is as you agreed."

Pitts hunched over Feng's notebook and stared at the screen. "It is indeed, gentlemen. Once my unit is ready and you trigger the transaction, I'll have little Mark brought down. And as soon as my account reflects the activity, I'll be wishing you all the best and will be out of your hair."

"Just so you know, Mr. Pitts," Boone said, "I'm going to slip into the other room before the boy arrives so as not to confuse him and to give Wang his personal moment with him."

"How thoughtful," Pitts said. "A capital idea. All right, it looks like I'm up and rolling. Whenever you're ready, sir."

Feng rubbed his hands together and dramatically pushed Enter. Pitts pulled his cell phone from his breast pocket, punched a key, waited, and said, "Ms. Shi, please bring the boy."

Boone shook with anticipation as he slipped into the next room. How would he be able to keep from rushing out and enveloping Max? *God, help me!*

A few minutes later he heard a tentative knock. Pitts opened the door and said, "There's the little man! Come in, come in! Now, come on; don't be shy! I'd like you to meet someone. . . . Well, naturally he's a little scared. Ms. Shi, just leave him with me, and thank you again."

"Good-bye," she said.

"Bye," Max said, and Boone's throat caught. He sounded so tiny, timid, scared.

"Why does everybody lie to me?" Max said, and Boone clenched his fists, fighting the lump in his throat. "She said I was going to see my daddy."

"This is your new daddy, son!" Pitts said. "Look what he's got for you over there!"

"I don't need a new daddy! I've got a daddy!"

"He's confused. He'll be all right."

"No, I'm not!"

"Wait, wait," Feng said. "This not child you promised."

"Sure it is!"

"Why hair is the short and black? Picture was blond!"

"You know kids. They want what they want. His real hair is blond; it'll grow out."

Feng was perfect, Boone thought. Resisting showing his ID and reacting to Max's hair was just enough to make Pitts work, the perfect prescription for an effective sting. But now Boone just wanted the phony transaction to go through so Pitts would get out.

"I want my mommy and daddy!" Max wailed, and Boone clenched his teeth, trying to keep from sobbing. Enough already!

"There it is!" Pitts exulted, and Boone could hear him slapping shut his computer and yanking cords. "The boy will be fine; the hair will grow out—blond, I promise! I just know you're all going to be happy. All the best now!"

As soon as the door opened and slammed, Boone put his hand on the doorknob of the room he was in. To keep from scaring Max to death, he had to endure a few more seconds.

"What's gonna happen to me now?" Max said.

"I know real name, son," Feng said softly.

"What?"

"Your name Max. Your daddy policeman."

"Yes!" Max was crying.

"Everybody lie to Max."

"I know!"

"Not me. You tell me you want Daddy; I show you Daddy."

"I want Daddy!"

"Here I am, Max," Boone managed, tears streaming.

The boy looked up, eyes wide, and ran to his open arms.

Boone had to hand it to Jammer Pitts, scoundrel that he was. He knew enough to coach his people on how to treat a young boy so he wouldn't panic and cry for help at every new venue. Boone had agonized over what he assumed was Max's fear and trauma over being kidnapped, but the truth was—to hear Max tell it—he had proved the perfect victim.

"I liked Uncle Alfonso," he told Boone. "He was fun. Is he with Mom?"

Boone was at a loss. How much to say? He wanted to tell Max he would never see "Uncle Alfonso" again, ever—that the man would not likely see freedom in his lifetime.

And Max had also liked the woman he thought was "Miss Virginia," though he didn't remember much about her. "I was so sleepy." He said the "old lady babysitter" talked funny but gave him good snacks. "She seemed worried all the time. But she kept telling me I would see you very soon. Uncle Alfonso said he was taking me to see Mom. Miss Virginia said that too. Then the old lady said I'd see you. I didn't believe her 'cause it was like everybody was lyin' to me, even though they were nice. Mr. Feng finally told me the truth."

Boone considered it had been by the grace of God that Max was too young and naive to realize the danger he had been in. Regardless, he had been away from his parents long enough to now be clingy. He sat on Boone's lap on the bullet train back to Beijing, and when Boone treated them to a night in a luxury hotel, he slept in Boone's bed.

Max was excited about getting to "fly on the big jet" again and fondly remembered the food. But he stayed close to Boone and often sat on his lap when the seat belt signs were off.

When Max finally slept, Boone asked a flight attendant for a pad of paper. It was time to get back to his letter to the boy, and it was also time to deep-six what he had started with and begin again.

Keeping in mind that Max would not be reading this until he was at least twelve, Boone wrote:

> My beloved Max, the first thing you need to know and understand is that the story I'm about to tell you is nobody's fault. It's certainly not Aunt Flo's fault, though she blames herself. We were all the victims of very cunning con artists, and if you don't know what that means, you will by the end of this letter.
>
> As you know by now, you didn't become my son in the usual way. You came into my life when I fell in love with your mother. The first thing I wanted to do after we married was to adopt you, give you my name, and make you my forever son. . . .

Later in the letter Boone told Max why they were flying back from China at the time of the writing and that he was about to tell Max what had happened to his mother. That prospect gave Boone some sleepless hours, even when the letter was finished. No way would he take a sleeping pill on this flight.

Jack met the flight at O'Hare, having been brought up to speed by Boone via texts.

Max looked surprised when Boone sat in the backseat with him. "Need to talk to you, bud," Boone said. "I have to tell you something about Mom."

Boone was careful not to make Haeley's condition sound as serious as it was. The boy had been through enough, and as it was clear that Haeley was slowly getting better and would be conscious soon, there was no point in telling him how close to death she had come.

"Has she got a bump on her head?" Max said.

"A pretty big one, actually. And her face is bruised. She's going to be sleeping for a few more days, so do you want to wait and see her when she wakes up?"

"No! I want to see her now."

"I'll have to think about that."

Boone called Nurse Chaz Cilano and then Dr. Sarangan. Both thought it would be all right for Max to see Haeley, and the doctor said, "For all we know, it might be good for her too. She may hear his voice, feel his touch."

One thing was certain: Boone decided to say nothing about Max's little brother or sister, leaving that for Haeley to tell him.

Three weeks later, Florence Quigley's apartment at Bethune Arms was so crowded her twenty-one guests had to sit in shifts. She had worked with Boone on the invitation list for an open house to honor Haeley's first outing. All had been briefed on the fact that Max had only a vague idea of what his long, mysterious trip had been all about.

Haeley's amazing recovery was in full bloom, and while she still had to sit most of the time—nobody could pry Max off her lap—and use a cane when she walked, her mind and her speech were nearly restored. Everyone promised to give Haeley some space, but over the course of an hour, everybody got to greet her.

Florence stood at Haeley's side, shyly meeting two of Haeley's doctors and her nurse, Boone's former boss and his wife, one of Boone's detectives and his wife, and the Drakes' pastor and his wife.

Florence's own pastor and wife were there too, and at one point she had to pull him off to the side and tell him to "quit apologizin'. None of us meant no harm, and there's enough blame to go 'round."

Florence even invited Willie and Scooter, telling the wino, "They's no alcohol up in here, and don't be bringin' your own." He was the first to leave, and Willie had to get back to the desk.

The strangest trio, to Florence, was an older gentleman with a funny name whom Boone called Rags, his wife, and a woman named Brigita. Rags was the one who brought a computer and connected with the guy in China Boone had worked with to get Max back. Florence's guests seemed excited about the video conference with Feng Li, but Florence found him hard to understand.

Fortunately for Florence, only seven of the guests were staying for dinner. When everybody was gone except the Drakes, their friends Jack and Margaret, and Pastor Sosa and his wife, Florence told them to give her a little time to finish at the stove and she'd finally keep her promise to Boone.

Finally they all crowded around her table, and after Pastor Sosa prayed, Florence set a heaping, steaming pile of pigs' knuckles before them and beamed in their laughter.

"I jes' got to say, Haeley, " she whispered while Max was distracted, "one thing that nasty con man got me on bad was knowin' about your unspoken prayer requests. He said they was about him, but you didn't even know him. What were they?"

Haeley chuckled, and as everyone strained to hear her still-weak voice, Max perked up and listened too. "I was just praying I could have a baby with this man," she said. "And I'm going to. A healthy one in spite of everything."

Everyone clapped and cheered, and Max raised both fists and said, "You're havin' a baby! Yes! A boy or a girl?"

"We don't know yet, honey," Haeley said. "But you'll be the first person we tell."

Jack Keller cleared his throat. "I'd like to say something, if you don't mind. Pastor Sosa sent me a verse—as he likes to do—in the middle of all this, ah, stuff, and I memorized it. It goes, 'You will seek me and find me when you seek me with all your heart.' Well, I'm doing that. With all my heart."

Pastor Sosa said, "He keeps his promises, Jack, so watch out. Now can I give you all one more verse?"

"Nobody better say no," Florence said.

"Ephesians 3:20 and 21," he said. "'Now to him who is

able to do exceedingly abundantly above all that we ask or think, according to the power that works in us, to him be glory in the church by Christ Jesus to all generations, forever and ever. Amen.'"

TYNDALE HOUSE NOVELS BY JERRY B. JENKINS

- *Riven*
- *Midnight Clear* (with Dallas Jenkins)
- *Soon*
- *Silenced*
- *Shadowed*
- *The Last Operative*
- *The Brotherhood*
- *The Betrayal*
- *The Breakthrough*

THE LEFT BEHIND® SERIES *(with Tim LaHaye)*

- *Left Behind®*
- *Tribulation Force*
- *Nicolae*
- *Soul Harvest*
- *Apollyon*
- *Assassins*
- *The Indwelling*
- *The Mark*
- *Desecration*
- *The Remnant*
- *Armageddon*
- *Glorious Appearing*
- *The Rising*
- *The Regime*
- *The Rapture*
- *Kingdom Come*

Left Behind Collectors Edition

- *Rapture's Witness* (books 1–3)
- *Deceiver's Game* (books 4–6)
- *Evil's Edge* (books 7–9)
- *World's End* (books 10–12)

For the latest information on Left Behind products, visit www.leftbehind.com.
For the latest information on Tyndale fiction, visit www.tyndalefiction.com.

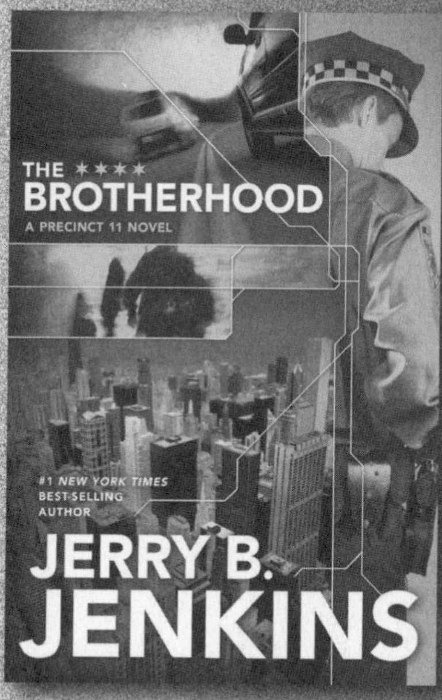

"AS A LONGTIME CHICAGOAN, THE SON OF A POLICE CHIEF, AND THE BROTHER OF TWO COPS, I FOUND THIS WRITING A LABOR OF LOVE."

Jerry B. Jenkins

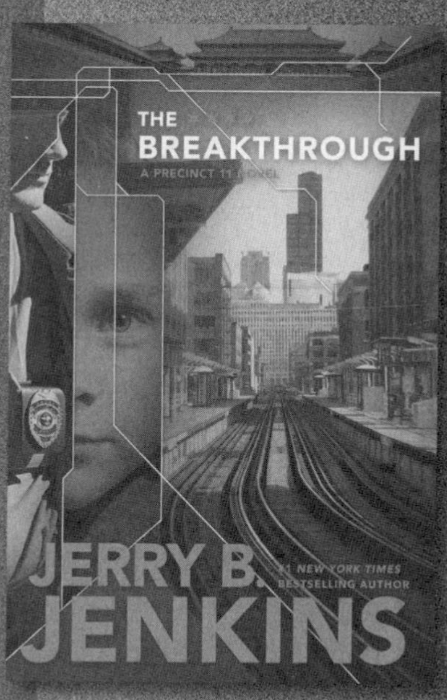

WHAT IF IT HAPPENED TODAY?

NEW LOOK! COMING SPRING 2011

REDISCOVER THE TIMELESS ADVENTURE.

RELIVE THE ETERNAL IMPACT.

Leftbehind.com

CP0117